Lindsey Barron Series
Volume 5
The National
Healthcare Program

Vic Broquard

Artwork by Crooked Willow Studios.

Published by:
Broquard eBooks
http://Broquard-eBooks.com
author@Broquard-eBooks.com
103 Timberlane
East Peoria, IL 61611

For Morgan and L. Ron Hubbard

Table of Contents

Chapter 1—Prelude

"Hello, this is President Missy Snow," the harried woman spoke into the telephone, which an aide had rushed to her.

"It's Simon Mac Fluide! You *have* to take this call," the brunette had just urged her boss. "No one ever gets a call from *him*!" Missy twisted her hair again, thinking hard. For days now, her mind was focused solely on how to best get her promised National Health Care Program past the Congress. She needed millions of dollars for its initial funding—dollars she did not have, nor could her Secretary of the Treasury, Herman Smiley, find it for her.

She knew about this incredible recluse—this Simon Mac Fluide. Wealthy, famous, Simon ran his huge enterprise by telephone, refusing all outside contact with other people. Some said that he became a recluse twenty-five years ago after some kind of illness. Others said that he had an immune system failure; the merest contact with outside germs would make him deathly ill, if not outright kill him. Others said that he hated people. Missy sighed, reluctantly putting down her calculator and the impossible figures. She took the phone and identified herself.

"Good afternoon, President Snow. Simon Mac Fluide here." His unidentifiable scrambled voice annoyed Missy, but she could understand him. He continued, "I'm calling today regarding your proposed National Health Care Program. You're still attempting to push it through, are you not?"

"Why yes, yes I am. It is the first major policy action that I promised my voters," she replied, wondering why he asked. Everyone knew she had been and still was pulling every string she could, trying to convince half of Congress to go along with it, but with little success.

He continued, "We share the same goals: a healthy, robust population, free from disease and from crime as well. If every American in our country was totally healthy and no one dreamed of committing any crimes, then even I could walk freely in our land without fear of contamination."

Missy smiled, thinking to herself, "So he does have an immune system disorder after all." She replied, "Yes, a healthy citizen is a valuable citizen. However, I'm not sure that merely being healthy can wipe out crime. That is a very lofty goal. Right now, I just want to get all Americans healthy, reduce this mammoth load on our health care system, which drains trillions of our taxpayer's dollars every year," she automatically spoke her political speech.

"Yes, I understand that. As the head of this large corporation, I have a vested interest in all my employees being totally healthy. Correct me if I am wrong, but is not the sole stumbling block the Congress, which refuses to fund your pilot health care program?" Simon asked.

"Yes," Missy sighed, "they offer as many reasons against it as I can come up with reasons for it. Why?" she added a little infuriated, as much against her own failure to convince the Congress as the Congress' failure to fund it.

He didn't answer her, which annoyed Missy slightly. He continued, "Am I correct in assuming that you, as President, could dictate this Health Care Program, but you are being held back because of lack of funding? Is this not why you are having to deal with Congress instead of making a Presidential decree and getting on with the establishment of your proposed National Health Care Program?"

"Yes, and yes," Missy replied, growing even more annoyed that he was being so utterly blunt about her failings. At least he ought to be more polite with his criticism of her, she thought.

"I thought so. President Snow, how much money do you need to get the pilot program operational?" Simon asked.

"Right now, we are looking at ten million dollars to fund the pilot. Of course, once it has proven its worth, then millions more will be required. Why?"

"President Snow, if you will call my Executive Director with an appropriate bank account, I will see that ten million dollars are deposited there for the sole purpose of funding your pilot Health Care Program. Consider your financial barriers completely removed. Forget Congress and get on with your promise to the citizens of our great country."

Missy nearly fainted. She took several deep breaths, which only made her more lightheaded. She swallowed and finally got her voice back. "You—you will donate such a sum? Simon, this is the greatest gift I have ever had! On behalf of the entire country, I thank you!" She finally recovered her political sense. "However, I must ask you, are there any strings attached? People do not just go around donating ten million dollars every day."

"No strings. You have nothing that I need. My enterprises are huge. However, President Snow, I believe that I may be of even more assistance with your program. One of my subsidiary companies, Aetna Pharmaceuticals, has developed a new wonder drug. We have just finished all the secret testing phases as required by law and have now passed all the FDA requirements. However, we have not yet announced this new wonder drug to the world nor have we given it an official name. It is known internally as Saude Dourada."

"Our initial findings, from extensive and exhaustive testing studies, indicate that Saude Dourada makes the recipient 100% healthy, no disease, no colds, no flu, no cancer, just perfect health. However, we have also discovered that Saude Dourada has a unique side effect on all those who have taken it: total elimination of criminal thoughts and actions. Indeed, we are now conducting further tests in an undisclosed prison to see if it has this same effect on hardened criminals. If it does, not only will they become perfectly healthy, but also those who were criminals will become honest, contributing members of society once again. Further testing will give us better knowledge on just how effective this new wonder drug will be on mass populations. What do you think of this new development?" After a pause and hearing no reply, Simon said, "President Snow? Are you still there?"

For the first time in her life, Missy Snow was speechless! Cure all diseases? Cancer? Remove criminality? This was the greatest gift to mankind she had ever heard of! Gasping, she replied, "Yes! Yes, I'm overwhelmed! Cure disease is fantastic, but to also cure criminality? Simon, this is almost a gift from God! I don't know what to say. The benefits for our country are beyond staggering!"

"Ah, we think alike. Yes, that, too, is how I see it, staggering. What is even more incredible, Saude Dourada is incredibly inexpensive to manufacture. However, there is one problem, a serious one, from my point of view, being staunchly American. The moment that Aetna Pharmaceuticals releases this drug on the market, many other countries will want to purchase vast quantities of it for their own use. Where will our country be if all the citizens of all the European countries are perfectly healthy and have zero crime? Worse, what if China pursues this? Our beloved country, I fear, would quickly become a third world country! That is why I have withheld all news of Saude Dourada."

Missy jumped on his patriotism instantly. "Oh I quite agree! We cannot allow this to go to other countries, not until ours is well on its way to being completely healthy and without crime. We should be the ones holding that banner high. Look to the United States, for they are the ones who have brought heaven to all the peoples of Earth."

"Ah then, perhaps we think alike in the initial distribution of Saude Dourada," Simon replied. "What would you say if I were to donate all the Saude Dourada you could use, free, no charge, as long as I have your guarantee that none of it would ever be shipped outside of the US? Once our country is a shining example of healthy, crime-free citizens, then Aetna Pharmaceuticals would become the sole providers of Saude Dourada to the rest of the world. In other words, President Snow, we will donate all the drug needed for the entire US. Once the rest of the world desires the product, we will begin to sell Saude Dourada abroad, recover our costs, and make a very handsome profit as well."

"I would say that your offer is the most generous I have ever had. I give you my word none will leave the States. You and your pharmaceutical company will become incredibly famous, but your generosity should not go unrewarded, Simon."

"Reward enough for me when every citizen in the States is healthy and crime free. I will keep our company in the background. No limelight, please, low profile. Keep my name out of it, just refer inquiries to Aetna Pharmaceuticals; they will handle the press."

"Incredible, Simon, incredible. Seldom have I met such an honorable man as you, generous beyond imagination. You have the welfare of our citizens at your heart. One day, our country will likely erect monuments to your undying love and help for the US."

"Thank you, President Snow. As far as the details go, we ought to follow your pilot National Health Care Program. I believe it is most workable. Every citizen shows up once a month at the clinics to obtain their supply of Saude Dourada. How large an area were you planning for this pilot program? I ask, because we need to begin commercial production of the wonder drug and will need time to be able to mass-produce hundreds of millions of doses. All that takes time."

Missy answered, "My initial plans called for implementing the program in one state first. After a trial period, analyze the effectiveness of the program. Then, go from there. I had thought that we could try it on both New York State and the DC area. DC has one of the highest crime rates as well as poverty level. New York is not far behind. How soon would you be able to ramp up production to service that many people?"

"Excellent plan. I believe that we may be able to fulfill that initial request within a few months. It will likely take you and your staff some months to prepare anyway. Do we have a deal then?"

"Oh yes, we most certainly do have a deal, Simon. Of course, there are myriads of details to iron out. The Department of Health will need to examine the drug's testing and safety reports. Methods of delivery will need to be worked out."

"Thank you. Just refer all future questions to Aetna Pharmaceuticals or to my Executive Director, if you need to reach me. They have all the data that you and your staff could possibly want. I will issue the orders to begin ramping up production sufficient to handle New York and DC. Aetna will be able to let your people know when to expect the first deliveries. Oh, one minor detail that you should hear directly from me. There are two forms of the drug, one for normals such as us and another for those who practice magic. It seems there is a significant difference in body hormones between the two. Hence, the scientists have worked out the proper formula for each type. I don't begin to understand the science behind it, only that it has worked perfectly for both and passed all FDA tests. It has been a pleasure talking with you, President Snow."

"Oh no, it has been my greatest pleasure talking with you, Simon!" She heard the phone click; he'd hung up. Missy sat there holding her phone in the air for a minute. Her aide came in to the room. "Pinch me!" Missy said. "You'll not believe the deal I have just made for us!"

Chapter 2—The Pilot Program Begins

"It sure is quiet around here this summer," Lindsey Barron said to her friends, while she changed her year old, little brother's dirty diapers. Like her friends, she was sixteen, and this fall they would begin school at Arthur Bradbury's School of Magic as fifth year students. Lindsey had long brown hair, which she continued to let grow as much as it wanted. It now reached down to her the small of her back. After her first experiences with magical hairdos for the Presidential Inaugural Ball last January, she continued to use Full Body on her hair. Now it looked rich, thick, and silky. Her eyes were blue, but she had stopped growing taller. She was five-nine, but now her youthful body began filling out in all the right places, as her friends told her.

Her sister, Ashley Stokes-Compton, who her parents had adopted over a year ago, was holding Jonathon's hands as he playfully wiggled them. Ashley, who had lost her arms and both parents in a traffic accident when she was two years old, now had magically regenerated arms, good as new. Since she had met Lindsey some two years ago, she had been allowing her light brown hair to grow longer as well, though hers was wavy. Her hazel eyes only added to her mystique. Last January, Ashley had become a fashion model for Teen Fashion Magazine. Yes, she was a very beautiful young woman, though she was still growing taller. Currently, she was all of five-five.

Lindsey was learning how to become a Dispeller, following in her deceased father's footsteps. Sam Barron had been the world's most famous Dispeller, before he was murdered. A Dispeller is one who dispels attacking wizards and witches spells, keeping his or her friends alive so that they can capture the evil parties. Meanwhile, Ashley was definitely well on her way to becoming a Class 4 Diviner, one who can predict where and when something bad will happen.

For several years now, another young orphan teen,

Audrey Lemon was staying with them as well. Lena and Lloyd Compton, Lindsey's parents, had become Audrey's foster parents. Audrey was a silent girl, with sad looking, blue eyes. Average looking, Audrey was a brunette, short and curly. Audrey was a master wood carver, able to take a block of wood and turn out the most incredible carvings of animals imaginable. She now had her own website, an online store, where she sold them, usually making five hundred dollars a figurine. Audrey had a keen sixth sense. That is, she could sense whether she should be where she was. If something bad was going to happen in her vicinity, she knew about it instantly. While nowhere near as accurate and precise as Ashley's vivid premonitions, she nevertheless could sense when danger was near. She had stopped carving and had come to watch Jonathon a while.

Lena was a rugged Colorado ranch woman, whose spread was five miles square just north and east of the High Plains town of Arapahoe. She had three one-mile in diameter irrigated crop circles, which produced an abundance of crops. Her husband, Lloyd was actually a Security man working for the Department of Security, Magical Branch, High Plains, who was permanently on assignment here at the Compton ranch. His job was to guarantee the safety of Lena, Jonathon, and the girls when they were here during holidays and summer vacations. Why? The evil wizard Dominus Malefic had several times attempted to kill Lindsey and now Ashley, as well as another of their friends, Pam Betts.

Pam and her family were also staying here on the Compton ranch. Their home in Sterling, Colorado, had been attacked and was now being watched by the Death Stalkers of Dominus. Many times now, Pam had been instrumental in uncovering various plots of Dominus, causing numerous complications to his plans. She was a budding Sleuth. Dominus wanted Lindsey, Ashley, and Pam dead, but had been unable to succeed in that desire thus far.

Pam's father was Fred Betts, the head of the High Plains Department of Magical Misuse, a key position. He was usually gone most of the day. Her mother, Polly, now helped around the house, freeing up Lena so she could work the fields. Audrey, a plant expert, handled the ever-growing organic garden.

Pam, a computer expert, was melancholic today and had walked out to the living room to see what the others were doing. She felt rather lost. For the last four years, she had been in love with a gorgeous blonde, Monique Blackburn. Monique had just graduated from Bradbury's and had decided to become a Magical Doctor, like her father, Henry, who worked at Greeley General Hospital. Now that Monique was gone as well, Pam felt very alone. All these years, only Monique really loved her and appreciated her as she was.

Pam was homely. Her height was right, five-eight, as was her weight. Her large front teeth with their gap only added to the homeliness of her round face. That her black hair was more flyaway than hair made things worse. However, she had been allowing it to grow longer and had recently discovered that longer, it was a bit more manageable.

Also staying here with them was Pam's Aunt Wilma Welsti and her two older boys, who were being paid to help with the heavier ranch chores. Both boys were now nineteen. Wilma was also a member of Sam Barron's gang, called the Rat Pack. Wilma was their Eliminator, the one who did the actual capturing of the evil doers. Her disguise was that of Bill West. The fourth member of the Rat Pack was Able Monument or really the disguise used by Monane Tumble, an Apache woman and the Rat Pack's Tracker. A Tracker has the ability to see and follow the faint traces left by the magical energies of cast spells. Monane was now staying with her brother's family, Running Bear Whitewater, R. B. for short.

R. B.'s ranch was next to the Compton's ranch, also north of Arapahoe, but on the small Indian reservation. Some five hundred Native Americans lived on this reservation, and they owned and operated a gambling casino in Arapahoe. R. B. had nothing to do with the casino, however. He was a highly skilled magical item inventor.

His wife was Lucinda Morning Dove, Luci for short. Their oldest boy Tom had married Sandy Rains, an Arapaho, and the two were now in Denver going to college, their second year. Both Tom and Sandy opted to attend summer school this year, in hopes of graduating in three years, not four. His youngest son, Jim, who just graduated, was Ashley's boyfriend. Jim was off getting his Department of Security training, preparing for a career protecting others, especially from the likes of Dominus and his Death Stalkers.

Their eldest daughter, Amanda, was Lindsey's dearest friend. Amanda was tall, six-one, though she too was now filling out instead of further upwards. Amanda had thick lips, darkish skin, and very long, thick black hair. She and Lindsey were in an unspoken competition to see whose hair could grow the longest. Amanda was also a bit melancholic these first few days in June. Her boyfriend of four years, Henry, had just moved away to Chicago. Amanda was a beginning Tracker, like her Aunt Monane.

Her little sister, Fern, two years younger, had adopted Audrey as her closest, dearest friend. Indeed, they both had a love of plants in common. As much as possible, Fern hung out with Audrey.

Around the Whitewater ranch, things were particularly quite this June. All last year, the Blackburn family had stayed in R. B.'s second house. Now all four of them were gone, three back to Greeley, while Monique was in Denver going to a Magical Healing college. Jim and Tom were gone; the three foreign exchange students were gone; the place seemed horribly empty to Amanda and Fern. Even Monane, Luci, and R. B. felt the change. Luci encourage the girls to use their Teleport Pad, invented by R. B., to go over to visit with the Compton's as frequently as possible.

The monotone voice spoke, "Amanda and Fern are arriving." This magical warning system was devised by R. B.

"In here," Ashley called out. "Lindsey's changing Jonathon's diapers. We're all in here." Amanda and Fern joined them in the living room, just as Lindsey finished with Jonathon. Ashley picked him up and snuggled with him.

"What's up?" Lindsey asked, knowing that sounded awfully lame.

Amanda shrugged her shoulders. Fern asked, "Audrey, how's the elephant carving coming along? Want to see my deer? I'm nearly done." Audrey and Fern disappeared into

Audrey's workroom, where the two did their carvings together. Audrey was teaching Fern how to do it.

"Boy it sure is awfully quiet around here," Lindsey offered. "It feels so weird, so few around."

"Like a morgue," Pam mused.

"We have the chores done, so we are free to play, as long as we take care of Jonathon for mom. She's working the fields now," Lindsey explained.

"I miss my brothers," Amanda admitted. "I never thought I would, but with Jim gone too, it's so lonely around our house."

"Yes, and Henry dropping that bomb on you, telling you at the last minute that he was moving to Chicago, that certainly doesn't help either," Ashley added.

"Well, he only found out about it a few days before he told me," Amanda stuck up for her former boyfriend.

"What shall we do?" Lindsey asked, bored.

"Dunno," Pam said morosely.

"Dunno," Amanda added, not quite as morosely. Then, she asked, "Hey Ashley, have you decided anything about those modeling offers you got yesterday?"

Ashley had received two offers thus far. One was for Teens and the other for a follow up photo shoot with the original magazine, Teen Fashion. "I'm not sure about Teens, their models reveal more of their bodies than I feel comfortable showing. Teen Fashion's offer is a bit strange. It seems that they got a tremendous response on that one photo of me when I Morphed back into my old self, when I had no arms. Their offer wants me to model predominately that way, armless. Kind of strange, but they are offering me fifteen thousand dollars to do it. I haven't decided yet."

The four girls sat on the couch quietly doing nothing for several minutes, a total lull in their conversation. Finally, Ashley had an idea. "Say, why don't we go look at all those fetish clothes that Nadia van Nye Malefic gave to Lindsey? We can get a good look at them. After all, we've never really had the time to just examine them before now." That brought all four of them up to curiosity, and they headed to Lindsey's room to do just that, Ashley carrying Jonathon in her arms.

Since Ashley wanted to look too, Lindsey cast her Move Object spell, bringing the playpen into her room. Ashley put her little brother in it, and he got excited with his little toys. Meanwhile, Lindsey unlocked the small briefcase and spoke its command word, Open. At once, the case began unfolding until it occupied nearly half of the room, over fifteen feet long, but three feet deep.

"Wow, look at all the outfits!" Pam declared.

"And the heels!" Ashley added.

"Wow!" Amanda added. Lindsey smiled. She had many expensive clothes in there, including the four thousand dollar gown that she had worn in January to the Inaugural Ball.

"We should organize them," Lindsey suggested. "I understand them all better now. Nadia said some of these are only worn in private for your partner. I can certainly see why. Let's put that kind in one area. Let's put the ones that one of us might possibly wear to a dance over on this side."

She added hastily, "But be sure to move all the accompanying accessories as well. Nadia has these very well organized and color coordinated. She has a real sense of fashion, I'll give her that."

Many dresses were satin. Some were latex, while a few were of other materials. Some were long and form fitting. Others were very skimpy in length. "Golly, if I wore that maid's outfit, I wouldn't dare bend over! You could see everything!" Pam declared.

"Maybe you aren't supposed to bend over," Amanda suggested.

"Unless it is for your partner," Ashley teased them. "I bet if I wore this for Jim, well. . ." she didn't finish her sentence. She couldn't. All four giggled loudly.

"Oh, I just realized something. These corsets that are so colorful—they are supposed to be worn on top of the dress, while these other plain ones are worn beneath the dress. I get it," Lindsey explained her realization.

"Oh, I've seen that type before," Pam pointed out. "It's called a cat suit. Sure is fetish."

"Say, when Monique wore her boy's suit at the dances with you, wouldn't that qualify as a fetish outfit?" Lindsey asked.

Pam blushed, but answered, "Yes, she wanted me to look as good as I could. That's why she did it. It helped a little." Pam suddenly was lost in thought.

"What?" Lindsey nudged her, curious about what she was thinking about.

"Well, when we were at the Ball wearing these four thousand dollar dresses, compete with those really high heels, why, I felt beautiful. I can't explain it. It defies all logic. I was still me, but I felt so utterly different, you know. Weird," Pam explained.

"I felt sexy!" Amanda admitted. "*Really* sexy. I saw lots of men stealing glances at me too." They all giggled again.

"Twenty outfits," Ashley finished her tally. "You realize there is not one pair of heels in here shorter than five inches? Gosh. Half are even taller! I mean we were having a tough time managing the oxfords with five-inch heels."

"I imagine these others are more for private times," Lindsey concluded, though she had seen Nadia and Jolina, Nadia's constant companion and dear friend, wearing heels as high as the tallest in this collection. However, they were wearing them around the house. No—she now remembered that Nadia wore the six-inch heels at the Inaugural Ball and needed her to support her. Still, Lindsey could not imagine actually wearing them in public.

Sorting through the clothes, admiring them, arranging them, took all of an hour before the girls were bored once more. With all arranged properly, Lindsey shut her magical closet. The four wondered what to do next.

Lindsey sighed, "Well, I ought to practice on my harpsichord, and I ought to work on learning all those Grade 5 spells sans wand, sans words."

"Hey, let's work on the spells," Amanda said. Magic always had her interest.

"Yes, and I will see if I can learn any more that way too," Ashley added.

"I suppose that I ought to go do some more research," Pam sighed. "I've still got Governor Alister's special request to learn all I can about Dominus Malefic's Restricted Wish spell.

13

And then there is still the puzzle about why the Mac Fluide Enterprises is dealing with Dominus and loaning him money to start up a fishing business. You all go practice, and I'll watch over Jonathon for a while and do my research."

"Thanks, Pam," Lindsey replied. The three girls headed outside to practice spell casting, Pam cast her Move Object on the playpen, placing it in her room near her computer.

"Okay, Jonathon, let's see if Pam can figure out anything useful today," she talked to the year old baby as though he were grown up. A bit later, Pam told Jonathon, "Well, little fellow, Pam can't really do anything more on the Restricted Wish spell until I get back to the school's library. I guess I ought to see what more I can find out about Mac Fluide Enterprises, don't you think?" She looked down at the tyke. He looked up at her with his big brown eyes and smiled.

"Oh you want to be up here with Pam, do you? How can I turn those big brown eyes down?" Pam picked up Jonathon and sat him on her lap. At once, he began to reach for the keys of the keyboard, managing to pound a few. "Oh, you want computer lessons right away! Well, I think perhaps you need to grow a little, but Pam will teach you all she knows when you get bigger. Say, what have you done here?"

The baby had managed to task switch her laptop over the MagNews. Hugo, white teeth gleaming as usual, was reporting, "President Missy Snow has just unilaterally bypassed the Congress of the United States, which has for months balked at providing the needed funds to launch her ambitious National Health Care Program. KMAG News has just learned that the billionaire philanthropist, Simon Mac Fluide, has just donated ten million dollars to President Snow's program. This is the precise amount that she was seeking to get from the Congress. Bertha Dors, Secretary of Health, has just announced that the National Health Care Program will be launched in two weeks throughout the entire state of New York and the DC area."

"Here is an excerpt from the speech that the Secretary gave earlier this morning. This is Bertha Dors." Hugo gave a charming smile, as the screen switched to the prerecorded video shot earlier today.

The large woman spoke before a wall of cameras. "This is the pilot program. We will be carefully monitoring the results over a four-month trial period. After that, we will carefully evaluate the results and make a recommendation for the next phase. Beginning on Monday, every resident of these two areas will be asked to visit their local Health Care facility. The plan calls for monthly visits. The cost to the residents for all these visits is zero. All costs are fully covered by President Snow's plan. Of course, we realize that many will have difficult times getting to their local Health Care provider. They will not be left out. Anyone who cannot easily get to their local provider should call this number, and once a month, a traveling physician will visit their homes."

"The health care covers everyone from age three to ninety-nine. Smaller infants are exempt and should be handled by their pediatrician. Please note: this plan is not voluntary. Rather it is the civic *duty* and *obligation* of every resident of the state of New York and DC to see their local center within the next month. After that time, the Department of Law will compile a list of those who are violating the plan. During this pilot phase, those unwilling to follow the plan will be given a choice: follow it or move to another state. We expect to see tremendous benefits from this plan, absolutely mind blowing benefits, though I'm not at liberty to discuss those benefits with you just now. We are not just talking saving billions of dollars; no, we are looking to improve the overall health of every resident of these two areas."

"By October, the results of this first pilot program will be announced. President Snow plans to address the nation, presenting the results personally and announcing what the next phase will be. Thank you for your time."

Immediately, the reporters volleyed many questions her way. "What happened to freedom of choice? Are you making it against the law not to participate?" One reporter called out loudly.

Bertha turned to answer that one. "The benefits of the plan will only be seen in time. Honestly, do you really *want* to be ill? If our plan will guarantee that you will not get sick, not even a cold, wouldn't that make it valuable to you? Only with

100% participation can we cut the staggering cost of health care in this country. Let me put this to you another way. You are paying one third of your yearly income taxes on health care for either yourself or others who cannot afford it themselves. This is a staggering amount. What if that expense became zero, nada? Your taxes could be lowered by that amount, giving you that much more of your own hard earned dollars to spend on yourselves. Allow a handful to not participate and the cost of their emergency treatment begins to eat up all that savings. Do *you* want to give one third of your taxes to support those few who refuse the free health care? I think not."

"Secretary Dols," another reporter yelled the very instant she thought Bertha had finished, "What has Aetna Pharmaceuticals got to do with the program? Sources inside the White House tell us that they are deeply involved."

Bertha replied, "At this time, I not at liberty to say what their participation in the program will be, only that they are heavily involved. Their role will be fully explained by President Snow at the October Press Conference, where she will present the pilot program's results to every citizen of our country. Now, I have much work to do; this is a broad and sweeping program. Thank you very much." She stepped away from the microphones. Hugo's smiling face reappeared.

"You heard it, mandatory participation of every resident of New York state and DC! Yet, she has a point. We cannot allow a few individuals, who refuse to participate in the health care program, to run up such huge medical expenses that the rest of us have to pay for it out of our income taxes. Ladies and gentlemen, if I could save one third of what I pay in taxes each year, I could afford to buy a new car! It is my humble opinion, that if President Snow's program does indeed cut the astronomical health care costs in this country, then we must insist that the government lowers our taxes by that very amount. I put this very question to the Treasury Secretary an hour ago. Here is what Herman Smiley had to say." Hugo faded out, and the balding man appeared.

Herman said, "Once the program has been fully evaluated and the financial picture is clear, it is the expressed wishes of President Snow that the income tax rates be lowered accordingly. You suggest the figures that Secretary Dols has announced. If that holds up, then, yes, the President will be asking Congress to lower your taxes by that amount. In doing so, think of the economic impact that will have on the country's economy!"

Hugo reappeared onscreen. "I find this incredibly interesting news. I have asked our reporters to present us with an in depth study of our current health care system and its staggering costs. Tonight, I will present those results and compare it to what the Secretary of Health, Bertha Dols, today has suggested the savings may be."

Hugo leaned forward, moving in close to the camera, as if he were moving close to the viewer, sharing some important secret. "Personally, just between you and me, I don't see how just visiting your local health care center once a month will suddenly slash all of your medical expenses to zero. Doesn't this sound more than highly unlikely to you? Well, it certainly sounds preposterous to this reporter! Unless President Snow and Secretary Dols are outright lying to us about her health care program, there must be something else going on here that they are *not* telling us! I promise you that KMAG will get to the bottom of this. We will find out what *is* going on and report it to you immediately! Stay tuned to KMAG News. This is Hugo Whitefield reporting." A commercial for a breakfast cereal appeared on the screen, and Pam clicked the window into the background, de-activating it for now.

"This is scary, Jonathon! Mandatory participation, that's un-American. Just what are they going to do at the monthly doctor visit? How can one trip to a doctor each month keep anyone from getting a cold or flu? Hardly likely. Worse, Jonathon, I don't trust this Mac Fluide Enterprises at all! They have been funding Dominus Malefic and even letting him use their Florida studios to make his presidential videos, hijacking the commercial satellite feeds. We know that Snow is now a puppet of Dominus. She has one of his rings on her finger or rather imbedded in her finger. I don't trust any of this, do you little one?" She looked lovingly at Jonathon, who was sitting in the playpen looking up at her now. She had put him down when she became engrossed in the newscast.

"I know, I know. I should do more investigation of them. Okay, but I've been over this a hundred times already." Pam sighed and brought up their home page and stared at it. The screen title in bold, black lettering read: Simon Mac Fluide Enterprises Worldwide. Pam stared at the screen, hoping for some inspiration that she had not yet had before, something she could track down, some clue that she had overlooked during all her other research efforts into this corporation.

Minutes went by and still her mind was a complete blank. She smelled something foul, looked down at Jonathon and grinned. "You need a diaper change and some dinner, don't you? All right, Pam comes to your rescue." He cooed.

Having handled Jonathon and pelting him with kisses, Pam carried him back into her room. As she put him back in his playpen, positioning him so he could see her, she commented, "Boy, I sure do need to know the answer to this one, don't I?"

Like a bolt of lightning, it struck her! They'd learned a new divination based spell this past spring, the Know Answer spell. "What the heck? Why not?" She waved her wand and said, "Know Answer: Simon Mac Fluide Enterprises." Her wand activated, but she didn't see anything really happening at all. Thinking that this was a total bust, she sat down and stared at the screen.

Suddenly she saw double. There was the web page line and another ghostly line appeared just below it. They read:

Simon Mac Fluide Enterprises

Dominus Malefic Enterprises

She stared at these double images. Now the letters seemed to move apart until she saw:

S I M O N M A C F L U I D E

D O M I N U S M A L E F I C

"It can't be!" Pam mutter, hastily writing out the letters, Simon Mac Fluide. Then she began crossing out the letters as she spelled out Dominus Malefic. "Oh my god! Oh my god!" exclaimed Pam. "He's done the same darn thing that Sam Rabnor did, scrambling his letters to form Barron, just like Wilma and Monane did too. All four did the same thing with their names. Oh dear god, Mac Fluide Enterprises is Dominus's own huge corporation! Oh no! Now he is giving Missy Snow ten million dollars for the Health Care Program! Oh no, no, no! Jonathon, this is horrible news. I have to let everyone know about this right now before it is too late!" He cooed again.

"Where is a Mass Message spell when you need one?" Pam said disgustedly. At once she began a litany of Message spells. Only after firing off twenty identical Message spells did Pam finally calm down. She'd notified her father, Governor Alister, the faculty at Bradbury's, her friends, and even her Dutch foreign exchange students from last term.

She'd no more than finished sending the last ones, when Messages began appearing before her eyes. Governor Alister's message read:

Brilliant Pam. Will Message the others and will meet with Rodents tonight after supper. A.

Instead of replying, Lindsey, Ashley, and Amanda came running inside to see her, joined on the way by Fern and Audrey.

"Pam, how on earth did you figure this out? It's so simple, we all should have seen this ages ago!" Lindsey declared.

"I know. I feel like the world's biggest idiot," Pam replied. Wilma and Monane poked their heads into the room and overheard her comment.

"Pam, it is Monane and I who are the idiots! We never dreamed that he did the same thing as we did with our names. I feel like an imbecile! However, Pam, this discovery is monumental in its importance!" Wilma exclaimed.

Monane added, "Now we have a clue to Dominus's next action. It has something to do with this National Health Care Program. Brilliant, Madam Sleuth! Did you get Alister's Message about meeting tonight?"

"Yes, I got it."

Ashley commented, "I told you all this was really, really bad, but now it is so much more worse that I am getting really scared again. This enterprise corporation of his is huge! Our battle has gone from trying to capture and defeat one man to an entire corporation. I'm scared!"

Audrey was just extremely pale. She didn't have to voice her fear; it was plainly visible.

"Ashley, you have every right to be scared, honey," Wilma replied. "Personally, I am too. We all are. You are right. We are facing a whole corporation, not one man. Now for the first time ever, I can see why we have been having such a hard time tracking this man down and bringing him to justice. He has his hands in many, many other countries as well as ours, access to nearly inexhaustible resources. Yes, Ashley, I'm very scared. I hope Alister can calm us all down tonight!"

"Oh no! My dad!" exclaimed Ashley, who was having a flash of insight. "He was investigating that corporation and was about to expose who Simon really was! No wonder dad and mom were murdered! Darn you, Dominus, I'm going to make you pay for what you did to my mom and dad!" Anger seethed in the young teen's body; her fear had given way to a total hostility.

"You are right! Now it makes complete sense—why your folks were murdered," Lindsey replied.

Ashley became down right antagonistic. "Yes, it sure does make sense! I'm relieved in a way," she sighed. "You know—knowing the real reason why. Well, I'm ready to do my part in putting this man where he belongs. I hope we can get on to it sooner than later."

"Say, I heard Hugo say something about one of their affiliated companies was going to be involved in this Health Care Plan, Aetna or something like that," Pam stated flatly, finally calming down. "I'd better see if I can find out what their connection is supposed to be." She returned to her laptop and began searching for this company. The others decided to have some sodas to calm down a bit, before resuming their spell casting practice, leaving Pam alone with Jonathon and her computer.

An hour later, a frustrated Pam picked up Jonathon to take him for a walk. She just could not find a way to hack into the Department of Health's system nor into Aetna Pharmaceuticals to see what was going on between the two. She thought about seeing if some hacker in the Underground would do it for her, but thought better of it. Breaking into those departmental systems carried huge penalties if caught. Hacking into Aetna's would be a direct challenge to Dominus, putting the hacker at a severe risk of being hunted down and murdered by Death Stalkers. She valued these anonymous hackers too much to sacrifice their lives.

Lena came in for a break. "Lena, I think that Jonathon might be hungry again," Pam ventured. He was being very fussy just now.

"Yes, I figured so. Hold him while I heat up his grub." While Lena began fixing his baby food, she asked, "Say, having any luck on that corporation of Dominus's?"

"No, I can't get into Aetna's site or into the Department of Health. Hence, I am still in the dark, but there must be some awful connection, I just know it."

Taking Jonathon from Pam, Lena began feeding him. "Well, they make drugs, don't they? I mean, that's what pharmaceutical companies do."

"Sure," Pam answered, not seeing where Lena was going with her question.

"Well, if they make drugs, it stands to reason that they need to then ship those drugs to their destinations. If you can't find out from either the source or the recipient, then there are always the transportation companies. Someone has to handle the shipping."

"Brilliant, Lena! Yes! I'm off. Oh, when he's fed, you can bring him back. I'm watching him, and he's watching me."

"Okay, but it is time for his nap. He can sleep in his playpen I guess," Lena replied. Pam dashed off to check on trucking companies.

Pam didn't need to Google on trucking companies. She knew there were thousands of them, anyone of which might be making the deliveries. Instead, she went to the GEOSAT tracking site. All trucks these days used the GEOSAT system. The drivers punched in their origin point and their destination point, and the GEOSAT system handled the driving. Accidents had been reduced to nearly nil as a result.

Pam had no idea where the Aetna laboratories might be located, so she again browsed their website. While their research labs were in South Florida, she found that their manufacturing and distribution center was in Macon, Georgia. She entered that as the source location. The destination location was more problematical. The Health Care Program was to be implemented in all of New York and DC. She assumed that there could be many drop off points for such deliveries. Hence, she decided to try just the DC area first.

Minutes later, she had the real time map of all trucks in transit between these two locations. "What'cha doing?" Lindsey asked, whispering softly so as not to wake up her sleeping brother. They had finished their spell casting practice sessions, and she had come to see if Pam wanted to go swimming with them.

"Trying my best to find out what's going on between Aetna and the Health Program. Here are all the trucks in transit between Macon, Georgia and DC—lots of them to choose from. However, they might not be shipping today, so I will have to look at all the traffic say for the past month and see if I can find out something."

"That sounds like a long project. We are going for a dip. Want to join us?" Lindsey asked.

"No, I'd rather work on this. We need everything we can find out, if we are going to have any chance of stopping him," Pam said with a sigh.

"Don't they have all that stored in a database somewhere? Wouldn't it be easier if you got a copy of that database and then wrote a program to go find what you are looking for?" Lindsey asked, unwilling to let Pam just sit inside on such a fine June day. Besides, she knew that Pam was feeling terribly lonely now that Monique had left.

"Well, actually, Lindsey, you are quite right. I will be wasting tons of time doing it this way. Thanks for the tip."

"Okay, so why not come outside with us and get some space and fresh air?"

"Okay, okay, as long as I can just sunbathe. You know I don't really like to go swimming," Pam agreed at last. Lindsey moved the crib into the kitchen area where Polly was working on making dinner for everyone. She agreed to keep an eye on the sleeping baby.

Soon they joined the others who were already splashing in the waters of R. B.'s large pond. Pam put her towel onto the grass at the side of the pond and dipped her feet into the water. "There, I've been in the water, satisfied?" she teased Lindsey, who threw her towel down beside Pam's. Lindsey giggled.

"Say, can I ask you a really personal question, Pam? I've been wanting to ask you for years, but I just never got the chance."

"Sure," Pam replied, wondering what Lindsey wanted to know about her.

"Were you and Monique in love with each other, like Tom and Sandy who got married last summer? You don't have to answer me if you don't want to. I mean, I've got no right to ask you this. It's just I've been curious about it for years. If you were, I can understand what her going off to school means to you."

Pam's face felt very hot, but she replied anyway. "Yes, I thought that we were in love. I mean she's the first person who really cared for me, good old homely me."

"But that's not true, Pam. I care for you very much, so does Ashley and Amanda. We care a whole lot."

"Yes, but that's not the same thing. I was, well, attracted to her. She's beautiful. She is older and wiser about many things. She's very good with computers like me. We had a lot in common. I, we, sort of fell in love with each other, but. . ." Her voice trailed off and she became silent.

"But?" Lindsey asked.

"Well, I'm now all confused. It happened at the Ball, you know. I saw that new guy she met there, that Ace Brill, of the Colorado Department of Defense, Magical Branch, kissing her—kissing her like we kissed! I could tell that Monique feels towards him as she felt towards me. Now that she is gone off to school, I've lost her. I know it. Ace will be probably courting her; I'll bet anything on it. I saw his eyes. He was really taken with Monique."

"Gosh Pam, I didn't know. I'm so sorry for you." Lindsey didn't know what else she could say to her dear friend.

"What makes it horribly worse for me is that for the

very first time in my life, I felt really beautiful at that Ball. You know, we were so fancied up. I never had long nails like that or a dress even remotely like that one, let alone those high heels. For the very first time, Lindsey, I felt that I was truly worthy of Monique."

"That must be devastating to you! I didn't know," Lindsey repeated herself.

"It was like someone threw a snowball into my face!" After a pause, she added, "But then there was the boy our age who was dancing with me, Tom Ryker. He's the son of the Arizona Department of Law head, Bill Ryker."

"What about Tom? He danced with you all night long," Lindsey asked, wondering where this was headed.

"He and I got on very well. I mean I don't usually get along well with boys. They take one look at me and go yuck. Lindsey, I really like Tom, but then I don't suppose that I will ever see him again. After all, he's in southern Arizona, Phoenix School of Magic, he said. But he's the nicest guy I've met yet."

"Well, why don't you email him? Start up a chat or something. Maybe he feels strongly about you too?" Lindsey suggested.

"Yes, but what if he doesn't? What if he was just dancing with me, like he said at first, to avoid having to dance with his mother?"

"Then, you will be crushed, Pam, but at least you will know how he feels and you can move on from there," Lindsey advised.

Pam flashed a smile, "Better to have all the crushing news right now, isn't it? I mean how much more crushed can I get?" A bit later, Pam sent an email off to Tom Ryker.

That evening after supper, Polly had the girls help her brew a large batch of tea. "We are expecting a lot of visitors this evening. We need to be prepared. I've baked up a bunch of pies. Hope they will be enough." The girls giggled and lent a hand. Shortly after six, people began arriving.

Governor Alister arrived, bringing Deiter Cross with him. Minutes later, most all the professors from Bradbury's School of Magic arrived, but not Professors Blake and Janice Smith—the latter was disliked by Lindsey and her friends.

Doctor Henry Blackburn arrived at the same time as Jim Whitewater. Jim at once gave Ashley a loving, long kiss. Tom and Sandy Whitewater came and were immediately surrounded by R. B., Luci, Fern, and Amanda, asking them lots of questions about how college was going for them. Tom began explaining how they could graduate in three years not four, if they did summer schools each year.

Lindsey was very surprised to see the other arrivals. Fred Betts brought along his boss, the head of the Colorado Department of Magical Misuse, Casper Williams, his peer, Rachel Smith of Denver, and Governor Lacy Broom, the US Governor General over all the magic schools. Not long after that, Pina Pong, Governor General of the Southeast Asian schools also arrived, along with Ace Brill, Colorado Department of Defense, Bill Ryker and Kathy Jacks, Arizona and Colorado Departments of Law, respectively.

This was the largest assemblage of people yet here on the Compton ranch. Just the introductions alone took nearly a half hour. At last, Alister rose, sitting his teacup aside. "I have called this meeting of the Rodent Pack because of the startling revelation made by Miss Betts this afternoon. We have all been underestimating Dominus Malefic so enormously that it is not even funny. So many events in the past have now become strikingly clear to me. For example, fourteen years ago, Ashley's father, a deep undercover agent for the Chicago Department of Law, was on to Mac Fluide Enterprises. His last journal entry suggests he was about to disclose just who Simon Mac Fluide really was, Dominus Malefic, though perhaps it is the other way around. He was summarily murdered along with his wife. Many things are now clear to me."

"Until today, I was under the misguided notion that we faced one man and his Death Stalkers. Now, I realize just how wrong we have all been. Behind the scenes for many, many years, Dominus has been establishing an entire network of 'legal' businesses, from banking, to pharmaceuticals, to airplanes. The list of companies under corporation ownership is staggering. He has built an entire network of companies. Why?"

"I thought about this for some time, before I sent you

today's summons. All this elaborate planning can only be direct towards his stated Manifesto, his so called Golden Path, a path which puts him as the dictator of the entire world. Last year, we thought it was the height of folly for him to run for President. Yet, that too is part of his overall plans. Now we know that he has millions of Americans under his direct control via the rings that he gave out under the cover of Dominus for President. I must tip my hat to Dominus. That was one very clever bit of planning. We never saw it coming."

"Today, we have had our first break. Via Pam's revelation, we can now connect the dots, as she would say. This mandatory National Health Care Program of President Missy Snow is funded by Dominus. His Aetna Pharmaceuticals company is playing a major role in that program. However, just what that role may be, we do not yet know. I've called everyone here for a major strategy and planning session. What should we do now? I throw the table open to suggestions." Alister sat down.

Ace Brill, whom Pam thought was now Monique's boyfriend, replacing her, spoke up first, "I would like to add a little more facts to what Governor Broadwell has said. As head of the Colorado Department of Defense, I have been issued some orders connected with the rollout of this Health Care Program in New York. All the state heads have been ordered by the Secretary of Defense to summarize the crime rates in our states fully and completely, going back over the last ten years. We were told that these data will be later compared to the rates found in New York and DC after the pilot program is over in October. As far as we know, the program is to start on July 1. I've discussed this with a number of other state heads and our conclusion is that this Health Care Program is somehow expected to lower the crime rates drastically in these two test areas. No one will give us a direct reason why this may be."

Old Casper Williams rose next, "This gets curiouser and curiouser. I have a connection over in the Department of Records. Right now, Sam 'DNA' Spade has everyone working overtime compiling lists of all known wizards and witches living in DC and New York State. I don't know what this has to do with anything, but it is somehow connected to the Health Care Program." He sat down.

Governor Lacy Broom rose next. "As you know, I'm in charge of all the schools of magic in the US. I report directly to Thomas White, the US Regent, whom we know is under the direct control of Dominus. He has given me direct, specific orders regarding the implementation of the National Health Care Program in New York, as it relates to the New York School of Magic. He has made it clear to me, and I have been forced to make this clear to Governor Alice Walker of the New York School of Magic. All students and all faculty and staff who are wizards or witches must report to their Infirmary monthly. He said that they must receive the B pill. All non-magically endowed staff must also report monthly to receive their A pill. By his orders, anyone failing to comply will be expelled from school or, if they are faculty or staff, arrested."

"I tried to get him to discuss what these pills were, would do, or anything about them. He flatly refused to divulge any further data. Obviously, we can now presume this Aetna company is manufacturing them. What in the world are these pills anyway?" No one knew.

After the conversation died down, she continued. "Of course, this is going to pose severe problems for the New York School of Magic. Alice Walker bitterly protested to me, but there is nothing I can do about the ruling. She and I came to a compromise. You didn't hear this from me," she cautioned.

"Many feel that their rights are being violated by this mandatory pill taking, especially when the contents and effects of said pills are not known. Hence, you may expect a very large number of transfer students this fall. Shortly, I will be drafting a letter to all the US magic school Governors telling them to expect a sizeable number of transfer students. This also includes faculty. According to Alice, she expects that half of her faculty will either retire or move to another state. Some will need jobs, so my letter will also alert you to this possibility as well. As far as the norms there, we don't know enough about norms to answer that one."

"Well I do," Professor Herbert Mac Elroy, Lindsey's math teacher, a sixty-four year old, grey haired non-wizard, rose. His wife, Professor Elaine, was a witch and taught English. "We don't take kindly to being ordered to take unknown pills or anything. You may expect a sizeable number of ordinary citizens will be so outraged by this move that they will pack up and move to another state. The surrounding states ought to be forewarned; they may see a sudden population explosion in the next three weeks. Whatever is our country coming to?" he sat down, quite angry.

Professor Delius Dogs rose, "If I may make a suggestion? At this time, we ought to obtain some of these 'pills' and analyze them. Just what will be their effects? I find it very disturbing that there are to be two pills, one for those of us who control magical energies, and one for those who do not. Very disturbing."

Pam rose. Lindsey opened her mouth to say something, but quickly shut it. Among all these important adults, Pam felt a bit daunted. "I'm researching what trucking company they are using to transport the pills to DC. Once I know that, I can tell you just what truck is on its way and precisely where it is located at any point in time."

"Brilliant," Delius rose again. "May I suggest that a few boxes of these pills magically disappear from the shipment? Once we have them, where can they be analyzed? Do we have any laboratories that we can trust this to be handled secretly and safely?"

No one had an answer. Finally, Doctor Blackburn rose. "Well, I am a facial reconstruction specialist, but we do have limited facilities at Greeley General Hospital. I know some lab folks who could perform some basic tests on the quiet. This would be a start. Another possibility to keep this out of the major labs, which will likely be being monitored, would be to make use of some CSI lab. They are fully equipped to analyze unknown substances."

After some further discussion, Fred Betts rose, "I know a fellow I can trust in the Colorado CSI unit in Denver. Get me some samples, and I'll see what can be discovered about them as well."

Professor Cho Lin rose, "You know, something Lacy mentioned is bothering me. It is this exodus thing. Personally, if I were on the New York faculty, I would depart rather than be subjected to taking unknown pills. Should we be making some kind of contingency plans to house and care for those who chose to evacuate New York and have no place to go or stay? What if this goes nationwide? What then? Is Singapore School of Magic hiring," she jested to Pina Pong, who grinned back.

Lena rose to speak, a mere norm among these powerful wizards and witches. Lindsey was very surprised as she rose, still cradling Jonathon, who was asleep in her arms. "We have a lot of space here. I would be more than willing to provide shelter for anyone in need. Perhaps with R. B.'s help, we can add another home like this to house them."

Before she could sit down, R. B. rose, "Excellent, Lena. Yes, the Compton and Whitewater ranches are perfect for this—remote and out of the way. I will see to it that we have enough of these energy efficient homes to meet the needs, within reason of course. We can live nearly independent of civilization out here, if we must, though getting the kids to survive without sodas and pizzas will be tough." All the teens chuckled.

Alister joined them, "I will see to the expansion of our dorms. Bradbury's could accommodate many more students, if need be."

"Thanks Lena, R. B., Alister. I feel better about it now," Professor Cho Lin replied.

Pina Pong rose, "May I make a suggestion? What about making a worldwide attempt to choke off the basic supplies that this Aetna company needs to make these pills? Lord knows how badly we want to put Dominus out of business. He's wanted for a dozen murders and nearly fifty robberies in Southeast Asia alone."

Deilus added, "She's got a valid point. Once we know what raw materials are needed for their manufacture, we should do everything possible to cut them off."

"We'll have to do it in secret, vigilante style," Kathy Jacks rose and replied. "As it now stands, the Departments of Law and Misuse cannot touch it in any way. I don't condone taking the Law into your own hands, but in this case, I don't see any other viable way. Dominus now has control over the normal law enforcement lines."

"In a related matter," Lacy rose once more, "I have visited with all the US Governors. All pass the sub-dermal ring test. Evidently, Dominus cares little about the magic schools."

"Well, that is a bit of bright news, Lacy. Thank you," Alister complimented her efforts.

She added, "They are taking a cue from you, Alister. Each school is holding a physical exam week at the start of the fall term. Any student who has such a ring will be given the choice of having it cut off or leaving the school. I insist that we have no hidden Dominus controlled students on any of our campuses. I don't want a repeat of the bombings that you had at Bradbury's, Alister."

"What about their faculty and staff? Are they to be examined as well?" Delius asked.

"Yes, I'll not have a Dominus-controlled professor teaching our children. I have put my foot down on that one. However, I have no intention of ever telling my boss what I've ordered. I feel he has no need to know how I run my magic schools, none of his business," Lacy replied. Lindsey noted that Professor Delius seemed very relieved.

Bill Ryker rose when she finished. "In late August, all the heads of the state Departments of Law will be meeting in Chicago with Geneva Holmes. At that time, I will endeavor, with Kathy Jacks assistance, to find out which state Department of Law heads are not under the control of Dominus. By late fall, we should know better just how bad the rodent infestation actually is." Several chuckled at his jest.

Professor Delius rose once more, "Governor General Lacy, I would like to make a suggestion for your consideration. At Bradbury's, we ran mock battles last year. Every five weeks, all those in a specific year who wanted to participate, joined in mock combat situation. I refereed them. No spells are ever actually cast. The five-minute combat is recorded, and the students review the recording afterwards. It has been incredibly instructive and very productive, perhaps one of the best educational drills we have ever had. My suggestion is that you suggest that the other schools of magic adopt a program similar to ours. If you like, the teens here tonight have been participating all last year and can give you their own point of view on the mock battles."

"Yes, I've heard about that program. Let's discuss this in detail after the meeting. It may well come down to the kids versus Dominus," Lacy replied.

The adults chatted a bit more, and then the meeting broke up. Polly, Wilma, and Monane served up pie and hot tea. During the informal hour, Delius and Lacy talked at length about the mock battles. Lacy wanted to hear just how they were done. After that, Lacy chatted with Deiter, Lindsey, and Ashley, getting their opinions on the program. When she left, she was firmly convinced this program needed to be adopted at the other schools. She vowed to make it so, if possible.

Since Deiter came with Alister, he had to leave when the Governor did. As he left, he called out to Lindsey, "I'll be coming round tomorrow morning about ten to show you something. Bye for now."

"What's he going to show you, Lindsey?" asked Amanda.

"I have no idea." Lindsey hated being left in a mystery. She wanted to box his ears for leaving her like this—wondering all night.

After the last guests had left, Lloyd sat down with Ashley. "Have you reached a decision on the offers for more modeling, dear?"

"I'm definitely not going to do the one where they want me nearly naked!" Lloyd grinned, thankful for this decision. "But I can't make up my mind on the other one. I mean it will be fall clothes and all that—nothing wrong with that. It's just that they want most of the shots to be me without arms. I can't figure out why? What do you think, dad?"

"It's up to you. You really don't need the money, so you should do what you really desire to do. If you feel uncomfortable with it, then say no. I'm sure other offers will come along sometime."

Ashley giggled, "So you aren't going to tell me if I should or not, are you?"

"Nope." She gave him a big hug, realizing that he was

treating her as an adult.

"Well then, I think I will do it. I thought about it, and there are other women who have disabilities as well, like missing arms and such. If they see me as being comfortable with it, perhaps it will help build their own confidence. If just one teen does, then it is all worth it. That's how I see it."

"Admirable reason to do it. Shall we sign the papers and let them know?" Lloyd asked. They did so. The next day, they learned the shoot would take place on June 22 in Hollywood, which excited the teens all the more.

The next morning around ten, Lindsey was waiting for Deiter to show up with his surprise. All the teens wondered what he was mysteriously going to show Lindsey. They heard a low flying airplane outside, but thought nothing of it until the monotone voice announced "Deiter Cross is arriving."

Lindsey dashed to the front door. Opening it, she was taken by complete surprise. A small single engine Cessna had just landed on their mile long drive, taxing up to their front door. Everyone ran to the plane, and a very proud Deiter climbed out, standing tall on the footpad on the wing of his plane.

"Hi ya! Like my new plane? Dad got it for me. Got my license to fly too. Been soloing for a couple of weeks." He climbed down, the girls swarmed around him, anxious to see a real airplane up close.

"Well, you sure surprised me, Deiter. How many can it carry?" Lindsey asked.

"Three including me. Miss Barron, Miss Stokes-Compton, would you care to go for a fly and see what your ranch looks like from the air?" Deiter asked, scarcely able to contain his enthusiasm. They didn't need to be asked twice! He showed them where to step, and soon Ashley was in the back seat, while Lindsey sat beside Deiter.

He talked them through the starting sequence, checking each aspect of the plane before he started the engine and then took off, roaring down their long roadway. From the air, Lindsey got a spectacular view of her ranch, the Whitewaters, and Arapahoe as well. After the short ride, Deiter took Amanda and Audrey. Next, Pam and Fern got a ride as well.

"Well, that's all the gas I've got. I have to head over to Lamar to fill up before I head back to Colorado Springs. Isn't this the greatest thing, flying in a plane, I mean?" Lindsey had to admit that she had a ball. Deiter volunteered to come again another day and bring his plane.

"Well, that was sure a surprise," Lindsey said, waving goodbye to Deiter as he began rolling down their road again.

"No kidding, makes me want to cast my Fly spell and zoom around here a while," Ashley commented.

Pam was mostly unmoved, "Honestly, I prefer my Fly spell. There are just too many mechanical things on which he has to depend for that plane to fly."

Chapter 3—A Rare Day in June

Pam set to work attempting to determine the trucking line being used to bring the pills to the DC or New York areas. This, she soon discovered, was going to be trickier than she had anticipated. This whole business was shrouded in secrecy. Aetna Pharmaceuticals used more than one trucking company and had no set delivery pattern. While she was able to spot a truck that left the distribution center in Macon, Georgia, when the truck stopped at a weigh station along Interstate 95, the weight indicated the truck was empty and the driver declared an empty manifest. She began to wonder if the trucks were just dummies. Perhaps they were making the deliveries by use of Teleport spells. This, she reasoned, would not only be safer but also secure as well as secret. It would certainly be the method that she would use.

Her computer beeped indicating that she had incoming email. Pam tasked switched over to Agent and saw a new arrival. Her heart skipped a beat. It was from Tom Ryker. For a moment, she sat there not willing to read it, fearful of yet another round of crushing news. "Might as well get it over with," she muttered to herself. She clicked on it and began reading.

Hi Pam,

Really super to hear from you!

I rather figured you probably weren't interested in someone like me, which is why I didn't write. Girls around here aren't interested in me. Just between you and me, I'm not much interested in them either.

Every girl I've met here in Phoenix is an airhead, you know. They seem proud that they don't know what a hypotenuse is or how to prove the earth moves around the sun or why everyone's fingerprints are different. They are all into looking fashionable, being hooked up with fancy houses and all that. Yes, I know Phoenix has some incredibly expensive homes.

Me personally, I rather live with someone I respect and

admire. That means more to me than marble tiled floors and gold plated faucets in the bathrooms.

Our chat on the dance floor about why the CSI's use different colored fingerprint powders was incredibly stimulating. I thought about it until I fell asleep that night.

I must admit, Pam, I have never met a young woman quite like you before. In fact, I think that you are far more brilliant than I am, which I find humbling.

My dad's now under an awful lot of stress. His boss, Geneva Holmes is Dominus controlled. He swears that she is watching him like a hawk. Is it the same with your dad?

I know you probably won't be interested in dating a computer geek like me, but I would be really honored if we could just be friends. I know you mentioned that you were good with computers. I plan to be a Mag Computer Engineer, which of course turns off all the girls around here. That is, until their computer goes on the fritz. Then it's "Oh help me please, Tom!"

I've been doing C++ programming since I got my first computer when I was six. Right now, I have been taking Advanced Computer Engineering as my electives ever since third year when we finally could have that option.

I've already written and sold one of my programs. You've probably have never heard of the surveying company called Belliard's. They make the Marshal Angles, which is a surveying tool that makes surveying field work a breeze, thanks to my software. It measures line of sight angles. I made ten grand on that sale. I think that programs ought to make life and work easier for people. Anyway, that's the aim of my software. I will probably open my own business when I graduate.

However, mom and dad, they want me to go into either the Department of Law or Magical Misuse. We've had arguments over this. They want me putting my skills on detecting, finding, or trying criminals. Me, I want to make people's lives and work easier. Ah well, parents.

Anyway, Pam, I am attaching a photo of me working away on my computers, in case you forgot what I look like. If you wouldn't mind, I would really love to have a photo of you, but I'll understand if you don't want to do that.

Your friendly Phoenix computer geek,

Tom Ryker

Pam let out a little squeal as she finished reading the email. She double clicked and launched her image viewer to see Tom's photo. He was acting silly in front of several monitors. He evidently had several.

"What's up?" Lindsey asked. Passing by Pam's door, she'd heard the squeal.

"Tom sent me a reply and his photo!" Pam said, trying to conceal her excitement.

"Can I read it?" Lindsey begged. Pam moved back so Lindsey could see her monitor. "You really talked to him about CSI fingerprint powders while you two were dancing?" Lindsey asked, rather floored by the topic.

Pam blushed, "Well, yes, we did."

"Hey, he is deep into computers too. That's got to be a plus for you, right?"

"Well, yes," Pam admitted. "I can't believe that he was the one who wrote the software for those Marshal Angles. I gave one to Amanda and Monane to help them with their tracking. Small world!"

"I remember. Wow, he wrote the program, cool! Pam, I think that he is interested in you. Are you going to write him back? You should tell him how into computers you are. Honestly, I don't know anyone better with them than you, Pam."

"You think I should? Write him?" Pam asked a little insecure, after all this was a boy she was writing to, not Monique.

"Sure, why not? Tell him about yourself, I suppose. As long as you are honest with him, then you can't be hurt. If he doesn't want you, then that's the way it goes. I'd at least chat with him," Lindsey suggested. "He is kind of cute. Say, what does he mean by a computer geek?" Lindsey had not heard that term before, but then she'd never had or used a computer until going to Bradbury's.

Pam giggled, "I'm considered a computer geek.

36

Someone who is deep into computers. Usually, it is a derogatory term, like his term airhead. Okay, I'll write him back."

At lunch, R. B. joined them, bringing a set of plans for expansions. "The first question, Lena, Lloyd, is do you want a separate house or would you prefer this house expanded double?"

Before Lloyd could respond, Lena asked, "Isn't one larger home more easily defended than two separate houses?"

"Very true. Even if the two houses are joined via a common hallway, you still have two separate entrances to guard. One larger place is more defensible," R. B. pointed out.

Lena looked at Lloyd and said, "Then, let's go more defensible. I don't mind more people around. Perhaps we can find a way for them to still have some privacy as well."

Lloyd agreed, "Yes, one large unit, but isn't it risky only having one exit? Perhaps we build an extension on either side of this house. We could have two more front porches or rather one long one, and then have three front doors. Inside, the rooms can connect, allowing free passage as needed, yet giving the other residents some privacy as well."

"It sure is a good thing that I followed Audrey's suggestion to grow more vegetables this year," Lena commented. "We've now got all twenty-five square miles or sixteen thousand acres irrigated, not just the three circles. The crop circles are in wheat for flour, and the rest is vegetables. I think by harvest that we'll be able to support quite a lot of people in these new buildings. Say, what about Wilma's boys? Won't they have to be moved?"

"Yes, we can move them into one of the new spaces when it is finished," Lloyd replied. "Say what about making a long hallway and then having two bedroom apartments coming off that hallway? We could fit more families this way."

"Scrap my first plan," R. B. chuckled, turning them over, he began to sketch out another idea. "Look, one long hall goes down the length of either side of your house, connecting doors in several of your existing rooms. We then divide the ninety-five by two hundred foot section into four equal sized homes. Each can have a huge living room and another large room behind that, leading to a long hallway. On either side are the bedrooms, say four of them, two baths, ending at the combination dining room, kitchen, and pantry. Given that Wilma's boys will take over one home, that means you can add seven more families without the slightest crowding."

"How much is this going to cost us?" asked Lena, always conscious of the finances.

"What say you if I use adobe for the inner walls? That will accomplish two things, lower the total cost dramatically and add a good measure of soundproofing," R. B. suggested. "I bet this way that we can do it all, including the furnishings for twenty grand, maybe less. I believe that I will also do the same thing to my ranch. Then, we can buy in bulk and get better deals."

Lindsey was about to volunteer the needed funds, but Lloyd spoke first. "Perfect, I have more than enough to cover it in my account. Let's get started as soon as possible. Undoubtedly, folks from New York are going to begin evacuating soon, certainly by the first of July, three weeks from now."

"Hum, manpower, Lloyd. We are going to need some workers. We can use Wilma's boys. It would be ideal to have another pair of strong arms."

"I will ask Deiter and Emilio if they are interested," Lindsey finally said something. "Besides, Kathy might want to come to help too, since she is going to go with Ashley to the photo shoot."

"Okay, then shall we get started yet today? I will bring my Magical Digger over here and we can get going," R. B. replied.

Luci teased, "Lena, you'd best keep an eye on R. B. and that digger of his. Before you know it, he will have dug three ponds for you as well!" Everyone laughed. R. B. did love to play with his invention, one of the more enjoyable of his inventions.

Lindsey emailed Deiter, Emilio, and Kathy. Andy had already left for another archaeological dig, so he was out. At one, R. B. had his Magical Digger in operation. Deiter, Emilio, and Kathy arrived, eager to help. At first, everyone stood around watching R. B. play. Okay, he really was digging the physical space of the new addition on the east side, a hole twenty by forty feet. Once he had a quantity of dirt removed, everyone began magical creation of adobe bricks, following R. B.'s instructions.

"Thanks for asking me to help," Deiter said to Lindsey, as the two worked on preparing their first batch of bricks. "I really want to help out. Besides, this is going to be fun. We can see how R. B. magically creates the inside space five times the physical dimensions. That ought to be a really cool piece of magic."

"You bet. I missed it all when they built our current home," Lindsey replied, and then said commanding, "Mix." Her wand flashed, and the dirt and water began stirring itself. "I'm sure glad you are willing to help. He says we should be able to take seven large families in here, without using any of our existing space."

"That's really generous of you and your family. I mean to offer a home to those who may need it. Besides, I couldn't possibly turn down a reason to spend a lot of time here with you, Lindsey." Lindsey flushed and gave him a sideways glance. His eyes met hers, and he grinned. Lindsey felt a rush of warmth flooding through her body, and it was not from the sun overhead.

"I bet we get to learn some new construction type spells too," Deiter added.

"I like how cheap it is to build and how self-sufficient it ends up being," Lindsey chatted while her first batch of mud was mixing. "Do you realize that it cost mom and dad a total of one hundred dollars for all their utility costs the whole last year? Heating and cooling and electricity. Most was gas for cooking."

"You're kidding? Right?" Deiter asked a bit confused. "We pay three times that for one month!"

"Now you are teasing me, right?" Lindsey asked very seriously. Three hundred a month sounded huge. His face told her that he was not pulling her leg. "That's awful. Your dad must make a lot of money each month just to pay the bills."

"He does. He has his own company. The mortgage on

our house is a quarter of a million dollars. Mom says that he needs to earn three thousand every month just to pay the bills."

"Wow. Mom and I were always frugal. We own our ranch, no mortgage and hardly any expenses, compared to your folks, but then you probably have a really nice looking house in Colorado Springs," Lindsey replied, testing her adobe mud mix.

"I think I'd rather be like you, Lindsey, free, not behind the eight-ball every month like dad is, trying to make enough money. Say how's it look? I think this is cool, learning new spells. They don't teach us this Mix spell," Deiter said quite impressed with the spell. "I wonder how many more cool spells R. B. will teach us?"

"I think it is a specialized spell from the construction industry. I wonder how he gets the extra-dimensional thing inside done. Now that would be way cool to learn," Lindsey answered.

"Super way cool!"

Lloyd came over to examine their mixtures. "Okay, these are ready. Listen up gang," he said to all the teens, "new spell time. First, you use your Create spell that you already know to form the mud into bricks. We want them one foot long, four inches wide, and four inches tall. Use Create to make the bricks and then Move Object to line them up along the road. Once you have used all your mud, then I'll teach you the Fast Dry spell. Let's get to it."

Pam cast her Create spell and placed a perfectly formed brick on the road, beating everyone to it. However, the others were right behind her. Two minutes later, several hundred muddy bricks lay on the road, basking in the warm June sun. Lloyd had the group gather around him, and he explained the relatively simple Fast Dry spell. Via this spell, each mud brick became a solid adobe brick in seconds.

"Now you just go down the line of your bricks and cast Fast Fry on each in turn. Once that is done, Move Objects and start a pile over there. We will begin laying the outer walls and inner walls after you get the second batch done," Lloyd explained.

An hour later, several thousand bricks lay neatly piled. R. B. finally stopped his fancy digging machine. "Ah well, it was fun while it lasted. I do so like to dig holes." Amanda laughed; this she knew.

"Okay, kids, now comes the hard part," R. B. explained. "We have to lay in the outer walls and then the inner walls. Watch me and mimic how I'm laying them." He sat down on the ground, pulled out his wand, and began by first Levitating a brick and then using Move Object to place it in position. He interlocked the bricks until the outer wall was three feet thick. Quickly, the troupe joined in, but Deiter began laughing so hard he couldn't cast a spell.

Dozens of bricks were rising into the air, flying over to the ever-growing walls, floating down into position, all by magic. Soon, Ashley backed one of her bricks into Lindsey's, giggling. A short fight amongst bricks then occurred, until everyone was laughing hysterically. Thirty minutes later, they had used up all their bricks and had to go back to making more again.

"Excellent progress, kids. Tomorrow, it will be ready for the extra-dimensional enchantments. Anyone interested in learning how to do that?" Everyone chorused together, quite loudly. R. B. teased them further, "It's called Dimensional Shift, classified as a Grade 8 spell, but I believe you all may be able to handle it. We'll see."

"Wow, he's going to show us how to do that!" exclaimed Deiter.

By suppertime, everyone was pooped, but as one looked down into the hole, he or she could see the new walls, the long hall running down the side of their home, the four individual, new homes with their many rooms, all nicely outlined with adobe brick walls. As they ate supper, Lindsey said to Deiter, "You know, I hate to see you having to dash back home each day. If you want, why don't you stay here with us until we get this all done? You think your parents will allow it? I mean if you want to stay here," she added quickly, remembering to give him a way to go home if he preferred.

"Wow, yes I'd love to stay. I'm sure mom and dad will okay it. I'll need to go home and get clothes and things. I'll ask them now."

While he was asking, Lindsey asked Emilio and Kathy the same thing. Ten minutes later, all three teens had permission. Lena and Lloyd thought this was more than perfect, since after all the three were helping build the new homes. After dinner was over, Deiter asked, "Say Lindsey, as long as I'm going home to get my stuff, do you want to come along? I can show you my house, that is, if you want to see it? Maybe you are too tired tonight. We did a whole lot of work today."

"Mom, can I? Visit Deiter's place?" Lindsey asked.

Lena agreed, but Lloyd was concerned. "Security, Lindsey. Dominus and his cutthroats pose a risk every time you travel. Probably nothing will happen if you visit Deiter's house. However, some of us ought to accompany you, just to be safe. If this is okay with you, Deiter, and his parents, then let's do it." He tried to sound upbeat.

A few minutes later, Lloyd, Wilma, Deiter, and Lindsey arrived in a wealthy suburb of Colorado Springs. Here, all the houses looked quite elegant and large to Lindsey, who had seen very few houses actually. Their well-tended lawn was quite green. The home was tri-story brick with attached two-car garage. The entrance way allowed one to go either up or down.

"Welcome, come on in," Zelda Cross greeted them. Herbert was standing behind her and added his greeting to hers.

"I hope Deiter was of some assistance," Herbert said formally.

"Yes, he is quite the good worker," Lloyd complimented him. "Tomorrow, R. B. will try to teach him the Multi-dimension spell. You've a fine home here, Mr. Cross." While Lloyd followed Herbert, Zelda escorted Wilma to her kitchen, leaving Deiter to show Lindsey around.

"I am amazed, Deiter! Your house is so big and everything is so neat and clean, not at all like Tom and Jim's rooms." She remembered the perpetual mess that the Whitewater home had been when the boys lived there. This summer, their home was vastly neater—just Amanda and Fern

42

now, who preferred things to be orderly.

"Thanks, mom always insists that we keep it cleaned up. Here's dad's study. Can you tell he is an aviation engineer?" Lindsey saw many airplane models hanging from strings from the ceiling, a huge drafting board, and a wall full of books. Lloyd and Herbert were looking over a drawing chatting, so the two passed on to other rooms.

"Here's my room," Deiter showed off his room. His walls were plastered with Colorado Rocky baseball team memorabilia. One photo of Lindsey was also on the wall, but Lindsey pretended not to see it.

"What's all this Rockies stuff?" she asked. Deiter couldn't believe she didn't know about Major League baseball, but dutifully explained it to her. He also stuffed clothes and his computer and Staff of Power into a large duffle bag, but the staff wouldn't fit. He carried it instead. Lindsey noted that Deiter also kept his room neat, quite unlike the Whiterwater boys.

"Got to see my playroom and study hall," he said, leading her to the adjoining room. Here one wall held his entertainment center with probably fifty video games or more, all neatly arranged. His desk and bookshelf combination held numerous books. Many were biographies of famous people throughout history. He'd taken up guitar ever since his exposure to it in their second year.

"Here's our upstairs bath; we've a family and party room in the basement, pool table, poker table, games that sort of thing." He took her down to see.

"Ashley would love to come shoot pool," Lindsey teased.

"I know, but she'd skunk my butt." They laughed. "We'd better head back."

After Lindsey thanked Mr. Cross for letting Deiter come and help, the small group teleported back to the ranch. "Well, you and your folks have a fine house. Glad there was no trouble. Thanks dad, Wilma," Lindsey added.

After getting Deiter and Emilio settled in the spare bedroom, Kathy in with Lindsey and Ashley, the teens gathered in the family room to chat. "Say, anyone for a game of cards? I brought my decks," Deiter suggested.

"I know Canasta," Pam volunteered. Kathy also knew how to play, but Lindsey had never played a card game before. When she was little, she had no hands, making that impossible. Since she went to Bradbury's and had her hands re-grown, she'd had no opportunity to play games. Before long, Pam, Audrey, Amanda, Lindsey, Ashley, Fern, Kathy, Emilio, and Deiter were having a rousing game of Canasta, made all the rougher because nine were playing. Eventually, Lindsey ordered out for four pizzas—Lena expected that, though.

Early the next morning, Lindsey, Ashley, Audrey, and Pam raced through their morning chores, finishing just as Polly and Lena had breakfast waiting. The kids woofed down their breakfast, eager to get to work on the construction, the new spell beckoned to them all.

"First, it's time we learned Multi-dimension," R. B. explained. "Once we have the proper magical dimension expansion in place, then I must cast the Make Permanent spell, that's a Grade 9 spell, which I won't be teaching you today. After you finish your sixth year, you are welcome to drop by and see if you can learn that one. Very, very few wizards or witches are able to master that one, I'm afraid. Now, pay attention; here's how Multi-dimension goes."

Amanda found that her father had infinite patience when it came to helping someone learn a new spell. She had never seen this side of him. He went over and over it, especially with Kathy, who found this spell quite challenging indeed. "Don't fret so, Kathy. It is a Grade 8 spell, and you are ready to start learning only Grade 6 spells. It is three levels beyond your current education and training level." After hearing this, Kathy relaxed and finally got her wand to activate with this spell.

Because of the very large physical space that was being enlarged, combined with the five-fold increase in size, twenty such spells were required to alter the entire space. Finally, with Kathy adding the last one, R. B. then instructed them on how properly to analyze the results, making slight alterations here and there to make the combined inner space uniform. "It won't do to be walking down what is a five foot hallway only to have it suddenly become four foot-six part way down. Everyone, please check over all the twenty spaces now. You can avoid getting your stomach queasy by not looking outside the space. Once we get a roof over it, then the spatial disorientation problem goes away," R. B. explained.

Satisfied all was perfect, R. B. began a very long chant. Pam, eager to get a glimpse at the Make Permanent Grade 9 spell, listened intently, but she could not follow the spell's complexity. Finally, she just joined her friends who were sitting on the dirt pile outside, experimenting with the spatial distortion problem, looking partly at the world around them while also looking at the newly created expanded space of the home below them, and then trying not to be nauseous.

"Well, you can sort of get used to it," Audrey pronounced. Kathy merely vomited and gave up.

"I agree; you can get used to it," Deiter agreed with Audrey. Pam just shook her head at them all; she didn't bother with such silliness.

A bit later, R. B. finished and the space was finalized, ready for the roof and the inside work. "Okay, everyone, time for you to cast your Force Walls. We place these impenetrable barriers over the entire top. Then again, I cast Make Permanent on them. Once that is done, we cover the top of the house with three feet of dirt, sloping it to the back. Fern and Audrey can sew grass seed and water it."

After lunch, the real inside work began. R. B. put the boys to work on laying in the plumbing, while awaiting the arrival of the lumber truck. The girls studied how the inner walls were to be built. One person would use the nail gun, while the others would use their spells to bring the framing from the pile and position it for the nailer. Once the framework was done, then sheets of inside plywood were handled the same way. Of course, everyone wanted a chance to use the air powered nail gun. Around two, a semi pulled in with the wood for the two buildings here and for the two over at the Whitewater's ranch.

"This is incredible fun, Deiter!" Lindsey was taking her turn using the nail gun.

He grinned, "This plumbing stuff is not much fun. I

think you got the better job."

"Don't worry, tomorrow you will get a turn at the nail gun," R. B. chuckled. Deiter's grin broke into a very broad smile. He was definitely envious of Lindsey and what looked like real fun. Later in the afternoon, R. B. again fired up his digger to make a hole for the septic tank. That evening the plumbing was finished. The next day, the men went to work on the wiring, while the teens continued with the woodwork. At last, Deiter and Emilio got their turn with the nail gun.

After they each had their turns, both boys begged the girls to let them be the permanent nail gunners. Lindsey roared, "You want all the fun!" However, the girls let them do it. That evening, Lloyd turned on the power, and the four new homes had lights.

The fourth day, the women went into nearby towns to purchase fixtures, beds, dressers and other needed items to furnish the four homes or apartments. Polly suggested buying them from the Goodwill stores, keeping the overall cost way down. Lena agreed wholeheartedly with that suggestion. The teens were kept busy all day installing what the women continued to bring back each hour. However, Deiter and Emilio refused to help make the beds, which brought on a round of giggling from the girls. Instead, the girls made the boys install the toilets and sinks, which really made them work hard, as not too much magic could be used, just good old elbow grease.

As they all sat down to supper at the end of the fourth day, compliments of Luci, the first addition was finished. "You know it is utterly remarkable that we built this new addition, which is really four homes-in-one, in only four days," Deiter pointed out. "Normally, the normals build homes in closer to six months."

"Yes, Deiter, it would take us many months to build one like your parent's house," Lloyd explained. "These novel construction techniques have allowed us to put it up in four days. However, there is a huge difference in cost. If one were to purchase a home like yours, Deiter, I'd expect to pay at least three hundred fifty thousand dollars or more for it. If one were to purchase our home here, as large as it is inside, you might expect to pay four thousand for it. There is a huge difference in quality and marketability. Don't sell your home short. However, for our needs, homes like ours are far better. We can set in place far better security spells than we could on a home like yours. After all, look what three Disintegrate spells did to that home in Telluride, when you all rescued the three kidnaped girls. With these adobe walls, it is far, far harder to break through a wall to get inside."

"We've got three more of these to build, gang," R. B. said the obvious. "However, we will certainly have the other expansion unit here done before Ashley's photo shoot on June 22. Once you get back, then we need to add two to my place. I reckon that we will be finished by July 1. I'd expect that we will start seeing folks coming after that."

R. B. grinned and then added, "You kids have been really great workers these past four days, really good. If you all continue and help us get the other three done, I think that I will reward you. What would you say if I tried my best to teach each of you how to cast the Make Permanent Grade 9 spell? You won't be learning how to do it at school; it's beyond their skill levels, though at least two there know it."

After the wild cheering and thank you's died down, Lindsey asked, "R. B. can you tell us who at Bradbury's knows that spell, Make Permanent?"

"You are a curious one aren't you? Well, it is no secret. Governor Alister and Professor Cho Lin have mastered that spell. Just don't mention it to Professor Delius Dogs, because he is very sensitive about having failed on three occasions to master that spell." Deiter's eyebrows raised; he looked up to Delius. That he might have a chance to learn a spell that Delius didn't know filled him with an immense sense of pride and power.

When the day arrived for Ashley's new photo shoot, both additions were finished. All that remained was to punch entrances into the main ranch house so that folks could go from one addition to the other to the main house. This R. B. and the others would work on while the girls were off at the photo shoot in Hollywood. Again, Lloyd, Wilma, and Monane accompanied the teens. Besides Ashley, Kathy, Lindsey,

Audrey, Amanda, and Pam went along.

At eight that night, the tired teens arrived home. Kathy was on cloud nine. The fashions, the shoots, the sights they saw afterwards, as Lloyd took them on a tour of some of the more famous Hollywood sights, left her in a dizzying ecstasy. As before, Ashley returned with four new fall outfits.

"So how did it go dear?" Lena asked her young daughter.

"Really well, they took about half of the shots with me Morphed into my old self. I was wearing the sleeveless dresses for those. Honestly, if one other girl sees me like that and becomes braver as a result, then it was worth it. I just hope that I inspired others who are like I was."

"I hope so too, dear, that would be incredibly rewarding. Can I see your new outfits?" Ashley was very pleased to show them off to her mom.

"I'm giving this peach colored one to Kathy. After all, she got me this job in the first place," Ashley explained. Kathy was elated over Ashley's gift of the long gown. She promised to wear it at their first formal dance this fall.

Then it was back to work. R. B. had already finished the excavation work while the kids were off at the photo shoot. Hence, only seven days were needed to finish off the two expansion units on the Whitewater ranch.

As promised, on June 29, the group of teens gathered around R. B. and began taking notes, as he explained the theory and principles of casting the Make Permanent spell. "This is one of the more powerful alteration-based magical spells. It requires of the caster a *complete* conviction that it will be successful when cast. You see, it is your conviction that *powers* this spell. Your conviction must be as strong as the conviction that puts this physical universe here. It is my belief that most of those who cannot master this spell are failing just because their conviction is insufficiently great." He began outlining the lengthy chant, and each wrote down every word. R. B. reviewed what each had written, correcting the small mistakes, which would certainly cause the spell to fail. Once he was satisfied that they had the words down, he then went into the wand motions that were required. Even these were perhaps the most complex any of these teens had ever seen before.

After lunch, it was finally practice time, the moment of truth, so to speak. He had them Create Object, a small gold coin, perhaps a quarter of an ounce. Their objective was to Make Permanent the gold coin, which would otherwise wink out of existence in about five minutes. Deiter, Emilio, Pam, Ashley, Lindsey, Audrey, Amanda, and Kathy were trying it. Fern gave up; the spell complexity was too far beyond her skill level, regrettably. R. B. did promise her to teach it to her later on when she was older.

After a half hour of practice, R. B. was not prepared for what happened. Nearly at the same time, both Deiter and Pam had their wands activate, and their tiny piece of conjured gold had a magical energy flash appear around it for an instant. Everyone stopped and stared at the gold pieces to see if they really continued to exist. "You two actually did it?" asked Lindsey, gaping at their sudden and unexpected success.

"Duh, we must have!" Pam said, shocked that her spell had worked.

"Wow, that was very easy," Deiter admitted. "R. B., is it supposed to be this easy to do? Perhaps we did something wrong."

"One fast way to see. Cast your Dispel Magic on the gold nuggets. If your Make Permanent spell worked, the gold will be unaffected. If something went wrong, the gold will vanish. Go ahead, try it." He expected to see both gold nuggets disappear. Both waved their wands and cast their Dispel Magic spell. Both wands activated, but the tiny gold nuggets remained.

"We must have done it, R. B.," Deiter said cautiously.

"I'll be a donkey's butt! You two sure have done it. This is incredible. You two have no idea what you've done, do you?"

"Er, we've got a bit of gold here," Pam admitted. "I suppose we can sell it."

"The usual time to succeed in the first casting by a person who has completed the Grade 7 spell book is five days! You two took thirty minutes at most! This is unheard of! I don't understand this phenomenon at all. Perhaps, you two should try it again, maybe it was a complete fluke," R. B. suggested.

Pam and Deiter carefully conjured another small lump of gold. Next, they both went through the complex casting of Make Permanent. Once again, both their wands activated at nearly the same instant. Now they stared at two permanent gold nuggets.

"Er, R. B., we seem to have done it again," Pam whispered, very much afraid something was going very wrong with the spell. For her, it was so easy to do.

"This is completely unbelievable! But I've just seen it with my own two eyes. Incredible! I just do not understand how you two could have gotten such results so darn quickly. Well, be that as it may, continue to practice it until you feel really comfortable casting it."

"Way to go you two!" Lindsey complimented them. The others joined her in praising the two. Pam grinned and finally relaxed, likewise, Deiter. By the end of the day, Deiter and Pam had a rather large pile of golden nuggets in front of them. No one else did.

This was the topic over supper. Everyone was elated that Pam and Deiter had managed the seemingly impossible, learning this Grade 9 spell in one sixteenth the normal time that others, who were two years more advanced than they were, took. In fact, all the adults puzzled over this all evening long, the sole topic of conversation. "How is this possible?" asked Wilma, "I've never been able to get that one down, though I've tried at least fifty times."

"Dunno," R. B. said, scratching his head. "Defies everything I know. Yet, there's the pile of gold nuggets, probably a grand each, if they want to sell them. Now I could see Pam possibly doing this. She is probably the brightest of them all, but Deiter? Sorry son, no offense intended, but he isn't in the same league as Pam when it comes to that department. I'm afraid we need to rule out the intelligence factor, which is the most logical factor that applies to this spell. I mean it takes above average intelligence really to have any chance with this spell. I've seen plenty of brilliant wizards and witches still fail to master it. Take Delius for example, brilliant mind, but he hasn't gotten this one down yet. If we rule out intelligence, there's nothing left that I know about. How about you folks?"

"Don't look at me, I never was able to remotely learn that one," Lloyd admitted.

"I never even tried," Polly added, "but Fred can, though I remember it took him five days of hard work. He was a bear to live with until he finally got it down."

"Deiter, does your dad know this one?" R. B. asked.

"I don't think so, why?" the lad replied, wondering how it was that he and Pam had been able to do this so darn easily. "Maybe there is something wrong with me," he thought.

"We can rule out heredity—you know, picking up the skill from one's parents," R. B. said, "though I have never heard that that has anything to do with learning this spell."

Shocking Lindsey, Lena spoke up, "I'm sorry that I don't know anything at all about this magical stuff, but I can offer a suggestion. Perhaps there is some other as yet unseen factor that has allowed the both of them to succeed—something that they both hold in common."

"That has to be it," R. B. exclaimed! "Now what do you two have in common?" The next thirty minutes flew by as everyone jumped in with suggestions. However, all that they did was prove conclusively that Pam and Deiter were as different as a cat and a dog. Deiter loved baseball games; Pam had never seen any. Pam was a computer whizz; Deiter could barely run his. Pam was a gifted student; Deiter had to work very hard for his grades. Pam loved the sciences and math; Deiter was passionate about games. Well, they both liked to dance and loved magic. That they had in common, but no one thought that had anything to do with anything, since everyone here loved magic and liked to dance.

Just as everyone gave up and left the table, Ashley commented to Lindsey, "They have something else in common that lies behind this, only we haven't spotted it yet." Lindsey agreed with her sister. Pam and Deiter, concerned about their uncanny ability with this spell, were also slow in leaving the dining room and heard Ashley make her prediction.

Pam headed for her room, embarrassed sufficiently for

one day. Deiter, however, followed her, nervously. "Pam, a word," he whispered, not wanting anyone to overhear him.

She glared at him, as if to say "Haven't you caused me enough humiliation for one day," but allowed him to enter. He closed the door. He whispered, "There is one other thing that we have in common, Pam. It hit me when Ashley made her prediction thing a second ago. Remember, she said that we haven't spotted it yet. Maybe because we are keeping it a secret between the two of us. We've been to the Beyond and had an unusual look at this universe. You know, when we bent down, looked in, and our heads appeared upside down in the sky. That's hardly a normal thing to do in this universe. Maybe it's somehow changed us."

Pam's annoyance with Deiter vanished instantly. "R. B. said that our conviction must be as strong as the conviction that puts this physical universe here. Well, we sure have a different view now of what puts this all here. I think you may be right, Deiter. But how are we going to prove this?"

"How about taking someone else to the Beyond, showing them around, maybe meeting Greeley and the goggles? After that, see if they can now cast the Make Permanent spell. If this is the real reason we took to the spell so easily, then we can help Lindsey and the rest do it too," Deiter explained his flash of insight.

"You might have a point, Deiter. However, there is one fatal flaw in your plan. What happened to you when you first saw the Beyond and the goggles, eh? You went into convulsions, frothing at the mouth, and had to have emergency treatment from Doctor Caterwall, who as you can see, is not here at the moment."

Deiter looked crestfallen, "Oh." After a moment, he brightened up, "Yes, but when Greeley took us to the Beyond, that was your first time, and you didn't get ill nor did I."

Pam hated to be put on the spot. Deiter was indeed right. She had not gotten the slightest bit ill over the incident. Spooked, unnerved, shocked, surprised, yes, but definitely not the slightest bit ill, as had Deiter. He added, "I've always wondered why it was that you didn't get sick as I did when I first saw the Beyond, Pam." Her face grew very warm; she looked away from him.

"Maybe it was because you are so much smarter than the rest of us," Deiter suggested, trying to put Pam more at ease.

Pam looked at him, "You might be right. That might account for it. I can't imagine taking Emilio or Kathy to the Beyond. I'd bet anything Kathy would freak out, and Emilio would probably get quite sick."

Deiter agreed. He had been studying with them last year at school. Emilio was into desert survival, not physics and math. While Kathy was incredibly superb at potion making, she, Deiter thought, was more of an airhead, when it came to math and science and how things worked. Hesitatingly he suggested, "How about Lindsey? She is very bright and intelligent." He wanted to add and very pretty and very exciting and many other things, but refrained. Already his face felt warm. It wouldn't do to let his emotions show, not in front of the brightest Yellow Hall student. He was Black Hall, after all.

Pam evidently didn't notice his pinkish face. She was deep in thought. "Yes, Lindsey is the only one of us casting sans wand, sans words. She is already breaking the rules. Ashley does also, to some extent, perhaps Amanda. Audrey, no, I don't think so. Okay, Lindsey is our best chance at this. But Deiter, what are we going to do if she gets really ill like you did? We've no doctor, and how would we ever explain this to the others? One word of the Beyond and the adults will be all over us. We will be in the biggest trouble imaginable. They might even forbid us to Teleport!"

"I hadn't thought of that, Pam, but if we don't take one person, how will we ever know if this is the deciding factor? I would dearly love Lindsey to be able to cast Make Permanent. I felt so badly when we succeeded and she failed all day. That look in her eyes when she looked at me as we headed in for supper was devastating. If going to the Beyond will allow her to be able to cast it, I won't be able to live with myself if I didn't try to help her get it."

"Well, I don't know about this, Deiter," Pam hesitated.

"Let's at least explain our theory to her, Pam. Tell her

about the Beyond and Greeley. Let her make up her own mind. If she doesn't want to try it, then okay. I can live with that," Deiter compromised. Pam agreed and sent Lindsey a Message. A minute later, Lindsey knocked on Pam's door. Since Audrey shared this room with Pam, the three hastily went next door to one of the new apartments they'd just help build, where they would not be interrupted.

"So what's all this secrecy about?" Lindsey asked when Pam and Deiter finally were happy that they were completely alone. "What are you two up to anyway?"

Pam began to explain, as the three sat on the bare floor. "Thirty-five years ago, a British wizard named Greeley Longsteen made a startling discovery about the Teleport spell and how it really works. He published an article on it and was summarily ostracized as a crackpot, insane, and a bumbling idiot by the wizarding world. He was literally cast out by our society just for publishing what he had discovered. You know how bad prejudice can be." Deiter's face suddenly grew blazing hot; he'd done just that to Lindsey during their first year at Bradbury's.

"You know how we begin at the source origin point, hold firmly in our minds the destination origin point, and then cast the spell? Well, when the magic activates, we step out of our universe, move from the source origin point over to the destination origin point, and then reappear. If you step out of this universe, that non-space, for I don't know what else to call it, is known as the Beyond. It has no dimensions, no space as we know it. Everything there is controlled only by the power of your thoughts. You think and others can hear you. You think and it happens by your conviction."

"Well, Deiter and I did it. We visited the Beyond. We went in search of Greeley. That was the research project I was doing for him, after his accidental viewing of the Beyond. Greeley is really living there in the Beyond, we think, for these past thirty some years. He has kind of thunked up a cottage there in the nothingness and lives in it. Deiter got hungry while we were there, and Greeley had him think he was eating a subway sandwich, and Deiter was then very full. He's living with two friends he's made; they are called goggles—ghost-like dogs they look to us, very frightening when you first see them. I think that's what made Deiter so frightened when he accidentally saw them. Anyway, you can do strange things from the Beyond. I decided I was at my old home in Sterling. I imagined I was sitting on the ground, pulled my bed covers up, and peered under them, looking down onto Sterling. My head appeared in the sky, and I could see my house. I did spook a little girl playing in her sandbox though and quickly pulled my head out."

"Anyway, Lindsey, Pam and I think that this is why we both picked up the Make Permanent spell so quickly," Deiter hastened to explain. "We now have a very different viewpoint of our universe. We want to try an experiment, Lindsey. We want to take you there and then see if, after that, you too can easily cast this spell."

"To get there, you do what Greeley calls a Half-teleport. That is, once the magic activates, you totally stop concentrating on your destination, and you arrive in the Beyond, where everything is controlled by your thoughts and convictions," Pam continued her explanation for Lindsey. "Yes, we want to see if this is the connection. But Lindsey, this could be terribly dangerous. Remember how ill Deiter became after he accidentally saw the Beyond when we rescued Alister?"

"How could I forget that? Wait a second, you didn't get sick, Pam. How come you didn't?" Lindsey asked very intrigued by what these two had discovered. Further, she was amazed that they had kept this a complete secret for so long.

Pam didn't want to say because she was bright. "Greeley visited us in my room. His head appeared as if it was hanging from my roof, no body, just his head. Besides, he explained a lot about the Beyond before he helped us get there, and he helped us get used to it while we were there. Served us tea and all that, though I'm not sure if it was real tea, mind you, but it smelled and tasted like tea anyway. Perhaps that's why."

"He showed us the light show, people teleporting. It looks something like lightning streaks. They appear from their source locations and move across the Beyond to their destination points. Really cool to watch," Deiter added encouragingly.

"So you think that if you take me to this Beyond, then I will be able to cast Make Permanent?" Lindsey asked, twisting her long hair. She was very curious about this Beyond thing, but a little hesitant. After all, she remembered just how sick Deiter had been.

"Well, that's the theory," Pam said flatly. "However, I am very worried about getting you very sick, if we do it. We don't have Doctor Caterwall around here. Besides, if anyone finds out what we've been doing, they are very likely to ground us or worse, think we are nuts and send us to the looney bin."

"You didn't get sick, Pam," Lindsey thought aloud. "I've really got to see this place for myself. I'm game. When can we try it?"

"Are you sure, Lindsey? What do we do if you get sick?" Pam asked worriedly.

"Teleport me to Doctor Caterwall. Tell him I accidentally saw the Beyond—just not how," Lindsey replied. This would be the truth, just not all of it.

"Okay, I should Message Greeley and tell him that we are coming to visit him," Pam said. "I hate just appearing on someone's door. I have my list of questions for him to answer as well, if I can get a straight answer out of him. Don't let the two goggles scare you. They are very friendly and highly intelligent beings. They just have pretty weird bodies is all," Pam stuck up for the two friends of Greeley. She waved her wand and sent her Message to the elderly wizard.

A bit later, Lindsey was startled to see the head of an elderly man, wearing very thick lenses in his off-colored eyeglasses, appearing upside down in the empty apartment room in which they were waiting. "Ah, it is you, Pam Something and Deiter Something. Just checking, you know. You must be the new Something who wants to meet me." He looked at Lindsey.

"Er, yes. Hello, I'm Lindsey Barron, pleased to meet you Mr. Greeley Longsteen," Lindsey said politely, though she felt odd craning her neck upwards to look at the upside down head protruding from the ceiling.

"Very well. Grab hold of each other's arms, and I will

extend mine." Deiter grabbed Lindsey and Pam. Pam reached her arm up towards Greeley, short by about five feet, however. His arm appeared coming down from the ceiling a little to the right of his head. It kept lengthening until he reached Pam's hand. The next instant, Lindsey found herself surrounded in total darkness in all directions, including up and down. She felt very disoriented indeed.

"Ah here we are. What do you think of the Beyond?" Greeley asked. His mouth didn't move, but Lindsey heard him anyway.

"This is very disorienting," she thought.

"Blimey, then put a nice brick street under your feet," he replied.

Lindsey imagined a red brick street, and, presto, she had one under her feet. It felt solid and stabilizing to her. "Yes, that is much better. Thanks. Oh, what was that?" She'd just seen a streak of yellow light off in the distance.

"Someone's just teleported," Deiter explained.

"Ah yes. I remember! I'm bloody well supposed to offer you tea. I remember, Pam Something. This way to my cottage." Lindsey found that she was moving after this strange old wizard. She was mostly just floating along, but soon found it easier if she moved her feet. That felt far more natural to her. Ahead, she saw a quaint English cottage. This felt far better. She could relate to it, especially once inside.

"Ah, we have our guests back, plus one," Greeley said to the two ghostly, yellow furred dog-like creatures. "Mellor and Elmoid, my best friends," Greeley added.

"Yes, we see. It is Pam Something and Deiter Something. Back so soon or is it so late? We never can tell here, you see," Mellor explained and asked.

"Good to see you too," Pam replied. "This is our best friend Lindsey Barron."

"Well, which is it? Lindsey or Barron?" Elmoid asked of her.

"What do you mean?" Lindsey asked a bit confused.

"Are you Lindsey or are you Barron?" Elmoid replied.

"Perhaps she cannot make up her mind," Mellor suggested helpfully.

"That's my name, Lindsey Barron. First name is Lindsey. You can call me that. My last name is Barron."

"Two names? That must be most confusing to have to respond to two names, isn't it, Mellor," said Elmoid. "I think we shall just call you Lindsey Something as well." Pam chuckled.

Mellor asked, "Say what do you get when you cut a pie in half?"

Elmoid giggled. "Oh that's a good one, Mellor! Greeley taught us this one yesterday, or was it last week?"

"Last year," Mellor corrected him.

Lindsey was about to say a half of a pie, but thought better of it. She imagined a pie cut in half. You got two pieces, very large pieces, but surely, this was not what they were asking. It struck her, and she answered, "One PI." Both goggles roared with laughter, Greeley too. Pam smiled, getting the mathematical joke. Deiter looked dumbly at Lindsey. She explained, "Two PI radians in three hundred sixty degrees, a circle. Cut in half, you get one PI, its definition, really." Deiter now got the joke.

"Blimey, that is a good one. Lindsey Something is a bright one too," Mellor.

Pam pulled out her list of questions. "I have a few of my own, if you can answer them. First, this time thing. If I'm here in the Beyond, can I put my head into the past, and visit say ancient Egypt? Or can I put my head into the future and see what is there?"

"No and no. Better ask a proper question," Elmoid answered her.

Frustrated, Pam asked the next one, "Okay. Last time we were here, I wanted to know how long we had been gone from our world. You said as long as you wanted it to be. I don't understand, if you can't go into the future or past."

"Up here, there is nothing to measure the passage of time, which is objects moving in space. When you step out of your nicely measured universe, how much time passes while you're here is totally your consideration of it. It can be years or seconds," Greeley felt like explaining one of his discoveries that he made during his long stay here in the Beyond.

"Everything in the Beyond is what you consider it to be. Tea?"

At once a steaming teapot appeared along with cups and sugar, lemon, and cream. "Oh, I've decided that I took cream in my tea," Greeley explained. "Got the sugar right this time." Pam remembered that the last time he served tea, a twenty pound sack had appeared briefly. "Earl Grey this time, I do believe."

Lindsey sipped it and smelled it. She could not detect that it was anything but Earl Grey, however. Pam pulled out a plastic cube. "Mellor, Elmoid, I brought you a small present from our world. It is called a Rubik's Cube. Each face is now all one color. Now then, I will twist it a bunch of times like so." She fiddled with it for a minute. "Now, it's all scrambled. The objective is to get it all back to being one color on each side. It's a three-dimensional challenge."

"Oh goodie, goodie! let me see it!" exclaimed Mellor.

"No, me first, Mellor," Elmoid insisted. "I'm older."

"Since when?"

"Since now that I have said it," Elmoid replied, producing two long arms to take it from Pam.

"Boys, once you have each figured out how to get it back, then you can have a competition and see who can get it back to normal with the fewest twists," Pam challenged the two geniuses. Lindsey laughed, knowing that she never could figure this thing out. Pam had tried to show her how, but it eluded her completely.

"I can barely get one side all one color," Deiter admitted.

"Well, thank you for the tea. We need to show Lindsey how we can peek into our world, as you did a bit ago. Will you excuse us?" Pam asked.

A bit later, if a bit meant anything here in the Beyond, the three stood looking over the vast nothing. "Now pretend that you are sitting down, pretend you are lifting the covers on your bed, and then peer under them to see what's there. That's how it's done," Pam explained.

"But where am I looking?" Lindsey asked.

"It is where you decide that it is. How about us taking a peek at Bradbury's?" Pam suggested. "Just decide right here you are over our school, bend down, and take a peek.

Lindsey felt odd bending down in the nothingness, even odder as she imagined that she was peeking under her bed. Her head popped into the sky over Bradbury's school of magic. The sunset was rosy red. There were all the buildings. Her long hair, she considered, fell down over her head, since she considered that her head was now upside down. Just then, she spied Professor Cho Lin walking across the grass. Cho Lin looked and stared at the upside down head of Lindsey looking down upon her. Lindsey quickly jerked her head back out.

"Oh! Cho Lin just saw my head in the sky. I hope I haven't scared her!" Lindsey exclaimed, suddenly worried.

"Not to worry," Deiter consoled her. "After all, from her point of view, she thought she saw your head upside down in the sky. We all know that is impossible, now don't we? She'll just think she was imagining it, that's all." Lindsey felt better. He was probably quite right.

"We should be getting back," Pam stated. "Let's decide that we have only been gone a minute. We don't want others to come looking for us and find us missing or anything." The three did so and then appeared back in the empty room.

"Wow! Incredible! Beyond super cool!" Lindsey exclaimed.

"Hey, see, she is not sick," Deiter observed, highly encouraged and relieved.

"Yes, curious. Now we should go join the others, and then let's see if Lindsey is any better casting the new spell," Pam replied. They headed back into the main house.

"Ah there you are, we've been looking for you," Ashley exclaimed. We are starting a big Canasta game. Come on you three." Much to Pam's dismay, the decisive test would have to wait until the morning.

The next morning, June 30, R. B. again worked with the teens, trying to help them master this Grade 9 spell, Make Permanent. Lindsey's wand activated on her second try, amazing everyone, including R. B. "Well done, Lindsey! Incredible!" R. B. exclaimed. Now he had three who could cast it, although he didn't know quite how he had been so successful.

Everyone gathered around the dining room table for lunch, chatting about Lindsey's great success. Before her place on the table, she had ten small golden nuggets that she had conjured and made permanent. Lena asked, "Now is this real gold? I mean, can you melt it down and make rings and chains from it? This is a bit much to take in—why, you could always just make your own money this way. Just make a little gold and then sell it. Incredible what magic can do."

"Yes, well it is rarely done that way, Lena," R. B. explained. "While that could be done, you have to realize first that there are very few wizards and witches who can cast this spell. My guess is perhaps one in a hundred could, if even that many. Perhaps it is more like one in three hundred or even a thousand. Those of us who can, realize that if we went around creating mountains of real gold, that would have an adverse impact on the world's economy. Anyone who did this, creating a large sum, such as a million dollars' worth, would likely be apprehended by the Department of Magical Misuse on the grounds that he or she would be trying to destroy the world's economy."

"Well, then, that does make more sense," Lena seemed relieved to hear that there were restraints on the magical creation of pure gold.

"Say does Dominus know this spell, I wonder?" Pam asked.

Wilma answered her, "No. He does not know this spell, at least when we captured him. It is remotely possible that he has somehow learned it in these past four years, but not too likely. Most students get their chance to learn it in their sixth year. After that, the likelihood of picking it up becomes rather remote."

"That's good isn't it?" Deiter volunteered. "We have a spell that he doesn't. Can we use it somehow to capture him?"

R. B. chuckled, "Not likely making things permanent is going to capture him, Deiter. It does allow us to create better defenses that he cannot so easily break. This is one of the mandatory spells that any Governor of any Magic School must know in order to be appointed Governor. He or she must be able to protect the students fully by making permanent protective spells, as well as lowering them when needed and putting them back in place afterwards. We can use it to make protective magical items to help defend ourselves as well. Lots of good uses for the spell."

"Yes, but I am finding it is an awfully hard one to learn," Emilio added.

"Me too," Kathy said, not wanting to be left out.

"I'm sure that I will learn it in time," Audrey quietly pronounced.

Lindsey looked at her sister. Ashley was white as a sheet. "What's wrong?" she asked.

"I—I just had a vision! It's Nadia and Jolina! They are in big trouble, dying I think. They are somehow on their way here—in their car, I think. I hope they don't die on us." Ashley recovered from the shock of her vision, her premonition.

"Darn it! I knew they were in dire peril being around Dominus!" Lindsey exclaimed. "What do we do?"

Monane spoke calmly, "We should prepare. Let's get two beds made up where they can be made comfortable. We should alert Doctors Caterwall and Blackburn that their services might well be needed soon. I'll alert Alister, and he can see if Doctor Caterwall is available."

Lloyd added, "I'll contact Henry. Lena, what's going to be the best rooms to use?" The group sprang into action, preparing the first apartment off the new block to the east of the main ranch home. The end of the hallway that went past the girls' bedrooms and their many bathrooms had been opened and now led into the long two hundred foot hallway that went past the four new homes or apartments. Hence, they fixed up the very first one, Number Four, as that was closest to the girls' hallway.

Chapter 4—Nadia's Brush with Death

The second week in May, Nadia overheard the call that Dominus made to President Missy Snow. She was looking for Dominus to ask him what she should wear to the formal party that was set for this evening. As she got to his study, he heard him talking on a cell phone to the President. She began wondering why Dominus was calling himself Simon Mac Fluide. Curiosity roused, Nadia stood there quietly listening as Dominus offered her ten million dollars and something about pills that would make everyone healthy and remove all criminal tendencies. To her, this sounded like a miracle cure had been found. Yet, this was her husband, Dominus, not this Simon fellow. She began so suspect something was very wrong here.

Especially so, when he disintegrated the cell phone after he hung up. Worse for her, Dominus spied her standing by the doorway. "Taking to eavesdropping on me now are you, Nadia?" he growled at her.

"No, I wanted to know what you thought I should wear to tonight's formal dinner, Domi?" she replied. In the pit of her stomach, she felt a little frightened. Dominus seemed very angry with her.

"Bitch!" he yelled at her and slapped her hard on the side of her face. In the tight fitting dress and tall heels, she lost her balance, her little, short arms flailing as she fell, hitting the floor hard. "Get yourself up," he growled and left her lying there stunned on the floor.

Nadia lay there for a time recovering from the shock. At last, she tried to get up by herself. Effectively wearing two tight-laced corsets, one had been melded under her skin and was thus permanent, one she wore over the light blue, tight-fitting dress, which gave her that dramatic fetish look which she so admired, she couldn't bend much at all. Without the benefit of arms, Nadia found herself in a jam. Those Dominus had sliced off, while she was stunned, the sacrifice she had made to marry him. After much twisting, she finally rolled over onto her stomach and got her knees up under her. Only with a great effort was she finally able to sit up. Out of breath, she sat there for a time. Very carefully, she managed to regain her feet, standing at last. Nadia headed to the kitchen where her dear friend and constant companion, Jolina, was fixing their lunch.

"God, Nadia! What happened? Did you fall?" Jolina dropped everything, coming to the aid of Nadia. In whispers, Nadia told Jolina all that had happened.

The next day, after Dominus left for work, the two began wondering what was going on here. They found the Mac Fluide Enterprise website and that of Aetna Pharmaceuticals. That fit with what Nadia had overheard. A bit more web research yielded the fact that no one ever saw this Simon fellow. This worried the two women considerably.

During the rest of the week, Dominus acted as if nothing at all had happened. Not until the weekend came was he around the house a lot. On Friday night, he said, "Ah, my fair Nadia, I think it is time to add some more to your fetish scene." He blinded her. Jolina watched Nadia's eyes turn that cold shade of grey. He used his often-used Blind spell on his wife. Jolina was wise enough to make herself very scarce, only showing up when he called specifically for her. As Jolina left the area, heading for her room, he heard Dominus say, "Okay Nadia. Now you come find me and we can have some fun." She heard Nadia protest that she couldn't walk like this. His reply scared her even more, "If you don't stop that whining, I will have to permanently shut your mouth. Now move. Catch me."

Jolina laid down on her bed and sobbed to herself. Somehow, she had to get Nadia out of here. Lindsey was right; he was a sick, evil, sadist, or worse. They had been naive fools to have ever gotten involved with Dominus.

After a terrifying weekend, during which Nadia found herself blinded most of the time, as well as teased and taunted, on Monday, he dispelled her blindness and things returned to normal. Over tea on Monday, Jolina begged Nadia, "We need to get out of here now, before he really hurts you or me,

Nadia."

"Well, it wasn't so bad, really. I think he's gotten it out of his system now," Nadia defended her husband. Jolina dropped it, but began secretly making evacuation plans herself.

However, during the latter part of the week, Nadia spotted lipstick on his collar and face twice. It was certainly not her bright red shade. Nadia wisely didn't mention it, but Dominus noticed her noticing something about him. After checking the mirror, he knew that she knew. She overheard him say, "Nosey little bitch."

Friday night, Dominus came home with a new toy. A hard rubber ball was mounted to a leather head harness. He proceeded to gag Nadia. Once the straps were fastened, she couldn't undo it. Once more, he blinded her and played games with her throughout the weekend. More than once, though, he struck her, though he was careful not to bruise her where it might show up, if he took her out in public. This he stopped doing after that weekend in May.

On Monday, while he removed the gag, he apparently forgot to cancel his Blindness spell. First, Jolina fed her dear friend some solid food, because she'd only been able to sip with a straw all weekend. Then, she set to work on dispelling the Blindness spell. However, Jolina was taking a chance by doing this. She knew Dominus might return, possibly expecting Nadia to be blind still. However, she planned to say that they had to go out to get groceries, hoping that would justify her actions. After that, she did go out for a time, leaving Nadia alone for the first time.

"Look, I've picked up some PI equipment from Radio Shack. I'm going to put a microphone in your bedroom and one in his study. After all, most of the times that he beat you, Nadia, it was in your bedroom. If we are going to file for a divorce, we need proof, solid proof that he is beating you and worse. I will tape it and then we will have the goods on him," Jolina announced.

"But what if he finds out, Jolina? He will start in on you too!" Nadia cried, unwilling to have anything happen to Jolina. She realized very well that now armless, she was dependent in a large measure on Jolina. True, she could Morph herself into someone with arms, but not while Dominus was around, and she couldn't stay Morphed for long times for that matter. "What have I gotten us into?" she bawled, her emotions now very raw.

"Neither one of us has been any good at picking men," Jolina consoled her with the truth of their lives.

During the early weeks of June, they made some interesting recordings. True, they had captured some of the beatings and tortures that Dominus inflicted on his play toy, but they also taped some conversations that they couldn't understand—things about pills and ordering others to do things, mentioning names that they'd never heard before.

Mid-June, Dominus became furious with Nadia. Holding the microphone he'd found in their bedroom, he screeched, "What the blazes are you doing with this?"

Thinking fast, Nadia explained, "You don't love me anymore. You are being with other women. I wanted to know about these women. How are they better than me? Haven't I done everything for you, Domi?" She continued in this vein. Lucky for her and her friend, Dominus didn't see women as beings, as people, but as mere play toys, objects, something to fool around with and then discard when he became bored with them.

"Stun!" his wand activated. "Now I will stop you from ever spying on me ever again." He poked his wand into her eye and activated it. The magical energy fried her eyeball. Her sight went black in that eye. She thought, "Please don't do it to my other eye!" However, stunned into immobility, she couldn't speak. He poked it into her other eye and total blackness again flooded over her, only this time, she knew she would never see again. It couldn't be dispelled. He'd destroyed her eyes.

"Nadia, I swear to you that if you utter one peep, one cry, I will seal your pretty lips shut, just like I did with that silly, pesky teen, that Barron girl. You can spend the rest of your pathetic life sucking with a straw." Nadia, encased in total blackness, felt her stomach react with stark terror. Her mind now registered what Lindsey had told her that Dominus had done to her. All traces of doubt that her husband was indeed

66

guilty of every crime that anyone had ever suggested to her was true. He released her from the stun, but she didn't even notice it. She stood there petrified, unable even to move. He left her standing there and teleported away.

Shortly, Jolina found her, and together they bawled, Nadia resting her head on Jolina's lap. "I got all that on tape from the one in the study." Nadia, in her grief, didn't even hear her. "We have to get out of here somehow." She spent the rest of the day helping Nadia adjust to her new predicament.

"Your wand will always be here on the fireplace here in the front room, Nadia. That way you will always know where it is kept. Now we had better get our things packed," Jolina explained. She then Morphed Nadia into herself, hoping that Nadia could now see.

"My god, I still am totally blind!" screamed Nadia. Jolina felt crushed. She so hoped that Nadia would be able to see if she Morphed into someone else. So panic-stricken, neither woman thought of other potential spells that might enable Nadia to have some temporary vision. Instead, Jolina helped Nadia to sit down and went to start their packing. First, she ordered four more collapsible closets, similar to the one that Nadia had given Lindsey. During the next days, Jolina went from room to room gathering up the things that they desired, putting them into the open closets, which were disguised to look like shelving units.

Over one lunch, she explained her plan to Nadia, "Once we get everything organized and packed, I'll close all the cases and put them in our car. Then, we get you inside, and we take off, leaving this place forever. We can hide out somewhere, Nadia. I promise I will look after you."

"Jolina, we are going to need money, lots of money. Maybe a doctor can fix up my eyes, shrink my breasts a little, maybe we can get my arms back," Nadia suggested. She knew that there was no hope of ever ridding herself of the tight corset that Dominus had somehow melted into her body.

"Good thinking. I hadn't thought of money. I know. I will transfer all I can from the household account into my private account, Nadia. After all, Dominus owes us big time for the torture he's put you through." Jolina brought up Nadia's laptop and began checking the accounts. Dominus had made a slight mistake, she soon discovered. Knowing that Nadia had no way to every use her computer again, that is with no arms, he'd foolishly used hers one time to transfer some funds from his private account into their domestic account, from which Jolina purchased groceries and things for the house, as well as clothes.

"How does five million sound?" Jolina teased Nadia. Nadia didn't understand, and Jolina was too engrossed to tell her right now. She transferred five million from his account into the household account. Then, she emptied the household account into her main account in Denver. Then, she deleted the access to his account from the computer and packed up the computer.

Dominus came home that night, June 29. He found Nadia sitting as usual in a chair in the front room. She can do little else now, he thought. He didn't bother to say hello, but went to his study. Jolina ducked downstairs, where she still had the recording device concealed behind a stockpile of food bags. She eavesdropped on Dominus. Probably this is what saved their lives.

"Don Cassidy, this is your master Dominus speaking. I have a job for you. Tomorrow morning, I need you to come to my house here in Denver and eliminate Nadia and her companion. Make it look like a robbery gone bad. Beat their bodies up real good. Trash the place. I don't care what you do, as long as long as they are killed." Jolina took the earpiece out of her ear. She nearly fainted. Terror filled her mind. She just stood there shaking as fall leaves hanging on through a chilly winter's blast.

Sometime later, she regained her faculties. She stowed the tape in their car and went as quietly as she could up to her room on the third floor, turned out the lights, and got into bed. Pretending to be asleep, she ignored her evening duties for Nadia. She'd just have to manage for herself this once. Jolina knew that she dared not face Dominus. He'd see right through her, that she'd overheard his plans to kill them both tomorrow morning. He could just stun both women and leave them immobilized for his hired killer in the morning. No, she had to be asleep. She had to get into action the moment that he left in the morning!

Nadia knew something was wrong. Jolina had not checked on her for ages. Now she had to go to the bathroom badly. If she called out for Jolina and she didn't come, she would only get Jolina in trouble. Maybe Dominus had already harmed her? No, she had been listening intently. Dominus had entered, hung up his jacket, and went into his study. Then, he went into their bedroom and had not come out. Something was very wrong here somewhere. Slowly, she got to her feet, wobbling a bit as she fought to keep her balance. Taking the tiniest of steps, more like sliding one foot a few inches in front of the other, she made her way out of the living room and tried to find the bathroom.

After what seemed to her to be an eternity, she found it and the toilet. However, she was powerless to unzip her dress and lower her panties. Embarrassed, she went anyway. Why had Jolina not come for her? She could not tell time; she had no way to do that now. The house was exceedingly quite. More miserable than she had ever been in her life, she again made her way back to her seat before the fireplace. As she passed by his room, she heard him sleeping in their bed. It must be late, she concluded. Without Jolina's aid, she could not join him in bed. Of course, now she didn't want to. Instead, she sat back down in front of the fireplace. Why? Her wand lay somewhere in the blackness in front of her. She'd been forced to give up magic, and she fully realized the magnitude of her loss. She could not even Morph and be able to use magic again; she couldn't see. Nadia fell asleep sitting in the chair, her life a total ruin.

"Where's breakfast? Darn it, Jolina, you overslept!" the harsh voice of Dominus roused her. He was yelling. "Forget it! I'll get something on my way to work." Nadia heard him moving into the living room, heard him grab his jacket, and heard the door close behind him. Dominus had totally ignored her! He'd said nothing about her having slept in the chair all by herself. She panicked. Where was Jolina? Why had she defied him and not prepared breakfast?

Finally, her prayers were answered. She heard the

telltale click of Jolina's heels coming down the steps. "Is he gone?" Jolina whispered.

"Yes, he went out the front a bit ago. What's happening? Where have you been?" Nadia tried to control the panic in her voice.

"No time to explain. We have to get out of here fast. I overheard him talking to someone. He's ordered some man to come here this morning, kill both of us, and make it look like a robbery gone bad. I have to get us out of here. You stay put!" Jolina raced around the house as fast as her tightfitting outfit and heels would permit. She too had slept in the clothes that she worn yesterday. Trip after trip she made to their car in the garage, stowing their various briefcase closets in the back seat of their car. Finally, she only needed to get Nadia to the car. If only they had a few more minutes.

Jolina entered the living room, "Nadia time to go, get up." Nadia struggled to her feet. Just at that instant, someone smashed in their front door. The burglar alarm failed to go off, Nadia noted, as terror swept over her.

"Die bitches!" a male voice called out. Jolina, wand in hand, dove out of the way of a Disintegrate beam. Jolina knew that she was in a fight for their very lives. She shot a Hold Person spell wildly back in the man's general direction. It had no effect. He'd taken proper countermeasures before embarking on his assassination attempt.

Slowly, fighting back the terror in her stomach, Nadia moved towards the fireplace, intent on somehow retrieving her wand to help fight back. Fear turned to anger. No way was she going to die without a fight! She banged into the fireplace and now the extra heel height came to her rescue. She found that her tiny arms could just barely feel along the mantel for her wand. At last, she felt the familiar wood of her wand. Just as she managed to grip it under her shoulder, the man saw her and called out, "Stupid. How are you going to use that? Push!" Nadia felt the full effect of his spell. She fell hard onto the floor, her wand falling beside her. She hit her head hard on the marble floor and was stunned temporarily unconscious.

How long was she out? Nadia had no idea. Her head was pounding. Something wet covered her face. She heard

Jolina screaming in pain; she was hurt. "I'm supposed to beat you to a pulp before I actually kill you. Need to make this look real," the voice said. From the sounds, Nadia believed that he was kicking her with his foot. Nadia tried to get up, but the pain in her head prevented it. She felt her wand brush her right stump. She struggled, wiggled, and managed to get the wand grasped under her arm. With all her remaining strength, she rolled over and sat up. Jolina was no longer making any sounds, but the kicking continued. Nadia sensed Jolina was nearly dead already.

Holding her wand under her arm, she realized that there was only one spell whose wand motion she could make. She cast it, "Disintegrate: man!" she called out and felt the magical energy flying from her wand. "Disintegrate: man! Disintegrate! Disintegrate! Disintegrate! Disintegrate!" she screamed over and over, each time her wand activating. Several minutes later, she heard nothing and finally stopped. Her head was pounding in pain. The wetness tricked down her chest between her breasts. She suspected it must be her own blood.

Nadia could not see what she had accomplished however. The killer had been taken by complete surprise. His lifeless body lay on the floor near Jolina's. Four gaping holes streaked into the framework of the house. A hissing sound was all that Nadia could hear. She'd ruptured the main natural gas line, though she didn't know it. "Jolina! Jolina!" she called out, but silence and total blackness was all that she sensed. Clumsily, she tried to get to her feet, but gave it up. Her head pounded so, and she was very dizzy. Wiggling, she managed to move along the marble floor over to where she thought Jolina was lying. She bumped into her body. Wet stuff was all over the floor beside Jolina. It was her. She smelled her lilac-scented hair. Awkwardly, Nadia sat up and tried to feel for signs of life. Her large breasts felt Jolina's faint breathing.

"Car! Got to get to the car. How?" Nadia thought. She knew that she had to get Jolina and herself out of here fast. Eventually, someone would come by to check on the killings. She couldn't sit here hoping Jolina would regain consciousness and get them to the car. At last, Nadia did the only thing she could think of doing. Using her teeth, she gripped tightly onto Jolina's dress and began wiggling herself across the floor, pulling Jolina's limp body with her. It was horribly slow going, and more than once, Nadia nearly fainted from the pulsating pain in her head. The only thing that allowed her to succeed was the fact that the floors were marble, which allowed their bodies to slide along relatively easily. Had it been rugs, Nadia would have failed.

She reached the stairs to the basement. She lowered her body down a ways and carefully dragged Jolina's with her. She couldn't tell if this was damaging Jolina further or not. It didn't matter. There was nothing else Nadia could do. An eternity later, she landed on the floor. She scooted over to the car. Finally, Nadia got her first real break. In her haste to get them out of here, Jolina had left the doors open, ready to put Nadia safely inside.

An eternity of pushing, shoving, butting with her throbbing head, Nadia somehow managed to get Jolina into the car and the door shut. Exhausted, she still could not get to her feet and so continued her wiggling, sliding action to get to the other side. Bracing her body against the car and its seat, Nadia managed to get her pain-wracked body up. In the tight fitting dress, getting herself inside was even more problematical. Finally, she managed, although her head protested madly in this upright position, throbbing hideously. That she had a very bad concussion never entered her mind. She leaned forward, feeling with her right arm, and found the GEOSAT console. Using her arm, she fumbled until she was able to press the large activate button.

"Take us to the Fire Department at our top speed," she called out.

A moment later, the monotone voice said, "Your door is ajar." She couldn't close it even if she had wanted to do so. Now something else came vaguely to her attention. Her nose? Yes, she smelled something awful. What was it? Her mind was shutting down. Nadia tried to focus on the smell. What was it? The monotone voice continued, "Shutting the car door now. The garage door is opening. Program is now active. Fire Department. Top speed. Say abort or press the abort button to cancel." She sensed the engine starting up and heard the noise of the garage door opening.

Just as the car began to move, her ears heard a massive explosion. Her neighbors saw their expensive home literally explode in a giant ball of fire. Out of the flames and smoke, the hot Ferrari shot, zigging and zagging down the residential streets of Denver, until it reached the open highway. The computer then kicked the red Ferrari into ninth gear. The car's speed, if you could actually measure it as it traveled through magically altered space, exceeded two hundred miles per hour.

Nadia felt the car's motion. Then, she succumbed to the massive throbbing in her head. She too passed out, slumped over in her car. Everything was now in the hands of the GEOSAT computer.

Chapter 5—The Arrivals Begin

Based on Ashley's premonition, Governor Alister rounded up Doctor Caterwall. The two teleported to the Compton ranch. "Wow, tripled in size. Impressive," the older man said, as Lindsey met them at the door.

Grinning, Lindsey replied, "Thanks for coming. Yes, we've been working hard and have just finished it. We have four homes in each addition, but we could pack more folks in, if need be. Come on in."

Governor Alister greeted Ashley first, "Hello. I hear you had a premonition." His kind voice was very reassuring to Ashley. She at last calmed down.

"Yes, something terrible has happened to Nadia and Jolina. I know it. They are on their way here in their Ferrari, but something is terribly wrong. Lindsey and I both sent them a Message. Nothing, sir. Nothing came back. They might be dead."

"Do you feel that is so?" he asked softly and politely, but also with intention.

"Well, no, but why else won't they reply?" she asked.

"Many reasons. Perhaps they are hurt. It couldn't be that they don't want to chat and drive at the same time?" This brought a giggle to Ashley. She'd been taught not to chat while manually driving a car.

Just then, the monotone voice announced, "Red Ferrari is approaching at a high rate of speed. Registered to Nadia van Nye Malefic and Jolina Wessel."

Everyone raced outside, just as the red car covered in black soot materialized. Its motor automatically turned off, as the GEOSAT announced in a monotone voice, "Fire Department has been reached. Disengaging in thirty seconds. Press abort to continue activation."

The whole group looked inside the windows. Nothing could have prepared them for what they saw. Blood covered both unconscious women. Dried blood was on the outside of both doors. Governor Alister opened Jolina's door first. The slumped body of the woman lay in a weird position. She was covered in blood, and her arms appeared broken. Shoe prints were all over her bloody blue dress. Doctor Caterwall felt for a pulse. "She's alive, barely." Alister went to the other side to check on Nadia's condition.

Her face was covered in blood from her broken nose. A huge swelling distorted her head. As he straightened her up, he saw the burn marks where her eyes had been fried. "She's alive too. Doctor, very bad condition, probably head concussion."

"These women belong in a hospital," Doctor Caterwall whispered, "but I don't think that they will survive long enough to get them there. Best do emergency stabilization here, and then decide what's best."

"Levitation?" Alister asked.

"Right, avoid further injury and trauma," the doctor replied.

Lena spoke up, "We've a room all prepared for them. Lindsey, show them the way. I'll start water boiling." The ranch woman was levelheaded in a crisis, Alister observed.

Alister cast his Levitate spell on Nadia and began extracting her from the car. Lindsey followed suit with Jolina, only she didn't say anything or raise her wand. With both women now floating above the ground, Lindsey cast her Move Object spell and Jolina reappeared above one of the two beds that they had prepared. Since Alister was not familiar with their new construction, Lindsey did the same with Nadia for him. Everyone followed Lindsey, except Audrey.

Audrey was just as shocked at the appearance of the near dead women as everyone else was. However, she felt like she needed to remain with the car. "Why?" she said to herself. Inside, blood covered both seats. Mechanically, she began casting numerous Clean spells. Suddenly, she spied the cassette tape lying on the seat, right where Jolina had dropped it. She picked it up and knew that this was what she was meant to find. She carried the tape inside.

Audrey found everyone gathered around the two women in the new apartment, now called Number 4. "We have to get the swelling on her brain down fast or she will die,"

Doctor Caterwall was saying.

"Okay, I'll fetch the blood from Greeley," Deiter volunteered. Pam had already sent word to Doctor Blackburn that they needed five pints of type A blood. Doctor Caterwall muttered his thanks.

"Alister, we need to very carefully undress both patients so I can examine them. Could there be traps in a situation like this?"

"Kids, let's check for traps, shall we?" Alister asked. At once Lindsey, Pam, Ashley, Emilio, Kathy, Amanda, Fern, and Audrey cast their detection spells. A few minutes later, everyone agreed there were no traps.

"Girls, I think it best if you removed their clothing. I am not familiar with their outfits and how it should be done," Doctor Caterwall asked, a bit baffled with their fetish outfits. The girls giggled and, with Lindsey carefully Levitating each girl, they began undoing their clothing. Jolina was finally lying naked on the bed for the Doctor's careful examination. "Internal bleeding, I thought so. Darn, she took one heck of a beating. It's a wonder she isn't dead."

"Hello. Oh my god! What's happened here?" the voice of Doctor Henry Blackburn spoke. He and Deiter had just arrived, Deiter carrying the precious bags of blood.

"Severe beating on this one; she's bled a lot externally, but now from the discoloration, she's also bleeding internally," Doctor Caterwall gave his quick analysis.

"Nadia's ready," Lindsey announced. Pam had finally gotten the unconscious woman's smelly underpants off.

"Good god! What has he done to her?" exclaimed Doctor Caterwall. Indeed, everyone stared at Nadia's waist. Beneath the skin around her waist, they could see a wasp waist corset. It had been melted into her body, similar to the way that the rings of Dominus had melted into the wearer's finger. He began outlining his findings anyway. "Severe concussion, broken nose. No signs of any beating. Eyes burned out, arms amputated, waist—well, you can see for yourself on that one. We have to reduce the pressure on her brain or she'll die.

"We need to get them into the emergency room fast," Doctor Blackburn said.

"Don't think they will last that long," Doctor Caterwall answered. After a short examination, Henry agreed. "Okay, which case do you feel the most comfortable handling?"

"I'm a facial reconstruction expert. I'll take the internal bleeding case," he replied.

"Boiling water, doctors?" Lena, Wilma, Polly, and Monane entered, carrying a large number of boiling pots of water and a stack of towels.

"Thanks. Kids, put a dozen permanent Light spells on the ceiling over our heads. We are going to need tons of light." At once, the shocked teens obeyed, and the room grew intensely bright. "Ladies, you are hereby appointed our nurses. Kids, it's best that you leave. This is not going to be pretty." Doctor Caterwall suggested the teens leave. Alister went with them, as well as Lloyd and R. B.

"Sir, I think you should listen to this tape," the meek voice of Audrey broke their silence as they walked down the long hallway past the girls' bedrooms. "I found this in their car. I sense it is important." She handed the cleaned tape to Governor Alister.

"We've got a tape player in the family room," Lloyd took charge. Everyone now had something to do—listen to the tape. Deiter needed this for he was turning several shades of green. Kathy stopped off at the bathroom to vomit. Audrey and Fern went to aid her.

Listening to the short phone call that Jolina had recorded snapped the teens out of their initial shock at seeing the women so badly wounded. "So Dominus ordered their deaths," Alister mused. "Jolina must have recorded this, probably last night. There was a lot of stuff thrown hastily into their back seat. Jolina must have been packing for them just before their attacker came, probably at the very last minute. What I don't grasp is that Nadia was driving. Considering the beating that Jolina has taken, I don't believe she was conscious when she was put into the car. Could someone else have put them in there? What was that bit about having reached the Fire Department?"

"I can explain that," Lindsey answered. "I gave her my address here at the ranch, and Jolina programmed it into their

GEOSAT machine, filing it under the address of Fire Department, in case Dominus ever checked. If Jolina was unconscious, how could Nadia have ever gotten her into the car, let alone operate it?"

Pam interrupted them, "Hey everyone! It's on the news!" Everyone gathered around the big screen TV. A Denver announcer was showing live video of the violent fire. "This morning, the house of Dominus Malefic was struck by a natural gas explosion, which leveled the tri-story home in the plush suburbs of Whitegate. Initial reports indicated that Mrs. Malefic and her maid were home at the time of the blast and were certainly killed in the explosion and fire. As you can clearly see from this footage, nothing at all is left but the concrete basement floor and foundation walls. The intense fire has incinerated everything. It took Denver Gas and Electric an hour to get the gas turned off, finally shutting down the entire subdivision as a precaution. Fire fighters worked all morning to save three neighboring houses from severe damage. Their siding has been scorched. Windows have been blown out in every home within a two-block radius. Speculation is rampant over the cause of this explosion and blaze."

"Dominus Malefic is said to be in shock at this hour, claiming that his wife and servant were home at the time of the blast. Investigators on the scene tell us that it may well be several months before the exact cause of the blast is known. As a safety precaution, Denver Gas and Electric has already begun a full inspection of all homes in the subdivision before they turn the gas back on, hoping to prevent a similar occurrence. Now a word from our sponsors. Stay with us we'll be right back with more on this disaster."

Pam turned the volume down. "Well, we can't take the women to the hospital, that's for sure," Governor Alister said softly. "I'd best relay this to the doctors."

Lindsey looked at Lloyd questioningly. He replied, "There simply aren't enough Security men to prevent Dominus from finishing their murders while the women are at the hospital. Sorry. Besides, Dominus now thinks that these two are dead. As long as he thinks so, they are far safer, if they survive their injuries, that is. They look awful."

78

"How could anyone do that to them?" Deiter finally spoke what his heart said. "I mean they were both really beautiful women. Why beat them to death and torture them? Dominus must really be one sick person."

Lloyd replied, "Aye, Deiter, that he is. I wish you teens had not seen them like this. No one should see anyone beaten as they have been. Grizzly sight even for me," he replied.

"What can we do? To help?" Deiter asked.

"I know, why don't you kids go clean up their car and bring all their things inside," Lloyd thought fast, giving the teens something to focus on, something to do. Grateful, the bunch headed outside to do just that.

"Are they going to make it?" asked Deiter, as he helped hand items out of the car to Lindsey and Ashley.

"Dunno, they look terrible," she replied.

Inside the well-lighted room, Doctor Blackburn wiped his hands, as Polly and Monane began casting Clean spells. "That was tricky, but she's a fighter. I think she will make it." The two doctors had finished their initial attempts to save the two women and were double-checking each other's work.

"I swear that corset, strange as this sounds, saved Jolina's life. Those steel stays displaced some of the kicker's force over a wider area. Otherwise, those kicks would have been fatal. She has several cracked ribs. One punctured her left lung and poked into her liver," Henry explained.

"Pretty ingenious way to get the blood out and the lung expanded," Doctor Caterwall complimented him. "Magical spells to the rescue, eh?"

Henry chuckled, "Necessity is the mother of invention, as the old saying goes. She has her right arm broken here and her left one, here. Defensive wounds, I would guess. Left leg is probably broken as well, but without x-rays, I can't tell for sure. I have her stable. If you concur, then I will administer the heavy duty healing potions and get her body on the mend."

Doctor Caterwall looked Jolina over from head to toe, making sure nothing was overlooked. "Yes, I agree. Dose her and then have a look at mine. Nadia is a mess." Henry put a large potion bottle on the IV rack and opened its valve, allowing the concentrated healing potion to begin to drip into her system. Already he had put four pints of blood into her system, replacing the significant blood loss she had suffered. His estimate was the Jolina had another ten minutes to live before he gotten to her; it was that close. Now he turned his attention onto Doctor Caterwall's work on Nadia.

"Excellent handling of the head, Frank, brilliant. How do we proceed with her?" Henry found no other immediate injuries. The concussion was the worst, and Frank's handling already had the life threatening swelling rapidly going down. The problem was an obvious one; medicine had no way to deal with the strange melding of the corset into her body.

"I don't dare regrow her arms, Henry, not with that corset inside her. Lord knows what the potion would do to her. Can it be surgically removed?" Frank asked.

"Darn it. I don't see how. I agree, administering nearly anything will carry a huge risk. I see you are gambling with her eyes?"

"Yes, local application of a mixture of healing and re-grow. I figure that if I can get her sight back, she can at least get by until we can figure how to get that thing out of her." The two discussed the situation further and both agreed, sending for Alister.

"How do we get this out of her?" Frank pointed to the corset.

Sighing, Governor Alister answered, "We just don't know. It is likely the same spell that he used to meld the rings to the fingers of his supporters. Once we solve that riddle, we can use it on her. Anything else you can do for her?"

"Too darn risky to try. Heaven knows what the re-grow potion will do with that in her system. I know it is a bit of a risk with her eyes, but I've been keeping the potions locally applied, not internally, cutting down the risk."

Henry suggested, "You know, Alister, the way things are going, it might not be a bad idea to establish a secret emergency room here to treat patients on the side. Frank and I just worked under the worst imaginable conditions to save these women's lives. Oh yes, by the way, Alister, Jolina came slightly around as I was working on her, she mumbled something about transferring money out of her account. I don't know what she meant, and she went under after mumbling it. I'll leave that one to you."

"I believe you have a valid point. Please, will you and Frank get together a list of what you think should be here, and I'll see that we have an emergency treatment center set up here," Alister suggested. The two men agreed, and Henry left for Greeley, before his presence was missed.

"Pam, by chance did you kids find Jolina's computer in their things?" Alister asked a minute later. The teens had all the women's things in the front room. They were just finishing cleaning the blood off of them.

"Yes, this one has a 'J' on it, probably hers," Pam said.

"Would you be so kind as to get it up and running? Jolina mentioned something about transferring money from her account. We don't know what that means, but let's see if we can see what she might have been intending, shall we?"

"Wu hoo, another mystery!" Pam exclaimed and began booting up Jolina's laptop.

"How are you going to get in, Pam? It's asking for her password?" Deiter asked. All were looking over Pam's shoulders.

"Several ways, but I'll try the obvious first." She typed in "Jolina" and then "Nadia," both failed. Then she typed in "Ferrari," and the laptop continued to boot up. Pam had a satisfied look on her face.

"But that's not a good password," Deiter remembered his school lessons on computer security.

"Most people can't remember a really secure password, Deiter. So they use one they can remember, usually something common and significant in their life. Here we go. She has a link on the desktop to her bank account. Up came the Denver National Bank page, again asking for login information. Unfortunately, for security reasons, though beneficial for Pam, Jolina had the RememberIt software package installed, which automatically filled in her logon and passwords for the secure sites that she visited. "So much for security," Pam commented flatly. Even Deiter knew this was just asking for trouble.

"My god! She has over five million dollars in her account! Let's look at the history. Oh, she just transferred the five million into her account this morning! What should we do, Alister?" Pam asked.

"Hum, if you will allow me?" he said. Pam moved out of the way. He sat down and set up another automated transfer of funds. After clicking the Do It button, her account was minus the five million, holding just the few hundred dollars she had in it before this large transfer.

"Where did you send the funds?" Pam asked, curious about the transaction.

"Until we know the true story with these funds, I thought it best to make a donation to the Arthur Bradbury School of Magic. Legally, she has just made a new endowment for our school. However, if the funds are hers, I will transfer them back later. Now then, I had best be off. Message me when they regain consciousness. I wish to question both of them." He then left, and the teens went to check on the two women.

"Let's put all their things in their new apartment," Lindsey suggested. They spent the rest of the day fixing up the Spartan rooms for the two women. Nadia and Jolina remained sleeping all the day, while Frank hovered over them, checking on their vital signs. Periodically, he administered more of his potions to the women.

Lindsey kept an eye on the news, hoping for further word about what happened to Nadia and Jolina. The only additional tidbit was the discovery of the burned shells of their two wands. Unexplained was also the presence of a third wand shell. Speculation of a direct attack on the women and Dominus began because of this discovery. Both women were now presumed dead in the fire, for no witch would ever leave her wand behind, ever.

However, the larger news coverage was the launching of President Snow's National Health Care Program tomorrow. This initial phase covered all residents of the state of New York and the DC area. Many residents were interviewed, expressing the whole gamut of opinions about this mandatory program. By far the most common opinion among the normals was "let's wait and see how this works out." The wizarding community held the most divergent opinions—from this could be the best thing for everyone to this is the worst possible thing that could ever happen.

July 1, the two women finally were allowed to wake up, under Doctor Caterwall's expert care. "How are you feeling today? You're safe on the Compton ranch. I'm Doctor Frank Caterwall of Bradbury's School of Magic."

"My head hurts so badly! Jolina! How is Jolina?" Nadia asked.

"She is recovering nicely, very close call, mind you. Your eyes will be back to normal in a few days, Nadia. However, until we can get that corset out of your body, we dare not attempt to re-grow your arms. I guess you will have to be patient a little longer. You had a very nasty concussion. Your head may ache for several days yet. Ah, Jolina is waking."

"Welcome back, Jolina," he repeated his introduction. "Don't try to get up. You have a number of broken bones in your arms and leg. They will heal in a few days. You have several cracked ribs as well. We nearly lost you. Another ten minutes and you would not be here today."

"How—how did I get here? Nadia? I saw you fall."

"I can cast a Disintegrate with my arm. I got him. He's dead. I dragged you to the car and somehow got us here, but I passed out after the car started moving," Nadia explained.

"Well, you both are now safe. Governor Alister wishes to speak with you as soon as you are able to handle it. All the kids are just as anxious to chat with you too. I think it wisest if Alister meets with you first. Relax. You are completely safe here on the Compton ranch. No one knows you are here or are alive."

A half hour later, Governor Alister sat between the two beds. After a brief pleasant chat about how they were doing, he explained what he knew. "As far as the news is concerned, the explosion and fire destroyed the house. They found the remains of your wands in the rubble and have pronounced you both dead as a result. Your car brought you here, and we summoned our school doctor and Doctor Henry Blackburn, Monique's father, here to treat you. Audrey found your tape. We all heard Dominus ordering your murders, so we dared not take you to a real hospital. Jolina muttered something about her bank account and transferring funds. Pam discovered that you had just transferred five million dollars into your account. To play it safe, I transferred it to Bradbury's. We can handle further transfers when you are well. Now, that about tells you everything that we know about your situation. What can you tell me about what happened to you two?"

For over an hour, Jolina and Nadia told Alister everything that had happened, beginning with Nadia's accidental overhearing of the phone call to President Snow back in May. Nadia ended, "I have been a complete and utter fool. Look what I have brought down on us! I nearly got my very best friend killed, and me—look at me. I can't even cry with these bandages over my eyes. I'm so sorry for what I have done. Jolina, can you ever forgive me?"

"You saved my life, Nadia. I don't know how you could possibly have done it, but you did. That is more than enough thanks, dear. I grabbed us five million in compensation though. Alister, is that legal? I mean I transferred it from his account into the household account and then into mine. Should I give it back to Dominus?"

"You are in charge of maintaining the household. You are Nadia's official keeper. I think that officially the transfer will hold up in court as a valid transfer. You are simply providing for her continued care." His eyes twinkled, and she giggled briefly, but her sides ached so badly the giggle stopped at once.

"I'll get the teens. I know they are dying to see you. However, the first order of business. I need those tapes that you made of Dominus. Can you tell the girls where to find them, please?"

Eagerly, the teens filed into the room to see their guests. Alister said, "Miss Betts, I would like you to return with me to Bradbury's. I have an assignment for you to research in our library. Nadia has just given us a valuable clue. When Dominus put the corset on her, his command word was 'Meld.' Because of that, the corset became as it is now, beneath her skin. I believe that is also the same spell that merged the rings onto the wearer's finger. We must find that spell and figure out how to reverse it. Are you up to a challenge?"

"You bet! Cool! I'll find it, Nadia. Then, we can get it off of you," Pam promised.

Minutes later, with the many tapes in hand, Alister and Pam left. In the last two hours, he had discovered more information about Dominus and his plans than he had uncovered in the last month. He had work to do and to do fast. He delegated the lesser research project to Pam, for now at least.

Around four, Amanda got an interesting Message from her father. "Gang, looks like dad is taking in a family from New York. Come on. Let's go lend a hand. They are from Utica, dad says."

The group of teens headed over to the Whitewater ranch. Already, numerous boxes and crates lay on the ground outside their ranch house. R. B. and Luci were watching them. He explained, "Hi all. Eli is transporting his whole house I believe. I think this is their last trip. Ought to be here shortly, if nothing goes wrong. They are Iroquois, Seneca, I believe. He got a hold of me via the tribal council, desperately seeking sanctuary. Ah, here they come." Four people suddenly materialized near the large pile of boxes and crates.

Lindsey saw at once that they were Native American as well. "Here we are none too soon, that was a close escape," the older man said. "Whoa, you've got quite a crowd to meet us," he said, looking at all the teens. He was still holding onto his wife, who was crying.

"I am Eli Orondarka, Department of Security, Magical Branch, New York. Oops, ex-Department of Security. I just quit." He looked to be forty. All members of his family were definitely Native America, darker skin tones. "This is my wife, Kimi. She does not use magic and is an attorney." Lindsey noted that this was his polite way of saying that she was a normal. The whole family had black hair and dark eyes. While Eli had very short hair, Kimi's hair was shoulder length, well cared for as befitting a professional woman. Lindsey noticed that she was rather distraught.

"Our children, Ahana, sixteen, and Orenda, fourteen. Both were students at the New York Magic School." Ahana was tall, at least two inches taller than Amanda was. He was handsome, and he smiled a lot, Lindsey noted. Orenda was also cute, wearing her hair like her mother's hair.

Eli continued, "I'm afraid that Kimi is not doing too well. You see, we were ordered to partake of this infernal health care plan. Early this morning, we did as ordered, reported to Utica's Health Care facility. Gave us all pills. However, Kimi, not a witch, was given the normal pill. It was awful to behold. She turned into a walking zombie. I had to cast Cure Disease on her to rid her system of that pill's effect. Kids didn't seem to be effected by their pills. However, I faked taking mine. Good thing. We got out of there in short order. Is there any doctor around who might look after Kimi? See if there are any lingering aftereffects?"

"Bradbury's school doctor is over at the Compton ranch. We can take her there after we get you settled in. My wife, Luci, my two daughters, Amanda and Fern. Sorry, one boy, Tom, and his wife are off at college in Denver. Our other boy, Jim, is off getting his beginning Department of Security training. These others are our very dear friends and live next door to us, well from your perspective, a few miles," he grinned. These new arrivals were city dwellers not ranchers.

"Miss Lindsey Barron, Miss Ashley Stokes-Compton. They are the daughters of Lena and Lloyd Compton. Lloyd is with the Colorado Department of Security. He might be able to get you a job with them. Staying with them is their foster daughter Miss Audrey Lemon and Fred Betts and his family. Fred is the head of the High Plains Department of Magical Misuse. His daughter Pam is off doing some research on you know who. These are Deiter Cross, Emilio Lopez, and Miss Kathy Townsend—all good friends and who helped build these houses you will be staying in. Looks like we got them built just in time. Kids, will you lend a hand moving their things into unit Number One." This was the first of the new apartment homes they had built. "Eli and I will take Kimi to visit Doctor Caterwall."

"Hi, I'm Amanda," she offered her hand to Ahana.

He smiled and shook it, saying, "Pleased to meet you. You are nearly as tall as I am. I like that. Strange day though. Went to that stupid health care place at eight this morning. By nine, dad was Curing Disease on mom, and by ten, he had us packing up to move. Nothing like a wee bit of change to make your day. Say, where are we anyway? No civilization around here?"

They chatted as they began the lengthy moving of all their belongings into the new spacious home or apartment. "You are out on the High Plains of extreme eastern Colorado. This is a tiny Indian reservation. Our ranch here is at the northern edge of it. Lindsey's place is next to ours. We are all over at each other's place all the time. It's very safe here. Dominus doesn't dare come here. He sent a Death Stalker over to Lindsey's place once, but her mother, she's a norm too—she shot him dead with a shotgun because he was trying to kill Audrey here. So you are about as safe as you can be, I suppose."

"Say, you look familiar. Didn't I see you on TV? The National Track Meet in Des Moines two years ago?" Ahana asked.

"Yes, that's us. Lindsey, Fern, Ashley, Emilio, and me. Jim and Tom were on it too. We won First Place too."

"Yes, but how did you ever survive that explosion? Wait a second," he turned to Lindsey, "you're the Rat Pack's Sam Barron's daughter?" His eyes went wide open as he finally figured out who these teens were.

"Wow! Very pleased to meet you!" he stopped everything and shook Lindsey's hand again. "Sis, this is *the* Lindsey Barron!"

Orenda was rifling through one of her bags, chatting with Fern. She pulled out a magazine, just as Ahana called out to her. She grinned, looked at the magazine and then at Ashley. "You're *the* Ashley! The one in Teen Fashion!" she said, very awed at her discovery. Fern giggled. Ashley blushed.

Ahana, now very excited, added, "Wow! I thought dad was off his rocker, bringing us into the wilderness, just because mom got sick when she took that pill. Now I can see that we are the luckiest kids in the country. Amanda, you are one hot runner. I saw how you always run last, which means you are the best and fastest on your team. Incredible. I play basketball. I was the captain of our Yellow Hall team, but I guess that's a thing of the past now that we've suddenly moved out here. You don't have a basketball court around here do you?"

"Er, no basketball courts, I'm afraid, but we can probably make one for you," Amanda replied, a bit embarrassed by his elation. "We should try to get your house all fixed up for your folks. I imagine it has been a bit traumatic, what with a so sudden and unexpected move."

He sighed, "Yes, terrifying actually. The way mom looked and acted, I thought we lost her. I'm sure glad that dad knew what to do. Anyway, we're here, and mom's doing better now, so all's well with the world again." His cheery outlook came flooding back.

"Don't pay him any mind, Amanda," Orenda whispered. "He's always cheerful even when his team loses. Me, I'm still plenty scared, but knowing that this is where Ashley and Lindsey live, I feel tons safer, because everyone knows that Dominus is after them. Will we be going to Bradbury's this fall?"

"Probably. That's the only school around here, excepting Denver School of Magic," Fern answered her. "Everyone knows that Denver is a slum compared to Bradbury's. Do you like to grow flowers? Audrey is the expert, but I am right behind her. You have to see what I have done in my room. I have flowers growing in my walls."

The kids chatted away, as they began un-boxing all their household things. The larger furniture had been shrunk, needed to be un-shrunk, and moved into position. Orenda insisted that everything be put back in the same places that they were used to having them, as much as possible, since this was a different house.

An hour later, a very somber Eli and Kimi entered their new home for the first time. The teens had nearly everything unpacked and in its original locations as best they could. "Oh, it looks like home!" exclaimed Kimi. This was the first smile Lindsey had seen on the poor woman's face. "Lindsey, your mother is so nice! She and I are alike, married into a family of wizards and witches. She made me feel right at home, but I still have the shakes."

Eli continued, "Yes, Doctor Caterwall gave her a complete physical, as best he can outside his facilities. That pill was laced with a low dosage of heroin! President Snow is turning all our citizens into heroin addicts, if nothing else! Kimi will be fine in a few days. Withdrawal symptoms, kids, that's what the shakes are coming from. Darn that Dominus anyway."

"Yes, but those poor women, Eli!" Kimi added.

Eli explained, "They are taking care of Dominus's wife, Nadia, and her companion, Jolina. You know, they were supposed to have been killed in the explosion and fire. Well, that was no accident. Dominus ordered a hit on his own wife! Glad it failed. Golly, they are in terrible condition though. You'll get to meet them. We are having supper over at the Compton's tonight. Say, you kids should try out R. B.'s fancy teleport pad. It goes from one family's front room to the other. Clever. R. B. is an inventor, kids."

"Come on; we'll show you," Amanda couldn't help herself from saying to Ahana. "We'll be over at Lindsey's." She led them all to their teleport pad, explaining how it worked as they walked.

Just as they arrived in Lindsey's front room hallway, Pam walked in the front door, heavily laden with large books. "Oh, you must be the new Orondarka's. Hi. I'm Pam Betts, pleased to meet you. Doing a bit of spell research for Governor Alister at the moment."

Grinning broadly, he replied, "Hi. I'm Ahana, my sister, Orenda. We've heard a lot about you. You were the one that brought ex-Governor General Albright to justice, weren't you?"

"Yes, that's me. If you will excuse me, I have lots of research to do just now. I have to find a cure for Nadia and everyone who was stupid enough to put on one of Dominus's rings." She headed on down the hallway to her room. Ahana stared after her, though.

Lena, Wilma, Monane, and Polly were introduced to the two teens. "Boy, your place is huge inside!" Ahana commented, impressed with the spaciousness.

"We just got done adding two wings on either side that are also the same size, only we divided them into quarters so we could house eight families. Alister thinks there will be a lot of people needing refuge," Lindsey explained.

"Go cheer up Nadia and Jolina a bit, kids. We are working on supper," Lena suggested. Lindsey led them on a short tour of her house, and then went through the new doorway into the eastern wing. At the first door, she stopped and knocked. Jolina and Doctor Caterwall replied, and the group entered.

"Hi, Jolina, Nadia, we're back." Lindsey added, "We have some new neighbors who have just come from New York to stay. This is Ahana and Orenda Orondarka. This is Nadia van Nye and Jolina Wessel." Lindsey was careful not to say Malefic. Nadia had had enough of that name and didn't need to be further embarrassed by it. The two newcomers now understood why their folks had returned looking so somber.

Lindsey wondered how she could cheer up the two women. To her surprise, Ahana did. He got over his shock of seeing them in such bad shape quickly. He said, "Say, I bet you to like to rock and roll, to dance, am I right? You just look like the type."

"Ja, sure ve do, all de time," Nadia replied, her head was still throbbing, causing her English to slip slightly. "Jolina is better than I though."

"Well, today is your luck day! Ever heard of Eli's Rockers?"

"Who hasn't?" Jolina replied. "Just one of the up and coming hot bands. I like the way that they play many of the Antique Rock songs. Nadia and I are passionate Antique Rock lovers. Why?" Even Lindsey knew of this youthful rock band. Tom had played several of their songs during their many dances.

"Well, like I said, this is your lucky day, ladies."

"Oh boy, here we go again. Audrey, why don't you show me your wall flowers," Orenda said.

Ahana got out his wand and commanded, "To Me." Suddenly, a classical guitar appeared in his hands. "You are looking at the founder and leader of Eli's Rockers. How about a solo? The rest of the band is still in New York." He began to play the introduction of the Antique Rock song Aqualung, by

Jethro Tull.

"God, it's him!" Nadia exclaimed, recognizing his voice. Her eyes were still bandaged up.

Pam, hearing the sound of her favorite Antique Rock group, stopped everything and came running into the room. She held her hand over her mouth to keep from shrieking and interrupting Ahana. When he finished, she finally let it out, "It's you, Eli's Rockers!" Nadia and Jolina were grinning from ear to ear.

"Ja, ve love Antique Rock. Ve got hundreds of disks in our collection," Jolina replied. Pam finally found someone else more devoted to Antique Rock than she was.

Amanda, just as awed as the rest, including Deiter, said, "Why are you called Eli's Rockers? I didn't recognize you until you played."

"Because who's going to call themselves Orondarka's Rockers or even Ahana's Rockers, eh?" Everyone roared with laughter, even Jolina, whose sides ached, and Nadia, whose head throbbed. He played several more songs until the call to supper came.

"Thank you so much for sharing your home with us," Kimi said as Eli helped her sit down. "I am feeling better now. That potion is taking effect. I don't know what came over me today. It was just a pill, supposed to prevent all sickness," she explained. "Eli says that there was heroin in it. That's criminal. I'm an attorney, you know, but I guess we are fugitives now, I suppose."

"No dear, we just moved. It's still legal to move," Eli replied.

"How are you kids getting along?" she asked. "I'm so sorry that I got sick, and we had to move so quickly without any advanced warning. You had to leave all your friends behind."

"Coolest mom. Do you know who these are?" Ahana cheered up his mother. He explained about Lindsey, Ashley, and Pam. Hence, Lindsey felt obliged to relate her many adventures with Dominus, attempting to show the rolls that Deiter had played in them as well. Eli was incredibly impressed that so many of them had a Staff of Power. Both families shared stories for well over an hour. Finally, Lindsey ended with the sad tale of Nadia and Jolina, bringing them all up to date on the latest happenings.

After the extended meal was over, Kimi excused herself and went to visit with Nadia. "I'm a federal attorney, Nadia. They've just told me about your situation with Dominus. I want to help you."

"Jolina thinks that we can now get me a divorce, what with that tape where he ordered us to be killed," Nadia said quietly, rather embarrassed by the whole thing.

"Say, I've one question first. Remember, we are under client privileges here, so I can't be forced to repeat anything you tell me here in confidence. Did he sign your wedding papers as Dominus Malefic?"

"Yes, why?"

"Because he just committed fraud, if his birth certificate says his legal name is Simon Mac Fluide, and he has not formally and legally changed it. If so, we can easily get an annulment; no need for a divorce. Since it appears that Dominus is controlling so much of our government—Eli says everyone has orders from the President not to bother Dominus—an annulment would be the easiest to secure. If you choose not to divorce him and he is killed, then you would legally be entitled to inherit his estate. However, if his legal name is Simon, then that would surely be contested in the courts, to say nothing of all the other people he has killed or harmed who might also seek compensation. Honestly, I think an annulment is the best way to go, Nadia. Later, you would be free to file your own petition seeking compensation from him or his estate."

"That sounds good to me. Thank you so much. I have been the dumbest person in the world for having ever been mixed up with him. I was such a fool."

"Haven't we all at some time or another in our lives?" Kimi replied, putting her more at ease.

As she left, Deiter entered. "Hi ya. I brought you a small TV so you can watch the news and stuff. Er sorry, listen to the news," he hastily added, flushing.

"Thanks Deiter," Nadia replied. "Can you set it up for

us? I'm not allowed up yet, and Jolina probably can't manage it." Deiter turned on the KMAG news for them and rejoined the others, feeling content that he had done a little something for the women.

At eight, the monotone voice began announcing more arrivals. Governor Alister had called another meeting of the Rodents Pack. As soon as the large group arrived, Professor Delius asked, "Have you been watching the news today?" No one had, unfortunately. Hence, they all crowded around the big screen to get the latest update.

They were interviewing a man who had cancer before today. He talked in a slow, monotone voice, "I am very happy now. I am very well. I want to work hard now. I will do my job very well. I will make my family prosper." He stared off into space while the words came out, seemingly detached from what was going on around him.

The announcer from New York added, "Physicians can find no trace of his cancer and have pronounced him healed or at least in regression. The same story is being told countless places around DC and New York. It does seem that those taking the pills are indeed now healthy, even if they were not when they reported to their local clinics. KMAG asked the same question many have been asking all day today. Has a new miracle drug been discovered by Aetna Pharmaceuticals? A spokesperson at Aetna told KMAG that they had no comment until the pilot program is completed and the analysis done."

"Countering these miracle cures, others are calling this a debacle, turning out automatons not people. Walking zombies, others have called them. One employer who chose to go on record had this to say, I quote: 'They have lost their ability to think and act independently. No creativity. I'm afraid that I will have to fire all of those who are on the health care pill. We can't have mindless zombies operating this heavy construction equipment! It's far too dangerous.'"

For a half hour, everyone listened to the various sides of the big debate. Finally, Alister called the meeting to order. "I'd first like to welcome the four newest members of the Rodents Pack." He introduced the Orondarka family.

"They have given us our first real break. Until now, we have been completely stymied in getting a hold of these pills to analyze them. Kimi received a month's supply this morning, and Eli has given us the remaining twenty-nine along with all of those intended for him and his children. We now have an adequate supply for testing. Each pill has a letter stamped prominently on it, A or B. We know the A pills are for the normals and the B pills for those of the wizarding world. Fred has taken a sample to his friend at the CSI lab, and Henry has taken a few to his hospital for analysis."

"Henry reports that each pill contains a low dosage of heroin, which makes these pills highly addictive. That is, once the person begins taking them, they will most certainly crave to continue them. Henry also reports that they contain a highly concentrated form of the Heal Disease Potion that is routinely used in Mag hospitals. That's all his lab is equipped to detect. Fred will be along later with the results of the CSI analysis, if it gets done in time."

"From Nadia and Jolina, we now know that Dominus arranged for this whole National Health Care Program, paying ten million dollars to finance it, to say nothing of providing the pills. Those two have provided us with a wealth of information. We now know that Dominus alone has the controlling device that permits him to force his will on his ring bearers. He speaks orders directly into this device. It is a small, handheld device."

"Nadia was with Dominus when he activated the rings. It took place right under our very noses in Montrose—in a factory there. Apparently, Dominus had one Chief Engineer Smythe St. Johns, PhD, design and build these rings. At least from what Dominus said that night, Nadia believes he was the architect behind it. Delius is now researching this doctor to learn all that we can about him. Perhaps a clue will emerge."

"The exodus from the affected areas has already begun. Bradbury's has accepted fifty new transfers above our maximum number of enrollments. Looks like a busy fall term. Oh yes, I have Miss Betts researching the spell used to meld the rings onto fingers. We may have a lead finally. I believe that about summarizes it." After this, they broke into small groups and chatted.

The next morning, Kimi borrowed Nadia's car. Dressed in her professional grey suit, black hose and low heels, Kimi headed for the county seat and courthouse in the small town of Cheyenne Wells, the county seat of Cheyenne County in which she now lived. First, she filed her federal papers, making it official that she lived in the county and could conduct her law business from here. Second, she did a thorough search of the official records. By ten, she returned the ten miles to the Compton ranch.

"It's official. You are eligible for an annulment. He used the wrong name on the marriage license. I've taken the liberty of filling out the forms for you. The signature is the problem. You are supposed to sign here. Under the circumstances, I'm having Jolina sign for you. If you don't mind, I will attach a photo of you with it as proof." Nadia felt embarrassed about having her picture taken looking like she assumed that she did, bandaged up, no makeup, but Kimi was discrete; the photo only showed her from the chest on up. "Back in an hour with the papers filed." Kimi whisked out of the room, light on her feet. For a change, she felt she was making a difference in the world. True to her word, she returned an hour later. The form had been accepted. Nadia was no longer married. Nadia wanted to cry, but still could not because of the bandages over her eyes.

On July 7, the bandages came off of Nadia. "Oh my god! I can see again! Oh thank you Doctor Caterwall! Thank you!" Nadia was ecstatic.

"Now about your breast size. Would you like them reduced?" he said politely.

Nadia grinned, while Jolina gave her a quizzical look. A few minutes later, Nadia was satisfied, and Frank ended the reduction spell and fixed it. He thought for sure that Nadia had kept them much larger than she originally had, though.

Jolina was also fully recovered, though still a bit weak. Finally, the two women were able to get back to caring for themselves. Alister had brought them both replacement wands, which worked perfectly. At once, Jolina and Nadia began to fix up their new home the way they liked. The eager teens brought in groceries and other supplies that Jolina requested.

That evening, Jolina and Nadia were able to join the others for supper. Of course, both women wore their fancy tight fitting fetish outfits, complete with heels. After supper, in celebration, they held a rock dance. Pam had now become their very good friend. The three were heavily into Antique Rock music. In fact, Pam practically lived in their apartment, until she had heard every one of their hundreds of disks, compiling her own "must have" list. So it was Antique Rock night at the Compton ranch.

The girls, not to be outdone by Nadia and Jolina, quickly changed into their formal gowns, donning their finest black hose and wearing their five-inch oxfords from the Inaugural Ball. Since Orenda didn't have anything quite appropriate, Ashley gave her one of her free Teen Fashion dresses, and Jolina found a pair of heels that fit her.

Meanwhile, Deiter, Emilio, and Ahana setup the music system and moved the furniture back in the front room. Lloyd explained, "Usually, we erect a sound divider. On our half, we have nice waltzes, and we let them all jump around on their half. However, tonight, I guess we can watch or wiggle too."

Eli chuckled, "Kimi, we used to wiggle quite nicely, didn't we." She blushed and agreed, remembering their many dates so long ago.

When the girls made their grand entrance, Ahana was not prepared. He just stared at the gorgeous looking teens. "Well, are you going to dance with me or not?" Amanda coyly approached him. Still gaping, Ahana took Amanda in his arms to dance. He never let her go the entire evening.

During the evening, Jolina and Nadia taught the teens several new dance moves. This was one of their favorite pastimes, dancing. For the first time in nearly a year, they were completely relaxed and truly happy.

Chapter 6—July's Mess

Ahana and Orenda adapted well to ranch life. Having been given a complete tour, both pitched in to help with ranch chores. R. B.'s ranch was barely a ranch. He didn't farm really, unlike Lena. Afternoons, the teens all went swimming. Each Friday night was formal dance night, waltzes predominating. Each Saturday night was rock night. Deiter, Emilio, and Kathy now spent time at their own homes, returning to spend the weekends on the ranch. None of the three wanted to miss any of the dances.

Having more hands to work the fields was heaven-sent for Lena, who was still caring for year old Jonathon. This morning, Nadia joined her in the kitchen as she was feeding him. The teens were out doing chores. The two were alone in the quiet house.

"Do you have parents back in the Netherlands, Nadia?" Lena asked.

"Ja, but they hardly count as parents. Dad's a normal and a drunkard. Mom divorced him a long time ago. She runs a teashop, but she and I parted ways when I was in magic school. I haven't heard from her in five years. She didn't approve of my dressing like this."

"Well, I must admit you look tons better with your current breast size. That must have been awful to have them so huge. I will admit, though, I've never had any dresses quite like yours. I've been a ranch woman all my life. Most of the time, I was on my own. Raising Lindsey—why, I was lucky to make five thousand dollars a year. I had to make her dresses myself."

"You are kidding? Wow. No one can live on that tiny amount! How could you survive?"

"Worked hard, saved every penny. Now with Lloyd, I feel so happy and free. Still I find it hard to not count pennies," she chuckled.

"Have you ever worn a fancy dress like Lindsey, Amanda, and Ashley's?" Nadia inquired, already suspecting the answer.

"Heavens no. I could never afford even the cheapest of their dresses."

"But you can now. Yet you don't?"

"I, well, I don't know if I would look good in one. It would be such a waste of money to buy one and then never wear it. Say, have you thought any about what you want to do with your life, now that you are free of Dominus? I know it is rough not having any arms. Lindsey was born without hands, and I raised her that way. She didn't get them, as they say, regrown until she went to Bradbury's. Then, along came Ashley who had no arms at all, not even little ones like you. So I do know how hard it is, but I also know the barrier can be overcome, if you wish it."

"There are not words to thank you all for giving us back our lives, Lena. Nothing can ever thank you all enough, not ever. One thing is for sure, we both love to dress like this. It is us. That, we've decided, we won't change."

Lena smiled, "Well, you sure are good looking, I'll admit. Even Lloyd has a hard time taking his eyes off of you." The two chuckled. "But if you could do whatever you really, deep down inside wanted to do, what would it be?" Lena asked in her motherly way.

Nadia looked at Lena, this unassuming normal woman, and was touched. "You really want to know that? Will you promise not to laugh? I mean I haven't ever told anyone this before."

"Your secret is safe with me, Nadia."

"I have always dreamed of writing children's books, uplifting stories that keep their attention and leave them feeling happy when they finish reading it. Honestly, Jolina wants to someday be an illustrator, but don't tell her that I told you. I know, it's a silly dream. Jonathon is so precious; it makes me want to do something good for him, you know. Can I touch him with my arms?"

"Sure you can hold him if you like, while I clean up the mess. Just lie back, here he comes." She laid the small boy on her chest and her short arms cradled him.

"Oh you are a fine lad, Jonathon. You are going to grow

up big and strong like your mommy and daddy." Nadia's little arms rubbed his sides and back lovingly. "Nadia would sure like to write stories for little guys like you."

A bit later, Lena put him down for his nap. "I know you cannot type, but Pam can make your computer voice activated. You could talk your story, and the computer can type it for you. I've seen Ashley doing that a couple times. If you like, I can ask Pam to fix yours up for you."

An hour later, Pam had Nadia's computer rigged for voice activation. After showing her how to operate it, Pam left Nadia and Jolina, resuming her spell research. It was slow going, Pam thought, though she was learning something.

Her world of magical spells had just taken an unexpected turn. It seemed that there was a vast array of other spells not found in the standard Grade spell books. In fact, as she had discovered, nearly every profession had a few unique spells of their own. Seal was the spell that Dominus had used to seal Lindsey's lips shut. It came from the packing industry, where palettes of boxes would be shrink-wrapped and sealed for shipment. Pam knew that out there in the professional world, somewhere wizards and witches were using a Meld spell, melding one thing into another. Her problem: finding that profession. No one had ever bothered to compile a complete list of all these specialized spells, which made her research so time consuming.

Two days later, Pam let out a shriek. "It's not Meld, it's Melt! It comes from the baking industry. Melt is used to melt chocolate bars into a cookie mix, to melt butter into a flower mix. That's why the rings appear to be un-solid and Doctor Caterwall's needles go through the rings; they are melted onto the fingers! Yahoo!" Lindsey cheered her, as did Ashley. Pam fired off a Message to Alister announcing that she had found the spell.

"How do you undo it?" Ashley asked.

Pam's excitement vanished. "Er, that's what I am on to next. I hope there is a way to undo it." Ashley chuckled; if there was a way, she felt sure that Pam would find it. The teens left Pam alone and rounded up everyone else to go for a swim over at Amanda's.

Later, Pam's elation vanished. When a baker made a mistake, he cast Solidify on the mixed chocolate and then poured the mixture through a sieve with the now-hardened chocolate being trapped in the sieve. This would never work to undo a ring or Nadia's corset. She went back to Bradbury's library and went through every baker's spell book there. She came home dejected. There was no direct counter spell in the baker's field.

Pam wandered over to the Whitewater's to see what the others were doing. To her amazement, she found that they had built a basketball court, well, half of one anyway. Ahana and Amanda were sweating profusely, playing one on one. When she approached, the two stopped and took long drinks of water. "How do you like our new court? Ahana is teaching me how to play basketball. I'm not very good at shooting baskets yet."

"Cool. Has anyone else played?"

Amanda laughed, "Ahana won't let Lindsey near the court anymore. He tried to teach her how to shoot baskets. Guess what she did? She used her silent Move Object spell to make all her shots go into the hoop. It looked silly. Some of her shots were nowhere near the net; yet she just moved the ball up and in. He called it cheating, and Lindsey just laughed."

"Darn right; you're not supposed to use magic to get the ball through the hoop. I didn't know she could cast spells like that. We aren't supposed to even try until our sixth year," Ahana added, jovially. "Let's take a swim and cool off, Amanda." The two headed for the pond where the others were splashing each other in a big water fight. Pam wanted no part of that so she wandered inside to chat with Luci.

"Hi Pam," Luci said; she and Kimi were chatting in the kitchen. "Why so glum?"

"I found the spell Dominus used to get the rings melted onto fingers and that corset melted onto Nadia. Only there isn't a reverse spell in the baker's spell books, well not one that will work. I mean suppose that you are making cookies and accidentally melted the chocolate into the batter only to discover you weren't supposed to do that. How do you get it out?"

100

"Simple, throw that batch out and start over," Kimi replied, "though I don't think that will work in this case." She grinned, bringing a grin to Pam as well.

"I have some ideas if I could only experiment. You see, you could first cast Solidify on it and then Rise to Surface. That might work. However, I don't dare experiment on Nadia. If it didn't work right, I could end up killing her. I suppose it wouldn't be quite so dangerous with a ring on a finger, because we could always cut the finger off if it all went wrong."

"Dear, don't go Melting anything onto yourself to experiment with," Luci cautioned Pam, who grinned. She had been thinking along those lines, however.

That evening Alister came by, and Pam discussed all her findings with him, including her speculation on how it might be undone. Alister actually thought her idea might have merit, and the two began a lengthy discussion with Doctor Caterwall. "If it becomes solid again, a real corset, sub-dermal, and all else fails, I could then surgically remove it, Pam. The only complication would be what happens when I cut the bindings and it tries to expand. Still, if that corset was solid again, it could be removed, though it might be painful to her."

Alister decided to try it. The three then had a long chat with Nadia, outlining the risks. That it could be removed, once it was solid, convinced Nadia to try it. Doctor Carterwall gathered all his surgical instruments, and Lena and Polly prepared a lot of boiling water, ready for the operation, should it come to that.

"Nadia, I don't want to sedate you. If something starts going wrong, I need you to tell us at once. Can you withstand a bit of pain? We have no idea whether or not this will hurt you." Nadia had little choice; she wanted to be free of this diabolical trap. She loved to wear corsets, but also to be able to take them off when she desired.

"Wait a minute!" Pam exclaimed as she was about to cast the spells. "Look, if I cast Solidify first, it's likely to tear her apart when I cast Rise to Surface. Perhaps it ought to be cast in reverse, Alister."

"I do believe you are right. Do it that way." Alister didn't mention the fact that he already knew that this was the right procedure. He had given Pam this assignment as a test of her skills. Alister had a reason for his methods, though he confided it only in Professor Cho Lin.

Pam waved her wand and commanded, "Rise to Surface: Corset." Her wand activated, and she prepared to scream out "Cancel!" at any second. All three watched Nadia's waist closely. Slowly the corset seemed to flow through her skin until it was finally exterior once more. "Solidify: corset!" Pam commanded, making the proper wand motion. Again her wand activated. The corset appeared to be a normal white wasp waist corset.

"What's happening?" Nadia asked. "It has just been feeling kind of funny and itchy."

"I think we are in luck. Let's roll her over onto her side," Doctor Caterwall suggested. Pam untied the carefully tied knots, and then she loosened it. At last, she was able to undo the busk, and she removed the corset.

"God I can finally breathe again. I love corsets, mind you, but I need to be able to take them off too. Thank you Pam! I am indebted to you once more. Thank you all!" Nadia exclaimed.

"Well, now that was interesting. Now at last I can finish my work," Frank said. He retrieved his bag of potion bottles. "Nadia, I will be giving you potions to re-grow your arms. For the next two days, I need you immobile so the arms can't be accidentally damaged. You will need to consume as much of my special fortified milk as you can. Are you ready?"

Back in the Compton's home, Alister praised Pam for her excellent work. Lindsey and Ashley cheered her, while Amanda gave her a big hug. Audrey yelled out, "Way to go hot shot!" Pam felt like she could conquer the world. The feeling that she had when she freed Nadia was why she did everything that she did. Endless hours of study resulted in success, her kind of success anyway.

By July 17, Nadia van Nye had her life back. She was healthy, and her arms were fully healed. Nadia knew that she owed all these people not only her life but also the quality of her life. She would never forget that.

That night, they again held a celebration party, only this

time it was waltzes only, though the teens wondered why Nadia insisted on waltzes not rock. In secret, Nadia and Jolina had made some clothes purchases. After supper was finished, the teens did up the dishes as usual, before changing into their fancy dresses and heels. Nadia and Jolina pulled Lena back into their apartment.

"Surprise, Lena. Look what we have for you." Nadia gaily announced.

Sometime later, the impatient fellows got the music going, and soon the teens made their grand entrance as they usually did. In waltzed Ashley, Audrey, Lindsey, Pam, Amanda, Kathy, Orenda, and Fern. Deiter and Emilio had come as well to celebrate. Ahana latched onto Amanda as soon as she appeared, Pam noted.

"Where's our guests of honor?" asked Lloyd, noticing the Nadia and Jolina were absent. He assumed that Lena was off feeding Jonathon or changing his diapers.

Just then, arm in arm, Jolina and Nadia led Lena down the hall into the living room. She wore an elegant brown silk dress, fine nylons, and matching pumps with four-inch heels. Nadia had decided that since Lena had never worn heels before, they should keep them lower. This was her idea of lower.

"Mom! Oh my god, you look beautiful!" exclaimed Lindsey, staring at her mother, as if she had never seen her before.

"Wow, mom! Sexy!" Ashley added. Lloyd gaped, stunned breathless.

Recovering for the shocking surprise, Lloyd came to her and added his compliments, whispering them into her ear. Lena actually blushed. Lloyd never let go of Lena the entire evening. Indeed, Lena was the talk of the teens this evening. Lindsey and Ashley were very proud of their mom; she looked gorgeous to them. Once more, Lindsey felt the world was finally at peace.

That fleeting peace was shattered the next day. Lloyd came in from working the fields. "Lena, message from Alister. We're going to have guests in a little while."

"What's up dad?" Lindsey asked. Ashley, Pam, and

Audrey were right behind her. Lena, holding Jonathon, came into the room, diapers half on.

"Seems a family had to make an emergency evacuation from the Big Apple. Husband's having a bad reaction to the health care. Expect four."

"Girls, go make up Number 3, next to Nadia's. Make sure there's toilet paper and all that," Lena ordered.

A bit later, when the alarm announced Alister's arrival, everyone headed to the front room to meet the new arrivals. Nadia and Jolina, wearing their everyday fetish outfits and heels, brought up the rear. A slightly portly man, well dressed in a fine business suit, was led inside by an equally well dressed woman, wearing a grey skirt, black pumps of moderate height, and her hair done in a bun. Her makeup was barely noticeable. Both were at least fifty, Lindsey estimated. Behind her came two young men, Nadia's age, she guessed. Twins, that was certain. Both were also well dressed, but not as if they were businessmen; rather one wore an expensive silk suit, the other a suede suit. The older man seemed very disoriented.

Alister did the introductions. "I am honored to present Mr. John Hampton, his wife Department of Law, New York City Branch, Mary Hampton, their twin sons, Bailey and Barnaby."

In a monotone voice, though urgent, Mr. Hampton said, "Where are we? I must get to my bank. I have never been late. I must work hard. I must support my family. I can't find my car. Has anyone seen my car? Mary, are you taking me to my bank? I am late. It is nearly ten thirty. I need my pill. I haven't had my pill today, have I? Where have my pills gone?"

Mary said, "Normal, withdrawal symptoms. Those darn pills are laced with a narcotic."

"Allow me, Mrs. Hampton. I'm Doctor Caterwall. Mr. Hampton, please come with me. I have your pills."

"Oh. Well, in that case, I should have my pill. Take one every day—that's what they told me. I've never felt better in my life, except now I'm late for work. Do you suppose you can write me an excuse I can show the teacher?" His voice trailed off as he walked down the hall with Frank.

"Please have a seat. Can I get you anything to drink?" asked Lena.

"Thank you, some tea perhaps. This has been a nightmare." Mary slumped onto the couch. One by one, Alister introduced the group to Mary, Bailey, and Barnaby.

"I say, are you those Bradbury students who nearly got blown up at the Nationals a while back?" asked Bailey, recognizing the names.

After Alister confirmed that they were, Barnaby replied, "I say, Bailey, we are in good company. They've had more TV coverage than we've been able to get."

"Perhaps we should ask them for tips, Barnaby," Bailey joked.

"Boys! Please be civil; this is horribly serious!" Mary barked at her two sons. Both twins sat stiffly in their seats with a solemn look on their faces. It lasted only a minute before they both burst out laughing.

"Sorry mom," Barnaby finally said. "We're promoters, Bailey and Barnaby and Barnaby and Bailey Promotions. That's our company, well, until two hours ago anyway."

"Which is it?" Pam asked confused. "I mean is it Bailey and Barnaby or is it Barnaby and Bailey Promotions?"

"Oh, it's Bailey and Barnaby and Barnaby and Bailey Promotions," Bailey replied. Pam looked very annoyed.

"Boys!" Mary said sternly.

"We couldn't decide whose name should be first, so we named our company both ways. This way, neither has top billing." Pam finally understood, but was still a trifle annoyed with them.

"What do you promote?" asked Polly.

"Until two hours ago, it was comedy clubs in the Big Apple," Bailey sighed.

"But we weren't really successful at it," Barnaby admitted.

Mary put in, "John and I have been trying our best to get them to get decent jobs, normal jobs, but we've failed utterly. First, they tried promoting gambling halls, then it was floating casinos, then it was rock and roll bands, then it was, well, I've now lost track. Lately, they are failing miserably promoting local comedians. Honestly, boys. Times like these, I could disown you. For once, act your age. This is terribly serious!"

"Mom, we know it is serious! We are just trying to lighten things up a bit. Say, you look an awful lot like that wife of Dominus who got herself blown up a couple weeks ago." Barnaby commented to Nadia. "Except she had no arms and had these huge knockers."

Lindsey wanted to crawl under the table, thinking Nadia would be so embarrassed.

"Hey, that's me, kiddo. Got my arms regrown and boobs resized to where they ought to be. Dominus tried to kill us, but failed completely. As you can see, I look very good. Jolina, too."

Barnaby's face turned red as a beet. Bailey's too. He apologized, "I'm sorry, Nadia. I didn't mean, well you know, to offend you. You look positively smashingly—you too, Jolina."

"Seldom have we seen women as sharply dressed as you two are. Going to a party soon?" Bailey asked.

"No, these are our everyday outfits," Jolina answered. Both men were finally silent, but neither took their eyes off the pair.

Mary explained, "John is president of the First National Savings and Loan in New York City. He's been on this despicable drug for two weeks. It's turned him into a zombie. He walks, he talks, but he is useless at work. So is every normal who works at the bank. They brought in a couple of wizards to take over the real decision making yesterday. John doesn't know that yet. We are under orders not to leave the city, but well, I knew Governor Alister from years ago and asked him for help. I guess now I'm a fugitive from my own Law department."

"We had to leave everything behind. I'm afraid we don't even have a change of clothes. Whatever are we going to do now?" she added.

Surprising everyone, Kimi answered her in a very professional manner. "Mary, I am a federal attorney, now officially stationed here in Cheyenne County. Don't ask how I pulled that one off. Let's see, he's the president of the bank, so he has come here to establish a branch office in Colorado. I will get that affidavit sent off first. Of course, as his wife, you are obligated to follow him here. I will send in a transfer form so stating. Alister, should it be the High Plains branch or the Denver branch office of the Department of Law?"

"High Plains might cause less of a stir," he replied softly, a twinkle in his eye. Kimi was working out very well, he thought.

"High Plains it is. Next, I will send them a copy of your transfer request. If they are on the ball, you should receive a Message from them by tomorrow, Mary. Is this acceptable to you?"

"You, you can do this?" Mary looked at Kimi, hardly daring to believe that she was somehow narrowly escaping becoming a fugitive herself. "Yes, yes. Oh thank you, thank you!"

Kimi headed off to make the arrangements, returning a while later for her signature. She already gotten John's signature after telling him he was supposed to be opening up a new branch office. He readily agreed and signed. Doctor Caterwall then continued his work on John.

"Now then, it seems the most critical detail is with your possessions," Alister suggested.

"Yes, I guess we can transfer funds to a bank out here somewhere and then buy all new things."

"Hum. I have an idea how we may get your household items moved out here, Mrs. Hampton. Let me check on a few things and get back to you after lunch. Perhaps, Lena and Lloyd would like to show you around their ranch. I'm sure you will be safe here, no matter what happens." Alister left.

"This is our living room, though on the weekends, of late, we have been using it as our dance floor," Lena began to give them a tour. Mary gave Lena a strange look and a coy grin.

As the twins rose to follow, Nadia slipped her arm around Barnaby, while Jolina slipped hers around Bailey. "We need a bit of steadying in these outfits," Nadia whispered to him, but with a wry smile on her lips. Meanwhile, Lena and Lloyd gave them a guided tour, eventually showing them the home that they could live in until it was safe for other arrangements. Even the twins were impressed with the main ranch home and its twin additions.

When they finished the tour, Mary went to check on her husband. Nadia and Jolina led the twins into their new apartment, offering them tea and pastries. The twins needed no urging at all. Sipping tea and devouring the delicious pastries of Jolina's, Barnaby said, "You were really married to Dominus. Wow, that must have been awful." The four chatted away for some time.

"So honestly, Barnaby, what do you and your brother really want to do?" Nadia asked.

Barnaby sighed, looked at his brother. "We want to make people happy, cheerful. We want to have fun while doing it too. Everyone is so serious these days."

"Getting worse every year," Bailey added.

"Only we can never figure out how to really do it—make people feel happy," Barnaby finished.

"Dad's been pressuring us for years to join him in the banking industry. Claims we will be rich. Have you ever seen a cheerful, happy, rich person walking out of a bank?" Bailey explained.

"No," Barnaby continued. "Mom has been constantly on our case to join the Department of Law of Defense or Magical Misuse."

"Make something of yourselves, she says," Bailey went on with their story.

"We just want to be us, but no one understands that," Barnaby finished.

"We do," Nadia and Jolina replied in unison. "You just described us. We want to just be ourselves."

"Oh yeh?" Barnaby asked very curiously. The four began a serious discussion.

Alister returned with good news. "Mrs. Hampton, it's all arranged with Ace Mag Movers. They will get to your home tomorrow, pack, and move everything in the house. Expect them to arrive here the day after tomorrow. Century2200 will be arranging the sale of your home after that. All that remains is for you to open a back account and transfer some of your funds." He discussed the cost of the movers, which he had already handled.

After expressing her undying gratitude for coming to their rescue, she said, "What about John? Once he is recovered, he's going to be very frustrated and upset."

"Doctor Caterwall tells me that he will need at least a week or more to come down off of the heroin, perhaps more. Kimi only needed a few days because she had such a minor dose. Once he is back to normal, he will need to set new goals for himself and the family. You are used to the big city, correct?" She nodded. "I might suggest that he goes ahead and tries to establish a branch bank in Denver. However, Dominus is known to be operating out of Denver at times. He used to have a home there, before it exploded. As long as you are careful, you ought to be safe."

"Where does the High Plains Department of Law have their offices?" she asked.

"Greeley or Sterling. Mr. Betts still conducts his business out of Sterling, but the main offices are in Greeley."

Satisfied, they checked on how John was doing. "I have him sedated at the moment. The DTs are running out now. You can see for yourself." John's body lay on the bed, but his limbs were shaking slightly. Today will be the worst for him, but after this, it's downhill. I'd like to give Dominus a taste of his own heroin!"

Two dances and a week later, John had fully recovered. Mary had re-established their household in Number 3 and had begun work in the Greeley Department of Law offices. Although feeling fit physically, John was more subdued than he had ever been in his life. He moaned, "How could our President do this to us? She should be impeached, tried, and convicted." After watching catching up on the news, he realized the magnitude of the problem.

All normal members of Congress and the Justice system were now automatons, mere zombies perfunctorily going through the motions. Many of the wizarding world loyal to or controlled by Dominus had been called in to work behind the scenes drafting bills and such, giving the final products to the elected members of Congress to pass, which they did, stating they were working hard for the people. John was scared now, rightly so. "Governor Alister, how can I, we, my family, help bring down Dominus and President Snow?" He asked the burning question that had occupied his mind since watching the news.

"Go ahead with the deception of yours. Open a branch bank in Denver, transfer as much funds as possible and be prepared to finance covert operations as needed. You are not alone. A resistance movement is slowly building. Dominus will be stopped. Already, we are putting a plan into action. The immediate goal is to cut off the supplies needed to manufacture these drugs in quantity. If we can keep his production levels low enough, perhaps we can keep this outbreak contained to the east coast."

He agreed and then said, "Lena, I've talked this over with Mary. After what I've been through, I just would not feel safe living in a big city any longer. Could we trouble you to rent us Number 3 for some time, until this all gets handled?"

Lena smiled, "Mr. Hampton, it was for people like you that Lloyd, the kids, and I built all these extra homes. Of course, you may stay here, stay as long as you like. Mind you, it gets rather wicked in the dead of winters sometimes. However, this ranch is one of the safest places in the country."

Lena was shocked to discover that John had deposited fifty thousand dollars into her account the next day. Using his fancy Cadillac2200 with GEOSAT controls, he commuted daily to Denver. By the end of July, his bank was up and running with five million in seed money in his vaults, ready to help finance the resistance movement.

Of particular note, John and Mary attended the next Friday night dance. The twins observed that their dad and mom were actually dancing and flirting with one another, something they had not seen since they were little boys. Their dad looked years younger, a spring in his step the next day. The twins decided immediately to put their promotional plan into action. Of course, Nadia and Jolina lay behind that plan and soon became an integral part of it.

On August 1 while everyone was enjoying a dinner together, Bailey and Barnaby made their announcement.

"Ladies and gentlemen," Bailey rose formally.

"May we have your attention," Barnaby added.

"We have an important announcement to make," Bailey went on.

"We are very proud to announce formally that we are now opening," Barnaby continued.

"B&B Dance Hall, located in downtown Denver," Bailey pronounced.

"No alcohol, no drugs, no weapons, just fun dancing," Barnaby went on with the description.

"One night will be Romantic Evening, a formal affair," Bailey explained.

"One night will be Teen Formal Evening, again a formal affair," Barnaby carried on.

"One night will be rock and roll, not so formal," Bailey continued with the explanation.

"One night will be live rock bands," Barnaby finished up.

"So what do you think?" both said in unison.

"Well I'll be!" John exclaimed, very surprised that his boys finally were doing something sensible, as he saw it. "For once, I do believe you have something worth promoting, don't you think, dear?"

Mary grinned, "Well done, boys. When will it be ready?"

"We have the location picked out. Nadia and Jolina are going to be partners with us. If all goes well, we will hold our grand opening on the August 15," Bailey explained.

"Much do between now and then. We need to hire a number of wizards and witches to provide protection, catering staff, sodas and pizza on teen nights, tea and pastries on other nights," Barnaby added.

"Ahana, can you get Eli's Rockers together for our first live band night, say on August 21?" asked Bailey.

"Of course, you are all invited to opening night, a formal dance night," Barnaby insisted.

"We will be deeply offended if you do not come," Bailey teased everyone. "Ours will be the premier place to be on the three weekend nights in Denver."

Chapter 7—Counteractions

By the third week in July, the pills had been analyzed as well as could be done without raising any alarms within the now compromised Departments of Law and Magical Misuse. Governor Alister sent the findings to all his overseas friends. With the rapid disintegration of Congress and the judicial branch, something had to be done quickly.

Professor Delius suggested cutting off Aetna Pharmaceuticals sources of raw materials, which they needed to make the diabolical pills. To this end, Alister suggested his friends look into doing just that. He decided to take a two-prong attack stateside. First, stop the inflow of heroin coming in to the US or drastically reduce it. Second, he considered the possibility of somehow damaging Aetna's processing facilities. Distribution interference had been ruled out by Pam. Her guess was that teleportation was being used to move the pills from the manufacturing plant in Georgia to the New York area, not the trucking industry.

The so far unfettered Department of Security was given the task of reducing the incoming heroin. This fit perfectly into their overall charge, to protect the United States and its citizens. After few well-placed calls to several heads, the Security forces began stepped up operations. By the end of August, they estimated they had lowered the inflow of the drug into the States by five hundred percent. Dominus would have a hard time attempting to convince anyone that stopping the inflow of illegal street drugs was a bad thing.

However, damaging Aetna's capability to produce the pills was fraught with ethical dilemmas. At one of their Rodents Pack meetings, Alister presented some of these problems. "You see, we have Aetna mass producing these pills, which some of us realize are terribly harmful and may ultimately lead to the destruction of our entire country. Yet, they are well within the law; the government has ordered these pills and is overseeing their dispensing. The Law is on their side, I'm afraid."

"I would like nothing better than to attack these facilities outright, destroy their production machinery, and put them out of business. Yet that would put us on the wrong side of the Law. We would become the criminals, just as Dominus has been. Do we stoop to that level?"

No one wanted that onus on them. "Why not just get everyone together and go after Dominus, eliminate him and his thugs?" asked Eli.

Pam explained didactically, "Well, for one thing, whenever Dominus appears at a public function where we could get at him, there are always Secret Service men, Security people, and police present, to say nothing of his own forces. We would have to battle our own people before we could get to him. He's hiding behind men and women that we would not dare harm, yet they are under orders to protect him."

She went on, "And then there are the news reports. After his house in Denver blew up, Dominus has made it clear that he is keeping where he now resides a total secret, allegedly to prevent that from happening again. When he is not in the public view and we could get at him, we don't know where he is. This has been the problem since his escape from prison four years ago. No one knows where he is. Even so, if we should manage to get to him, he always has his Restricted Wish spell lying in reserve, and can extricate himself from our grasp."

After more discussion, the consensus was to see if their friends abroad could cut down on the delivery of raw materials, see if the Department of Security could further curtail the importing of heroin, and try to raise public opinion against this National Health Care Program and its pills.

By August, deep divisions in the fabric of the United States began appearing, without any assistance from the Rodents. Of course, many of the elected officials and key opinion leaders—key influential men—were now under the control of Dominus. These men became vocally outspoken for this wonderful Health Care program. Others began standing up, arguing against what they rightly saw as good intentions gone extremely bad. Demonstrations began popping up in the larger cities across the country. Talk shows had a field day bringing together some of the protest leaders and those under the control of Dominus for their live programs. It made for good entertainment at least.

The challenge heard repeatedly—the most often defense of the program was: "Wait until the pilot program is completed and the final results are presented. Then make your decision." This wait until the pilot phase results are tabulated pacified many people. No one thought that President Snow could possibly ignore the horrendously bad effect the program was having on normal citizens.

Mary Hampton soon discovered that she was privy to a wealth of new information from her position at the High Plains division of the Department of Law. She explained it this way at one of the Rodents Pack meetings in August. "Given that the normals who have entered this Health Care Program have uniformly become friendly zombies, unable to think for themselves, to effectively solve problems, a vacuum is being created at the key positions within both the governmental and private sectors. Corporate executives are now unable to be effective leaders. Companies are now offering top salaries for qualified and not so qualified wizards and witches to step in and fulfill those shoes. Likewise, we have seen that every Representative and Senator, who is not of the wizarding world, has now hired a wizard or witch to direct them, to tell them what to do, basically being blunt about this."

"I've been doing some checking and it seems that these positions are being filled by seedier wizards and witches. I am having Pam cross-check their names against known Dominus supporters, since all records of Dominus and his crowd have been ordered purged from departmental computers. Initial results show that sixty-five percent of the new hires either support Dominus or have very questionable backgrounds."

"What I find scary is that major financial markets are in the Big Apple and are rapidly becoming either directly controlled by Dominus or by his supporters. I fear that if they are not careful, they may cause a total financial meltdown of our country! Dominus may be unstoppable at this point."

She finished, "It's funny. Dominus is now in a position where anyone who takes action against him is forced to break our own laws!"

"No, it is a brilliant move on his part," Governor Alister corrected her. "I have always said that the man in extremely intelligent and extremely methodical. I'm afraid far too many have overlooked this aspect, preferring to label him merely an evil sadist and criminal. It may well be that his fourteen years of imprisonment may have been planned all along. Everyone certainly forgot about him, leaving his companies free to finish developing the rings and the drugs, completely neglected by everyone, including me."

"Yes, Mrs. Hampton, Dominus has made what I believe to be his ultimate 'Check' move, forcing the Law to be on his side, protecting him—the ultimate slam in our very faces. It forces us to become the 'Law Breakers' if we try anything to stop him," Alister replied to her statement finally.

"You are saying that our country, good old USA, is a country of rule by Law, not by Justice?" Mary asked.

"You as a member of the Department of Law ought to know that is the way it is. Seldom, if ever, do the victims of a crime ever get justice from the criminal," Alister replied, his eyes sternly looking down at Mary.

"Yes, but we used to often lock the guilty in prison," Mary protested. "Isn't that some form of justice?"

"Last October, the teens here rescued six women who had been kidnaped by Dominus. He cut off their arms, blinded them, made them wear confining clothing, and repeatedly raped them. Yes, they were rescued and healed of their wounds and severe emotional trauma. However, I ask you, if you were one of those women, would you feel that you had obtained Justice if Dominus merely went to prison?" Alister asked the leading question.

"Yes, I heard about those poor women. No, I see your point; merely having him in prison hardly compensates me for what he did to me. If I were one of those women, I would be howling mad about now, since Dominus has received a full pardon from the President."

"Right, Mrs. Hampton, you certainly would be, and rightly so. Another point, Congress has been inventing and passing Laws for nearly four hundred years now. Some complain that soon there will be laws dictating what we have for breakfast. Indeed, isn't the Law structure of our country now so complicated it takes attorneys to figure anything out, if at all?"

Mary grinned, and Kimi, the attorney, chuckled, "Well, yes, it sometimes takes us two weeks to figure out sections of the Law," Mary agreed.

"The bottom line is that I believe this latest move of Dominus is coldly calculated to bring about the total downfall of our country. However, I may just be overreacting, all doom and gloom. Time will tell, as they say," Alister grimly said.

"But how do we stop him? How do we prevent the US from collapsing?" asked Professor Cho Lin, deeply concerned that Alister was correct in his conclusions.

Fred Betts spoke up, "At this point in time, there are deep divisions with the rank and file of the Department of Magical Misuse. Many of us are getting more and more frustrated at the injustices we are being forced to dole out in the name of Law. Of course, the Dominus supporters and those he is controlling see it completely opposite of us. I don't know how much longer the department can withstand this dichotomy, this awful disparity. Only today, I was barely able to prevent one of our junior officers, who is on our side, from outright attacking Felix James, head of the Denver department, who is under the control of Dominus. Tempers are really flaring. One of these days soon, the whole thing is going to collapse."

"It's the same in the Department of Law, Fred," Mary added. "One day it is just going to explode. Is this what Dominus is hoping will happen?"

Professor Delius spoke up, "My money is on that, Mrs. Hampton. If those two departments break down, what's left to control our country? Only Dominus and his supporters. He will, in effect, be the dictator or supreme leader, seen as one who can bring order to the chaos—the strong, the powerful bringing order. After all, people prefer order to chaos. No matter how awful that regimented control actually is, it is preferable to anarchy and chaos. This will be especially true, if vast numbers of the normals are drugged zombies or automatons."

"Already we are seeing vast numbers of witches and wizards moving into the positions of power and control, replacing the normals that used to hold those positions," Delius pointed out. "This fits in with his stated manifesto, wizards and witches being the 'master race' and all that malarkey."

"I agree, Delius," Fred nodded. "However, what do we do about it? How do we counter Dominus?"

"What about getting some wizards who also know the Restricted Wish spell and have them cast it, capturing Dominus for us or bringing him to us so we can capture him?" Lindsey suggested. She finally asked the question that had been in the back of her mind for quite a long time now. After, all, if Dominus could cast it to capture Governor Alister, why not use that same spell against Dominus?

"Very, very few wizards or witches ever bother to learn that spell," Delius answered her question. "Besides being a tough spell, every usage prematurely ages the caster. Mostly, it is Black Hall graduates who attempt to learn it, those seeking personal power and might. Further, once you can cast that spell, you are required by Law to register with the Department of Magical Misuse. They keep records of everyone who can cast it."

Fred butted in, "Right now, there are ten in the US that are still alive and can cast it, including Dominus. However, I believe that they are all siding with Dominus at the moment."

"Well, isn't that a find howdy-do!" Lindsey replied, her bright idea suddenly dashed. Delius smiled at her reaction, which he fully expected from the young witch.

Governor Alister stepped in at this point, "Honestly, everyone, what matters most is your own actions. Always be true to yourself, no matter the consequences. If you always take that action which helps more broadly than it harms, you will always be at peace with yourself. Not only does it help yourself, but it should also help your family, your friends, the various groups of which you are a part, our country, all mankind—there are other countries, mind you, plants and animals which share our world, and even the material universe itself. If your action helps more of these than it harms, your action is an optimum one, and you can have no regrets about having done it."

He continued, "Personally, I believe that we should focus our attention on Justice and not on the Law. That is, concentrate on bringing about just and fair treatment, the deserved punishment. Since Dominus is incapable of doing this himself, we must find a way to make him do this. I don't have the answers at this time, only the direction that I personally will be following. If my body is slain, I will be content that I have done my best and have no regrets, no shame, and no blame. Your own personal integrity is worth far more than your immediate life, but then that is just my opinion."

"Say, on a different matter," Wilma changed the topic to one on which she was keenly interested, "Professor Delius, rumor has it that the Idaho Red Brigade Militia has deployed. You knew their commander, Field Marshall Erin Saks, right? Any idea what they are planning to do?" Pam had never heard of this group before and quickly typed the names into her notebook on her laptop.

Eyeing the number of confused looks from around the room, Professor Delius explained, "Erin and I went to school together, Black Hall, Boise School of Magic, small school. He joined the Idaho Red Brigade Militia and has become their leader at this point. He has always believed that the strong survive, might makes right, and that our government is selling us out. I believe he has been labeled a Right Wing Conservative or some such name. His base was around Idaho Falls. Last I heard, his group had about two hundred like-minded men and women in it. He often tried to get me to join up, saying their goal was to protect America when the time comes. Yes, I heard that rumor too. I did a little checking, Wilma. It seems that their barracks is empty. They have cleared out, taking everything with them, guns, ammunition, food, materials, vehicles, the lot. It is almost as if they have deployed into the field."

"Do you think he is going after Dominus himself?" Wilma asked what she had been speculating for days now.

118

"I wouldn't put it past him. I know he has been extremely angry over the Presidential Pardon, and now that the initial reports are in on this drugging of the New York and DC areas, I wouldn't put it past him to take matters into his own hands. I can't blame him. Dominus has turned the members of Congress into walking zombies, who now only do what their wizard and witch advisors suggest. He probably believes this is a major threat to our country, which it is."

"Is he powerful enough?" Monane asked, her tone was very serious. "I mean to take on Dominus directly?"

"There isn't a wizard or witch alive who could take on Dominus, Monane. I don't think that Erin Saks is that foolish. He is probably up to something, but what? I don't know." After that, the meeting broke up.

The next day, Pam shared her latest research finding with her friends. "Lindsey, I've figured since Dominus is really Simon, we ought to know all that we can about Simon's background, so I have been digging away."

"Cool, Pam, good thinking," Lindsey acknowledged, wishing she had thought of this.

"He was born in New Orleans, in 2138, which makes him really forty-four years old, though he looks to be at least sixty. He was captured in 2163 and spent fourteen years in jail. His parents were Ross and Jacqueline Mac Fluide, of Scottish descent on his father's side. Unbelievably, he went to Bradbury's School of Magic! He was here from 2150 to 2156, and Governor Alister was running our school then, so he knows Dominus first hand! No wonder they are old rivals or enemies."

After the comments and curses died down, Pam continued, "Now I did some digging. Evidently, Ross was also a pervert or a sadist. His wife Virginia contracted diabetes, and the doctors had to amputate her arms below her elbows and her legs below her knees. Ross, who should have cast Cure Disease on his wife, didn't, sending her to the normal's hospital instead, where they had no choice but to amputate to save her life. Instead of later regrowing her lost limbs, Ross kept her like that. All this was when Simon was ten years old."

"From old photos, he did allow her to wear prosthetic

legs, but not arms or hooks. She wore corsets and fancy dresses, though I can't tell anything about shoes. Dominus probably saw his dad treating his mother like a toy, and he's following his father's example. In addition, I found that his father was twice warned by the police to stop beating his son, but that was before his mother got sick. I expect Dominus was traumatized by his father, and maybe that's what triggered him to become such a sadist. He may be trying to bring back alive his mother with all these women he brutalizes."

"Gosh, that throws some light on his sadistic behavior anyway," Lindsey replied. "Now he makes a bit more sense."

"Yes, but he's not going to stop it—that sadistic behavior towards women, I mean," Ashley added, putting two and two together. "Look, he's gotten rid of his wife, whom he tried to make into his mother, sort of. Nadia said that she spotted lipstick on his collar back in May. This is now August; he's had over three months to kidnap and make a new bunch of play toys."

"You mean he's kidnaped some more women and cut off their arms and stuff?" asked Deiter. "Darn him anyway! We should try to find them and rescue this new bunch. Anyone got any ideas where to look?" Deiter was ready to swing into action once more.

"Wait a minute, Deiter. We don't know if any have been kidnaped or where they might be. Surely, he will leave his toy house much better protected this time. After all, we did capture his last one," Lindsey replied hastily.

"If I knew who was kidnaped, I might be able to use my skills to locate them," Ashley added helpfully.

"Okay, I get the message. Pam needs to see if there have been any recent kidnapings that meet our criteria," Pam teased her friends.

"Can you have that for us in say five minutes?" Deiter teased her. The girls giggled.

Audrey said quietly, "I think you will be successful. It feels right." She went back to her whittling. Pam headed for her computer in her bedroom. Deiter and Lindsey headed outside to help Lena and Lloyd in the fields, while Ashley was on Jonathon duty.

The next day, Pam had news for the group. "I've searched the FBI's missing files, narrowing it down by women between twenty and twenty-five. There are only something like two hundred or so in the last four months, countrywide. Right or wrong, I eliminated witches and wound up with one hundred ninety-two. Next, I decided to eliminate the not-so-pretty women. After all, someone as homely as me would never attract the interest of Dominus or any other one for that matter."

"Pam!" Lindsey said sternly, her hands on her hips. Pam ignored her and continued. "Now we are down to around fifty possibilities—forty-seven to be precise. Next, I looked at any follow up actions, such as receiving a random note, phone calls to home, things like that. The list is down to a dozen likely candidates."

"What about the recovery of body parts? Like arms?" Deiter interrupted her, anxious to get to the crux of the matter.

"Don't rush me, Mr. Cross," Pam teased him. "The arms of Miss Lyn Zhu of Los Angeles were found by a fisherman. She is a likely candidate. However, I found something much more interesting. It seems that all spring, Dominus was spending quite a lot of time with Miss Lisa Marton, that's Senator Bart Marton's daughter. They were seen at several fancy DC affairs in June, and then she went missing. Now get this! Dominus has put up a reward of a half million dollars for her safe return! Naturally, everyone thinks that he is the distraught boyfriend of Lisa's. I'll bet anything he has her."

"Cool, Pam! I knew you could do it," Deiter praised Pam, who could not help flash him an appreciative smile. "Now all we need to do is figure out where he's holding them and go rescue them. Say, maybe we can even collect his half million dollars while we are at it. Wouldn't that be weird?"

"Okay, I have enough to work on," Ashley said. "Don't anyone disturb me for a while." She left and laid down on her bed, relaxed, closed her eyes, and began her premonition work. Ashley and Professor Mary Ann had worked long and hard last spring to train her to get premonitions when she chose, instead of just when they happened to come to her. She opened her mind and concentrated on Lisa Marton. Where was she? What shape was she in, dire peril, great pain?

A half hour later, one very pleased Ashley rejoined her friends. "I did it! I actually did it! Just like Mary Ann has been teaching me. It worked! Yahoo!"

"You found the women?" Lindsey asked her very excited sister. "You're okay and all that?" She remembered the horrible times that Ashley had previously had when awful premonitions came to her.

"Never better. She's imprisoned in a house in an Atlanta, Georgia, suburb. It's a stately, old mansion home, at least a hundred years old, maybe more. She's throwing off waves of terror and fear, gang. That's how I found her."

Everyone patted her on the back. "Well done sis! Incredible. I don't know how you do it," Lindsey was very pleased with Ashley.

Pam typed furiously on her computer, following down links. "Got it! The Mac Fluide Enterprises owns a mansion there, a Colonial era copy, done by the architect Godfrey Laminos. It's one hundred twenty years old. Now what do we do?"

Just then, the monotone voice activated, "Jim Whitewater is arriving." Ashley let out a shriek and dashed for the door. When she opened it, there stood her boyfriend. She jumped on to him, putting her legs around his waist, her arms around his neck, kissing him.

After he put her down, he teased, "Gosh, I didn't think you'd miss me, Princess. Guess what? I'm done with my training. I've now got a permanent security assignment!"

"Terrific!" Ashley exclaimed, and then realized that he could be posted nearly anywhere. Her smile faded. What if he were posted in New York or Florida?

"Here. I am assigned to help Lloyd protect these two ranches." The relief on Ashley's face was huge; she kissed him even longer this time. Everyone else came to greet Jim, who had been gone nearly ten weeks.

"So what's happening around here that your top gun Security man ought to know about?" Jim teased. At once, Deiter explained about their discovery of another group of women that Dominus had kidnaped and that they were about to go to their rescue.

"Now isn't the right time," Audrey said softly, causing everyone to pause and stare at her. She repeated it.

Deiter accepted Audrey's pronouncement. "Well, we should at least put together a raiding party so when the time is right, we strike." He smashed one fist into his hand for emphasis.

Jim agreed and then asked, "Say, have you heard anything about the Idaho Red Brigade Militia? The Department of Law is all over this one. Apparently, we are to report any sightings of these men immediately." Lindsey relayed to Jim what little they knew of these men.

With Jim now the center of attention, Deiter turned on the TV to catch the latest news and soon dozed off. "Hey, wake up," Jim roused the boy. "We got a job to do. We're going to case this mansion." It was an hour later.

"Way cool!" Deiter jumped up and grabbed his Staff of Power. "What's the plan?" he asked as they stepped outside.

"Audrey is convinced now is not the time, so we are going to locate it, and see if we can see anything—you know, case the place. Then, when it is time, why, we'll know where it is and the what-evers."

Deiter didn't quite know what the what-evers might be, but was excited about checking out this mansion. It meant action to the Black Hall boy. A minute later, they teleported to the suburb, and then went in search of the mansion. "Here, we are looking for this place. Pam printed it out for us." An hour later, the two finally found the site. Located on two acres and surrounded by a low stone wall, the stately old home looked vacant. Pecan trees dotted the green grass with red dirt showing in places. The two hopped the wall and crept up to the house.

All the windows were covered, but they could hear voices inside. With their Invisibility spells in force, the two felt confident that they could not be detected, at least as long as they remained outside. Undoubtedly, Alarm spells would be activated if they actually tried to enter.

"Yeh, they are okay. Took them their lunch. Pathetic bunch, sure don't see why the Master gets off on them," one voice said.

"Ours is not to question, only to do. At least, there's no danger with this assignment. The pill runners—now those guys are taking a big risk. I heard Sam nearly got robbed dropping off his load in the Big Apple. There are still plenty of norms who are fighting us there, but we're slowly rooting the rats out, I hear," a second male voice said.

"Well, we'd best get things cleaned up around here. The Master is due here tonight," the first voice suggested. Deiter heard the men moving around inside, then a vacuum cleaner drowned out all further conversation. Jim decided he'd heard enough, and the two returned to the Compton ranch with their news, picking up several boxes of pizzas on the return trip.

The next evening, while everyone was eating their dinner, Fred Betts received an urgent message. "Darn it! What next? Sorry, I have to go. It seems that the Idaho Red Brigade Militia is attacking the Aetna Pharmaceuticals processing plant in Georgia as we eat. It's on TV, breaking news." He hastily kissed Polly and Pam, then left.

Audrey said quietly, "Now is the right time, if you still want to do it."

Lindsey looked at her and realized what she meant! Time to rescue the kidnaped women. This time, Lloyd, Monane, Wilma, and Jim went along with Lindsey, Amanda, Pam, Ashley, Audrey, and Deiter. Ahana insisted on coming along as well as his father, Eli. Both Fern and Orenda begged to be allowed to come, but their fathers refused. R. B. insisted that they stay behind to guard the ranches and to prepare the rooms for the women. Satisfied that they had some purpose, they set about fixing up room number 8, which was the last one on the western side, adjoining the long hall and bedrooms of the adults.

Two minutes later, the large group arrived beneath the stately pecan trees. Lights were on in some of the mansion's first floor rooms, though no one was on patrol outside. "We stick to the plan," Jim whispered. The teens cast their Invisibility spells, while the adults cast their Disguise spells. Jim, looking like a normal policeman, walked up to the front door. His gun was real—the one that Ashley had given him as a graduation present. Behind him, the others gathered, their guns were just an illusion, as was their disguise.

Jim knocked loudly and called out, "Police. Open up." Adrenaline began to flow. Jim was enjoying this immensely. Presently, a man came to the door. Jim recognized his voice as one of the two he'd heard before. "Police. We got a call of a burglary in progress here at this mansion."

Taken by complete surprise, the man said, "I don't know what you are talking about. We've heard nothing. Who reported it?" He was not making room for Jim to enter, and he held his wand at the ready.

"Got an anonymous tip from a jogger that someone was breaking in a basement window in the rear. Sir, how many of you are inside? I need to have you show us to the basement and then get yourself and the others outside, for your own protection. Please be quiet. We don't want to alarm the burglars into harming anyone," Jim said very formally. Invisible, Ashley smiled. Jim sounded so official, so believable, and so gutsy.

"Just me and Jerome. You wait here; we are the caretakers. Allow us to deal with this matter ourselves," the man said. Seeing that the wizard was not about to allow Jim inside, Wilma cast her old standby spell, the one she had used to capture many of the Death Stalkers fourteen years ago, the Grab. A giant claw-like hand grabbed a hold of the man around his head, temporarily covering his eyes and mouth. Monane cast her Disarm spell at the same time; his wand flew to her. Jim merely knocked him over the head with his gun butt and caught him from falling, handing him back to Lloyd. The Security man handcuffed him and laid him just outside the door.

Jim, Monane, and Wilma walked inside. They were in a large entrance hallway. Suddenly, the other wizard shot a Hold Person spell taking Jim off guard. He froze in place, as Wilma and Monane dove in different directions, avoiding the spell. At once, the others, still invisible dashed inside, Lindsey pausing over Jim to cast her silent Dispel Magic.

A Disintegrate spell narrowly missed Wilma, who was still rolling out of the way of the shooter. Several Magical

Missiles and Arrows of Acid flew back at the wizard, which had no effect. He had already cast his magical protections. Lindsey realized that probably nothing below a Grade 5 spell would have any effect on this wizard.

He shot off two spells in rapid succession. Ashley commanded her staff to suck up his Cloud of Poison Gas with which he attempted to slay everyone in the room. His rapid-fire second spell shot a wall of sticky webs over the bunch, which Pam absorbed barely in time. While none were in danger of becoming entangled as the wizard intended, the mass of sticky webs would make it difficult for them to disperse.

Deiter fired off his Cold Ray spell, which sent a blast of super-chilled air at the wizard, who was unprepared for it. His face froze in a silent death scream; his body slowly collapsed onto the floor. "Oh my god, I've killed him," Deiter muttered, suddenly terrified of what he had done. Until this instant, it had all been more play than serious life and death battles. As he looked at the frozen face of death, he felt awfully sick. Monane hastily took him outside, where he did vomit up his supper. Wilma joined them and suggested Monane would be of more use inside. Wilma, the old Rat Pack Eliminator, put her arm over the boy's shoulder.

"First kill is always bad, Deiter. You did what you had to do. He was aiming a Disintegrate at Lindsey, who was helping to free Jim," Wilma said softly.

"Did, did you see his face? Horrible, I'll never get his look out of my mind!" Deiter wailed.

"I know that you would like me to say, 'yes you will, give it time,' but that's not true. Taking another's life is always haunting. That's why I always used to spell to disarm, not to kill, though I have killed. It is never a pleasant thing, not something to be proud of or brag about, Deiter. It says you didn't have enough skill to take him down without killing him. These feelings are what separate us from Dominus and his gang. They relish and enjoy torturing and killing other people, but we hate it."

"I don't like to kill. Now that it has happened, I'll do my best not to kill in the future," Deiter promised and felt a little better, though the image of the frozen face still was vivid in his mind, as though he were still facing the dead man.

Inside, Jim and Lloyd began searching the first floor, calling out "Clear," as they verified each room in the spacious mansion held no further surprises. The others remained on the alert for surprise attacks. None had any idea if there were other wizards lurking about the mansion. A few minutes later, all were satisfied the first floor was clear. Now came the rough time. Lindsey suspected the women were kept upstairs.

For the sake of the women who were likely being held captive, Wilma and Monane led the girls up the stairs, though Lloyd protested against this as well as Jim. Both were worried about the women being taken by surprise. As she reached the top of the stairs, Lindsey knew they were likely to find the women here. The walls were done in the same plush red, velvet-like wallpaper that she had seen before.

After checking master bedroom and bathroom, Wilma opened the next door. She quickly put her hand over her mouth to keep from terrifying the prisoners with her gasp. Four mutilated women, wearing similar clothing and shoes sat on chairs around a table. On a low pillow sat another woman, her legs were missing. She looked up at Wilma and smiled a rather silly smile. Pam recognized it instantly! The woman was under the same spell that she had been, Idiot Mind.

"Who's there?" one of the four women nervously called out, pointing her sightless eyes more or less towards the door.

"Which one does he want tonight?" asked the woman who had no legs. "They are all ready."

"Ladies, we are here to rescue you and get your bodies healed up. I'm Lindsey Barron. We've rescued others who were just as you are now. The first thing we need to do is get you safely out of here. Trust me. You are now safe, but we have to get you out of here quickly."

"But we can't see and can barely walk," the same blonde haired woman said, looking sort of in the direction of Lindsey, who could see the telltale grey clouded eyes of the Blind spell in the woman's eyes.

"Leave that to us. Each of us will put our arms securely around one of you and lead you to safety." Lindsey put her arms on the shoulders of the woman who had been brave enough to talk to her. At once, Ashley, Amanda, Audrey, Wilma, and Monane went to the others, Wilma lifting up the legless woman.

Pam stated, "I'm going to do a quick bit of evidence gathering once you are gone. I'll go tell the guys."

"Guys?" the woman Lindsey was helping to stand up said nervously. "I don't think we have any panties on. Are we nearly naked? It feels like it."

Lindsey's heart went out to her, but she felt the woman needed to know the truth. "We know. You are wearing a very tight corset, hose, and impossibly high heels, nothing else. We promise not to let the guys see you like this." Hearing this, all four visibly relaxed.

Lindsey grasped her woman securely around her waist, the woman's greatly enlarged breasts pushing hard against her. "Teleport: Home." As she cast her spell, she heard four other's saying similar words. She landed her rescued woman onto the ground holding her tightly, since the blind woman, totally disoriented, could not keep her balance in her heels. Within seconds, the other four were standing beside her.

"One step up onto the porch. I'm right here. I won't let you fall. Yes, there it is," she saw the woman desperately feeling with her shoe. "Little higher. Good. There you go. Now up we go." It was all she could do to keep the blind woman from falling. Slowly, ever so slowly, shoes mostly shuffling a few inches at a time, they entered the house. Fern, Orenda, Polly, and Lena were waiting for them. Lena held her hand over her mouth. She'd had never seen anything like this before. Neither had any of those four. Fern's eyes watered, as did Orenda's.

Meanwhile back at the mansion, Lloyd, Deiter, Ahana, and Jim stood guard, while Pam took fingerprints, photos, and ten DNA samples from the red satin bed sheets. Satisfied she had a good representative sample, she joined the others. "Okay, done. Now what?"

"Jim and I will contact the authorities and deliver these to two them. Join you in a bit," Lloyd replied. The teens teleported back, while Lloyd contacted the Atlanta Department of Security. Thirty minutes later, they teleported home too.

"He'll be freed before morning," Jim predicted, "just as soon as they find out that he is a Dominus man." Lloyd grinned and agreed.

"That was pretty gutsy, Jim. You went ahead and filed for the reward on rescuing Lisa Marton. I hope she was one of the women they rescued," Lloyd added. Jim certainly hoped she was.

Lindsey finally had her woman safely inside the large front room of the vacant apartment. Fern and Orenda had five beds waiting. Now came the awkward moment: how to get her safely onto the bed.

"I know how now," the woman said meekly. "Position me so I can back into the bed." Lindsey did as she asked. Once her legs touched the bed, she bravely sat down, but rather hard, without arms to steady, guide, or ease herself down. Once she was lying down, Lindsey pulled a sheet over her. Meanwhile, the others were also helped into their beds.

"Okay, first we are going to get your vision back by undoing the Blind spell that was cast on you," Lindsey explained. "Just lie comfortably, and let us work our magic." Indeed, they had to work at it. Canceling such a powerful wizard's spell proved challenging, though they all knew that it was possible, just not likely from attempt to attempt. Lindsey wondered if she would need to make twenty tries to succeed, that being the 5% that her professor had drilled into her head. Her patient regained her sight after Lindsey's tenth attempt.

Once all four could now see, Lindsey said, "Okay, I'm Lindsey Barron." She introduced the others. "Now then, we need your names so we can notify your families."

"I'm Lisa Marton. My dad's a Senator, but can we see how we look? None of us knows what we look like. We were all blinded," the blonde said bravely. Lindsey lifted the blanket so she could see herself. However, the huge size of her breasts prevented her from seeing much. One by one, the women looked over at their companions and gasped. "What's happened to us?" Lisa began to cry.

"Dominus Malefic kidnaped you and did this to you. Don't worry; we will be getting you all healed up. Now the next thing we need to do is get these shoes off you and the corsets. If Dominus did to you like he did to those that we rescued last January, they are booby trapped." Lisa gave her a strange look, so Lindsey added, "Yes, they were just like you are now, only one had her right arm cut off along with her legs. Grim. Okay, gang. Let's start with Lisa. Check for traps on her heels."

Pam came along later and took copious notes. Lisa Marton was twenty-one with shoulder length, very blonde hair, and deep blue eyes. Melissa Blackhawk was twenty-two, a raven-haired beauty, who had won several pageants, most recently Miss New York. Lyn Zhu, twenty-one, from Los Angeles, had long brown hair and eyes. Twenty-two year old Cherrie Athos, from Florida, had a tan and blonde hair as well. The fifth woman, Ellen Sprague, was the oldest at twenty-three. She had long brown hair and still could not understand what was happening to her. The Idiot Mind spell turned her mental capacities to that of a very young child. She had been trained to help the others with their bodily needs, including brushing their hair, fixing their makeup, and feeding them. That routine gone, Ellen was a mountain of confusion. Her southern accent suggested that she was from Georgia, but she didn't know what city or who her parents were.

Detecting the traps and then undoing them proved very challenging for the teens, even with Wilma and Monane helping out. Eventually, the women agreed to allow the guys to lend a hand, especially once Lindsey and the others began to find the traps laid by Dominus. The heels were doubly trapped, while the corsets were triply trapped—all designed to prevent them from being removed. By ten that night, all had been removed, much to the great pleasure of the women. Next, Lindsey found them all panties and shorts that fit. Finding tops proved next to impossible; their enormous breast sizes proved daunting for normal clothing. Nadia came to their rescue, digging out five of her older blouses, which had yet to be altered to her now drastically smaller bust size. At last, the rescued women felt properly clothed.

Since it was late and everyone was famished, Lindsey led them into her home and to their dining room. Lena and Polly had foreseen this and prepared a nourishing, hot meal for everyone. Of course, the five had to be fed. Lindsey did the honors for Lisa. "I don't know how to thank everyone for rescuing us. It's just a miracle. How did you ever find us?"

While they ate, Pam gave her explanation, outlining everything. "Tomorrow, our school's doctor will come and check you over physically. He'll probably start your arm re-growing process then too. A week from now, you should be as good as new."

"But I am perfectly good. There is nothing wrong with me," Ellen protested. All ignored her comments. Pam grimaced, suspecting that this was what she must have sounded like when Dominus had turned her into an idiot.

The next morning, Governor Alister and Doctor Caterwall arrived early. Alister had bags under his eyes. "Not been to bed yet. Seen the news?" Lindsey admitted that she hadn't. Pam raced to catch the news, leaving Lindsey to handle the explanations and introductions.

"You took a risk, Miss Barron, but I see how you minimized the danger. Clever of you to time your rescue when the Idaho Red Brigade Militia was making their attack on Aetna Pharmaceuticals processing plant," Alister said. His usual twinkling eyes were dulled this morning, Lindsey noted.

"Yes, Audrey's doing. She told us when it was the right time to go," Lindsey explained. Next, she introduced the women to Alister and the school's doctor. While the doctor gave each woman a thorough examination, Alister quizzed Lindsey about the traps that they had found. Deiter backed up Lindsey, explaining each one they had found and de-activated.

"You've all done well," Governor Alister complimented them. "Bold move by Jim, claiming the reward should go to your group of Bradbury students. Yet, it calls the attention of Dominus once again to you and Ashley, Miss Barron. That might not be so wise. Nevertheless, it's done."

"Excuse me," Frank interrupted him. "The women are in amazingly good condition, all things considered. I've reduced their busts to normal. Doctor Verner should be here shortly. I will begin their healing process, once he's finished. Can't have them jerking their bodies around while their arms are re-growing."

"Wow, you got Doctor Verner to come again? Thanks!" Lindsey exclaimed, really relieved that these women's emotional trauma would also be handled.

"Yes," Alister replied, "can't have them half-cured. Besides, he was making his rounds today anyway. I just added one more stop on his trip. Ah, here he comes now." Lena entered bringing the old gentleman with her.

"Here's your other doctor," Lena said, grinning at some jest he had made while they were walking down the long hallway.

"Guten morgen, I see ve have more to do. Same as before, Alister?" Doctor Verner tipped his out of style felt hat. Alister shook his hand and ushered everyone out of the room, leaving the doctors to work their respective magics. However, he prudently cast a Silence spell at the door, muffling the relived trauma that the women would soon be re-experiencing as the pain was erased from their minds.

For the rest of the week, the recovering women needed round the clock assistance, which the teens willingly provided. However, Pam hooked up a TV for the women to watch. She wanted them to become educated on just what the situation was in New York and DC, namely that the population had been turned into what she called zombies or automatons. "Lisa and Melissa can't go back to their homes in the Big Apple," Pam explained, "not unless they want to become zombies too."

The afternoon that their healing began, Pam brought everyone up to speed on what happened that night. "The Idaho Red Brigade Militia struck the Aetna manufacturing plant, which is making those evil drugs. They sent in two hundred zombies and skeletons, resurrected from the local cemetery! While the guards were fending off the undead monsters, they attacked and set off charges, probably C-4 would be my guess. Initial reports suggest that they really crippled the plant's production capabilities. That ought to slow Dominus down considerably."

"Cool. But what happened to the militia?" Deiter asked.

"Got clean away. No casualties, as far as the news can determine. The Department of Law said that they will be tracking them down, treating them as criminals," Pam continued indignantly. "No one knows where they are now. Half the country is cheering them on and the other half cursing them. Question is, where will they strike next?"

"Got to hand it to them," Deiter replied, "they sure slowed down Dominus."

The last week in August, the five women were fully recovered. Lyn and Cherrie returned to Los Angeles and Florida, respectively, but with a full time Security woman posted as their personal bodyguard. "I can't go home," Lisa fought back tears. "Look what's happened to mom and dad!"

"Me either," Melissa added. "I'm the reigning Miss New York, but I don't dare go back. What are we going to do?"

Pam had the answer for both. "I've been researching you both a bit. Hope you don't mind. Melissa, weren't you planning to enroll in college this fall?"

"Yes, elementary education. Why?"

"Why don't you both go to Denver University? I know it is a bit late, but perhaps under the circumstances, they will accept you both," Pam replied. "I've made a few inquiries, and the Dean suggested that you contact him if you are interested."

Kimi offered, "Kids, I can help you with those details as well as getting your funds transferred from your New York banks to new ones in Denver. Legal things are my specialty." Indeed, Kimi really wanted to help. Not being a witch, she felt more than a little left out of things.

Both decided to take Pam's advice. Ellen could not return to Georgia; too much was happening there. Instead, she had her boyfriend move to Denver, and they hastily got married, assuming that once married, Dominus would have no further interest in her. Once more, the lives that Dominus had confiscated had been returned to their owners.

On August 26, a certified check for a half million dollars arrived for Lindsey. Dominus kept his word, primarily, Pam thought, because he had made such a big deal about offering the reward in the press. Lindsey sent one hundred thousand to Bradbury's to compensate the school for their medical assistance. Each of the five women was given fifty thousand each to help them get restarted financially. The remaining one hundred and fifty thousand, she divided among all those participating and helping, each receiving a share, including Fern and Orenda. All were pleased to receive around twelve thousand dollars. For most of Lindsey's friends, this was a huge sum, not necessarily so with Lloyd, Wilma, Monane, and Eli.

Chapter 8—Ahana Scores a Hit

The end of the third week of August was the grand opening of B&B Dance Hall in downtown Denver. Bailey and Barnaby ran into a few more complications than they had first anticipated, delaying their opening by a week. Nadia and Jolina were their constant companions, lending advice as well as assistance. Baily and Barnaby saw at once that these two women knew precisely how a dance hall ought to look and operate for maximum pleasure of the dancers. Hence, they quickly left the interior design, layout, furnishings, and catering arrangements to the women, while they worked on what they did best, promotion. By the Friday August 21, nearly every quarter of Denver had heard of their grand opening.

Friday night was billed as the Romantic Formal Dance night. A live rock band was on for Saturday night. Barnaby and Bailey decided to hold just two opening nights this first week to see how everything went, ironing out any kinks. The following week, if all went well, would see three nights of action. For the first time in their lives, both Hampton brothers were nervous about the grand opening.

"I'm shaking life a leaf, Nadia," Barnaby said to her. All four were in Nadia's home, next to the main Compton home, trying to get dressed and ready. Nadia began fixing his cummerbund and then his tie. "I mean this time it really *means* something to us, you know. Well, it's not as if our other projects didn't mean something, but this is it, the really important one."

"I know, Barnaby, this time you are doing what your heart is telling you to do, not what your pockets are asking," Nadia whispered in his ear. "Nadia and I feel the same way, you know. We've been searching the world for something like this, a place to go, dance, and have a fabulous time, no strings attached, just for the pure enjoyment of the dance. Look, there must be many folks who, once they know about this, will die to come. Have faith. You build it. You've brought it to everyone's attention. We've got it decorated perfectly, so when they come and see for themselves, you'll see. They will come back and bring their friends too. You look handsome," Nadia added, kissing him on his cheek.

"Thanks, Nadia, you look, well stunning doesn't even say it all. You know that B and I could not have done this without your help and Jolina's too, don't you? You are as much a part of this as we are, maybe more so," Barnaby added.

"We know; it is our heart's fondest desires coming to fruition. Come on. Let's see how Bailey and Jolina are making out," Nadia replied. Nadia wore a billowing light green, satin ball gown with a matching light green and white striped outer corset also made of satin, adding just a touch of fetish to her appearance. Her tall, spiked heels matched, as did her oblong emerald earrings.

Arm in arm, the two walked into their front room, where the other half were making their final preparations. Bailey was also a nervous wreck, but Jolina had already gotten him calmed down. Jolina wore a light blue outfit, exactly matching Nadia's, but with light blue emeralds, altered by a Color spell. The men wore formal tuxedos with a stovepipe top hat, reminiscent of the 1800's.

"Are we ready?" Bailey asked, his voice had a tremor in it.

"All set here; let's do it," Barnaby replied. The four held hands, and Nadia teleported them to their new dance hall in Denver. Already, the newly hired staff had arrived. Outside at the teleport arrival pad, right near the entrance, three Security men had taken up their position.

"Good evening, bosses, you four look quite sharp indeed. How big a crowd are you anticipating tonight?" asked Melvin, the lead guard.

Nadia replied, "Time will tell. A packed house would be nice, but we'll just take what comes. Keep us safe, Melvin," she grinned.

"Yes, boss. Drug and alcohol sensors are operational, as are the weapons and bomb detectors. We'll be casting our See True spells, once folks begin to arrive. I'll be honest, I've not seen this kind of security excepting at Presidential affairs."

Searchlights streaked across the sky, attracting

attention to their main entrance and an antique-style neon sign clearly identified this as the B&B Dance Hall. The two couples went inside the spacious building. Nadia had redone the floor in a oak wood finish, with matching draperies. Overhead, a dozen chandeliers with fancy light bulbs provided the illumination. Just now, they were on full, as the ten inside staff hastily finished last minute preparations. One wall housed the DJ and the massive studio-quality sound system. He was in charge of playing the music. His orders were simple, play a wide variety, see what the group responded to best, and then play more that was similar.

The opposite wall held a number of elegantly styled tables and chairs, while behind them the caterers would serve the refreshments. The actual food would be matched to the crowd. That is, tonight tea and coffee predominated, along with healthy and nourishing treats. Tomorrow night, teens would predominate and thus sodas and pizza would be served primarily. All the dishes were fine china. Sterling silverware lay neatly arranged on each table. A vase of flowers and a candle provided the final touch on each table, whose covering tonight was red velvet. A faint odor of fresh flowers filled the spacious room.

"Well, everything seems to be in order," Nadia said, having eyed all aspects of the room. "Shall we take up our positions?" The four moved over to the entrance, one couple on each side. Their plan was personally to greet each person when they entered, though they too would join the dance once people stopped arriving.

At six-thirty, the first group arrived, the combined Compton-Whitewater group. First to walk inside was John and Mary Hampton, the twin's parents. "Welcome, mom, dad, to B&B Dance Hall," the twins said in unison.

Nadia added, "So glad you could be the very first to enter. I know Barnaby and Bailey are very proud that you came."

"We hope you enjoy the dance," Jolina added.

"My, you ladies look lovely tonight," Mary replied. "Boys, your father and I are—well, let's say that for the first time in a dozen years, we both totally approve of this venture of yours. I do hope it is a successful one."

"Yes, sons, this place is amazing. Well done indeed, though I do detect that Miss van Nye and Miss Wessel must have handled the interior decorating. Lady's touch I see. Splendid, ladies, amazingly splendid," John, the conservative banker said, more joviality in his voice than the boys could ever recall hearing.

Behind them, Lena and Lloyd Compton entered, followed by Wilma and Tom Weltsi, Monane and Rufus Tumble, Luci and R. B. Whitewater, Polly and Fred Betts, Kimi and Eli Orondarka, and Lottie and Henry Blackburn. All wore their finest suits and gowns, ready for what had been promised to be a romantic evening of dance.

The teens followed them; Deiter escorting Lindsey came first. "Wow! Way super cool, Nadia, Jolina!" Lindsey exclaimed, as her eyes took in the expansive room.

"Glad you like it," Nadia beamed. "All thanks to you." She gave Lindsey a big hug and whispered in her ear, "You gave me my life back. I can't tell you how much that means to me."

As Deiter led Lindsey inside this elegant room, he commented, "Lindsey, this is so rich, so luxurious, so—I don't know what. You look terrific, and this place does you justice. Thanks for letting me bring you. Anytime you want to come, just let me know! I'll be here with you. With you on my arm, I'm the luckiest guy in the whole world!" Indeed, Lindsey thought that he couldn't possibly stand up any straighter, but she managed to smile instead of giggle. She felt butterflies in her stomach, but didn't know why, only that she dearly loved dressing up like this and going to a formal dance. Deiter did look handsome in his tuxedo, she thought.

Ashley and Jim followed Lindsey and Deiter, chatting furiously with each other. Ashley wore her expensive Inaugural Ball gown and Jim, his light blue tuxedo. He'd only been gone for a couple of months, but the way these two chatted, one may have suspected it had been a lot longer.

Kathy and Emilio, dressed in their finest, were right behind them. "My gosh, Nadia, this place is incredibly fancy. Will it look like this tomorrow night for the live rock?" he asked as they shook hands with the four owners in turn.

Nadia chuckled, and said mischievously, "Oh, you'll just have to come tomorrow and see."

"Wild horses couldn't keep us away!" Kathy pronounced.

Ellie and Orenda, dressed also in their gorgeous gowns that Lindsey had given them entered next, escorting each other. Orenda had not met many others beyond those on the two ranches, since her family moved from New York. Though a Red Hall beauty, Ellie still didn't have a steady boyfriend and decided that she and Orenda ought to come together. With luck, they might meet some boys, though both girls thought that their chances would be infinitely greater at the rock dance tomorrow night.

Amanda, wearing her Inaugural Ball gown and tall heels, held onto the arm of Ahana, who had asked for her hand this evening, as well as tomorrow night at the rock dance. At her side, Pam, likewise wearing her expensive outfit with equally high heels, held on to Audrey, who wore the fancy gown that Lindsey had given her. Audrey commented, "Pam, you should have worn more sensible, lower heels, like I am."

Pam ignored her comment, replying, "I do hope he will come." As soon as she said that she wished she'd kept her mouth shut. She had emailed Tom Ryker, telling him about this grand opening. Pam still didn't know how she had ever gotten the nerve a to ask Tom to meet her at the dance and be her date. Yes, she had actually asked Tom for a date, though she knew that it was supposed to be the other way around. Still, with the ability to hide behind an email, that is, not facing him directly, she had found the courage at least to ask.

Amanda said, "Well, he replied that he would, Pam. We will wait here with you. After all, you are going to have an awkward time in these heels and dress if he doesn't." She clung to Ahana for support. "Honestly, Pam, I think you did the right thing. After all, he did seem to love dancing with you at the Presidential Ball. How soon is Bill coming, Audrey?"

"Ah, here comes Bill now," Audrey flushed, her boyfriend Bill Williams just appeared on the teleport pad nearby. He wore a dark blue tuxedo.

"Hi Audrey, wow, you look great!" he gave her a hug. She latched onto his arm, very glad that he had come. They had not seen each other all summer and quickly began chatting.

Tom and Sandy Rains-Whitewater apparated on the teleport pad. Sandy wore an inexpensive gown, but looked very happy. "Tom!" Amanda exclaimed and gave her big brother a solid, loving hug. "Long time no see. You look great, Sandy."

"Gosh, sis, you look incredible, fantastic," Tom replied.

"Thanks, you look fabulous, Amanda. So do you, Pam, Audrey," Sandy added. "Those the gowns for the Presidential Ball, right?" Amanda nodded.

"We're hitting the books really hard, sis, trying to get our degrees in three years. Hope we beat Dominus and the President, before they turn everyone into automatons," Tom explained why they had not been home for visits since heading to Denver University last year.

"Mom and dad are inside, so is Jim. Ashley did another photo shoot too," Amanda explained. "Oh, Ahana, this is my older brother, Tom, and his wife, Sandy. This is Ahana Orondarka. He and his family are staying with us. They escaped from New York."

Tom and Sandy shook his hand, and Tom said, "You take good care of my big sister, Ahana." Both boys laughed, and then Tom and Sandy headed on inside to find the rest of Tom's family.

Pam was getting nervous—would Tom actually come? Just then, Tom Ryker appeared on the teleport pad. He wore a slightly out of date tuxedo. "Hi Pam. You look terrific! Sorry I am a bit late. I had a hard time finding a tux. This was the only one they had left that would fit me. Thanks for asking me." He slid his arm around her, just as he had done at the Presidential Ball.

Grinning and trying to keep her heart from racing, Pam put hers around his. "Didn't know if you'd want to come. I'm very glad you did. Nadia and Jolina have done a really super job of decorating this place." Arm in arm, the two followed Audrey and Bill, and Amanda and Ahana inside.

"Sure glad you asked me, Pam, though I didn't think you would really want to see me again—you know, being the computer geek that I am and all that," Tom said. "I just can't believe my luck; you are the greatest girl I've ever known."

Pam blushed, "Well, I'm a bit of a computer geek myself too."

"I suppose I should tell you, Pam. I'm a member of the Voodoo Underground Website. It's a site where the best computer hackers of the world meet online. I'm called Dingo there, just thought you ought to know," Tom admitted, wanting to be up front with Pam.

Pam choked, and Tom kept her from losing her balance. "I'm—I'm Madam Fingers," she whispered. Tom's eyes opened wide; his mouth opened to say something, but nothing came out.

"You, you, Madam Fingers? I thought so! God, do I love you!" He picked her up and twirled her around twice. "You hired Dingo to hack into ex-Governor Albright's email system and get all his emails. Later on, I saw on the news how you had met with the Board of Governors and presented all that evidence against him. There were those same emails I retrieved, so I kind of guessed Madam Fingers might be you." Tom admitted his hunch, which had paid off royally for him.

Pam, still flushed, replied, "You are one of the best hackers I know of, Tom." Her arm tightened around him, as the two finally joined the large gathering.

Promptly at seven, the waltz music began. After an hour, the DJ had worked out that the older couples preferred the slower waltzes while the younger set liked the faster ones. Well over eight hundred were in attendance tonight, more than half were not teens. Hence, slower music prevailed.

For once, Lindsey was grateful for the end of the dance. It was midnight. She and her friends had been dancing almost all night, five hours in their heels. "Thanks, Barnaby, Nadia, Bailey, Jolina," she complimented the foursome as her large group finally was able to exit, being nearly the last to leave. "Tonight was just super cool! We'll be back as often as we can."

Deiter added, "You bet, only we can't come during school, but we'll be here during Christmas break and all summer long!" A bit later, when they were a part from the others getting ready to use the teleport pad, he added, "Lindsey, thanks for a really great night. You are the best! You look so sexy, so attractive in your gown and all that I can hardly stand it! I didn't want the night to ever end!"

Lindsey flushed, but quickly replied, "You are a really good dancer, Deiter. I feel very safe with you. Thanks. Let's do this as often as we can! Guess we'll get to rock tomorrow night, right?"

"You bet!" She didn't let go of him, still keeping her arm firmly around his waist all the way home. Even after arriving at the ranch, she clung to him, suggesting they get a midnight snack before he headed home. He didn't need to be asked twice.

While they were sitting at the kitchen table, drinking a soda and munching on fish and chips, they heard the clicking of heels headed their way. From the sounds, Lindsey guessed it could only be Nadia or Jolina. Nadia's face was flushed, Jolina's too. They were walking together, supporting each other. "Lindsey! You'll never, ever guess what happened to us tonight, right after the last one left!" Lindsey had never seen Nadia this excited before, or Jolina, for that matter.

Nadia and Jolina flashed their ring fingers, displaying a pair of large diamond rings. "Barnaby got down on his knees to me and proposed!" Nadia gushed.

"Bailey did the same with me, at the same time," Jolina added, just as excited as Nadia.

"Wow! Congratulations, both of you," Lindsey exclaimed, surprised as well.

"Hey, I could see that one coming a mile away," Deiter added. "It's like you were made for each other. I saw that when I met the twins. Congratulations indeed. When's the wedding going to be?"

Bubbling with excitement, Nadia explained, "We want to hold it when all of you can attend. Lindsey, I want you to be my maid of honor; Jolina wants Ashley to be hers. How does June 15 sound to you? You'll be back from school and settled in by then."

"Great! Thanks, er. I'm not sure what a maid of honor is

supposed to do, though, Nadia," Lindsey replied.

"Don't worry, Lindsey, we have nearly a year to figure it out. Honestly, neither of us does either. We've got to find Ashley and ask her," Jolina answered her. The two ecstatic women left to find where Ashley and Jim were located. They were in the front room having a good night embrace. Lindsey heard the squeal from Ashley and knew that she had just heard the good news. Finally, Lindsey led Deiter to her front door, still holding on to him, as they stepped outside so that he could teleport home.

"I can't go home if you don't let go of me," he teased her.

"What if I don't want you to," Lindsey replied, wondering why she said that.

Deiter reached a decision, something he had been working up the courage to do all evening long. He leaned forward and gave Lindsey a loving kiss. She found her arms moving around his body, holding on tightly, returning it. At last, the two parted, and he disappeared, teleporting home. Lindsey floated back inside and all the way to her room. There she found Ashley, still wearing her fancy gown and heels, just lying dreamily on her bed. Lindsey threw herself down on her bed too.

After a bit, Ashley cooed, "Jim is mad about me. I kind of thought he might find someone his age when he left, but he's still in love with me. I'm sure of it. Of course, I'm crazy about him, too."

Lindsey mustered the courage to say shyly, "Deiter just kissed me—I mean, passionately."

"Well, it's about time," Ashley replied haughtily. "Everyone can see he's in love with you. Didn't you know it?"

Lindsey flushed; she hadn't realized this! The next thing both girls knew, it was morning; Lena called for breakfast. Hastily, but dreamy-eyed, the two changed their clothes and raced out to get something to eat before it was all gone.

They barely had chores done when Amanda, Orenda, and Fern came over. "Ahana kicked us out," she explained. "It seems his whole band just arrived, and they are practicing for tonight's concert."

"We tried to get their autographs," Fern added, "but failed. Wait til tonight, he kept saying. Rats."

"They always have a practice session before gigs," Orenda explained. "I always get run out too. Boys!" They spent the day with the five patients, whose arms were being regrown.

At six thirty prompt, the teens, accompanied by Lloyd, Wilma, and Monane headed for the rock concert and dance. The adults were unwilling to allow the teens to go alone, for the threat of Dominus was too strong. This time, Tom Ryker was right on time. All the teens were wearing jeans. The four owners met them at the door as they had the night before.

"Wow, what a look, Nadia, Jolina!" exclaimed Lindsey, as she shook hands.

"Knockouts!" Deiter added. Indeed, both women wore shiny latex, tight fitting cat suits with matching striped latex corsets and matching tall spikes. Nadia's was forest green, while Jolina's was sky blue. The twins wore suede brown jackets with matching pants.

"Thanks, this is the look we love. Anyway, hope you like the live dance. We are hoping that Eli's Rockers is a strong opening band," Nadia replied.

"They wouldn't let us anywhere near their practice session today," Amanda growled, still a bit miffed at having been run off her own ranch for much of the day. "Hey, this place is filling up fast; we better see if we can get closer to the band." The large group slowly made their way to the stage area, located at the back wall opposite the entrance.

Gone were all the romantic decorations from the previous evening, replaced with spinning, reflecting lights and two wall screens on either side of the stage. Streamers of colored lights, which flashed in synch with the rhythms, hung from the ceiling. The front-most section was marked "Reserved for Amanda Whitewater's Group."

"Hey, way cool!" Fern gushed, as she spied this unexpected touch. Amanda and her friends squeezed into this section, accompanied by numerous catcalls, one of which was "Lucky Dogs!" By seven, the hall was packed with teens and a few in their twenties. Lloyd, Monane, and Wilma took a seat at the very back near the entrance doors where a dozen other security personnel were also stationed in case of trouble. Lights dimmed and a large flash, reminiscent of an explosion, hid the stage. Appearing amid the dimming flash, Eli's Rockers took the stage.

"One, two, three, four," Amanda saw Ahana counting. He held his guitar marking the proposed rhythm. The crowd yelled and whistled, as they recognized the introduction of one of Eli Rocker's biggest hits, "Rolling Home." The concert and dance began with a solid, rocking song, sure to please their fans.

After the thunderous applause, yelling, and screaming died down, Ahana, spokesperson for the band, called out, "Special song for a special person!" Again, he gave a count down. However, he was singing this song while playing the acoustic guitar—the lead in to the larger sound of the foursome. The tune was an Antique Rock song from ages ago.

"This song goes out to the one I love," he crooned, all the while his eyes focused solely on Amanda. In fact, throughout the song, his eyes never left hers. Amanda blushed, but then blushed even more as she saw hundreds of other fans straining to get a glimpse of whom he was singing the song for, her.

"We've had many requests for Antique Rock songs," Ahana called out after the thunderous applause and yelling died down enough for him to be heard. "This song goes out to a trio of fabulous girls here tonight, Pam, Nadia, and Jolina." He began his acoustical lead, and then began, "Sitting on a park bench." At once, the crowd knew this famous song; they yelled and screeched so loudly that he was nearly drowned out. This time, Pam flushed; it was her favorite Antique Rock Jethro Tull song, Nadia's too.

When the noise died down, the keyboard member began playing a slow piano jazzy sounding lead in for their next song. Over the music of the solo piano sound, Ahana called out, "This is for all you Dominus resisters out there, especially L and D, my personal favorite JT tune, Locomotive Breath." Once the piano intro finished and the wall of sound, heavy, fast, one-two pulsating beat began, the crowd went wild, yelling, singing along, and dancing furiously to the simple rhythm. Lindsey and Deiter realized this one was meant for them, as they danced as madly as the throng around them.

Their rendition of Free Bird came next, then a batch of Rolling Stones hits. Midnight came far too soon for the entire crowd, who yelled and begged for encores long after the band had left the stage and began packing their gear. While the crowd of well over five thousand began leaving, as expected, Eli's Rockers then lined up at a table to sign autographs, which they did after every concert. Amanda and her friends brought them plenty of sodas and pizzas. All were famished after that long show.

After the last customer left, Lindsey's group, the band members, and the owners all sat down. Bailey said enthusiastically, having already counted the receipts, "I say, we are definitely going to have to get you guys scheduled here again!"

Barnaby continued, "Smashing success, turnout exceeds all expectations."

Nadia added her opinion, "Obviously, we need a bigger dance hall, fellows!"

"Cool! Thanks for giving us the gig. Largest crowd we've ever played," Ahana explained.

"See, I told you Antique Rock is really big," Nadia teased Barnaby, who grinned and kissed her.

Committed to getting more live concerts from Eli's Rockers, Jolina quickly suggested, "How about three performances over Christmas holiday break from school?"

"Yes, you must do at least three," insisted Bailey, grinning because Jolina had beaten him to it. Naturally, the band agreed.

At one in the morning, the teens finally arrived home. B&B Dance Hall was a smashing success. Sunday afternoon, Ahana worked out rehearsal ideas with his band. Noshi Fry, bass, Chogan Jeans, drummer, and Phil Huritt, keyboards, were all transferring to the Toronto School of Magic. Their families had also packed up and moved out of New York, avoiding the National Health Care fiasco. Governor Alister accommodated Ahana by allowing him to travel to Toronto one weekend each month so the band could practice. In return, Alister wisely asked that the band play for Bradbury's Christmas dance.

Chapter 9—Back to Bradbury's for the Fifth Years

The familiar Bradbury school bus materialized in front of Lindsey's front porch. It was August, and as Yellow Hall Floor Monitors, Lindsey, Fern, and Pam had to return a week early. Ellie was now a Red Hall Floor Monitor, something her older sister, Monique, never was. Their job was to help all the new students during orientation week. School began on September 1 as usual. They loaded their numerous duffel bags, while Ahana gave Amanda a long farewell kiss. Ahana and his sister, Orenda, were new students and had to attend orientation week.

Clipboards in hand, Lindsey took charge of the new older students, while Pam and Fern handled all the new first year students. Pam truly enjoyed helping the first years last year and insisted that she do so again this time. Lindsey checked off her two new students, Ahana and Orenda, "We are always the first to board, since we're just about as far east as you can get. Golly, we have more stops than usual this year," she added.

"Must be all the new transfers, Lindsey," Pam suggested, counting her list. "Unless there are disproportionately far more students on the High Plains this year, we are going to have a whole lot more students to handle. I have thirty first years on my list; twenty will be on this bus. How's your total look?"

"I've got fifteen counting Ahana and Orenda. Wow, there must be a whole lot of transfers from New York." Then, Lindsey suddenly recognized one name on her list and broke into a big grin, though she said nothing about it to Pam, hoping to surprise her later.

The bus made nearly twice as many stops as usual; most were at smaller towns on the High Plains. Even Deiter was too busy helping the many new Black Hall students to spend time with Lindsey after he boarded in Colorado Springs.

By the time the bus made its last stop and began the final long haul to Bradbury's, over sixty were on the bus. As they finally settled down and Deiter could come to join Lindsey, Ahana's comment was, "Jeesh, we really are living in the wide open spaces, Lindsey. There's virtually nothing out here. Now the mountains, they are really cool. Does Bradbury's have tall mountains around the campus?"

"You bet. One twelve thousand plus mountain is just to our east," Deiter explained. He and Ahana chatted away about the magnificent scenery passing by the bus windows. Finally, at Cortez, the bus took the state route 145 up towards Telluride. Ahana and Orenda stared at the magnificent mountains, so close that you could almost touch them—her words. Finally, the Ophir Loop came and went through the San Juan Mountains and Forest. The picturesque drive up to near Telluride went without any attacks on the bus, much to Lindsey's relief.

As the bus pulled into the staff parking lot, the dark grey walls surrounding the campus commanded the new arrival's attention. Now the Floor Monitors really had a workout. As each new student found all their bags, Lindsey, Deiter, Pam, Fern, Ellie, and Emilio had to find what room the person was assigned and Move Object their bags into their room for them. Finally, with all bags handled, the Floor Monitors gathered the students assigned to their specific Hall. "See you all at dinner," Deiter called out, as he led his throng of Black Hall students onto the campus.

Pam and Fern led the large group of first years, with Lindsey and the older transfers following. They listened to Pam's explanation to these younger students. "Bradbury's outer walls are heavily enchanted to protect all of us inside. There is no way to fly over the walls or climb them. This is the main gate, which leads to the parking lot, where you will see many of the professor's cars. The shape of these outer walls is that of a pentagram. Inside, the buildings also form an enormous pentagram."

"Now, here is the Administration Hall. It's where the professors meet and such. One room holds all the trophies and awards that we have earned. Please note this is the bottom left corner of the pentagrams of buildings. Straight on across this bottom in the middle of the bottom is the Infirmary. If you get sick or injured, you will be brought here."

They had walked past the Administration Hall and turned north or left between this two story modern looking building and the single story brick Infirmary building, which looked the least inviting of all the buildings. "Here is our heated swimming pool. No swimming unless there is a lifeguard on duty. Just north of the pool is our dorm pentagram building, the five-sided building." Each side looked much like any other modern college campus dormitory, however. Each fifth was painted a different color.

Pam continued her explanation, "Yellow Hall is for those wizards and witches who are brave and fearless, who prefer thought as a means of solving a problem, who are cheerful, who like light and air. In contrast, Blue Hall is for those who love water, who are compassionate and caring, who believe that emotions should be used to solve problems. Many in the Blue Hall are healers, succoring those in need. Now Red Hall is fiery for those who believe passions rule, who believe love is what rules, and that hot emotions should be used to solve problems. Brown Hall represents the earth. Here are those who love to grow things, both plants and animals. They are stalwart and dependable to a fault. They believe honest efforts solve life's problems. Those in Black Hall stand for pure logic. They see themselves as all-important; some are foolhardy and take risks to solve problems. Might and strength, effort in other words, is their hallmark. Dominus came from Black Hall."

"Here we are. In the very center is this pentagram dorm building where we students all live. Each side is a different hall color. Black Hall is at the bottom of the dorm pentagram. Blue Hall is on its right, while Brown Hall lies to the left. Above Blue Hall is Yellow Hall and above Brown Hall is Red Hall. Yellow Hall and Red Hall adjoin each other. In the center of the dorm pentagram is the courtyard and the large dining hall, where we all meet and eat our meals. First, we will visit the dining hall, then it's find your room time."

"After showing everyone to their rooms, Pam and

Lindsey took them all on a quick walk around the campus. "Here is our stadium," Lindsey explained as they walked north out of their dorm building. "To our right is the Book Store, which we will visit to get you your books. If you need any supplies, clothes, or such, just go there and ask. Due north of us is the Stadium. Your PE classes will meet at the Stadium. Due west of us is the library. It looks small, but it is huge inside, magical expansion. Due south of us is the swimming pool."

They walked to the northern point of the Bradbury pentagram of buildings. "Here is the Math and Science Hall. Math classrooms are on the third floor; the others are for science classes." This building looked just college science buildings, many steel and glass windows, rather modern looking.

They walked southwestward to the next building. "Hall of Alteration Magic. As you can see, this building continually changes its appearance each day. One day, it looks like a castle but today I'd say it looks like a rocket ship or something. It keeps changing its appearance." She led them on southwestward to the next building in the line, which marked one of the five corners.

"Here is the Hall of Illusional Magic. Each day, it changes its color scheme." The building looked like a grand old mansion, today constructed of red-brown bricks. Ivy grew up one side of it. Walking along a southeastern line to the next building, Lindsey said, "This is the Humanities Hall. English and Literature classes are held here. It looks like an English manor house." Ivy completely covered all sides of the building.

"Further along this southeast line is the Hall of Invocation-Evocation Magic. It looks like a dragon and the main entrance is through the dragon's gaping mouth. Now, on southeasterly is the bottom east corner of the pentagram of buildings, the Administration Hall." They walked along the bottom of the pentagram of buildings past the Infirmary building, which looked like a norm hospital. Continuing eastward, they got to the bottom east corner building. "Here is the Hall of Necromancy, the dark arts, entirely black." Stone serpents climbed up the walls on either side of the doors.

Human skeletons were carved into the stone walls at periodic intervals.

They continued northeastward. "Here is the Hall of Divination Magic." It looked like a crystal ball sitting in the ground, a giant translucent sphere rising from the ground. On northeastward, they came to the Hall of Abjuration Magic, which always looked like a miniature castle. "Now over there are the Dark Woods. See this dense patch of woods here? It stretches from here all the way to the mountainside and all the way down to the outer ramparts wall that surrounds Bradbury. It is dangerous, primarily because wild animals sometimes come down from the mountains around us."

"Now on northward and all the way to the eastern ramparts wall are the Formal Gardens. This is one really cool place to spend time," Lindsey explained. A little further along, they came upon the easternmost corner building. "Here is the Hall of Charm and Enchantment Magic. It looks like a small English cottage, but that is only its enchantment. Inside it is really large."

From here, they moved northwest. "Here is the Hall of Conjuring and Summoning." It resembled a Greek building with many marble columns and arches. Part was out in the open, part was enclosed.

"Now in bad weather, we all use the extensive underground tunnel system." They led the students down the stairs beside the dining room. At this huge hub, the many tunnels were clearly labeled with large signs. Five could walk abreast in here. Periodic lamps provided good illumination vast tunnel network connecting all the buildings on campus. "The outer line of tunnels goes from building to building in a giant pentagram of tunnels. However, there are numerous cross tunnels, the shortcuts, as we call them. Right here is the most confusing location on campus, the tunnel hub underneath our dorm." The hub was an underground room nearly as large as their dining hall above them. All around the perimeter of the room shortcut tunnels sprang; all twelve of them were clearly labeled. Hence, one could not get too lost down here.

Finally, Lindsey, Pam, and Fern got some time to visit

their own rooms. "We are in Number 20 this year," Pam announced as they reached their room. Fern was in Number 14. "Oh, it looks like we are five to a room this year," she added when they entered. Pam checked her room assignments and smiled. "Kathy is back in with us this year." Lindsey smiled. She liked having Pam, Ashley, Amanda, and Kathy as her roommates. The two set about organizing their many possessions.

"How come every year our stuff seems to multiply?" Lindsey asked, remembering her first year here, when she had only one small backpack to her name. Now she unpacked nine large duffle bags, including the briefcase closet that Nadia had given her. Pam chuckled.

An alarm sounded, "Let's get a move on it. Another bus is coming, more students," Pam announced. She cast her Magical Door spell, and Fern, Lindsey, and she stepped through it, coming out beside the main gate. Only now did Pam survey the names of the new arrivals on this new listing. She let out a squeal of surprise. "Tom's on the list! He's supposed to be in Phoenix!"

Just then, Tom hopped off the bus. He was sitting at the very front to be sure he was off first, hoping that Pam would be waiting for him. "Hey Pam. Surprised to see me?"

Pam flushed, but recovered her poise quickly, "Sure am. How come?" She didn't get to finish.

Tom quickly explained as the other students clambered off the bus. "I used some of my money to help defray the cost of coming here to finish magic school. Mom said I could, if I paid the difference myself. I wanted to be with you." Now it was his turn to flush, but he said what he had intended to say. "You are the greatest, and I just have to be around you, Pam. Hope you don't mind."

"Cool, Tom. Great. Perfect in fact. Oh, I'd best be doing my Floor Monitor duties," Pam quickly saw the many students were now waiting on her. After the bags were moved to their rooms, Fern led the way with the first years, so that Pam could walk along with Tom. Emilio, who was in charge of the boys, walked ahead with Fern. Lindsey brought up the rear with ten more transfer students, though she smiled when Tom took

Pam's hand.

That afternoon was filled with orientation duties. The students had to get their schedules, their books, their supplies, their new computers, and their cell phones. Lindsey was very glad that there were more Floor Monitors than normal, since there just had to be many more students this year than last.

All the next day, Lindsey, Pam, and Fern were kept busy with the new students. Each had to be shown around the campus and walked through their class schedules, until they were satisfied that each new student could find their way from class to class. Then, it all had to be redone using the tunnel system. Finally, that second evening, Pam fixed up Tom's computer, though he had already done much of it himself. Then, she fixed up Ahana's computer and finally Orenda's. "There, now you can send cell phone photos to your computer with the push of a button. Also they boot up faster, without all that extra overhead of stuff you don't need."

"How about showing me around the Formal Gardens?" Tom asked shyly. Pam grinned, suspecting there was more to it than a walk. She agreed, but found that Ahana and Amanda were also heading there along with Deiter and Lindsey. The three couples walked among the flagrant flowers of late summer, as the sun hung low in the west. One by one, the guys led their girlfriends apart from the others, until Pam found herself alone with Tom.

"I'm in love with you, Pam," Tom whispered. "When I saw you on that dance floor at the Presidential Ball, I nearly fainted. I think you are the greatest young woman in this entire world. I just had to be with you, no matter what. I hope you don't think I'm being too forward, Pam. Emilio's been filling me in. I'm sorry that Monique isn't here with you anymore." Pam looked at him, and a sly grin came over her face. "What?" he asked, blushing.

"I'll bet you're not sorry Monique isn't here. I, well, you know, I'd be with her and not you." His face turned even redder. "But I've somehow changed since then, Tom. I'll bet anything that Ace fellow is courting her now. Besides, when I was dancing that night with you, I felt different. Tom, you make me feel really special, just like Monique used to do."

Tom's face broke into a smile. He gently pulled her close to him, and the two passionately embraced. Not far away, the other two couples were doing the same thing. Only when the sun set did the six head back to the dorm.

The Floor Monitors were busy again. Many buses brought all the other returning students back several days earlier than normal, which had been the practice since security had been heightened four years ago, just after the prison escape of Dominus. Finally, everyone was on campus. That evening, the full faculty met the returning students at the first formal dinner. Lindsey was sure that the dining hall had been enlarged. At least one more row of tables had been added to each hall's tables. There seemed to be many more students piling into the dining hall tonight.

Soon well over eight hundred students, their Floor Monitors, and the Hall Mothers and Hall Fathers gathered at the five different colored tables. All eyes started at the long table at the head of the dining room.

Sixteen adults sat at the professor's table, they were discussing things among themselves. All student eyes focused on the man in the middle, the oddly dressed man in his fifties, Governor Alister Broadwell. While everyone else wore their wizard robes, he was dressed in an out of style, by several hundred years, black business suit complete with a top hat that a norm magician might use to pull a hare out of a hat. Lindsey noted that he wore the same outfit at the start of every term.

Lindsey had grown to love his kindly look, with his black moustache and goatee beard and long sideburns. She noticed this year that he had twinges of grey in his hair and beard. To her, his eyes looked very tired. At last, he rose, and a complete silence fell in the dining room. Alister spoke clearly and slowly, as if each word held some kind of magical power behind it. Lindsey realized it was nearly the same speech she had heard during her first year here.

"Fellow professors, Hall Mothers and Fathers, Floor Monitors, and first year students, welcome to Orientation Week at Arthur Bradbury's School of Magic. I am the Governor, that's head man to you students. . ." That last was a sort of joke, and the many adults present chuckled.

"I am Governor Alister Broadwell, and it is my pleasure to welcome everyone to yet another term at Bradbury's, even if it is in these most terrible and difficult of times. You must forgive my appearance. I have just come from an important meeting with the Department of Defense. Dominus Malefic, alias Simon Mac Fluide, continues to give everyone the willies."

"I assure you all that you are all going to be quite safe here at Bradbury's. I know that you have heard that we were the target of several bombings in years past, but I point out that not a single student suffered any permanent damage. There will be none of those diabolical pills Dominus is handing out in New York on this campus, not as long as I am alive."

He grinned broadly and said, "Now Professor Elaine Mac Elroy, your English and Literature teacher, has accused me of not being romantic enough, so I dressed for this occasion. How is this, Elaine?" He looked at one of the older teachers, who grinned back and shook her greying head at him. Lindsey realized that she too was growing older. "Oh, you mean I am several centuries off?" Now the whole group of teachers chuckled. Even Lindsey smiled, for he did look terribly old fashioned, but it was the same joke he had played each year.

"Ah, then how's this?" He waved his hand and in a flash, he was wearing his wizard robes, looking much like the other teachers.

Alister continued, "Ah, still not romantic enough for the professor, so try this." He waved his hand and thousands of small candles burst into flames high over the heads of everyone, while the normal lights turned off. The room took on a distinctive yellowish glow, a warm glow at that. Several students cheered and broke out into a clap.

"Allow me to introduce our faculty to you," Alister continued. "Starting here on my right is Professor Blake Smith, Conjuring-Summoning. Girls. You have no doubt noticed just how handsome Professor Blake is, but unfortunately, he is married to Professor Janice Smith, sitting next to him. She is your Charm-Enchantment teacher. She also will be teaching you your Grade 0 and 1 level spells this year. She is also in charge of the Red Hall." Lindsey looked at her. She continued to present the appearance of a glamor queen or model. However, her smile appeared forced or faked, even more so this year. Lindsey wondered if all this Dominus business was finally impinging on her.

"Next to her is Professor Jerry Thalmus, Abjuration. He also will be your History of Magic teacher and is the head of Blue Hall." He looked to be around fifty years old, and was quite bored with this whole meeting. "Next to him is Professor Mary Ann Thornby, Divination." Her hair flew off in all directions, as if she'd just had an electric shock or something. She seemed very nervous. Lindsey could see her trembling slightly, which she now knew was normal. However, this year, Mary Ann seemed more nervous than ever before.

"Next to her is Professor Delius Dogs, Necromancy and head of Black Hall." He had a dark complexion and an antagonistic stare. However, he received a round of applause from the many Black Hall students. He managed a smile. "Next to him is Professor Arthur Thornby, Alteration, and head of Brown Hall." Several Brown Hall students clapped for him, but once again, Lindsey wondered why he was not sitting beside his wife.

"Now on my left is Professor Huan Su Sung, Invocation-Evocation, and beside him is Professor Cho Lin Sung, Illusions and head of Yellow Hall." Not to be outdone, those around the Yellow Hall including Lindsey began loudly clapping. Cho Lin looked directly at Lindsey for a moment and smiled, but also gave her a curious look. Lindsey wondered if she remembered seeing her head looking down on the school from the sky and the Beyond.

"Next to her is Professor Herbert Mac Elroy, your Math teacher. Students take note; he is not a wizard. He will tolerate no monkey business in his classroom. Next to him is Professor Elaine Mac Elroy, English-Literature; she is a witch, mind you." Several on the staff chuckled, but Lindsey wondered what was funny, and she still did not know the answer. This year, Lindsey noted that both he and his wife looked very old indeed. "He is now past retirement age," Pam whispered to her. Lindsey wondered if he was sticking around to see her class through their sixth year.

"Next to her is Professor Jasper Jones, Science. He is also not a wizard. Let me warn you all. Do not call either Professor Jones or Mac Elroy a norm or you will find yourself in detention." This was a stern warning.

"Next to him is our Librarian, Lillian Angel Jones, who will assist you in finding your research and study materials. She would like me to remind you that the library closes at ten p.m. Next to her is Doctor Frank Caterwall, our resident physician. Let us hope that none of you need to visit him this term." He grinned, and many chuckled, for who wanted to see a doctor? Andy now did, but for an entirely different reason. Frank taught his archaeology elective courses.

"Finally, at the far end are Hank and Betsy Walls, your PE teachers. New students," Alister winked at them and leaned forward as though he was letting them in on a secret, "let me warn you in advance, those two are fitness freaks! They are even trying to get me to lose some weight!" At that, the staff all chuckled.

"You see, Bradbury's has a very wide and talented set of professors, perhaps one of the best in the United States. I suspect that is because we are in the Rocky Mountains. After all, isn't this the vacation spot of the country?" Everyone chuckled.

"At this time, I would like to extend a warm, friendly welcome to all of those displaced New York and DC area students, who have transferred here to Bradbury's. As you may have guessed, we have more students than normal, which is why there are five to a dorm room in many cases. Let us all give a round of applause to welcome those who have transferred here." Lindsey clapped as loudly as everyone else did, making a ruckus to let them know that they were appreciated here, a nice gesture, she thought.

"In case you are interested, Bradbury's has accepted two hundred additional students over our normal maximum enrollment of six hundred. Your classroom sizes will be slightly larger this year, but the faculty assures me that this will not hinder them. Yes, times have worsened in our country.

However, always remember this, united, we are stronger than Dominus Malefic."

"Now then, on the announcement side, there will again be no National Track Meet this year. Same reason as last year, insufficient security. I'm sorry. On the lighter side, I am pleased to announce that for our Halloween Dance, you will have a live band, Eli's Rockers." He paused as the significance of his announcement sunk into the students. Suddenly, many girls let out shrieks of glee, while the boys clapped, stomped, and yelled their approval. Alister smiled broadly. "Let our feast begin."

Lindsey was now the Yellow Hall track and soccer team captain, compliments of Jim's last request as last year's captain. She took this opportunity to meet with her other team members whom she had not seen all summer. Dirk Dentwood, now a sixth year, was eating with his friends, when Lindsey came up to him. "Still planning on being on our track team this year, Dirk? Right forward position and the mile relay are yours if you want them."

"Hey Lindsey. Sure thing. We're still needing at least one more person, right?" he replied.

"Yes, we'll hold try outs on Saturday morning at ten. Spread the word. I really liked it last year when we had two on the bench to help. Maybe we can get some extras this year too." She moved on down the table to Lil Ames, a fellow fifth year.

"Hi Lil. How's your sister doing?" Lindsey asked. She had helped rescue Lil's older sister from the clutches of Dominus last year. He had worked his sadistic magic on her body, turning her into one of his play toys, until Lindsey and crew raided that house, freeing the prisoners and healing them.

"She's doing as well as can be expected. She doesn't trust men very much, still leery of men looking at her. The Security man is helping though. Thanks for everything, Lindsey."

"Cool. Say, you still on for track and soccer this year? You can have the left forward position and mile relay if you want them. We still need at least one more, though I'm hoping we can get a few more. It was great having two on the bench to help. I'm setting up tryouts for ten Saturday."

"Sure, thank. I'll be there. Sorry, don't know anyone who is interested, but I'll ask around," Lil volunteered.

Lindsey returned to her group and told the rest of her team the good news about Dirk and Lil. "Now we only need at least one more person—someone who can do the twenty mile relay."

"Good luck on that one," Emilio groaned. The runner had to race for five miles, grueling miles, as far as he was concerned. After supper, Lindsey and her friends congregated in the Yellow Hall study hall, comparing their class schedules.

```
 8:00 English Literature
 9:00 PE and First Aid
10:00 Advanced Earth Science
11:00 Beginning Calculus
 1:00 Spell Research I
 2:00 Potion Making II
 3:00 Spell Casting Grade 6
 4:00 Spell Casting Grade 6
 6:00 Elective
```

"Well, I am studying Egyptian archaeology as my elective," Andy told his friends. "I took a lot of pictures at my dig this summer. Anyone want to see them?" For a time, everyone watched his slide show on his computer, though no one was keen on seeing the old bones and pottery pieces. Still, the scenery captured their attention. Lindsey's elective was Dispeller Theory III; Pam's was Sleuthing Theory III; Ashley's was Divination Theory III; Amanda's, Tracking Theory III. Deiter, though a Black Hall student, joined them, along with Peaches, who now accompanied Andy wherever he went. Deiter proudly announced that his elective was Eliminator Theory I.

"Who's teaching you, Deiter?" Pam asked, very curious about this unexpected course of study.

"Dunno yet. Guess I'll find out Monday night. Guess you will be happy, since Professor Cho Lin is teaching our English Literature class, not Professor Elaine, who I expected would be teaching it. She's taught all the other English classes.

Just between us, I heard a rumor that both Mac Elroy's want to retire soon," Deiter answered her, but that raised even more interesting questions.

"I'm glad he is not retiring yet," Tom Ryker interrupted, "Professor Herbert Mac Elroy has offered to teach me Data Structures Programming as my elective! That's a college level course, way cool!"

For a time, they chatted about why they needed two class periods for spell casting. Pam's argument was adopted: the spells must be incredibly difficult to learn.

"Hey, did you see the announcement that Professor Delius put on the bulletin board?" Tom asked. "What's this about Mock Battles?" Pam explained them to him. "Way coolest! I'm off to sign up immediately! Best thing imaginable! Learn how to really fight back at Dominus!"

Saturday morning came at last. The decisive moment had come, as far as Lindsey was concerned. Would they be able to field a track and soccer team? Until last year when they had help from their foreign exchange students, Yellow Hall had barely made a team each year. Nine players were required.

Andy was their one hundred meter sprinter and goalkeeper. Fern and Emilio were two of the mile relay racers and played left and right midfield positions. Lil and Dirk were the other two of the mile relay racers and played left and right forwards on the soccer team. Amanda and Lindsey played center forwards and were two of the twenty-mile racers. Ashley was the third twenty-miler and played left fullback. They needed a right fullback and another twenty-mile racer. Lindsey and her crew arrived at the stadium fifteen minutes early.

Secretly, Lindsey kept her fingers crossed, praying that at least one more would show up. If not, she would have to try to find someone or forfeit their hall representation. As ten o'clock approached, they saw four walking towards them, all wearing track outfits. Lindsey held her breath.

When they walked up, she took charge. "Hi, I'm Lindsey Barron. Are you here to try out for Yellow Hall's team?"

None of the four had she seen before. Two were tall, African-Americans, twin sisters; she discovered that she could not tell them apart. One stepped forward offering her hand. "Hi, Venus Sams, second year from New York City. My sister, Ali. We were on the team last year."

"Hi, I am Alan Homes, second year and my friend Glen Welshby, first year. We're from Colorado Springs. We've been practicing all summer."

"Way cool! Thanks for coming," Lindsey said. She then introduced all the other team members, which took a few minutes. "I'll be frank and honest with you. We desperately need another twenty miler and to a much lesser extent a right fullback. However, if you all can pass muster, as far as I am concerned, you will all be on the team. Even if you are on the bench for a time, I promise you that everyone will get plenty of opportunities to race and play soccer. We took the Hall Cup in Soccer last year, and we aim to take it again this year, since the Nationals are out again."

"Yes, we saw your First Place race, Lindsey, on TV. Incredible race, but how did you ever manage to avoid being blown up?" asked Venus.

"Long story. I'll tell you all about it later. Right now, let's see what everyone can do. Lil's our sprinter. Andy, our goalkeeper, hates running, so he will be our timer. First, let's see the miler's race, and then we'll tackle the twenty-mile relay."

"Glen and I will try out for the mile relay," Alan said. "I don't think we can really do five miles." Lindsey accepted this, and she jogged to the finish line halfway around the track. Twice around was a mile. Each runner in the mile relay only had to race a quarter of a mile. Emilio, Fern, Lil, and Dirk took their positions. Alan and Glen joined them. Andy, holding a stopwatch, gave them a start.

As they crossed the finish line, Lindsey was not surprised to see Fern leading the pack. Next, came Lil and Dirk, evenly matched. To her surprise, Alan beat Emilio, with Glen coming in last. Puffing, Emilio called out, "Yes! Now you can replace me in the mile run. Alan can have my spot!" Lindsey chuckled and did just that.

"Okay, Emilio, but you are back up if any one of those four need help. Glen, you are second back up. I will still try to get you both into at least once competition this year, though. No sitting on the bench twiddling your thumbs." Both boys laughed.

Amanda, Ashley, Lindsey, Ali, and Venus warmed up for their five-mile run. Fern, clipboard in hand, became their official timekeeper. "Amanda is our finish runner. None here can take her, unless you two are hot runners, Ali, Venus."

"We know," Venus and Ali giggled, "we watched video replays when we learned that we were transferring here. Apache runners are hot. Let's do it!" Again, Andy gave them a starting count down, and the five runners took off.

After three miles, Ashley, seeing that both Ali and Venus were way ahead of her, dropped out of the race. "Yes! Now I can go back to running what I do best, the mile relay race." Fern giggled, glad that Ashley would be on her team again.

Venus and Ali kept the Apache pace for four miles before they began falling behind Lindsey and Amanda. The last half mile was the real test. As usual, Amanda easily edged out Lindsey by a good fifty feet. Both were several hundred feet ahead of the twins. Once they caught their breath, Lindsey yelled, "Yes! You are both our new twenty milers!" The twins pounded their fits into the air, a sign of victory on their part.

"Okay soccer time. What positions do you all feel you play best?" Lindsey asked.

After some discussion, Dirk decided to drop back and play right fullback, with Alan as his backup. Glen worked well as a middle fielder, while the twins were fierce competitors and ideal for forwards or for fullbacks, if the need arose. By eleven, they all headed back to the dorm for showers, yielding the field to Black Hall.

At this point, Deiter confiscated Ashley and the two headed off to play pool with Professor Jasper. Lindsey decided to fill Venus and Ali in on her many adventures. Alan and Glen chose to listen in as well. The small group sat around the dining hall sipping sodas, while Lindsey and Amanda told their stories. Lindsey wanted these new team members to have a good idea of her and her team mates.

Next, after lunch, she met with Hank and Betsy Walls,

along with the other four team captains, to work out the fall and spring match schedules. Hank had the sheets and explained, "As last year's winners, Yellow Hall gets to pick their play dates first. Lindsey, what will it be?"

Lindsey wanted to avoid playing in the cold, rain, snow, and mud. They'd done that already. "On the third Saturday of September, we'll take on Black Hall in track, and the fourth Saturday of September, we'll take on Blue Hall in soccer." The Blue Hall captain exclaimed, "Yes!" very glad to have a game not in the mud or snow.

Lindsey continued, "The first Saturday in May, we'll take on Brown Hall in track, and the second Saturday, we'll tackle Black Hall in soccer." The Black Hall captain also punched his hand in the air, pleased with Lindsey's choice. They would have their games in good weather.

As expected, at suppertime when Lindsey posted Yellow Hall's sports schedules, her team members cheered her. "Way to go, captain," Amanda exclaimed, "we are done after September and then only in May. Now we can put our attention onto these hard courses." Only Emilio groaned; he would have preferred as many distractions from schoolwork as possible.

Lindsey scheduled two practice sessions on the next two Saturdays and left the spring to take care of itself. Perhaps they wouldn't need any then. As she looked over her schoolbooks, she realized this year would be the hardest yet.

Chapter 10—Schoolwork Begins

"Welcome to English Literature class," Professor Cho Lin began promptly at eight on Monday morning. After introducing herself, she added, "I teach Illusion magic, music, and literature. This year we are exploring some of the greatest masterpieces of the world. We will begin with William Shakespeare and his famous *Romeo and Juliet*. You will need to read about thirty pages each night to keep up. During class, we will discuss what you have read. I will be evaluating your 'in class' answers as part of your grade. When each book is finished, you will have a comprehensive test over that masterpiece. Today, we are going to concentrate our studies on just why the characters are doing what they are doing, that is, the motivations behind their actions. Yes, this has everything to do with the situation today in our own country. You should look deep into the motivations behind other's actions. I guarantee you that all their motivations are age-old."

Lindsey noted an interesting thing on their way across the sunny campus. Andy and Peaches were holding hands, as were Amanda and Ahana, Pam and Tom, Kathy and Emilio, and even herself and Deiter. Strange how their lives were changing from her first year here. Pam commented, "What a relief! Finally, I have a class that will be extremely easy! Novels, yes!"

"Yes, but you are already a sleuth. You can figure all this stuff out. Think of the rest of us," complained Kathy. Lindsey giggled, but was glad Pam would have it easy, even if the rest of her friends didn't.

Betsy Walls explained, "This year we are going to learn how to play softball, at least while the weather cooperates. Then during the icy wintertime, we will take up your first aid training. As you can tell, we are running a combined PE class this year—that is two sections are meeting at the same time. This way, there will be enough players for two teams. Since Lindsey is the captain of the track team, I am appointing her the captain of one group, while Cyndi is captain of the second team. Now then, captains, choose your teammates, one at a time please." Cyndi was a Brown Hall girl whom had been in a different class section than Lindsey and her friends. Naturally, both began choosing those girls who were in their own section.

On their way to Advanced Earth Science class, Pam was exceedingly cheerful. "Golly, I finally have a PE class that I can enjoy!"

"Yes, but you mostly just stood around in right field," Amanda protested. "You didn't have much to do."

"Yes! That's the point!" Pam added. Everyone laughed. Pam was not into anything athletic, that was for sure.

"Welcome to Advanced Earth Science. I'm Professor Jasper Jones. Now that you have had your basic physics, chemistry, and biology classes, we can return to an in depth study of our own world. As you embark on learning the more powerful magical spells, many of which affect our physical world around us, it behooves you to know well how our world operates. Nothing acts *independent* of everything else. For example, without the sun drying the land, there would be terrifically lowered evaporation rates and thus less rain. If you raise the outside temperature worldwide by say ten degrees, what would be the result? Yes, Miss Betts?"

Pam's hand shot up like a rocket. "The polar ice caps and glaciers would melt, raising the sea level by several feet. This would drown many coastal cities, impacting millions upon millions of people."

"Precisely. Our world is a complex set of interactions, which we will be studying this year. Furthermore, each one of you will pick a specific aspect, a specific area of Earth Science that interests you in particular. You will be doing your own research into this area and writing a formal paper on your findings. During May, each one of you will give a thirty-minute presentation of your research project to the whole class. Fifty percent of your final grade comes from this research project and your presentation of it to the class." He paused while the class reacted, just as they did each year: moans, groans, cheers, and the whole spectrum.

"Now then, this first week we will review the major areas of Earth Science. On Monday, you must turn in to me a paper outlining what the topic of your research paper will be. After I review them, I will okay them, alter them, or reject them. Difficulty of the project plays a factor in the grading. That is, if you choose a trivial, simple project, then you had better produce stellar research, if you want a good grade. If you pick a particularly challenging bit of research, then you can get a good grade even if you don't totally succeed. Bear that in mind as you make your decisions. Mind you, that once I give my okay to your project, you cannot thereafter change it. Yes, you will be stuck with it. So class, give this project some serious thought this week!"

As they all walked upstairs for their math class, Emilio cheerily announced, "This will be a fun class. I already know what my research project will be about: rocketry. Woo hoo!"

"Yes, Emilio, we all know you had a blast making and launching rockets," Pam said sternly, "but this is a *research* project. You are going to have to do some *real* research. Rocketry can be very complex and mathematical, you know." Emilio refused to be disheartened, however, and entered math class smiling, for the first time in five years.

Herbert Mac Elroy, the aging math professor, began their next class. "Welcome to Beginning Calculus. I know that some of you dislike math, while others excel in it. As you know or suspect, I'm past the retirement age, but I've promised Alister to stick around through next year. So this year, I'm going to try something a little different—well, okay, *very* different."

"You see, like yourselves, I have been terribly worried about Dominus taking over control of our whole country. If all the math professors end up zombies, who will be left that can teach a new generation their math? I hope by now I have clearly shown each of you just how important a good understanding of math is in your lives. Yet I'm keenly aware that some of you have had a terrible time with these many math courses. I won't name names, as that is irrelevant. What is relevant is my goal for my last two years here. I want each and every one of you to be quite competent in math, to be able to use it to help you solve life's problems."

"After talking this over with my wife, I've decided what

must be done. Miss Townsend, I hope you don't mind my picking on you today. Back in geometry class, you ran into difficulty, which as I understand was handled by Miss Betts clearing up your confusion. You certainly greatly improved your math skills once that was straightened out. Since this phenomenon lies at the heart of what I'm attempting to do these next two years, I'll tell the whole class about that situation you faced, with your permission of course." Kathy grinned, nodding her approval; he had already spoken to her about it.

"Back in geometry, I gave out a problem called how to tell if two planes intersect. Miss Townsend said that was easy—just check with the air traffic controllers to see if two planes are too close to each other." The class giggled, but he only smiled and continued, "You see, her answer was perfectly correct. However, she was using the wrong definition of plane, airplane instead of a flat surface on which a straight line between any two points would lie. Using a wrong or only partially correct definition of the words of math will certainly lead to incorrect application."

"Today, each of you will take this comprehensive test that is designed to determine your weak points in math. Then, during the week, I'll meet with each one of you and work out a unique program of study for each of you. Our goal will be to have each one of you up to speed in math by the end of next year. As you take this exam, don't worry about not being able to answer some questions. You are not being graded at all on this test. Just do your best, and if you don't know the answer to a question, leave it blank." He passed out a very thick test booklet.

On their way to lunch, Deiter said, "Wow, that was really a hard test. I don't think I got half of them right. How about you, Lindsey?"

"I left way too many blank too. Maybe I'm not as sharp as I thought in math," Lindsey replied, a bit worried.

Pam broke in, "Well, I missed way too many too. I guess I really need some remedial help in math!" She looked dumb-stricken by her performance.

"Don't feel bad," Emilio added, "I will be lucky if I even

got a third of them done right. That was horrible."

All, however, were looking forward for the afternoon classes—all magic classes, especially their first one, Spell Research I. Professor Huan Su welcomed them, took roll, learning the names of the new students. "Traditionally, this class, Spell Research I, is taught in your sixth year. However, due to the country's current crisis, the administration has requested that this class be taught to fifth years around the country. You are very familiar with the traditional spells fully documented in the official Grades spell books. These are the agreed upon spells that every wizard and witch is taught in every magic school in the world."

"However, there are numerous other spells that have, for one reason or another, never found their way into these official books of Grade spells. For the most part, these are highly specialized spells, used in specific industries and for specific purposes. Outside of that industry, such spells have little use, which is why they are not contained in the official Grade books of spells."

"That said, Miss Betts has already had the opportunity to discover this for herself. She did a bit of valuable research this past summer, discovering the very spell that was used by Dominus to permanently bind those Dominus for President rings to the wearer's finger. Miss Betts, would you like to explain your findings for the class?"

Pam tried to hide, and no, she didn't like to explain it, but. . . "I went through the library and found that in the baking industry, they have a spell called Melt. When cast on say chocolate bits, they melt into the batter. This is the spell that 'melted' those rings onto their fingers. You see, Doctor Caterwall was able to push a sterile needle right through what had been the golden, solid ring before it was sub-dermal. The ring had been 'melted' into the body."

"Unfortunately, the reverse spell in the baking industry would not work to remove the rings. The Unmelt spell only solidified the melted bits, and then the bakers would use a fine sieve to remove the solid bits from the batter. I kept looking and discovered a Rise to Surface spell and then a Solidify spell. Combined, these two can be used to remove the rings." She did not explain that she had also used that combination to remove the melted corset around Nadia's waist. That was much too personal to reveal.

"Precisely so and very well done and researched, Miss Betts. This is the aim and goal of this class. Each of you will spend hours in the library researching all the specialized spells that you can find. The real problem is that no one has *ever* bothered to catalogue all these spells. Hence, it takes much research to uncover them. Some will be simple spells, bordering on Grade 0 useful spells in terms of difficulty. Others, well, let's say some will be very challenging indeed to master. Your task this year is to begin to construct your own listing of all these spells. One day, your list may prove invaluable to you."

"The format will be the spell's name, the reference in which you found it, the specialty area in which it is used, and a description of what the spell does. You may also find it useful, but not required, to write down all the details of its casting."

"Each day, I will look over your results of the previous day before sending you off to the library. Yes, most of this hour you will be spending in the library. At the end of each term, I will give you a test. I'll explain the details of that later on. So wizards and witches, let's get to work. Off to the library we go."

"Super terrific!" exclaimed Pam, as they headed over to the library, choosing to walk outside on such a nice day.

"This sounds like fun," Lindsey added, wondering if there was ranching or horse breeding spells that she could discover and perhaps learn to help more around the ranch.

On their way to Potion Making in the Hall of Necromancy, Kathy was enthusiastic about the past hour. "Do you realize that there are dozens and dozens of useful spells to help around the kitchen? Incredible! We've just got to learn some of these!"

"Well, I found a Glue spell for rockets!" Emilio proudly announced to everyone.

"Wish we had known about that one when we were making our rockets," Kathy answered. "Perhaps then my fins would not have fallen off." Emilio chuckled.

However, the group's mood sobered as they approached

the somber building with zombies and skeletons etched into the stone facade. Most all hated these dark arts, save the Black Hall students. Even Kathy was more subdued, though she loved and excelled in Potion Making last year.

Professor Delius barked, "Doom and gloom it is, students. This is Potion Making II, a class many of you will fail entirely. This year, the potions are vastly more difficult, but exceedingly more powerful than preventing one from sneezing. Those of last year may be considered trivial compared to this year's potions. Yes, Miss Barron, this year you will be learning how Dominus Malefic created that potion from your DNA, which allowed him to pass himself off as you on this campus for an indefinite time. Our Morph spell lasts only for a short duration, unlike this potion which lasts for a full day, before more potion must be consumed."

"Unlike the easy potions of last year, this time there are only twenty-five to learn to make each term. Your final each term will be as last year. I'll hand out a potion, and you have the class period to make it. Open your book to page one and begin." Delius didn't even bother to ask if there were any questions.

Halfway through the period, the vapors in the room were noxious to Lindsey, who couldn't wait for the class to end. However, Ashley looked up suddenly. She had been pouring in the twenty-five milliliters of water when she had another premonition. Quickly, she sent a message to Professor Delius, who acted at once.

"Lyle! Do not pour that liquid into your brew!" he bellowed so loudly that the entire class stopped and stared at Lyle, who was just about to add his carefully measured liquid. "Miss Stokes-Compton suggests that if you pour it in, it will explode. Now what have you measured in that vial?"

"W-water, sir!" Lyle stumbled, embarrassed once again. Potion making was not his cup of tea, either.

"Where did you get it?"

"From that bottle, see, it's labeled H_2O_2, water," Lyle explained, wondering what was going to happen.

Delius thrust his hands through his well-oiled hair in despair. "Lyle, did you flunk chemistry entirely? That is the formula for peroxide, not water!"

Even more red-faced, Lyle said meekly, "Oh."

"If you add peroxide to that brew, it will most certainly explode in your face. Do you have a death wish son? Pour it out and add water this time." Delius looked utterly exasperated, but sent Ashley a thank you message, causing her to grin.

Lindsey was very glad finally to be walking over to the Hall of Alteration for Spell Casting class. Her potion had been a dismal failure. "How on earth can we possibly make such a complicated potion in only fifty minutes?" Lindsey complained.

"Dunno, I didn't get mine done either," Pam admitted. "This is going to ruin my grade point average when I flunk Potion Making II," she said dejectedly.

"Well, mine turned out passable, but only a B," Kathy added. "I know that I was the only one to turn one in for a grade today. I'll just have to do better than that tomorrow." Pam threw her a dirty look.

"Welcome to Spell Casting Grade 6. I am Professor Arthur Thronby, for those of you who are new to Bradbury's. There are more alteration based Grade 6 spells than any other type, hence I am your beginning professor. Near the end of the term, Professor Jerry Thalmus, Abjuration, will take over until Christmas."

"As you have probably been wondering all summer, let me explain why there are two consecutive class periods devoted to learning these new spells. They are all complex and difficult to learn. Some of you may not succeed in learning some of these new spells, though I expect that you will make every attempt to learn them. Passing standard is to be able to cast three-quarters of the spells in your book. Yes, this year, the spells are much more difficult to master. As last year, as you master a spell, it will be noted in your grade book. There will not be a comprehensive final in which you must cast all the spells as you did for Grade 1. Some of these are quite deadly in their effect. Hence, we must take great care this year to make sure none of you are harmed."

"Today, we are going to learn the Disarm spell, a spell

which, when successful, removes the wand or staff from the hands of your opponent. Open your books to page one, and let's get started. Yes, Miss Betts?"

"Professor, is there any defense against this spell? I mean if Dominus casts it on me, do I automatically lose my wand?"

"First, we will learn to cast the spell successfully. Then, yes, we will learn to defend against this spell. If one is aware that the spell is coming, he or she stands a good chance of avoiding it. If taken by surprise, he or she will most certainly lose their wand. Now let's begin. Do not expect to succeed with this spell today. It takes an enormous amount of conviction on your part, as you are overriding your opponent's conviction that he or she is holding onto their wand or staff."

As they broke up into pairs, Lindsey again saw something completely unexpected happening. Deiter came over to be her partner, not Amanda, who went to Ahana's side. Pam and Tom paired up, as did Kathy and Emilio. Ashley and Audrey still were paired as usual, though. Their boyfriends were not in this class.

"Wand motion is a decisive jerk to the right," Deiter read aloud to Lindsey. Both practiced the motion. "Honestly, Lindsey, this doesn't seem all that hard. Let's try it. I'll go first, and see if I can disarm you, okay? Then, if something goes wrong, I'll look like the fool, not you."

Lindsey smiled; what a change in Deiter! Their first year, Deiter make a joke for the whole class over everything that Lindsey had done. Now he was protecting her. She took her position, pointing her wand at him. "Remember, Deiter, conviction. Concentrate on being really convinced that my wand will leave my grip," she coached.

Around them, both heard the sounds of others making their first attempts, "Disarm Ashley. Disarm Pam," and so on. Deiter concentrated, made the jerking motion, calling out, "Disarm!" His wand activated. The results shocked the entire class.

Instantly, Lindsey's wand flew out of her hand and halfway across the room! Not only that, but also every other student in the class, some thirty-three of them, had their wands fly out of their hands, scattering all over the room! Utter silence fell in this room in the Hall of Alteration!

Professor Arthur lost his wand as well, but he stood there mouth open, gaping at Deiter. He recovered first, "Mr. Cross, you need to be a bit more specific in whom you wish disarmed. It seems that you have just set two new school records. One, for being able to cast this new spell after about five minute's study, and two, for disarming the entire class. Can anyone see where my wand went to?"

Chaos ensued, as everyone scrambled around the room trying to find their wands. Five minutes later, the class was back to normal. Deiter tried it again, being very specific this time, "Disarm Lindsey!" Again, she lost her wand. After she retrieved it, Deiter said, "Now you try it. Make sure you use my name. That was really embarrassing."

"Yes, but think of it, Deiter! You disarmed the entire class! That has to be very important. Okay, okay. I'll give it a go." Lindsey made the motions with her wand until she felt comfortable doing so. "Disarm Deiter!" His wand flew across the room, just as hers had.

Professor Arthur stared at her, noting that she had done it on her first try. He watched as she did it a second time, then he came over to the pair. "Excuse me, but have you two been practicing this spell during the summer, before class?"

His face becoming red, Deiter said, "Er, no professor. I didn't even open this spell book until today. They all looked so hard, so I didn't bother to even read up on them."

"You Lindsey?" Professor Arthur asked.

"No sir. I've been too busy doing other things all summer. Besides, these are supposed to be really hard spells, and I wanted to wait until class time to try. We know we can get into awful troubles if we goof some up before we learn them, like the Teleport spell," Lindsey answered truthfully.

"Incredibly amazing, you two. I don't understand this, but continue, you are doing it perfectly, if only a couple of days too soon. Carry on." He left, scratching his head, puzzled by this strange turn of events.

Ten minutes later, Pam finally got her first chance to try the spell on Tom. He'd been hard at work trying to disarm

174

Pam, but failing, as expected. Pam gave the brisk wand movement and called out, "Disarm Tom!" His wand flew across the room, shocking both Pam and him. Professor Arthur just shook his head in complete disbelief. Three had this spell down almost from their first attempt! How could this be possible? He sent a Message to Governor Alister.

For thirty students, this was a frustrating two hours of failed attempts. However, near the very end, both Tom and Ashley finally had their wands activating and disarmed their partners one time. For Deiter and Lindsey, after the first half hour, both had it down perfectly and became bored.

"Say, Deiter, let me practice this sans wand, sans words, shall we?" Lindsey suggested. Eagerly, he agreed, watching her carefully in an attempt to see how this was done. He, like everyone else, knew that next year, as sixth years, they would finally get the chance to see if they could learn to cast a spell this way, though most would be utterly unable to do so. Deiter watched Lindsey intently, but saw nothing at all, except his wand leaving his hand.

After Lindsey did it a half dozen times, Deiter finally said, "How do you do that? Maybe I can learn how to do it your way. I don't see you doing anything at all. I've been watching you like a hawk."

"I don't know if you can do it. I mean when I had no hands, magical energies just trickled off the ends of my arms. I rather think that may have played a role in my being able to do these as I do them, but let's try anyway. I think you are pretty convinced that your wand needs to activate for the spell to work."

Sheepishly, he agreed with her. She suggested, "Okay, so let's see if you can disarm me without saying the words. Concentrate on the desired result. Picture it in your mind, and then wave your wand properly, Deiter." The two worked on this. By the end of the double class, Deiter cast his first spell sans words. He was jumping for joy, telling everyone about his incredible success. Professor Arthur again Messaged Alister about this even stranger turn of events in his class.

At seven that night, everyone finally gathered in Yellow Hall study hall. Many were just returning from their elective class. "You will not believe who is my teacher for Eliminator Theory I!" exclaimed Deiter, as he raced out of breath into their study hall from his class in the Hall of Necromancy.

"Out with it," Pam declared flatly. "I have been wondering that one all summer long." Everyone else stopped and listened for his reply.

"Your Aunt Wilma! She's my teacher. Incredible. I would never have predicted she would know anything about it, but she sure knows her stuff! Wow." Pam smiled; she didn't dare tell Deiter that he was studying under the famous Rat Pack Eliminator Bill West!

"Well, it seems that I've exhausted all that Alister knows about Tracking Theory," Amanda added. "So now my Aunt Monane is now helping me with the more practical applications. Really super cool." Again, she didn't dare tell the others that her aunt was really the Rat Pack Tracker Able Monument.

"Dispeller Theory is going to be even harder than before," Lindsey admitted. Delius was having her attempt nearly impossible things, as far as she was concerned. "He wants me to react faster than I can react." No one really understood what she was talking about, but they sympathized with her nevertheless.

Ashley said little about her new Divination Theory class with Professor Mary Ann. Tonight, Mary Ann had tested her skills from all previous lessons, and she had done well. "Now we are going to embark on a new phase of your training, the practical side. Let's focus on those people who are teleporting the Aetna drugs from their manufacturing plant to the distribution sites in New York. See if you can discover when someone is going to make a trip and their destination point and time of departure."

Professor Mary Ann then explained that she would forward that information on to others in the Rodents Pack. She didn't say who, but she was in direct contact with Field Marshall Erin Saks of the Idaho Red Brigade Militia, who intended to take action based upon these premonitions. Mary Ann and Erin decided to try to make a dent in the delivery of the pills, hoping to slow down the Health Care operation a bit.

In turn, this would give Ashley a lot of experience in knowing what others were planning and when. This ability would ultimately be the most critical of all, if Dominus was ever to be captured again. This was precisely what Mabel Pruit, the deceased Rat Pack Diviner, excelled at when she helped bring him down many years ago. However, if things went wrong, it would be on Mary Ann's head, not Ashley's.

Around eight, Pam declared, "Well, there that's done. I was an idiot today. Now I have to go back to the Library and redo all my spell research notes!"

"Huh? Why?" asked Tom. "I thought you had a nice list, Pam."

"Yes, but think about it, Tom. We ought to have a full and complete catalogue of these spells. I've made an Access database for mine. I've added a column for the type of spell, such as alteration, a column for estimated Grade. Honestly, we should write out everything we need to learn to cast each spell. Who knows when we might just need to cast one of these, like Rise to Surface and Solidify. Besides, I think that all these spells should be documented fully in some book. Maybe I can publish just such a book later on. You coming Lindsey, Deiter?"

"Coming," Lindsey packed up her laptop and followed Pam. Deiter was right on her heels, completely baffled why Lindsey was suddenly going with Pam to the library. Once the three were outside and away from the ears of others, Pam began whispering.

"Don't you think it was more than a little weird today in Spell Casting? I mean, it was just us three who were able to do it and do it in record setting time, to say nothing of Deiter's mass disarm. That was mighty cool, by the way, Deiter." He stood very straight. Pam just gave him a compliment!

"Yes, really strange. Deiter even got it sans words," Lindsey replied.

"Well, it is conviction based, and we three have been to the Beyond, now haven't we. We three picked up the Make Permanent spell too. I think that there is a strong connection between these spells and our having gone to the Beyond. However, I really do think we need to get all the details of all these new specialty spells into our laptop databases. Honestly, after next year, we won't have access to such a library as this one, at least not easily." Both agreed with her and followed her lead, adding all the information that they had not copied down earlier today to their own new spells database.

Later, Pam fell asleep reading *Romeo and Juliet*. This was going to be an arduous semester for her; she just knew it. She barely finished the required pages over breakfast.

In Beginning Calculus class, Professor Herbert looked more tired than ever. "Been up most of the night evaluating your skill levels. I believe that it will take me longer to setup each of your individual programs than I originally thought. Until I can get with you personally, continue working through chapter one. Miss Betts, I have your results first. If you will come here, I will go over it with you."

"See, I told you I bombed it badly," she whispered to Tom and Lindsey, as she dutifully walked to his desk, ready to accept her disgrace in math.

"According to your results, Miss Betts, you are far more advanced than the others in this class. You should skip the first fifteen chapters of the calculus book; start off on chapter sixteen today. If you run out of chapters, before the end of the year, I'll get you going on Intermediate Calc, getting a head start on next year's work." Pam stared at him in total disbelief.

"But I thought I flunked it. I missed so many questions, professor," she protested.

"Pam, if you had gotten all those questions correct, you would be finished with next year's math class as well!"

"Oh!" she exclaimed, suddenly realizing what he was saying and what the test was measuring. Calmly, she went back to her seat and opened her book to chapter sixteen. Ah, these problems were much more to her interest than all those elementary review questions back in chapter one.

He called Lindsey up next. "You are doing very well excepting when adding fractions, such as $5/8 + 1/3$. Yet, you are very good at basic algebra. Here's an alternative way to handle it. Obviously, we need to get the denominators the same so we can then add the numerators together." Lindsey nodded, to her, this was all a mystery; one had to sit back and guess things until it worked out. "Let's put it in algebra terms, shall we?" He wrote out:

5x/8x + 1y/3y

"Now we know that when we choose the right x and y, then 8x = 3y. Solve for x and we get x = 3y/8. Now let y be 8 so the 8's cancel out, leaving x = 3. Put them back into the fractions. 5*3/(8*3) + 1*8/(3*8) and we have it solved: 23/24."

"Oh, then there is no mystery here!" Lindsey exclaimed. "I kept trying to multiply the two divisors together, but that didn't always work out. I thought it was just a guessing game of sorts."

"Here, try this one: 5/8 + 3/16," he suggested.

Hastily, Lindsey wrote out 8x = 16y. "Oh, that becomes just x = 2y so if y is 1, x is 2 and we get 10/16 + 3/16. It's not a guessing game this way, is it?"

"No, not at all. Here, I want you to do these two pages of review problems. Then, you can safely begin chapter one of the Beginning Calculus text. Other than this lowest common denominator problem, you are right up to where you should be, Lindsey." She thanked him and returned to work on her new problems, finding them now vastly simpler to work out, now that the wild guessing game had vanished.

One by one, over the next few days, Professor Herbert did the same with the other thirty-three students. He handled those in the best shape first, knowing that students like Emilio and Kathy would require much more of his time. They had many out points in their math skills, and he was determined to remedy every one of them.

In science class, Emilio was the first to turn in his proposed research project. To his and everyone else's surprise, especially Pam's, Jasper accepted it, "Very nice idea, Emilio. Go for it."

"What're you doing?" Pam insisted on knowing, as they headed for lunch.

"The design of a self-sufficient desert ecosystem. I got the idea from helping R. B. and you building the new homes this summer. I like the desert anyway," he replied. Pam was awe struck that Emilio had really chosen a valuable line of research. She'd expected something silly about rocket designs.

Andy chose one related to his love of archaeology: rock identification as a method of dating strata. Tom chose to attempt to create a computer simulation of climate changes and its impact on the environment. Kathy's project would try to answer: Does the weather affect personality? Audrey chose to study plants and their reaction to light and stress. Lindsey finally settled on answering: Is there any real difference between organically grown food versus commercially grown using pesticides and growth formulas? Amanda went with an analysis of the aftermath of the hurricane that Dominus parked over the southeastern part of the country. Ahana chose to answer the question: What role does music play in human culture? He was stretching the envelope just a bit, however. Ashley went with the long-term effects of the de-forestation of the Amazon.

Pam just couldn't decide what to do. As the end of the week approached, all of her friends had made their decisions and gotten the go ahead from Jasper. She was one of the last students who had not yet made a choice. At the very last minute, she finally decided on the migratory paths of birds: genetics, inheritance, or learned.

In Spell Casting, by the end of the week, everyone had the Disarm spell down pat and most could resist its effect on them, as long as they knew it was coming. The second week of September, they tackled their next spell, the creation of a Fog of Death. Similar to their lower grade poisonous gas cloud, this time the distribution means was a dense fog, but the poisonous aspects were much greater. Professor Arthur had everyone stay continually alert for changes in the wind while they cast the spell. Each partner was charged with creating a wind gust, should the fog start to drift toward the line of students standing outside and casting away.

While Lindsey and many others did not like this spell, she found it useful to remove insect infestations in gardens. It obviated the need for pesticides, Pam explained. The third week was even tougher as they began to learn how to Control the Weather. At first, they were only able to make small changes to whatever the weather was each day that they practiced it. However, by the end of the week, they were able to make more substantial changes. Pam noted that the spell's effects were nothing like those that the Crown of Moses had caused. Why the top wizards thought that this spell was being used to keep the hurricane stationary was beyond her grasp. It was folly.

The last week of September was at least interesting. They learned how to cast Transparency. This spell temporarily turned solid objects into a transparent glass-like window so that they could see through it. They practiced the spell on the walls of the campus. Pam pointed out that if they used it to, say, spy on Dominus, it would be obvious, since, if the window allowed light to pass through to their eyes, it also allowed the outside light to shine inside. This was not going to be a "spy" type of spell.

Quickly, the group adapted to the demands of their course load. Each evening, they worked until nine together in the study hall and then headed off to the library to continue their various researches. Most chose to try to keep up on their heavy literature reading assignments just before going to bed. Often, however, they fell asleep while reading and then frantically tried to finish while eating breakfast. Indeed, fifth year was proving to be the worst yet in terms of their workload, just as Monique and Jim had told them.

During October, Lindsey learned the fundamental spell behind R. B.'s fancy digging machines, the ability to magically Move Earth. Next, the spell that was used to help free a nearly drowning Governor Alister, Part Water, was learned. These first two months everyone struggled to grasp these more involved, complex spells.

What of the sporting events? Yellow Hall easily beat Black Hall in their first track meet of the year. Their uneventful race was won with uneventful times. Their twenty-mile relay race time was substantially slower that it had been when Tom and Jim were on the team. Nevertheless, both twins proved to be excellent runners, matching those of Black Hall, allowing Lindsey and then Amanda to pull out in front.

The soccer game against Blue Hall the following Saturday was exciting but lopsided. Yellow Hall won easily.

True to her word, Lindsey allow each player to play at least half of the game, giving all valuable experience. Their workload was so great that most of Lindsey's group didn't even go to the other Saturday races or games. In truth, Lindsey found herself fully engrossed in her many subjects. They were becoming fascinating indeed, particularly the spell research project.

Chapter 11—The Pilot Program Report

The third weekend in October President Missy Snow's official National Health Care Pilot Program Report was made public. Much fanfare and debate accompanied its release. For days, the report was the sole topic on all news channels. The President herself broke the news in a live press interview. The whole school watched as she addressed the nation. In fact, viewer statistics recorded an all-time high in viewer-ship, approaching ninety percent of all households!

Speaking in the now familiar monotone of the automatons that the norm pills created, President Missy Snow began reading the report. Obviously some wizards or witches had written the speech for her, as she was now only capable of reading it. Her independent thought, gone.

"My fellow Americans, it is with the greatest of personal satisfaction and honor that I, your duly elected President, stand before our beloved nation today to outline the major findings from our National Health Care Program Pilot. As you know, the state of New York and the DC area became the first in our country to have my plan fully and completely implemented. For the last three months, I have had medical doctors and many others closely watching and observing the program and the effects it has had on our wonderful people in these two areas of America."

"I thought that the Big Apple ought to be one of the first cities to reap the full benefits of the health care plan. Today, the results are in, tabulated and cross-checked. The full report covers some three hundred pages, in which all aspects of the plan have been studied and analyzed in depth. I'm sure that you don't want me to stand here and read those to you." Missy flashed a fake smile at this point, as if rehearsed, and an applause machine added some chuckles and clapping in the background, totally fake sounding.

"Let me highlight the results for you. Here is a graph

representing the number of patients who needed hospitalization for whatever reason. On the left side are the numbers for all these two areas combined starting on January of this year. The pilot began in July. Notice the steeply descending line. Here on the right are the total numbers in all hospitals. Yes, it is ten people. Tens of thousands a month to ten. Incredible, beyond words, indescribable."

"This graph shows the number of combined doctor visits to all the various specialty doctors. As many of you know, after visiting your family physician, you get referred to many specialists. The graph combines all the doctor visits for each month. Again, you can see the numbers are in the hundreds of thousands at the start of the year. Here in September, barely twenty had to visit a doctor. Of those, most were accidents, such as falling and breaking an arm or leg. Impressive beyond words."

"As you know, drugs are a multi-billion dollar a year industry. This graph shows the millions of pills dispensed by various doctors and pharmacies. Notice that by the end of September, that number has decreased to nearly zero as well. Not included, of course, are the special pills that are a part of this program."

"This next chart represents the monetary savings. Please notice that during the three months of the pilot program, nearly a billion dollars in health care and related drug costs were not incurred by the citizens of New York and DC. Yes, we did not spend almost a billion dollars that would have been spent had they not been on this pilot program, one billion dollars!"

"Bottom line: the citizens of New York and DC are now totally healthy, disease free, able to work, and have saved a fortune in medical costs! But there is more, much more."

"The unemployment rate is shown in this next graph. By September, the unemployment rate is zero. Not one worker in these two test areas is jobless! Everyone is pitching in, working and earning for themselves and their families. No other city or state can boast such statistics!"

"All of this has come about through my National Health Care Program combined with the discovery of the new wonder drug by Aetna Pharmaceuticals, a subsidiary of Mac Fluide Enterprises. Kept under tight wraps until today, I am pleased to announce to the world their revolutionary new drug discovery, called Saude Dourada! This new wonder drug, combined with my Health Care Program, which guarantees every citizen complete and free health care, is responsible for this incredible result. Aetna has been donating all doses of this miracle drug free of charge to all citizens of New York and DC, these past three months."

"Yet, there has been an unexpected side-effect. This new miracle drug reverses criminality. Yes, you heard me. This next chart shows the crime rates over the last few years countrywide. In red is the crime rate for the test area. Notice that it is steeply dropping each month. I am now proud to announce that the crime rate is nearly zero at the end of the test period!"

"In fact, the many prisons in New York State now sit empty. Yes, empty. Every last inmate has been rehabilitated and is now working hard at his or her new job. Zero repeat offenders. Once on Saude Dourada, the criminals totally change their ways. Incredible, but true. Yes, this aspect has been very, very carefully watched by the Department of Law, I assure you. For the first time in the history of New York City, it is safe to walk down any street in any location at any time of day. In fact, I did just that last week, took a long stroll at night through Central Park. No crime!"

The combined effects of my National Health Care Program and Saude Dourada of Aetna Pharmaceuticals is monumental in its proportions! Every citizen is perfectly healthy. Everyone who wishes employment is gainfully employed, zero crime. This is truly the Miracle of the Century!" The applause machine worked overtime, simulating a large crowd.

"Now the down side. As you are well aware, this program has come under intense criticism from many quarters. This I fully anticipated. Look, we have just put tens of thousands of medical, hospital, and other health care workers out of a job. The massive drug industry is now suffering staggering losses. Even the police force has been forced to make drastic cuts in personnel, and I do mean drastic cuts. Yet, we have worked with these displaced workers to find them new, rewarding jobs. Many police have now joined their local fire departments, where they can still be first responders to emergencies, such as fires."

"I ask each and every American that, when you hear harsh criticism of this program, ask yourself this: Is this person tied to the medical or drug industries? They are becoming the 'Big Losers' in this program. You should expect a massive lobbying effort on the part of the major drug companies, who are making a last and futile attempt to prevent this program from totally wiping out their companies."

"What is our next step? I know many of you are asking that question. What do we need so that we can bring these incredible benefits to all Americans? Mac Fluide Enterprises and Aetna Pharmaceuticals have promised me that they will ramp up their production facilities and provide their new wonder drug, Saude Dourada, to every American. Once they have helped every one of our citizens, they will then market their miracle drug overseas, recouping their massive expenses."

"I will be asking Congress to pass an emergency spending bill to help establish the needed Health Care facilities in all states. Yes, this all will take time to implement nationwide, but you have my solemn promise that I will see this through to its end. I will not rest until each and every American is fully healthy and working, and until the nationwide crime rate is a thing of the past, where it is safe for every American to walk the streets of any town and city in America!"

"In the ensuing months, I will be meeting with the Governors of all the other states to work out details for bringing their state onboard. You can help me out by writing your Governors, your Congressmen, your Senators, telling them just how much and how soon you wish this program to be brought to your state, to your family. I know I can sleep nights knowing that my family is completely healthy and safe. Thank you for your attention. May God bless every one of you.

Good night, my fellow Americans."

Deiter called out jokingly, "This has been your local robot President speaking." The packed Yellow Hall commons roared with nervous laughter. This shocking news brought fear into many minds, grief into some, anger into others, antagonism into a few; none were unaffected.

"Maybe our family ought to have moved to Toronto with my fellow band members and their families," Ahana lamented. Gone was his eternal cheery disposition.

As Lindsey looked around the room at close to a hundred fifty of her fellow Yellow Hall students, she realized that they really needed some advice, some comforting words, and some kind of faint hope for the future. She thought, "Please, Governor Alister, say something," though she had no idea what he could say. Dominus had won; their world was crumbling rapidly.

"May I have your attention," the kindly voice of Governor Alister boomed loudly over the din of the chatting students in all five Hall commons. "Today's news, while it most certainly is not what any of us wished to hear, should not be seen as unexpected. The grandiose plan of Dominus and Snow has yet to materialize fully. What you have not seen on the newscast is that the Idaho Red Brigade Militia has been very active these past two months. Acting on delivery tips from various Diviners, they have been successful at intercepting actual delivery of these pills, crippling Aetna's delivery system. I believe that just barely enough pill doses are getting through to sustain those already hooked on the heroin pills in New York and DC to continue their addiction. Certainly, at this time there is no danger at all of Snow expanding the takeover to other states."

"However, methodical Dominus has undoubtedly foreseen this and will likely have other means of providing his drugs for the masses. We still have time to counter this mess. Do not lose hope just yet. What can you do? Study hard, learn your spells well, for one day, it may well come down to you, the young wizards and witches of our country, who will face off against Dominus. I will keep you informed of further details. The country has not yet fallen nor is it about to within the next few months. Take heart and continue your studies. Thank you."

"Yes!" Deiter pounded his fist into the air. "I knew it! Soon, we are going to get to fight Dominus, the Death Stalkers, and all the rest! Yes!" Several others shared his enthusiasm, Lindsey noted.

Just then, a Message appeared before Lindsey's eyes.

Please come to Admin Hall Room 312 immediately for a special Rodents Pack meeting. A.

Lindsey saw that all her friends also got the message. Quietly, they left the dorm. Lindsey opened a Magical Door to the Admin Hall. One by one, her somber friends stepped through. She and an excited Deiter were last. "I bet we are going to get our fighting orders, Lindsey," Deiter sounded hopeful and ready for a battle. Lindsey was not so sure this would be the case.

This room was the largest conference room on campus. Fred Betts was already present and was hugging his daughter when Lindsey and Deiter entered. Jim, Wilma, and Monane were also here, Ashley and Jim were also hugging. Lindsey smiled at the two. Alister looked even more exhausted than ever, but said kindly, "Students, please have a seat on that side over there. I'm expecting a large number of others today. Cho Lin and Huan Su are at the gates and will be Dooring them in here in secret. No one must know the identities of who is attending this meeting. You understand why, I'm sure."

Many other professors began arriving, taking their seats at the long front table, on either side of Alister. Just then, the Magical Door opened, and Santa Claus stepped into the room! Yes, everyone stared at the bulging belly, the red and white suit, the long grey beard, and roundish face, complete with a stocking cap with a jingle bell on its tassel on his head. He smiled, and Alister motioned for him to take a seat on the right, facing the students. He grinned and said, "Ho, ho, ho." Lindsey couldn't help by giggle. So did her friends.

"Some must come here in disguise," Alister explained. Lindsey noted that Santa Claus glanced around the room, his eyes fixed upon Professor Mary Ann, and he nodded to her. Lindsey saw that Mary Ann returned the slight head bob.

Ashley stared at Professor Mary Ann, a questioning look on her face. Lindsey wondered what was going on; who was this man or woman anyway?

The magical door opened again, and more people stepped into the room, taking seats near Santa, though they all smiled or chuckled when they saw him. Lindsey recognized Eli and Kimi. Then, Lloyd arrived along with R. B. Both gave their daughters a hug before sitting down. Mary Hampton came, bringing along Casper Williams, Fred's boss, and Rachel Smith, Fred's peer who was in charge of the Mountain section of Colorado's Magical Misuse Department. Lacy Brooms, the Governor General of all the US magic schools arrived, along with Bill Ryker, who shook hands with his son, Tom, before sitting down. Kathy Jacks, Colorado's head of the Department of Law arrived along with Ace Brill, Colorado's head of the Security Branch and Monique's boyfriend, Pam believed.

Ace stood up and shook hands with the next arrival, who Lindsey did not recognize. It was Misty Wells, the head of the entire US Department of Defense Magical Branch! Pam whispered who she was to Lindsey, who in turn stared at this most powerful woman. She and Lacy Broom were the two highest-ranking officials yet! Above them was only the US Regent, Thomas White, who was Dominus controlled.

Still there were many empty seats. Lindsey wondered who else was coming to this unprecedented meeting. The magical door opened again and two dozen men and women entered. Some wore obvious disguises, fake wigs, and such. Once inside the room, all discarded their disguises, however. Pam gasped, recognizing many of these people. There were twenty-three of them. She whispered to Lindsey, "That's Governor Al Waters of California, J.J. Julie James, Governor of Arizona, Arne Bellweather, our Governor. The others must be other state's governors!" Lindsey sensed this was not an ordinary meeting of the Rodents Pack at all. Something monumental was occurring here.

Still other scattered men and women arrived, though Lindsey did not recognize any of these. They looked awfully distraught and haggard, she noted. At last, Cho Lin and Huan Su stepped into the room, signaling that all were now present.

Governor Alister rose, "Welcome one and all. I have placed the very best security measures on this room. No one outside this room can detect who is here or what is said or thought. There is no safer location in our country at the moment. I must admit that this is the saddest day in my life, to have to host such a meeting as this. Nevertheless, it must be done. I believe we should begin with a few reports that will affect our thinking on this matter. I believe that Santa Claus wishes to speak first, Santa?" Alister smiled and sat down. Mr. Claus rose and walked to the center of the room.

"Pardon my disguise; it is absolutely necessary. If later on, Dominus learns that I was here, he'll not have my actual physical description. Field Marshall Erin Saks here." A furry of whispers echoed around the room. He went on, "As you know, we have become very successful at intercepting Aetna's delivery of the pills to New York, thanks to some excellent divination on the part of the staff here at Bradbury's." He nodded at Mary Ann.

"You haven't heard this on the news, but we have thus far destroyed over ten million of those pills! We are allowing sufficient quantities to get through to maintain those who are already addicted to the heroin. Not to do so would be inhumane of us; their withdrawal symptoms would be overwhelming to say the very least. I've no idea how you get millions off heroin, an entire state of addicts. Anyway, Dominus knows that he cannot use the normal trucking industry to make the deliveries. Now we have put a serious dent in his teleportation mechanism. I would anticipate that he will begin to develop other means of delivering the pills. Thank you." He returned to his seat.

Spontaneously, Governor Waters began clapping. At once, the other governors joined him, and then the entire room gave him a loud round of applause. Santa smiled and nodded repeatedly.

"Next, Governor General Lacy Broom wishes to speak," Alister announced. Lacy got up and faced the group. Her expression was grim.

"It is with a sad heart that I must announce to everyone that the New York School of Magic has closed its doors. All their students have transferred to other schools, many to Toronto. Some faculty have retired and left the state; others have resigned and moved away. A few have taken positions at other schools. I promise you that as soon as this Dominus plot is destroyed, I will reopen the New York School of Magic. Until then, it is impossible to keep it open." She looked crushed, but Lindsey saw the wisdom in it. How could a school operate if there were only a handful of students and little or no faculty left? Besides who would want to be taking those drugging pills?

She added, "I sincerely hope this is not the wave of the future or we are doomed."

Misty spoke next. "Hi, I'm Misty Wells, head of the US Department of Defense, Magical Branch. I'm pleased to announce that we have finished examining every wizard and witch in the bureau. We found ten who either support Dominus or wears an imbedded ring. These have been reported to Miss Betts. I'm prepared to dismiss these ten when the signal is given. Thank you." Lindsey found this encouraging. Dominus was ignoring these Security people, as well as the magical schools. Her uplifted feeling rapidly vanished, though.

Kathy Jacks rose next. "Hello, Kathy Jacks, head of the Colorado Department of Law. Well, it's finally happened. After the report was made public for us two weeks ago, massive in-fighting began. I have had to arrest forty people thus far. The Law Department is in shambles. As an operating unit of the US Department of Law, we are now completely non-functional. I have to make a bold move today or the whole department will be destroyed by tomorrow. I have had excellent support from Ace, who has sent several Security forces to guard each of the members within the Colorado Department of Law who are on our side against Dominus. I surely don't know where he found all these people, but they are preventing a massive magical battle that's for sure. I beg you to reach a decision on what to do next here today. I can't hold this position beyond today. Geneva Holmes, Dominus controlled, has given me an ultimatum: bring order by tomorrow or she will replace me and all those who do not support the current administration. That's her way of saying supporting Dominus, by the way. So, ladies and gentlemen, for heaven's sake, decide something today or you will lose the entire Colorado Department of Law."

"I'll second that," Casper rose. "Oh, yes, Casper Williams, head of Colorado Department of Magical Misuse. I have just managed by the skin of my shins to keep order within the whole department. Tempers are beyond the breaking point, I'm afraid to say. We must act today, if not, the Colorado will lose its Magical Misuse department within days. While I have outright lied about the extreme severity of the in-fighting to my boss, Karl Jous, the US head of the Department of Magical Misuse and Dominus supporter, others, such as Denver's head, Felix Jones, has been sending him reports behind my back. I might be able to stall for a few days at most. I'm open to any and all suggestions."

"Arne Bellweather, Governor of the great state of Colorado. I say why not launch an all-out attack against Dominus, his organization, and the drugged dopes in the White House? I've had about all I can stand of this stupidity and inaction!" He was fiery and angry.

"I understand your frustration, Arne," Alister spoke calmly. "If we attack the President, she will consider that an act of treason and call out the entire US Army to her defense. If we leave her alone and go after Dominus, she will also call out the army to defend what she sees as the miracle drug of the century. We can't directly attack either without severe repercussions. I don't want to fight and kill my fellow Americans."

Casper added, "It would be a slaughter of unprecedented proportions. The army would be decimated by magical spells resulting in a huge number of deaths. Going to war, in my humble opinion, is about the worst thing that we could do."

Other Governors reported similar dire situations within their states. Many suggestions were tossed out, but slowly everyone realized that any open, direct attack on Dominus would lead to war. Lindsey noticed that Governor Waters was closely watching his peers. At last, he decided to act.

He rose. "Governor Al Waters, California. California has no intention of ever subjecting its citizens to this vicious and destructive Health Care program or to give in to Dominus Malefic. I have discussed this with my staff, and I'm able to announce to you all that the great state of California is prepared to secede from the United States and form our own country, independent of the US. It is within the powers of states to so act. We are prepared to stand alone in this."

The room broke into an uproar of conversation! Mass pandemonium—everyone talking at once. Sometime later, Governor Waters pointed out, "Look, we secede and we take all trusted members of the Departments of Law, Magical Misuse, and Security with us. Form our own union; we can fight against Dominus legally then. The more states that join us the stronger we all are at resisting this takeover by Dominus and Snow."

Governor Bellweather, slowly beginning to side with Governor Waters, insisted, "Look, if we don't do anything, then the Departments of Law and Misuse are gone, replaced by Dominus supporters who will come after us, arrest us, or worse."

As the confusion began to die down, Governor General Lacy spoke up. "Governors, most of you are not wizards or witches. If you secede, Dominus may well react by having his Death Stalkers teleport into your governor's mansions and kill you and your families. That is a very real possibility."

"Yes, but," Misty Wells interrupted, "if we pull the entire Department of Security out of those states that do not secede, we will have more than enough to station many in all the governor's mansions. We can provide the best possible protections against Dominus retaliations. I would not hesitate for an instant to switch loyalties from Snow's version of our country to yours." This greatly eased the various governors' fears just raised by Lacy.

Misty added, "Your first action must be to purge all known Dominus supporters and those who wear his ring. True, we do not know all them, but certainly you can check on all of those in your governments, police, and other key officials."

"Yes, but what about Laws, our economic system, and money for heaven's sake," J. J. of Arizona asked. "Think of the immensity of problems we will instantly face without any advance planning. Chaos, chaos, chaos!"

Governor Alister, who had sat back quietly, finally rose. At once, the various governors hushed. "You are forgetting one important thing: you are not alone. When facing a critical crisis, one can do five things. He can attack it; he can flee from it; he can ignore it; he can lie down and give up; or he can find a way to go around the crisis. We are not about to ignore it, give up, or flee, at least not just yet. Hence, we can either attack it or find a way around it. Certainly seceding from the United States is one avenue you can take."

"I urge you to think this matter through in detail. As everyone now knows, Dominus or Simon has been miles ahead of us all along. I now believe that his capture and imprisonment years ago was merely a part of his grand plan! By taking the heat off him, we all thought the matter was handled. Yet in secret, his minions were off developing those diabolical rings and now this new drug. Indeed, I find the parallel to a game of chess appropriate here. He has placed us all in check, but that does not mean mate, game over, not yet. He is well on his way to installing his master plan for us: he as the supreme ruler, his wizards and witches as the dominate, controlling forces, the master race so to speak, and all the normal humans in their subordinate places, much like cows. In New York and DC, we are seeing in a microcosm his ultimate plans for the world, his Golden Path."

"Gentlemen, if all that has happened thus far has been according to his plan, Dominus must also have calculated very well what your move at this time would be. Expect then that he has long ago prepared countermeasures that will go into effect the very moment you take that anticipated action, all according to his plan."

"But what are you saying? Do nothing?" Governor Waters interrupted angrily.

"Certainly not nothing. Rather do the unexpected. Take an action that is not that for which he has planned," Governor Alister answered. "First, we must think like Dominus and see if we can make a guess what he is assuming will happen next. Key to this must be his control of the President, Congress, the Judicial System, and thus the Armed Forces. Thus, in my estimation, he is anticipating that you will rebel in some open way so that he can bring in the might of the US Armed Forces to quell any rebellion, under the guise of 'National Security.'"

"We need to take an unexpected action, one that his methodical mind has not presumed as a logical reaction on your part. Second, you are now well aware that he has millions of key men and women now wearing his magical controlling rings. These people are for the most part opinion leaders, one way or another, business leaders, government workers, and so on. Some are even your own aides. You can count on Dominus using those men and women to relay information to him about what you are actually doing. Spies, in short. Millions of them as near as we can tell. We have identified a quarter of a million, barely a quarter at most, of his ring wearers. Bottom line, Simon will know all of your plans almost as soon as you have made them."

"This all sounds so hopeless," Governor Waters interrupted. "So what *are* we to do?" He asked angrily. Many other governors echoed his feelings.

"If you were in Simon's shoes planning this all out in detail, what would you assume that the reaction of the rest of the country would be, once they discovered the truth of the Health Care Program? Anger, hostility, fight back, rebellion, attacks? I sure would, which is just what you have all been proposing, in one way or another. You are playing into his hand. No, we need to do the unexpected, something to help derail his Golden Path scheme."

"Suppose that instead of protesting and openly defying them, you come out in full and complete support of this Health Care Plan." Alister had to hold his hand up for silence; tempers suddenly raised a notch. "Further, you volunteer and absolutely *insist* upon sending people to New York to have them become 'perfectly healthy' in the name of State Welfare. The people you send will be all those that you can find within your administration who are Dominus supporters or who are wearing the rings." He paused a second to allow them to grasp his true intention.

"You absolutely insist, demand, and make a huge public show of getting these supposedly 'critically vital personnel' off to New York to become permanently healthy—put on enough of a public show so that they *cannot* refuse. Once you have verified that you have no others anywhere in your state governments, anywhere, you can then start in on the others who are key opinion leaders who are under Dominus control; ship them off as well. Make a big public show of their importance so that they too cannot refuse."

"Meanwhile, let's establish a State's Justice Department, a department that sits over all the states that participate in this action. Beneath the head of the Justice Department, let's have the Security Department, the Law Department, the Magical Misuse Department, and the Justice Department. The purpose is to establish a state controlled avenue for Justice for your citizens. Play it up big time, and you will be shocked at how well it plays."

"Let's take this opportunity to do it properly. The US currently is a country based solely on the Rule of Law. Over the centuries, the sheer number of laws has grown so out of proportion that now it takes teams of lawyers to figure out the simplest of questions. The average person has no idea what is and is not the law. Laws exist because the ruling government can no longer control its people. Laws exist as an enforcement mechanism to attempt to get citizens to do the right things. Yet we all know that those who would not do the right thing are not going to obey the laws. Hence our criminal system. Why should the average, honest citizen be burdened with the impossible to understand body of laws on which even the lawyers argue?"

"Even more importantly, what about Justice? That concept has evaporated from our legal system. Recently, some of our students rescued five women whom Dominus kidnaped, militated their bodies by cutting off their arms, blinding them, making them wear impossible clothing, and then repeatedly raped them. Yes, we've healed them, re-grown their lost appendages, and even helped them erase the severe emotional trauma. Yet, what about those women obtaining Justice? It isn't going to happen in the US. No, Dominus is now protected by President Missy Snow. Even if he weren't, what would our current legal system provide in the way of Justice, *true* Justice for these women? Two things, either the death of Dominus or his incarceration, at least until he again escapes. I ask you, if you were one of these women, would you consider *this* Justice? I know I certainly would not."

"Those of you in the Department of Law can tell us thousands of even worse cases. Honestly, all Justice has long ago left the United States. It is my humble opinion that if you put the central focus of this new state controlled Department of Justice on *true* Justice, not Law, you would find the common citizen hailing this as the greatest move ever. A storekeeper is robbed and beaten by thugs. Thugs are arrested and found guilty. Thugs are forced to work, and the greater portion of their pay is given to the storekeeper. They don't work; they don't get fed. They will work. How long? Until the storekeeper feels that he has had Justice served. People will really go for this."

"Now where do the personnel for this new state controlled department come from? All the current members of the US Department of Law, Magical Misuse, and Defense, Magical Branch. Have them all resign their posts and accept parallel posts in your new Justice organization. A sudden, mass exodus of all our people will certainly cripple Dominus and Missy! But it would need to be done as a coordinated action—all resigning at precisely the same day and time, across all current departments."

"Excellent idea," Governor Waters exclaimed! "We should have elected Governor Broadwell for President! Brilliant, man, incredibly brilliant. In one fell swoop, we end up with all the friendly personnel under our control and remove from our states those under Dominus control. Brilliant indeed!"

"Terrific plan, but we need to act quickly before the Department of Law and Magical Misuse collapse," Casper pointed out. "I doubt that we have days to delay, perhaps only hours. The situation is very grim indeed."

"I concur," Kathy Jacks added. "However, Casper,

perhaps we could privately explain what will be happening to the others that we trust. Let them begin their own preparations. Some are going to have to perhaps move out west from their endangered eastern state's homes, assuming that Dominus moves east to west."

"Let's set the transfer date of mass resignations and re-assignments to be the thirtieth of October, that is ten days from now. Until then, I will work on getting all those I can find who are under Dominus control shipped off to New York. You can count on full and complete support from California. All that remains is how to administer this new State's Justice Department and how to pay their salaries and such."

"What about the computer networks and such?" asked Fred Betts.

"Ah, I have been doing a bit of research, Fred," Professor Delius spoke up with a grin. "It seems that each state has been forced to pay for their local US department's computer systems. All those systems belong to the states, not the Federal Government. I suggest that at the same time as the resignations occur, each state file the appropriate papers to confiscate the buildings and the equipment they own. In short, kick out the federal employees who are Dominus controlled. Make them find new locations of their own." Fred chuckled; Delius was being incredibly devious.

"Misty, I suggest that you quietly review all the assignments of all the Security men and women in the US. When the mass resignation comes, you will want those who are protecting our folks to remain on their jobs, but pull all the others who are doing security work for the enemy off and put them onto protection of the governors who are onboard with us," Governor Alister suggested.

"I have already thought of doing just that," she grinned back. "About one third of our forces can be redeployed to help provide additional protection to the states and their governors. Governors, if you will be so kind as to notify me of your anticipated needs, I will see that they get filled on October 30 or shortly thereafter."

"If you will give your secure email address with Miss Betts, she will send you a copy of all known Dominus supporters, Death Stalkers, and persons who wear his ring of control," Governor Alister added. Quickly, they complied, and Pam and the other students and professors left the meeting. Jim blew Ashley a kiss as she left; he had to stay. The governors began working out the details among themselves.

Back at their study hall, Pam hastily sent out nearly two dozen copies of her ever-growing database to the governors. Finally, she and the others began to discuss what they had just heard.

"I just don't see how they are going to make enough of those drugs to give to so many millions of people," Pam commented. "They are certainly going to need many more production facilities, if they plan to expand to other states. I wonder how I can figure out where those new ones are located?"

"What if they haven't made more pill making factories yet, Pam? Suppose he was counting on the other states rebelling and then using the army to conquer the other states. Then, he wouldn't need more pills," Deiter suggested.

"Yes, but his plan to make normals into cattle is going to need those pills," Ashley countered. "After all, mom would shoot to kill, if he came around our place trying to make her into a second class citizen. Only automatons can be so easily controlled. Ultimately, he has to have a huge amount of pill production, that's what I think anyway."

"My thinking exactly. I'd best get on to it," Pam added.

"I'll lend you a hand," Tom wryly said, booting up his computer and sitting beside her so they could look over each other's screens. The others chatted about the significance of this meeting and what was in the offing, leaving the two computer Geeks working away.

The bombshell hit on October 30 as planned. Governor Al Waters of California led the parade of western governors, holding his press conference first. "Good day, ladies and gentlemen. It is with the greatest of pleasure that I stand before you today. Let it be known that the great state of California is fully behind President Missy Snow's National Health Care Program. So much so, that I have issued an executive order demanding that key personnel within my administration and within state government immediately move to New York. I realized fully that it will be some time before this program can be fully implemented across forty-nine more states. Hence, I greatly desire and insist upon these key personnel becoming perfectly healthy at once. One never knows when serious illness may befall one of us in government. This way, with my key personnel fully healthy at all times, should a catastrophe occur, they will be fully ready to step in on a moment's notice to take over the reins of leadership here in California."

"I have talked with many other governors, and we all agree that we must insist upon our sending our designated, key personnel to New York or DC. This represents the best imaginable safety factor for state and local governments. I'm sure that President Snow will fully agree that, until her program gets fully implemented in these western states, our key personnel must be kept healthy at all times. President Snow cannot deny us this opportunity to have our key backup personnel totally healthy and ready to go, I'm sure."

"Behind me stand a representative group of those key personnel here in California, whom I have ordered to go to New York to take early advantage of this wonderful program of our President. Let's give them a tremendous hand. They will soon be fully ready to take over in any emergency here in California." He turned and applauded the men and women behind him, including his Lieutenant Governor. Whether they liked this move or not, none showed anything but smiles and waves to the cameras.

"Next, in keeping with the overwhelmingly powerful Pilot report of President Snow's, we governors have decided to also listen to our citizens. For eons it seems, the average citizen, who is a victim of crime, has not received anything like Justice from the captured criminals. Until the President's plan is implemented nationwide and crime reduced to a thing of the past, we western governors are creating the States Justice Department. This new department will be charge with working out ways and means of not only capturing the criminals, but also of making those found guilty of said crimes make amends with their victims, so that victims will finally feel like they have gotten Justice."

"For example, you run a grocery store and a pair of thugs come in and rob you, stealing your money. Today, the thugs are captured, tried, and when found guilty, are sent to prison. While this gets them off the streets, it does nothing at all for the storekeeper! Under our new States Justice Department, these men and women will be working to make these thugs repay the storekeeper sufficiently, until he feels that he has had Justice served. Once thugs and criminals realize that they will have to make amends for their crimes, we hope that they will think twice about committing more. Yes, we realize that once President Snow's National Health Care Program finally reaches California, we should see the same dramatic drop in the crime rate. When that happens, we will then disband the States Justice Department."

"However, until then, our new program will offer the first real Justice for all those victims of crimes. I give you the new head of the States Justice Department, Amos Slaughter, one of the foremost leaders in his field." A loud round of applause greeted the sixty year old wizard as he smiled and waved before the cameras.

"Since our new department will need facilities, I have asked that the Federal Employees who currently operate out of state owned facilities to vacate those within two days' time. Already, most have left. After all, they will not be needed anywhere much longer, as soon as President Missy Snow gets her National Health Care Program operational nationwide. Also, many personnel with the federal departments of Law, Security, and Magical Misuse will no longer be needed, since the Health Care Program demonstrably removes nearly all crime. Thus, we will be accepting and offering those people a temporary job in our new States Justice Department. I say temporary, because once the program has finally gone nationwide, we, too, will no longer need this new department."

He then fielded many questions about this new department and how it would operate. While he was answering them, the newscasters cut away to Colorado, where Governor Arne Bellweather began his press conference. He followed the pattern set by Al Waters. By early afternoon, all the western states had followed suit, plus Illinois joined them.

That evening, Governor Alister held a short meeting with the Rodents Pack. Fred was very excited. "All heck broke lose today. No violence, thank goodness. Casper Williams was promoted to head the new Department of Magical Misuse, Pam. You are now looking at the new head of the Colorado Department of Magical Misuse! I've been promoted!"

"Wow! Way to go dad!" Pam exclaimed, giving her father a big hug.

He continued his explanations, "Actually, the complete transfer of the Security Branch went smooth as clockwork. Misty Wells handled it superbly, promoting those few within her entire branch that had ties to Dominus to leadership roles in the Federal Department of Defense, Magical Security Branch, which is mostly just a title now, since there are only a dozen now left in this Federal Branch." Everyone chuckled.

"Karl Jous, the head of the Federal Magical Misuse Department, was very upset with so many of us leaving, though I pointed out that he still commanded a sizeable group. I didn't tell him that they were all like himself, Dominus supporters. I guess he'll find that out soon enough," Fred chuckled.

"It was pretty much the same way in the Federal Department of Law," Kathy Jakes added. "Geneva Holmes was upset, but she could do nothing, not with all of us standing to lose our federal jobs just as soon as the Health Care Plan gets underway. She could hardly refuse us. I put a fly in her bonnet too. I told her that she ought to start looking for another job soon, because once it goes national in scope, she won't have any criminals to apprehend. She glared at me, but I caught a glimpse of fear in her face. Serves her right. The head of the States Justice Department of Law and Justice is Fred Angel, a good man. I've known him for years. He's from California. However, now comes the hard part, Fred. We have got to reorganize and actually work out ways and means of obtaining Justice for victims of crime."

Governor Alister commented, "Kathy, you should really do this new task well—the obtaining of Justice for victims. If we can defeat Dominus, many will be seeking Justice for what he and his associates have done to our country and people. The obtaining of Justice may well be what finally holds this country together in the end."

The group chatted for some time about the day's events. The complete results of this surprise action were not fully known until near Thanksgiving time. Forty states joined together in the new State's Justice Department, but only after the others also sent all the Dominus controlled or supporters off to New York as well. At the federal level, the Magical Security Department had only eighteen wizards and witches in it, all used to guard the President and her staff. In sharp contrast, the Federal Departments of Law and Magical Misuse had one hundred thirty-five and one hundred five members. Clearly, Dominus greatly desired to control these two key departments.

The states not on board were New York, obviously, and nine other nearby states, whose governors were tightly controlled by Dominus and his magical rings. President Snow was very pleased with the total acceptance by all the states. She, or rather her wizard and witch advisors, had expected a huge furor over it. Plans had been made to call upon the Armed Forces to quell rebellions. All were taken by complete surprise. President Snow had no choice but to accept all these new people moving into New York State, adding around a hundred thousand more residents there, and scarcely offsetting the many that had fled the state in the preceding months.

President Snow, whose intelligence level was now that of a five year old, just could not understand why Simon Mac Fluide was so upset with all this breaking news. Instead of a battle against these other states, why, they were embracing her Health Care Program. Perhaps, she thought, it had something to do with his company's ability to mass-produce their new wonder drug.

Chapter 12—Halloween Again

"What the bloody heck is going on?" screamed a violently angry Dominus. He was sitting in the President of Aetna Pharmaceuticals office. Surrounded by six of his most trusted Death Stalkers and company president Alfred Whitehall, he was watching the breaking news, as were so many in the United States this October 30.

"But sir, they, the states—they are going along with your master plan, are they not? Governor Waters is praising the Health Care Plan, sir. I, we don't understand," Alfred wiped the perspiration off his face. He was sweating profusely today, though it was not hot. He was nervous. He always got very nervous when Simon Mac Fluide's representatives came around his company. He didn't know that Dominus and Simon were one in the same person, however. Very few people did know that detail, very few.

"They were supposed to fight it, offer resistance, start a war, secede from the Union, any number of wild reactions—not support it!" Dominus growled. "Then, we would be. . ." He stopped from finishing his sentence, realizing he was around Alfred. He had made long-range plans to use the Armed Forces and the various National Guards to put down and quell all the riots that he anticipated would result from Snow's Pilot Report. Then, under that cover, he would quickly attain total control of the entire United States. He never had any intention of this pill business expanding beyond New York and DC. Now, it seemed his plan had worked too well, and all the other states were demanding to get on the program as well. This should *not* be happening! People should be outraged over what he did to the norms in New York, turning them into heroin addicts and automatons at best, requiring the use of wizards and witches, who were not on the pill, to tell them what to do.

"How could I have been so wrong? How could I have made such a huge, huge blunder?" he asked himself. None of the Death Stalkers said a word. They knew better than to say anything at all when their master was in this mood. "I need to go for a walk," he finally said more calmly. He, accompanied by his men, walked out onto the streets of Atlanta, Georgia on a cool, late afternoon. Dominus walked and walked, all the while reviewing his plans—plans that he had worked out so carefully for so many years. Yes, he had devised this plan some twenty-five years ago. Until this moment, every step had worked out precisely according to his plan. Even his fourteen years in jail had been perfectly timed. He had not broken out until he received word that the rings were ready to go into production and that the pills were nearly ready for testing.

All had happened absolutely, precisely according to his calculations, his Golden Path to world dominance. Until today, that is. How could these other states be demanding to be put onto these pills of his that turned norms into zombies? This defied all reason, all logic! After walking several miles, he came to the realization that the people in these other states could not really want to get drugged! Someone had become aware of his actual plan, his actual intent—to use the Armed Forces to take over control of the US, but who?

"It smells like a Diviner," he muttered to the sidewalk and promptly spat on it. "It has to be a Diviner. There is no other answer. After all, my true plan has not been discovered for close to a quarter of a century. There is no likelihood that it should become discovered this close to fruition. In six months, I ought to have been in total control of the US and working on expanding to other countries. No chance at all—they would have to be utter geniuses to have figured out the plan this far along. It has to be Diviners at work."

"Boss, there are no more Class 4 Diviners around. That Pruit woman, she was the last one," Ames Selig ventured.

"True, true, but there is this up and coming witch, the Barron's girl's sister, Stokes, yes, Ashley Stokes-Compton. You know, the one posing armless in the Teen Fashion magazine," Dominus replied. "She's already busted two of my whore houses. She and that Barron kid are becoming quite a nuisance. Plus, someone has obviously been tipping off the Red Brigade about our pill shipments."

"Hey, we all agree on that! We've lost eighty percent of

our shipments these past few months. Someone has to be divining when and where," Ben Johnston agreed. "Probably this Ashley teen is behind it. You want us to knock her off for you, Boss?"

"No, how many times do I need to tell you? I want to torture my enemies before I kill them. If one's enemies just up and die on you, it takes all the pleasure and fun out of life. I was planning a little surprise on their eighteenth birthdays. They would then be legal. Right now, they are just silly kids, pretty ones, mind you, but still kids. Never sexually mess around with kids. Only perverts do that. A little harmless torture, well that's okay, especially since they are girls and won't amount to anything anyway. No, I had big plans for that Barron kid and that Stokes kid when they are legal. However, Ben, if this Ashley Stokes is behind the pill thefts, when you couple that with raiding both my pleasure houses, that makes them plenty dangerous."

"What I don't see is how a teen girl could possibly have the intelligence to see through my grand plan, not at this late stage, when it was coming right down home stretch," Dominus pulled his hands through his hair and put his hat back on.

"Well, maybe they're working with their school's Governor Broadwell? Maybe it was he that took what those girls told him and figured out your plan," Ames suggested. Clearly, his boss didn't think the teens were smart enough to have done that. "After all, Broadwell has connections. It must have taken someone with a lot of pull to get all the western governors to do the very same thing on the very same day."

"I can see your point, Ames. I've already considered that aspect. I know that Broadwell is working closely with these teens. I don't know what the Stokes girl actually divined, but it must have been enough for Alister to work out what I intended to have happen next. If so, his countermove was a good one, I'll grant him that."

"Too bad he didn't drown when we had him nailed to the rocks on Cyprus," Ames cursed.

"Tisk, tisk, always make your biggest enemies suffer the longest and hardest. That's how I have gotten to where I am today. No, simple drowning was too easy for him. He just passed out from the cold water. If they hadn't come along when they did and rescued him, I was about to do so myself. I need, I want him to suffer real pain, excruciating pain, before I finally kill him," Dominus explained yet again. He knew his Death Stalkers would never understand this point. That's why they would never be anything more than his servants, though he never told them this.

"I think it would be prudent to get these two teens out of the way before I make my next move," Dominus thought aloud. "I don't want that Ashley divining my next move; it's too critical!"

Jumping on something he could grasp, Ben suggested, "Hey, you want us to grab them tomorrow? It's Halloween, and they'll be in Telluride again. We can pick them up and bring them to you."

"No, don't go near Telluride! Alister will have that place crawling with Security forces, even if they are now State controlled. I have other means of obtaining their presence. Now where? That is the question. I need them where we can keep them prisoners until they reach eighteen. Then, I'll add them to my next pleasure house, totally fitting for those two— to spend the rest of their days doing nothing but giving pleasure to me, until they beg me for release. The problem is all those darn Trackers are about. I need a special place that I can make secure from Trackers." Dominus walked along the street, deep in thought.

At last, he said, "I know just the place. Okay, men, we have work to do before tomorrow."

At nine in morning, all the third year students and above gathered in the dining room for their instructions from Governor Alister. "Today, the password is Mashed Potatoes. That will get you into the tunnel system and out at the other end. As always, I urge you to stay in packs of at least six. I have Security men in place, so your outing ought to be a safe one. Enjoy your day. It is sunny, and I hear Telluride has a light dusting of snow on the ground."

With that, the hundreds of students swarmed down the stairs to the tunnels and headed through the secret door into the kitchen area. From there, a mile long tunnel led into the back of a store in Telluride, where Jim was waiting patiently for Ashley, sipping a hot, spiced coffee. "Ah there you are, Princess!" Jim exclaimed, quickly taking her arm. Deiter already had his arm around Lindsey. Tom and Pam were holding hands, as well as Amanda and Ahana. "I wish I could come to the dance tonight, Ashley."

Ahana grinned, "Don't forget, gang, I have to be back at one to meet my band members and do a bit of practicing before the Halloween Dance." Amanda sighed, knowing that she had only four hours with Ahana.

"What's up first?" Ashley asked Jim.

"I thought that we should take them on a tour of the town first. After all these New Yorkers. . ." He didn't get to finish his sentence. They had filed out of the store and Ahana and Orenda got their first view of the mountains and the town. Both stood there speechless, staring at the mountains around the town.

"Holy incredible!" he exclaimed.

"Way utterly cool!" Orenda added. "So close, you can reach out and touch them!"

An hour passed as the large group wandered the streets of Telluride, checking out the scenery and the shops. They were walking east along San Juan Skyway just past the Fir Street corner and chatting away when it happened. Without any warning, without seeing anyone or anything, Jim found that he was holding onto Ashley's arm, severed at her elbows, while her other arm, similarly severed, fell onto the sidewalk. Simultaneously, Deiter found that he was holding onto Lindsey's identically severed arm, as her other one fell onto the sidewalk. Additionally, all their clothes and protective magical items fell onto the ground as well!

Pam and Amanda shrieked in terror. Orenda gagged and vomited onto the curb. Jim and Deiter waved their wands all round, but saw no one at all. Both boys began to panic, casting all manner of identification spells, finding nothing at all. "What's happening? Where did they go? Who is doing this? Anyone see anything?" Jim fired off questions for which he had no answers.

A small crowd gathered, forming a defensive circle around the others, but no one saw anything out of the ordinary! Pam came to her senses first and Messaged Alister. A return Message floated before her eyes. "Oh. Right. Makes sense. Gang, Alister is on his way. He wants me to get back to the safety of the campus. He thinks I might be next. I'm supposed to bring their arms back with me. God, who did this and how? Where are they? I didn't see anything!"

"Me either and I was right behind them," Tom, white with fear, added. "The arms—I mean that's all that's left of them. I'll help you and Orenda go back," Tom volunteered, picking up Lindsey's arms and their clothing.

Ahana decided to help his sister get back. "Amanda, I'll be right back, once I get her safely back inside the campus."

"Good lord!" Alister exclaimed, as he apparated beside the teens. "Pam, get going now. The rest of you, what happened here?" Though they all began talking at once, Alister didn't mind the confusion. They all told the same story.

"Okay, first, let's check for traps. It is possible that they walked over some kind of trap that triggered," he suggested. Finally having a reasonable spell to cast, dozens of Detect Trap spells activated, including his.

"Hum, no traps. Most curious. Amanda, let's you and I check for magical energy traces." The two did their Tracking skills. Jim had already verified that there were no unexplained footprints leading away from them in the light snow on the sidewalk.

"Weird," Amanda commented, "I see all our detection spells, but there are two really weird ones. I've never seen these before."

"I have," the stern voice of her Aunt Monane startled her. She turned around to see both Monane and Wilma, staves at the ready coming to them. Alister had notified them of the girls' abduction, and they had come at once. "You have too, Alister."

"Darn, darn, darn!" Alister replied, ignoring the fact that so many teens were gathered around. Word had spread that Ashley and Lindsey had been killed or mutilated. Hundreds now gathered around the scene, along with thirty

Security personnel.

Tom, the head of Telluride security, said sternly, "Alister, I swear there were no Death Stalkers or Dominus around this town. None apparated in or out either. What has happened here anyway?"

Alister explained, "Dominus used the one spell for which we have no defense." Wilma gasped; she knew what that one was. "I've seen that weird energy trail before. It's left when a Restricted Wish is cast upon someone or something. Dominus must have our girls and is obviously mutilating them once again. What surprises me is that Ashley had no premonition of this happening."

"I, I didn't either, sir," Audrey, now very, very pale, spoke up. "I mean we were just walking along. All was right and then this. I know that they are now in a very bad way, sir. How do we rescue them?"

"I'm already on it," Monane whispered. Soon, she was scratching her head. "Alister, Amanda, please follow my Message spell to Lindsey, will you? This is totally weird!" Monane cast another Message spell. Then, another and another.

"How—how can that be?" asked Amanda completely bewildered. "They all head off south by east, but then the first one veered northward, the second veered southward, and the third veered back on itself! How can they be in three different places at nearly the same time?"

"Dominus has gotten wiser," Alister replied. "He has taken measures so that Trackers cannot directly string a line to their location and thus go fetch the girls back. Darn it! I should have seen this coming. I have let the girls down this time." He sighed, showing his age.

Quietly, Monane cast another spell, "See through Lindsey's eyes!" she commanded. A moment later, she cancelled that one and cast one for Ashley, quickly cancelling that one too. "They cannot see, Alister, blinded I suspect."

She then cast a variant spell, "Hear through Lindsey's ears." She concentrated for a time. Since this was obviously meeting with some success, Alister and Wilma also cast it, as well as Deiter and Jim.

After a few minutes, Deiter, near tears, said, "We have to get to them fast!"

"I'll kill him myself!" Jim added, extremely angry at what Dominus had done to his Princess.

"Got to find him first," Amanda added quietly.

"Clues, clues, what did you all hear?" Alister asked.

"Well, they were talking to each other. Dominus must have left them," Jim began, trying to focus on what he heard, not his anger towards Dominus. "Sounded rather childlike, something about 'we have to learn to walk so we can go home.' That's what Lindsey was saying to Ashley."

"What does that suggest, Jim?" Alister asked pointedly.

"That both of them are under the Idiot Mind spell. That would prevent either of them from casting anything at all," Jim replied. Deiter, realizing that Jim was speaking what he most feared, agreed with him.

"How about other clues?" Alister persisted in the educational vein.

"Hollow sounds, like metal on stone. Perhaps they are somewhere underground," Monane suggested. "I don't quite understand what I am hearing."

"My feeling as well. I think they are in some underground chamber or tunnel complex. We at least have one clue. Thanks, Monane," Alister sighed again. "Now how the heck are we to find them?"

"Okay, Floor Monitors, round up everyone, Telluride Day is canceled. Everyone is to return to the campus. We have to organize a rescue party and find our missing students," Alister ordered, though at the moment, he had no idea on how the girls could be located.

Pam had recovered her shock by the time she and Tom walked into the Infirmary. "Here's Lindsey's arms," she laid them on the emergency table. Tom did likewise with Ashley's.

"Where's the rest of them? You don't expect me to re-grow the rest of their bodies from their lower arms, do you?" Doctor Caterwall teased. Neither reacted to his joke.

"We don't know what happened. Alister is investigating now, doctor," Pam explained. She and Tom told him what had happened. "One minute they were there, the next instant, both were gone, only their lower arms remained and all their clothes."

By the time that a solemn Tom and Pam returned to the dorm, Alister and the others were just arriving. She looked hopefully at him, but he shook his head. Pam knew something was very wrong. Alister asked Deiter, Jim, Tom, Pam, Amanda, Audrey, Ahana, Wilma, and Monane to follow him to his office. Professors Cho Lin and Huan Su were already there, hot tea ready for everyone. Professor Delius arrived shortly, escorting Professor Mary Ann. Hastily, Alister brought the professors up to date on the meager findings.

"Well, at least they are alive," Delius commented. "I'm sure that Dominus does not want them dying anytime soon. You know him. He'll want to torture them for a long time before killing them."

"Surely, he won't take undo advantage of them, sexually—I mean, rape them," Professor Cho Lin struggled to find a polite way of saying this, but could not.

"No, Dominus detests child pornography and child molesters," Governor Alister replied. Cho Lin relaxed noticeably; that was her worst fear—that he would molest the girls.

Pam said, "Sir, could we redo the Tracking of the Message spells, using the accurate angle measuring units I gave Amanda and Monane? I have an idea."

As Amanda and Monane got out their devices, Tom commented, "They are using the computer program I wrote for them." He was proud of his small achievement.

"Just measure the starting angles, please. Don't worry about them veering off in all directions. I want the initial bearings only." Pam booted up her laptop and brought up her mapping software, displaying the world. She centered it on Bradbury's and then waited for the two Trackers to give her their angles. Both reported the same value, one hundred fifty-five degrees.

Pam plotted the line on her map. "Now I need a cross fix, like maybe from London, England, that's close to ninety degrees from this line." Ten minutes later, Wilma and Amanda returned from their quick trip to London. Pam plotted their new line on the map. The two crossed somewhere in the mountains of Venezuela! This did not look good at all, she thought. "Could we get a fix from say Hawaii next?"

Monane grinned and teleported Amanda and herself once more. Ten minutes later, they returned with their angles, though Amanda commented, "Oh, you just *have* to visit there soon!" Pam plotted the lines. Because of the diverging spell on the actual location, the three did not intersect at precisely the same location, but still it was within about a twenty-mile area in the mountains of Venezuela.

"What does this tell us?" asked Deiter. "That we need to go down there and start a land search?"

"I'll get us some more measurements," Monane suggested. "How about from South Africa and Australia?" Pam grinned, realizing that Monane had figured out how Pam's triangulation method was working. A while later, two more lines merged, though it did not pin down the location to anything closer than a circle about ten miles across.

"I'm searching for known caves in the area," Tom said, MagGoogling away on his laptop.

Meanwhile, Alister begged Professor Mary Ann to see if she could get any kind of divination on the girls and their whereabouts. She sat down at the back of his office and closed her eyes. The data he asked for, such specifics, rarely came to her, for she was only a Class 3 Diviner, not a 4.

After an hour's concentration, Mary Ann reported what little she learned. "They are not in any serious pain. They are not radiating fear or terror, rather frustration and worry. I don't believe that their lives are in imminent danger. Both are radiating a strong desire to go home. That's about all I can get from them. I'm sorry, Governor, that I cannot be more helpful."

"Professor, thank you. This is indeed encouraging— knowing that they are not in grave danger right now. Perhaps we have some time to work out where they are being kept. I don't think I could have stood it, if you reported that they were in fear for their lives at this moment," Alister sighed, greatly relieved. Pam noted that he looked very tired and very old. This Dominus business was slowly sapping the life out of this man.

That night, the Halloween dance was canceled. Far too many were worried about the mutilation abductions. Many, including Ahana, were trying every conceivable way to locate the missing teens. Already, half of the school's older students had volunteered to go on the rescue mission just as soon as "they" had figured out where Lindsey and Ashley were being held.

At the supper hour, with Tom, Jim, and Deiter standing behind her, Pam finally broke down and began crying. Unable to withhold her raw emotions any longer she wailed, "I just cannot find them! I am so useless!"

As she slumped over her laptop, Tom slid his arm around her shoulders, comfortingly. "Hey, none of us have had any success either. Don't go blaming yourself. He used extremely powerful magic to snatch them, that Restricted Wish of his."

Pam wailed all the louder, "I know, I was supposed to be researching methods of countering that spell. Alister gave me that assignment, and now I have failed in that too! If only I had not failed, if only I had worked on it harder, longer, taken the whole summer off and spent it researching it, if only I. . ." She continued to cry even harder.

Real comfort for Pam came from an unexpected direction. Deiter said softly, "Pam. You know that Alister has been researching that Restricted Wish spell for many, many years before he gave you that assignment. Look how powerful he is. If he was unable to find a way to block it in all those years, you should not belittle your own efforts in so short a time. I think you have done very well so far. Have you ever considered that there might not be any way to block that spell? I have. That's the whole point of that spell. I've been reading about it, Pam. It is a wish spell, after all. If I knew it, I would willingly give up a year or two of my life to wish both of them back safe and sound. So would half of this school. Besides Pam, thanks to your measuring tool, we know that they are somewhere in that ten mile circle. We just need to narrow it down a bit more. Let's get some supper and then get right back to it. There must be some other way we can narrow it down further, don't you think?"

Pam wiped her eyes on her blouse sleeve. "Well, we could try to get more observations and see if they narrow it further," she suggested. "Maybe there are some other ways to triangulate on their position. I need to think about it."

"That's the spirit, Pam. Come on; let's grab some chow," Tom suggested. They headed over to the dining room together. Jim felt awfully alone. Ashley was not here. Amanda had him sit with Fern and her.

"We'll find her, Jim," Amanda consoled her brother.

Chapter 13—Trick or Treat?

Deep underground in the abandoned Umuquena mine, Dominus prepared for his work. Located at the end of the spur road off Highway 1 out of La Fria, Venezuela, Mac Fluide Enterprises had abandoned this gold mine after the entrance tunnel collapsed, killing ten miners. The loss of the mine was inconsequential to the corporation since it was nearly played out anyway. However, far below the rocky surface of the mountain, a large living complex had been carved out to support the miners. It consisted of a forty-foot square meeting area, a kitchen and pantry, a large bathroom facility, and a bedroom. Dozens of airshafts still provided air to the complex.

Dominus had turned this complex into a secret hideout, stockpiling provisions and installing nice beds and cooking facilities. The only way inside was via a risky teleport spell, assuming one knew precisely the location of the cavern, or by a Magical Door from the mountainside above it. However, he had arranged for weekly food deliveries from Umuquenta. Once a week, Palo, a local boy, went to one specific airshaft, which had a modified dumbwaiter system installed in it. If the contraption was at the surface, he would check if there was a note on it. The note was a grocery shopping list for Dominus. Palo would obtain the items and send them back down the dumbwaiter. For this, he was paid twenty US dollars, a handsome amount by his standards.

This system was needed because Dominus kept a woman prisoner down in the complex. Juanita Sanches-Remano had been imprisoned here for many years. When the mine collapse occurred, her husband was one of the ten who had been crushed to death. After escaping from prison, Dominus returned here to hide out. He needed a cook. Juanita was an excellent cook, and she was near starvation. With the jobs from the mines long gone, the people in Umuquena were in dire straits, many joining the drug lords to stay alive.

Sick and weak, Juanita was near death when Dominus called on her. He seized this opportunity. Pretending to be a doctor, he put her to sleep, amputated her legs below her knees and took her into the underground complex. When she recovered, he told her that the doctors had to remove her lower legs to save her life, but that he, Dominus, was coming to her rescue. If she would stay and live here in this complex, she would be paid a thousand dollars a year and have all the food she could ever desire. Her job would be to cook and keep house. To make it possible for her to do this, Dominus provided her with a special leg cushions. Essentially, these were leather socks that she could strap onto her thighs. The bottoms were heavily padded and had a hard leather, round sole. Wearing these, she found that she was finally able to walk again, albeit slowly and awkwardly.

Now thirty-three, Juanita had saved up her pay; she had five thousand dollars! For her, this was a huge amount, more than enough for her to live on her own for a very long time. Still, living mostly alone in this underground prison was hard on her, no one to talk to, nothing to listen to—just eternal silence. She relished the few days when Dominus or some of his men dropped by to stay a few days. Yet, in the last year, those visits had become exceedingly rare, though she knew not why.

Today, Dominus had returned. Juanita was overjoyed to see another human once more. "Should I fix you steak dinner, señor?" she asked cheerfully.

"No, I won't be staying very long. However, Juanita, I will be bringing you two new houseguests. I want you to look after them. They will need your assistance. Cook for them, keep them company, and look after their needs."

Company? Here? With her? Something to break the unending monotony of her existence? "Mucho gracias, señor, thank you!"

"If you will fix me some coffee, Juanita, I will get to work in the exercise room," he said. That was the name that they gave to the large, nearly empty forty-foot square room. It contained only one large sofa in one corner.

Dominus placed his newly acquired items on the floor, including two chairs, examining each to make sure all was in readiness. Until now, he carefully controlled his thoughts, never letting them drift off onto his intended victims. If this Stokes girl was divining, he wanted to give her no clues. After Juanita waddled in with his coffee, he asked her to leave him undisturbed. Now he set to work. It was after nine in the morning in Colorado, time for him to go to work. He waved his wand and began his very lengthy spells.

"I wish that Miss Lindsey Barron be brought here before me naked and with her arms removed at her elbows, nicely healed, but when she arrives, she will be under my Idiot Mind spell and under my Paralyze spell. My second wish is that at the same time Miss Ashley Stokes-Compton be brought here before me naked and with her arms removed at her elbows, nicely healed, but when she arrives, she will be under my Idiot Mind spell and under my Paralyze spell." He cast a pair of Idiot Minds spells and then a pair of Paralyze spells. Finally, the wish spells activated.

Magical energies flashed. Lindsey and Ashley, one moment walking along the street of Telluride and holding hands with their boyfriends, suddenly found themselves standing paralyzed and naked before Dominus in some underground cavern. Neither of their minds worked properly, but they could see that their lower arms were somehow missing. Both tried to talk, to react, to do anything, but were frozen to the spot, staring at him. Fear crept into both girls, but their minds no longer understood what was happening to them. Lindsey did notice that Dominus appeared to age several years before her eyes. His hair became significantly greyer and wrinkles appeared on his face, bags under his eyes. She wondered what happened to him.

"Welcome my pesky teens. You two continue to cause me enormous problems. Now I am rectifying that. You will be here with me for a time, but first we must get you more presentable. Pretty women ought to have small waists, so it is way past time for you to begin your waist training." Both girls felt him putting a wasp waist corset around their waists, tightening it until they nearly could not breathe, but were helpless to react in any way.

"Ah, much better, you are both sixteen inches around now. Your goal is to achieve a waist of fourteen inches. Once that is achieved, your waist training will be over." To the girls and their severely reduced mental capacities, this seemed a most reasonable statement. Just another two inches and they would be done with this horrible confinement.

Dominus waved his wand again and said, "Replace eyes with these pretty blue glass eyes." Suddenly, everything went totally black. Neither Lindsey nor Ashley could see anything. "Ah, much better, you both now have the prettiest light blue eyes imaginable. Very good, very good."

"Now you need proper shoes. It gets cold on these stone floors. I have some magnificent shoes for you both, really terrific." Dominus brought two chairs into the center of the room where the girls were standing like frozen statues. He sat each on down and then began putting on their new shoes. These were called in the fetish community ballet shoes, forcing the wearers to walk on their toes like a ballet dancer. Their heels were enormously tall and spiked. However, once he had finished putting each teen's new shoes on their feet, Dominus then cast another pair of spells on each girl: Shrink to Tight followed by Leather to Steel. His wand activated in four flashes of magical energy. Lindsey's feet felt funny, as if her toes were touching the ground and not her feet. Then, the new shoes seemed to become very tight on her feet. She wished she could see her new shoes, however. They must be pretty, she thought. Had she been able to see, she might not have thought so. Both leather shoes, which came up to their ankles, had now become very tight fitting and had turned into steel. They would be utterly impossible to remove now.

"Now it is a bit chilly down here, so I think a dress is warranted." Dominus slipped a pair of loose fitting, warm, cotton dresses over their bodies. He stood back admiring his handiwork.

Next, he retrieved the final components that he had carefully arranged on his floor. While he had cast numerous Dis-Locate spells on this whole cavern complex, he presumed that, given enough time, Governor Alister might be able to locate this place and attempt to rescue the teens, though he most definitely wanted to keep them until they were eighteen and he could culminate his plans for them. Hence, given this very remote possibility that the teens could be rescued, he wanted to make very sure that his very costly magical wishes were not undone. He could not afford to have these two back to battery after a rescue.

Carefully, he enchanted small plastic balls, each a quarter of an inch in diameter. The spells he had thought out carefully. The balls were melted into the ends of each girl's arms. Already the glass eye balls he had inserted in place of their own eyes contained the same small balls. Another pair he enchanted and melted into their waists between the opening in the laces. Finally, he melted another pair into each ankle.

Satisfied that all was in place, he canceled his Paralyze spell, allowing the teens to become active once more. "Oh!" exclaimed Lindsey, who found that she could now move and speak.

"Welcome Miss Barron and Miss Stokes-Compton. I'm so glad that you could come to visit me here," he said politely, though with a sneer on his face, which the girls could not see.

"Oh, we are visiting you? How nice," Lindsey exclaimed.

"Really, that is good, isn't it? I mean visiting you?" Ashley added naively. "I can hardly breathe, and I can't see. What happened to my arms? I am missing something, aren't I?"

"Yes, me too. I think I'm missing my arms. No, I have short arms," Lindsey said rather confused.

"You really do not need your lower arms and hands, now do you? After all, didn't Ashley here pose for Teen Fashion magazine without any arms at all?" he replied, barely able to keep from laughing at how well his Idiot Mind spells were working.

"Oh, yes, I think I remember doing that, Lindsey," Ashley replied, thinking hard. "Yes, he's right. We don't need hands and arms, not really."

"Good, good. Now I want to help you both become the best possible fashion models. As you know, the best models have the tiniest waists. So you must try very hard to get your waists down to fourteen inches; then you will be perfect."

"Oh, perfect? That sounds really nice. How do we do this?" asked Ashley, utterly unable to think how this might be done.

"In a couple of days, I will replace your corsets with ones that will allow you to achieve your goal. You need to get used to these first. I want to make getting a fourteen inch waistline as easy as possible for you," Dominus replied.

"Oh thank you, sir," Lindsey gushed. "This one is so tight. I can barely breathe. It will be good to get to a fourteen inch waist won't it?"

"Oh sure, then you will be perfect," Dominus replied, fighting hard to keep from laughing wildly. Under the Idiot Mind spells, these teens were totally accepting of nearly anything!

"Now girls, I am going to tell you something very, very important, something that I want you never to forget. Can you promise me that you won't forget what I am going to tell you?"

"Oh, something important. No, we won't forget, will we Ashley? I mean we haven't been forgetting something, have we? Are we likely to forget this?" Lindsey suddenly became confused about whether or not she had been forgetting something after all. Why was he asking them not to forget? She must be forgetting something.

"I don't think we are forgetting something, but then, how would we know if we are forgetting something? We would have forgotten it and so not remember we forgot it," Ashley said, becoming confused herself.

"Just promise me you will remember this." Both confused teens agreed. "Okay, do not ever let anyone remove your corset or shoes. Do not ever let anyone try to remove your fancy new glass eyes or allow them to try to re-grow your arms. Any attempt by anyone but me to do these things will result in a poison capsule exploding inside your body, killing you. I don't want that to happen to either of you, do you?"

"Oh! No, no, I don't want to be poisoned!" Lindsey exclaimed.

"Me either!" Ashley added.

"Good girls, just remember. Don't let anyone try to remove them or to try to re-grow your arms. You don't need the arms; your new eyes are so pretty, so photogenic; your waists will soon be perfect. Don't let anyone mess with them, all right?"

"I promise!" Lindsey replied.

"Me too," Ashley said very enthusiastically.

"Now then, Mrs. Juanita Sanches-Remano is staying here with you. She is a very good cook and will help you with anything with which you need assistance. You will like her. She will enjoy your company. Okay?"

"Sure, that will be nice. I like to eat pizza. Does she make pizza?" Ashley asked.

"I'm sure she does. Now one final thing, girls. I am sure that both of you want to go home as soon as possible, am I right?" he grinned. His definition of home and theirs were two entirely different things.

"Home? Oh yes, can we go home?" asked Lindsey, remembering her ranch.

"Yes, we want to go home," Ashley replied, "don't we Lindsey?"

"Good, I want you to be able to go home as soon as possible too, but in order for you to go home, you must learn to walk well in your new shoes. Just as soon as you can walk well in them, for say several hours, all by yourselves, then you can go home. I will take you there, unless you then want to stay here with Juanita. Okay? Promise me that you will spend lots of time practicing walking in your new, fine shoes, will you?"

"Oh sure we will!" Lindsey exclaimed, eager to please him and to go home.

"Yes, we know how to walk already. At least, I think I do," Ashley added.

"I'm sure you do know how to walk, but not in these fancy new shoes. So you both practice lots, will you?" Dominus talked as if he was addressing a small child, for that was really the girls' mentality at this point.

"I promise," Lindsey replied. Ashley did so as well. Neither had any idea what difficulties lay behind that promise, however.

"Okay, I am moving your chairs over against the wall. This room is nearly empty and is forty feet square. You can begin to practice your walking by walking over to the far wall and back to your chairs. I must go speak to Juanita now. I will come back tomorrow and check on your waists. If you don't eat too much, we might be able to get you both to fourteen-inch waists tomorrow and be done with your waist training. Wouldn't you like that?"

"Oh, you think we will? That would be really great! Then we would have perfect waists for modeling," Ashley replied, highly excited about the prospect of finishing the training.

"Good. Then, I will see you both tomorrow. Bye," he said and left them alone in the huge cavern room. He found Juanita in the kitchen and gave her very explicit orders about the two teens. He stressed that both would be killed if anyone tried to remove their shoes, corsets, or glass eyes.

"Oh dear me, what has happened to these poor girls?" Juanita said, feeling sorry for them.

"They are from the US and want to be models. They are trying to look just the way that models look up there. You know how girls are," he said.

She didn't have any idea of how people lived in the United States, but assumed he knew what he was telling her. She just accepted this as fact. Once he finished giving her the instructions, he then left. Now he could begin to take countermeasures against these unexpected moves by the western governors, secure in that Ashley could not interfere nor divine what his counteractions would be.

Left alone in their blindness, the two girls sat on their chairs. "Ashley, I cannot see anything, can you?"

"No, it's all black. I wonder if they forgot to turn on the lights?"

"No, we were seeing well before we got these new eyes. Maybe there is something wrong with them. We should ask him about that tomorrow," Lindsey replied.

"My feet feel funny, and I can't breathe well, Lindsey," Ashley said a little panicky.

"Mine too. I suppose that we should practice walking, though I am sure I don't know why we need to," she said.

"Maybe it is because we can't see. Do you suppose that's why we need to practice? We can feel things with our arms at least," Ashley suggested hopefully.

Lindsey held her short arms out in front of her and wiggled them. "Yes, I can feel anything that is in the way with my arms. Can you?"

Ashley moved hers around and agreed. "I suppose we should try walking in our new shoes." She tried to stand up and nearly fell over, her non-existent hands flailing around like mad. "Oh! I can't stand up. I seem to be trying to stand on my toes!"

"I'll try," Lindsey suggested and did manage to fall over, landing hard on the stone floor. "Ouch, that hurts. We are walking on our toes! How do I get up? I can't grab a hold of anything. My hands are somehow missing."

Ashley tried to lean over to help her sister up, at least as much as the tight corset would allow her to bend, but as the tips of their arms touched, she realized that she had no hands to grab a hold of Lindsey. With a great effort and with the touch guidance of their short arms, Lindsey managed to get back to her original sitting position on her chair.

Out of breath, she frantically struggled to breathe. At last, she calmed down. "This is going to be a lot harder than we thought," she said.

"I know. Maybe we should practice just standing first," Ashley suggested. "I wonder what these new shoes look like? Say, we can put our arms around each other and steady each other." Both girls rose, frantically wiggled their arms until they found each other, and took minuscule sliding steps to get side by side, where their arms could go around each other. They stood there for a minute.

"My feet are hurting and cramping," Lindsey complained.

"Mine too, but we want to go home, so we have to learn to walk, Lindsey," Ashley replied.

Just then, they heard a sort of shuffling sound coming their way. It was Juanita, her short legs encased in her leather booties making a scraping sound. "Hello, I'm Señorita Juanita. I'm cook and helper." She walked up to the two girls who were wiggling while trying to stand upright.

"Hi Juanita. I'm Lindsey Barron," she held out her hand

as she always had, forgetting that she had no lower arm and hand there. Juanita reached up and gently took her arm.

Following suit, Ashley raised her arm in the rough direction she though Juanita was located. Both girls still held each other with their other arm. "I'm Ashley Stokes-Compton, Lindsey's sister, though I don't remember why I am not called Barron. Golly, you seem awfully short."

Lindsey began feeling Juanita with her free arm. She seemed a very short woman. Juanita explained, "I lost my lower legs when I was so ill. Doctors had to remove them. Dominus made me these leather booties so I can still walk a little. It is slow and difficult, but I can manage. So I am short now."

"Oh that is so horrible, Juanita!" Ashley exclaimed, genuine worry and concern in her voice.

"Si, but I can still cook and clean. I'm looking after you girls now. I glad for company. I here by myself most time. You like Juanita's cooking, you see."

"I have to go pee," Lindsey suddenly said.

"Me too," Ashley added, not realizing it was part of the effect of their tight corsets.

"We have bathroom. I take you there. No pee on floor please. Juanita has hard time getting around and cleaning up mess. Please, I lead you to bathroom."

"Well, we are supposed to practice walking," Lindsey suggested.

"But we can barely stand up, and we cannot see anything. Why is it so dark in here?" Ashley asked.

"The lights are on. Dominus says you can no see no more. New eyes you have. Come, I lead you somehow." She moved herself between the girls and put a steadying arm around each girl. "Okay, take step, Juanita lead you. Small steps, Juanita take only small steps, please." Wobbling, waving their short arms wildly to maintain their balance, the two teens took very tiny, hesitating steps. It seemed like an eternity before they reached the bathroom. Both girls' feet were aching, but had now become rather numb to the pain.

The two realized without Juanita's help, they would be very helpless indeed, but now they both were hungry. It was well past lunchtime. Slowly, Juanita led the girls into the kitchen. "Juanita glad you both walks so slowly, keeps up with me. I so slow, but you slow too. I fix good food."

Both girls now smelled the aroma of something cooking, but discovered that they couldn't feed themselves. Juanita was able to get them to drink their own sodas, which she put into plastic glasses. Using their arms, they somehow managed this tiny action. Juanita had to feed them, but they all chatted away as she did so. Conversation was precious to this older woman.

Juanita explained the layout of the rooms carefully pointing out what was in each room. "While I do dishes, you two see if you can find the couch in the exercise room? That will be a very long walk for you to manage. Holler if you need help."

"Yes, we must practice walking," Lindsey merrily replied, having already forgotten how difficult it was and how badly her feet had hurt earlier.

"Yes, we must, but let's put our arms around each other, Lindsey. I'm steadier that way. Where are you anyway?" Ashley asked, waving her arms in search of her sister.

After some awkward steps, their waving arms made contact. Soon, they had their arms around each other and began making their way out of the kitchen. After sometime, Ashley felt the wall the kitchen, and Lindsey felt the door opening. After a little side shuffling, they entered the large room. "How are we going to find the couch?" asked Ashley, getting slightly afraid.

"She said it is on the opposite side of the wall from where we are entering now. I guess we walk across and bump into it?"

"But I can't see if I am walking in a straight line," Ashley complained. Nevertheless, she added, "I guess this is why we need to do so much practicing."

"I suspect so," Lindsey replied. Slowly, the two took the tiniest of steps, heading across the room. Perhaps a half hour later, they finally reached the couch and collapsed onto it, their feet aching, gasping for breath. "I hope I don't have to pee for a long time!" Lindsey suddenly realized that she was now really far from the bathroom.

"I want to go home, Lindsey," Ashley began crying. "I feel miserable. I hurt all over. This is not right. I know it."

Lindsey put her arm on her sister's shoulder, rubbing her back as best she could. "I know. Me too. I want to go home. He said we could go home just as soon as we can walk for a half day around this room. We will just have to work harder on our walking, sis, that's all. I've caught my breath now. Shall we see if we can go back and get to the bathroom? I think I may need to go again by the time we get there."

By bedtime, both girls were exhausted, drained of all enthusiasm. Yet, getting into bed also proved challenging without the help of Juanita. She helped them take off with their cotton dresses, and she slipped a silky nightgown onto each teen. After positioning each girl by her bed, she had them sit down, and then she tucked them in, pulling up the covers for them. Juanita could not help but give each girl a kiss on her forehead. "You plenty brave girls. You did well today. Tomorrow be better, Juanita hopes so."

The next morning, as the girls got out of bed, Juanita helped them to the bathroom. Almost at once and as if on cue, Dominus appeared. He had the teens stand, leaning against the wall while he undid their corsets. "Ah, I can breathe again," Lindsey said. "Are our waists now fourteen inches? Are we done with the waist training, sir?"

"Almost, we shall see how this one fits you," Dominus said, while grinning evilly at her. He waved his wand and commanded, "Close Fully and Tie." Lindsey had no choice but to exhale all her breath. It was forced out of her. If yesterday was bad on breathing, this new one was downright impossible!

"I—I can't breathe at all!" Lindsey hollered.

"Yes, you can, small breaths, dainty 'lady-like' breaths. See, you are speaking. Yes, perfect, fourteen inches, Lindsey. You are done. Now let me see how Ashley is doing."

"Oh! It's way, way too tight! I'm fainting!" Ashley exclaimed as his spell activated, constricting her waist to fourteen inches around. She felt like her middle was being cut in half.

"Perfect waist, Ashley. You should be very proud of your

achievement. You too, Lindsey. It is a remarkable woman who has her waist trained to be so dainty, so perfect," Dominus cooed to the naive girls. The Idiot Mind spell worked to perfection, he noted.

"Oh, it is—perfect then?" Ashley asked, taking fast, sort breaths, but feeling light headed.

"Absolutely perfect, Ashley, Lindsey. You should feel very, very proud," he poured it on, and the girls bought it completely.

He waived his wand and commanded twice, "Melt Corset!" Neither teen understood what he was doing. Nothing felt any different. However, had they had eyes, they would have seen that their corsets had melted beneath their skin, just as he had done with Nadia. Without the proper sequence of spells, these corsets were now a permanently part of their bodies. Further, any attempt to cast the Rise to Surface spell, which was the first spell in the sequence to remove them, would trigger the poison capsule to explode, killing the girls. Dominus gave an evil grin, as he admired his handiwork. He was finally getting his sadistic revenge on these two pesky, interfering teens. No longer would they be interfering with his plans! After all, they had somehow sabotaged his marriage to Nadia, raided two of his pleasure houses, stealing his women away from him. Now they would both pay the ultimate price for such meddling.

He put their cotton dresses back on them, lamenting that he dare not dress them fetish style, not until they were eighteen anyway. "Now do you still want to go home?"

"Oh yes," Ashley replied, gasping for a breath, adding, "very much so!"

"Good. So how are you doing on your walking practice?"

"We managed," Lindsey uttered the two words and stopped to breathe again, "to get across," gasping again, "the room once." She was finding it hard to say more than a couple of words without having to breathe. "This corset ... is too ... tight! ... Really, ... it is!"

"A perfect body has its price, Lindsey. But I promise you that in a day or so you will be quite comfortable with it. Don't worry; you'll be fine. Now I want you both to practice walking a lot. You can go home once you can walk around this room for a half of a day without stopping. I know I should make that a whole day, but you do need to have some time to eat. So I'm compromising with you, half a day non-stop. If you really want to impress me, then see if you can walk around the room non-stop all day. Juanita can feed you and help you use the bathroom when needed, of course. Now let's see you two go over to the couch and sit down. You said you managed that yesterday."

Lindsey and Ashley moved their arms about wildly until they felt each other. Carefully, they moved side by side. With an arm around each other, they painstakingly slowly headed off toward the other side of the room, hoping the couch would be there.

"Oh no, no, no. This will never do!" Dominus interrupted them. "You must be able to walk all by yourselves, if you want to go home. You can't be cheating by helping each other out."

"Oh!" exclaimed Lindsey. "I'm sorry. ... I didn't ... know that."

She and Ashley let go of each other. With their short arms moving wildly in all directions trying to keep their balance, each attempted to cross the distance. Dominus put his hand across his mouth to keep from laughing. His torture of these two was complete! "This is better than anything I have ever come up with in all my life!" he thought to himself.

Neither teen made it across the room. Both lost their balance, flailing wildly as they fell onto the hard floor. "Keep practicing," Dominus exclaimed and Teleported away. He could contain his laughter no longer. Laughing hysterically, Dominus entered an office to get more of his new plans into operation.

"I'm sorry ... sir. Are ... you there?" Lindsey, fighting hard to keep from crying called out from the floor. She heard no answer.

"I can't ... breathe like ... this," Ashley said, some distance away from Lindsey. "I think ... he is ... gone. Help ... me, please."

Unable to crawl in their dresses, Lindsey discovered she

could roll. Soon her body rolled into her sister. Together with a great effort, they managed to get to their feet. Locking their arms around each other for support, they continued their way across the room. When they finally found the couch, both collapsed into it in a faint. This had been exhausting work. Their new corsets were incredibly confining, more so that those that Nadia had worn. After a time they both came too.

Crying, Ashley said, "We'll … never get … to go … home."

"Yes, we … will, Ashley. … We just … have to … practice a … whole lot. … Besides, we … can't take … these things … off without … killing ourselves."

"Oh! Right. … Practice. … He said … we would … get used … to it," Ashley tried to be brave.

"Be brave, … Ashley. Practice … so we … can go … home. I … have to … go pee!" Ashley moaned; this meant they would have to walk a very long way immediately. The two got to their feet and, supporting each other, headed toward what they guessed was the doorway to the short hall that led to the bathroom. Every few steps, they had to stop to catch their breath.

After an eternity, they found the opposite wall, but not the doorway. Finally, they called for Juanita's help. She told them that they had gone the wrong way. After forty feet of torturous walking for nothing, this promised to be a horribly long day for them.

Chapter 14—Monane's Breakthrough

Pam had awful nightmares Saturday night. She kept seeing Lindsey and Ashley dying, reaching out to her, but she was unable to reach them. Three times, she awoke in a cold sweat. Nothing they had done after supper had made any difference. No one had any idea where the two girls were being held prisoner.

Sunday, looking for possible clues, Pam spent every minute on her computer. She did find out that there were a number of gold mines in this area. Tracking the foreign owners proved exceedingly difficult.

After lunch, the group met in Alister's office, though he looked like he had gotten no sleep at all. "I've decided that if we cannot find them today, then I will spend whatever it takes to purchase a Wish Spell Scroll. I want them back here soon."

"Alister, that will likely cost a half million dollars!" Professor Cho Lin gasped.

"I won't have them missing school. Besides, this is my fault, my lack of judgment. I should have cancelled Telluride Day this year. It is the only place that Dominus can get at them," he explained. The group discussed things to try during the afternoon, and then disbanded to carry them out.

All avenues had failed by the afternoon. After eating supper, Monane decided to try something different. She retired to Alister's office and cast her Hear What Another Is Hearing spell on Lindsey. She steeled herself for the worse and began listening in to what was going on around Lindsey, wherever she was located.

She heard the sound of their steel heels and toes against the hard stone, their gasping sounds, and their constant chatter about learning to walk so they could go home. Monane's heart nearly burst because she was so helpless to rescue them. Still, she steeled herself and listened for anything that might be useful.

Then, she heard the sound of a Spanish-speaking woman and suddenly came alert. This Juanita just helped them go to the bathroom and was now leading them into the kitchen for a snack. She listened closely to their constant chatter. When she thought that they were all seated, Monane cast another spell, "See What Juanita Sees!" Her wand activated. Suddenly, Monane could see everything! She cried out at what she saw though.

It was all Monane could do to keep her focus and to learn all that she could about this prison. Definitely underground, she concluded, after getting a good look at the walls, stone. Juanita was feeding each girl some chicken now. Then, a piece dropped onto the floor, and Monane gasped as she got a good view of Juanita. The woman had no legs! Well, that was not correct. She had her legs amputated at her knees. She moved around on some kind of leather pads. Otherwise, Monane noted, the woman seemed all right. She was not blind or deaf. But was she a witch? Was she in league with Dominus? These questions Monane needed answering. She continued to watch, re-casting her spell each time it ended.

She saw no wand anywhere. As the Tracker watched, Juanita slid down to the floor and, with an arm around each girl, led her into her bedroom. She watched as the kindly woman helped each girl to change into their nightgown. Monane gasped when she saw the melted corsets though and the steel shoes fastened to their feet. As Juanita leaned over to kiss each girl goodnight, she got a good look at each teen's eyes. Those were not human eyes, she guessed. They looked different. Then she realized those were merely glass eyeballs. Dominus had replaced their eyes with these fakes. No wonder the girls were blind. They had no eyes at all.

"The *** sick bastard!" Monane cursed to the office room's walls. She seldom got this angry, but now she was positively fuming with anger and rage, so much so that her spells de-activated, bringing her back to the present. She took a deep breath and recast it.

Monane now decided to experiment a little. While watching the girls in their beds though Juanita's eyes, she cast a Message to Lindsey. If the spell worked, she expected to see the little paper message appear before the glass eyes of Lindsey. No paper appeared, though her spell worked. This agreed with their Tracking observations, that is, the magic trail veered away from the intended recipient. Yet, she had been successful with two other spells.

If only one of the teens had the sense to ask Juanita where they were at, Monane would have the key answer she needed. Yet, there was no way to make either teen ask. Just then, Professor Cho Lin entered, bringing Monane a hot pot of tea. Monane asked her to cast her spell to see what she was seeing. Cho Lin called out, "See What Monane Is Seeing!" A flash from her wand and Cho Lin gasped, knocking over her teacup!

Juanita said, "Good night señoritas. Perhaps tomorrow you do better. I hope so. I thought you were both muy valiente today. You did not give up. Mañana be better, you see."

"Night Juanita, thank you," Lindsey replied, finally not gasping so frequently.

Juanita walked slowly and clumsily back to her kitchen, awkwardly climbing onto her chair. She continued to sip her tea.

"We need some way to get Juanita to say out loud where this place is at," Monane whispered to Cho Lin.

"Brilliant, positively brilliant, Monane! I know just the spell, my specialty."

Cho Lin carefully cast her illusion based spell. While the two women continued to watch and listen through Juanita, the Spanish woman thought she heard Lindsey's voice call out, "Juanita, where are we? What is this place we are in?"

Juanita was totally fooled by the illusion and smiled, "Señoritas, we are in the old Umuquena Gold Mine. The entrance collapsed years ago, killing my husband and mucho others. I used to be cook for miners here. But no more when collapse. Dominus found me and gave me this job to cook and keep this place clean. Pays me thousand dollars a year, mucho fortune. You sleep now. Rest tired bodies. Juanita goes bed soon too."

Pam was in utter exhaustion and despair. Nothing she had tried yielded any clues. It was now dark, and she figured that tomorrow Alister would spend a huge amount to get the Wish Scroll and that she had failed her friends utterly. Just then, a Message from Monane appeared before her eyes.

Bring laptop. Come at once to Alister's office! M.

Startled, she jumped up and grabbed her laptop. "Where are you going?" asked Tom, startled out of a doze here in their study hall.

"What's up?" Deiter asked, also awaken from an ill doze.

"Monane Messaged me. Something is up. She said to come to Alister's office and bring my laptop." Pam waved her wand and cast her Magical Door. Just as she was about to step through the door, Tom, Deiter, and Jim dashed through it before she could say no. All four arrived in Alister's office, where Monane was taking a cup of tea from Cho Lin.

"Ah, good news, Pam. I have gotten more data on where they are being held prisoner," Monane explained what she had been doing. "This woman is definitely Spanish and said that they are in a mine that has collapsed in the distant past. It used to be a gold mine called the Umuquena Gold Mine. See if you can locate that on your map. I hope it is within that ten-mile circle. I see the boys came too," she added with a smile.

Fifteen minutes later, Pam had the mine located precisely. Its collapsed entrance was clearly marked on her map and was squarely in the middle of their search zone, adding even more credence to the results. "I'm Teleporting there immediately!" Jim declared.

"Hold on nephew. The only entrance collapsed years ago. Probably the only way inside is to Teleport, and you know as well as I do that you have to know well the location underground before you cast it. I don't want my nephew materializing in solid rock!" Monane knocked the wind out of his sails. "Besides, there are a number of location blocking spells cast upon this place. Message spells are deflected as we know. However, a few others are getting through. Give us some time to work out how to get to them. Meantime, go find Alister and form up a big rescue party, Jim. Deiter, you go help him, will you? And send Amanda here at once."

Amanda and Alister arrived and were brought up to date on Monane's discoveries. That numerous location-confusing spells had been cast on this place made it very difficult for them to precisely locate the underground rooms. That it was now nighttime there only made matters worse. Alister vetoed going there at once because the terrain was mountainous and jungle, tricky even by daylight. Instead, they concentrated on finding ways to break through the enchantments that Dominus had placed upon this secret hideout.

Meanwhile, Pam ignored magical means, preferring to use normal Sleuthing methods. She and Tom began tracking down the old plans of the mine. They were not online, they discovered. Next, they tried satellite imagery. The nighttime views, when zoomed in fully, showed potential airshafts from which a faint light shown up into the sky. Pam found this encouraging. Leaving Tom to explore this more fully, she switched over to the radar mapping views. "Eureka! I've got it!" she called out, her fatigue and exhaustion instantly leaving her. "Here is the chamber."

Everyone gathered around her laptop and stared at the false image colors. "This is a radar mapping view, not what you can see with your eyes. This spot here—this must be the main exercise chamber. Here is the kitchen and one of these two is the bathroom and the other the bedroom. Got you now, Lindsey. Hang on a bit longer!" Pam exclaimed.

"I'll superimpose that image over yesterday's surface view, Pam," Tom called out, his fingers typing madly. Soon, he had the two overlain.

Indeed, it was rugged terrain! A forty-five degree rocky slope lay above their chamber. Even standing on the surface in the daytime would be challenging, let alone in total darkness. "To the rescue!" exclaimed Deiter, all traces of his own despair and exhaustion vanished.

"Caution, caution everyone," Alister spoke. "While it might be prudent and easier for us to make this rescue attempt in the morning, I dare not take the risk that Dominus will not move them to another location during the night. We certainly can Teleport to this location, but landing will be tricky. I suggest that we use a Magical Door to try to gain entrance into the complex. Yes, that will be the safest method. The place probably is illuminated by Continuous Light spells, so when you open the door, you ought to see light. If you see darkness, something is very wrong. Do not try to step though into solid bedrock."

"The girls have just gone to bed, so they are probably not yet asleep. I think it best if only a few go inside first. We do not want to scare this Juanita woman or frighten the girls," Alister said. "After all, we know that they are under the Idiot Mind spell and have greatly diminished reasoning faculties."

"Jim and I should go first," Deiter interrupted him. "We're their boyfriends. They will recognize us and not be scared."

Alister grinned, "Oh to be young again," he thought to himself. "Yes, that may be the wisest course to take. Jim and Deiter make first contact. "Please pay particular attention to this Juanita woman. We don't think she is a witch, but she may well be very frightened of strangers appearing in the middle of the night. Once you have explained to her that a rescue party is coming, Message us, and the rest of us will enter. Pam ought to get the chance to scour the place for any clues before we leave. After everyone is out of there, I intend to collapse it further, make this secret hideout no longer usable. Okay, let's get our things together; we've a rescue to perform!"

None needed his pep talk! Everyone was very eager to get underway. However, a few minutes were spent collecting some sacks, in case they found something to confiscate. Deiter, Pam, and Amanda went to get their Staves of Power as well, just in case of trouble. Around ten o'clock, the large party apparated on the side of the mountain in Venezuela. Most slipped and fell upon landing, however.

Pam then got her laptop out of hibernation and compared views. In the dark, she couldn't tell anything and resorted to good old GPS signals. "Follow me," she called out, though Tom had to steady her, because she had to hold on to her laptop and try to walk over this rough, rocky ground, sloping away steeply beneath her feet. More than once, Tom kept her from falling.

"Bingo. According to GPS, we are over the middle of the large chamber. It is directly below us," Pam called out.

How far down was the real question? Alister began to

create Magical Door spells, making each one about ten feet further down than the previous one. When he opened the door, blackness was all that was seen. He canceled that spell, casting another ten feet on down. At three hundred ten feet, light came out when he opened the door. Cautiously he stuck his head inside and looked around. He reappeared and recast the spell, lowering it by about three more feet. After taking another peek, he announced, "Okay, watch your step. It is about a foot above the cavern floor. Remember boys; be careful. Stay alert for traps and don't frighten the girls or Juanita. Let me know the instant it is safe for the rest of us to enter."

Deiter and Jim nodded and stepped through the door, quietly stepping down to the cavern floor. They saw a purple couch against one far wall, two chairs near them, and one exit to their right. "What should we do now?" Deiter whispered to Jim.

"Let's not startle them. Ashley, my Princess, are you here?" Jim called out, not too loudly, but gently. "Ashley, are you asleep or are you awake? It's Jim. I've come to rescue my Princess."

Deiter called, "Lindsey, you awake? It's Deiter. I'm here to rescue you. Where are you?"

"Who's there?" called out a voice with a decidedly Spanish accent. They assumed it was Juanita.

"Deiter? That you? Come to take me home?" the voice of Lindsey called out.

"Jim! I'm in bed back here. Please take me home," Ashley called out. Both girls struggled to sit up in their beds, suddenly becoming very cheerful and excited.

"It's okay, Juanita. We are their boyfriends. Jim and Deiter. We've come to take them home," Jim called out.

Shortly, he heard strange shuffling noises coming from down the hall. Wisely, the two boys decided to remain where they were. Presently, a very short, frightened woman, walking with a strange waddling gait moved very slowly towards them. "Hi, you must be Juanita. I'm Jim, Ashley's boyfriend. This is Deiter, Lindsey's boyfriend. Thank you very much for caring for our girlfriends."

"My god! What happened to your legs?" Deiter now saw the reason for her strange manner of movement. She had no lower legs and was walking on some kind of leather pads.

"Señors, es nighttime. They are in bed. This way. How you know my name? Dominus tells you?" she asked.

Deiter said, "Si," just to keep it simple at this point. Both boys had to suppress their urge to dash down the hallway to their girlfriends, but followed the painstakingly slow waddle of Juanita. Finally, they entered their bedroom and saw the two girls sitting on the edges of their beds, their heads moving slightly trying to face the sounds coming their way.

"Is that ... you, Jim?" Ashley called out. She could not see him and gasped for breath ever couple of words.

"Deiter?" Lindsey said questioningly, looking more at a wall than him.

Jim and Deiter rushed to their bedsides. "Yes, it's me, Jim, Princess. I've come to take you home."

"Lindsey! It's me, Deiter," he said, as he got to Lindsey's side. She was failing around with her short arms trying to feel for him. He took her arms in his hands and Lindsey attempted to stand up, nearly pulling Deiter over in the process.

"Deiter! Oh Deiter. ... I love you," Lindsey said naively, and did her best to feel for his face, eventually finding his lips and then kissing him.

Nearby, Jim, grasping Ashley's arms, pulled her up, and began kissing her. She threw her arms around him and held on to him for dear life, while kissing him passionately. Even though her passion didn't subside, Jim finally ended it, moving slightly to her side. "Gosh you are so tall in these shoes! How do you manage to walk in them?" he asked the obvious question.

"Oh, we are ... supposed to practice ... walking for a half ... day in the exercise ... room, then we ... get to go home. ... Jim, can you ... take me home now ... even if I cannot ... manage to walk ... much yet? ... Please, Jim, I ... want to go home." Ashley began begging him.

Deiter followed Jim's moves, but Lindsey nearly fell, forcing him to hold onto her very securely.

Lindsey said, "We passed one ... test, we have ... got

fourteen inch ... waists, but we ... can't breathe. ... Still, I love ... you, Deiter. ... Can you take ... me home? ... I want to ... go home, even ... if I can't ... yet walk there ... myself. I ... promise to keep ... on practicing ... walking when I ... get home."

"Yes, we came here to take you both home," Deiter explained.

"You will have to hold on to them," Juanita took it upon herself to explain. "They can only walk when they are holding on to each other. They fell yesterday when they tried to walk alone."

"Thank you, Juanita. Thank you. Say, we have some other people who would like to come and talk with you, and thank you for taking such good care of our girls," Jim said kindly. "Would it be all right for them to come inside now?"

"Si, but I don't know how to tell them to come inside," she replied, slightly flustered. This had never happened before, guests arriving so unexpected. Dominus always told her before when to expect guests. Always they had been rude men, she recalled, not kind ones like these boys.

"We know the way. I'll tell them to come on in. Thanks again, Juanita," Jim said softly.

"Si, I make coffee now," Juanita replied and began waddling towards the kitchen. When she had turned her back, Jim cast his Message spell to the others.

"Are we supposed ... to walk ... home now?" Ashley asked Jim. "I can't see ... anything anymore. ... We have these ... new pretty blue ... eyes. ... Do you like my ... fourteen inch waist? ... It is supposed to ... make me a perfect ... fashion model, ... but I can't breathe ... well at all."

"Princess, you look gorgeous," Jim said and gave her a reassuring kiss.

"Do you think ... I look like a ... fashion model, ... Deiter?" Lindsey naively asked. "My waist is ... also fourteen inches ... too and I have ... new pretty blue ... eyes too, but ... I can't see ... out of them. ... Do you know ... why that is? ... I can't breathe ... well."

"Lindsey, you are the prettiest girl in the whole wide world! I love you too. Yes, your eyes are pretty blue, but you can't see out of them because they are fake glass eyeballs. Darn

Dominus cut out your eyes and put these glass balls in your sockets."

"Oh, I thought ... his name was just ... Dominus, not ... Darn Dominus," Lindsey replied. Taking another breath she added, "What's a fake ... eyeball? ... What's a socket? ... Are they pretty? ... They're supposed to ... be pretty."

"Yes, they are pretty, but not as pretty as you are, Lindsey," Deiter replied, realizing just how badly she was under the effects of the Idiot Mind spell.

"Ah there you are, Miss Barron, Miss Stokes-Compton," the kindly voice of Alister broke in on them. "Governor Alister here with some others to rescue you two and take you home with us."

"But I want ... to go home ... with Deiter," Lindsey protested.

"Yes, that is what I meant, Lindsey," Alister quickly replied, defusing her protest. "Once we get you home, we'll get you healed up, arms re-grown."

"Oh! We were ... not supposed to ... forget!" Ashley exclaimed, stopping catch her breath again.

"Oh! Right, ... we promised not to ... forget, didn't we?" Lindsey added. "Can we go home now ... or sit down? ... It is hard standing ... like this."

"Señors, señoritas, se coffee is ready. Oh, so mucho hombres," Juanita exclaimed as she came back into the bedroom. Cho Lin had her hand over her mouth to keep from emitting her reactions to seeing her two students like this. Wilma and Monane stood there stone-faced, crying inside. Pam and Tom were both white-faced, holding onto each other's hands. Amanda and Ahana also just stared in disbelief, trying to grasp the tortures her two dear friends had undergone.

Kathy had stayed behind to help Doctor Caterwall prepare his potions. Inside the large chamber, Emilio, Audrey, and Professor Delius stood watch, looking for traps, and alert for unexpected arrivals. Outside, Huan Su stood guard under an Invisibility spell.

Audrey said, "Thank you Juanita, coffee would hit the spot right now or perhaps some tea."

Taking the hint from Audrey, Emilio commented, "Say, do I smell tacos?"

"Si, señor, tacos. I made some for my snack. Still warm. You like?"

"Sí, muchas gracias, Señora Juanita. Amo el tacos," Emilio replied, noticing that she was very pleased to hear someone speaking her own language for a change. Audrey and Emilio followed the slow moving, waddling Juanita into the kitchen.

Wilma followed them, having received a signal from Delius. He and Monane went back into the main cavern, the exercise room, to stand guard.

Alister took his cue from what the two girls just said. He move close to them and asked, "It's all right. Please tell me what is it that you were told not to forget."

"We will be … poisoned if … someone re-grows … our arms," Lindsey said, then gasped again.

"Same thing, if you undo … our corsets and shoes," Ashley added, stopping to breathe again.

"If someone … tries to do … something with … our pretty … blue eyes, they will … explode poison … into us," Lindsey began to breathe rapid shallow breaths, trying to recover from having said so many words without breathing after each.

"Please, we don't want … to be poisoned," Ashley added, also pausing to recover with many rapid shallow breaths.

"Don't worry, kids, we don't want you poisoned either," Alister replied. "Thank you both for telling me about it. Jim, Deiter, I think it best if you take the girls home now."

"Thanks! Home!" Lindsey exclaimed.

"But we can't … walk very far … yet," Ashley protested, "but we will … try! … Want go home!" Ashley was forced to breathe rapidly once more, having overdone it again.

Both girls, leaning on their boyfriends for support, began to take tiny steps, trying their best to walk home, where they desperately wanted to go. "Princess, will you mind if I carry you home?" Jim asked Ashley, after she was totally out of breath having taken numerous tiny steps amounting to perhaps five feet.

"Please!" she gasped.

"I'm carrying you, Lindsey," Deiter added.

Lindsey was too out of breath to reply, merely waiting for him to lift her up and take her home.

Alister added, "Jim, Deiter, through the Magical Door, teleport straight to the parking lot; get them to the Infirmary, but tell Doctor Caterwall about the poison traps!"

"Absolutely, sir. I don't want my Princess being poisoned!" Jim called back. The two boys carried their girlfriends out into the exercise room, stepped through the Magical Door, held open by Delius, and stepped outside in the night. Each waved their wand and cast their Teleport spell. A minute later, each boy laid his girlfriend down on one of Doctor Caterwall's exam tables. Jim warned him about the poison traps.

"Señora Juanita, these are the best tacos I have ever had!" Emilio exclaimed.

"Si, Juanita good cook," she replied with a smile.

The others now joined them, though Cho Lin made Juanita remain seated, while she brought more cups to the table. Cho Lin felt sorry for the poor woman who had no lower legs. Governor Alister, sipping the excellent coffee, complimented her on her brew and then chatted with her. Before long, she confided in him her life's story, which was altogether too short. She had married a miner and became the company's cook in this very kitchen. But when he was killed in the big collapse, she, like so many others, had been unable to find more work. She slowly starved and got sick.

Dominus came along. Here things got a bit blurry in her memory, something about waking up finding her legs gone, and Dominus saying the doctor had to amputate them to save her life. He offered her a godsend job as cook and house keeper here in this underground home, paying her a thousand US dollars each year. Yet, she admitted that she was terribly lonely and had loved every minute that the girls had been here. "Si, I miss them already," she valiantly held back tears.

Alister then said, "Juanita, I would like to make you a better job offer. I run a magic school in the United States. How would you like to come to the US with us and be one of our school's cooks? I will see that you are able to become a citizen, if you like. How does twenty-five thousand dollars a year with free room and board sound to you?"

As expected, her mouth fell open, she rattled off tons of Spanish, which Emilio alone understood. At last, she calmed down, "Si, fantastic. Si, Juanita loves to cook, good cook too. Come to America cook for students, mui good job, si. Muchas gracias!"

"Good, then there is only one small detail, Juanita. If you come with us, will you please allow our good doctor to re-grow your legs?"

She gave him a strange look, as if he was insane or ignorant. "Cada uno sabe que las piernas no pueden ser substituidas!"

Emilio quickly translated, "Everyone knows that legs cannot be replaced. Sir, I don't think she understands about magical re-growing."

Alister wisely let this slide until later. "Okay, let's gather your things, and we will go to America and my school. That's where the two girls will be. You can see them there, if you like, Juanita."

"Gracias, gracias, gracias." Cho Lin and Wilma began to help her pack up her things. When she went to the refrigerator to pack her spices, Cho Lin saw a gruesome sight: four eyeballs lay wrapped in a plastic bag. Juanita explained, "When Dominus left, I finds them on the floor. I keeps them in case he comes back for them." Cho Lin confiscated the bag and had Emilio rush deliver this to Doctor Caterwall.

Once Juanita had packed her few possessions and her savings amounting to five thousand dollars, Wilma, carrying her two bags of belongings, escorted her into the exercise room. "I need to carry you out of here. I'm afraid that you won't be able to walk." Reluctantly, Juanita allowed Wilma to pick her up. Her eyes opened wide as they stepped through the door that she had never seen before in the room. It all happened so fast that the woman could not grasp what had happened, but then she was walking into the Infirmary where she saw Ashley and Lindsey. She relaxed; she had grown fond of these two girls.

243

Just as soon as Juanita left, Alister gave the signal to search this place for all clues, to confiscate anything of any value. Pam went to work. After an hour, Pam gave up. "Sir, it is just what it appears to be, an underground hideout with nothing remotely of interest here. Bummer, I was hoping to find something useful here."

After the others left, Alister cast several Dispel Magic spells, dousing the lights, before stepping through his Magical Door. With everyone safely back at the school, his last spell caused the ground to shake, and the cavern hideout below him collapsed. No longer could Dominus and his men hide out here. He then headed to the Infirmary as quickly as possible.

He got in on the tail end of a conversation. "But I am ... perfectly healthy! ... I don't want ... to drink it! ... It smells awful!" Lindsey protested taking the potion that Doctor Caterwall was insisting she take. He knew that it was the potion to heal the Idiot Mind spell's effect on her.

"Señoritas, you should do as doctor says. He knows best," Juanita pleaded with her new friends.

"Okay," Lindsey finally agreed and drank the offered potion. Ashley followed suit.

"Juanita, perhaps tonight you would be so kind as to stay here with the girls?" Governor Alister proposed, quickly grasping the hold Juanita had over the girls. Besides, if she could just see the girls getting their arms and hands re-grown, she would understand what he wanted to do for her.

"Si, es el mejor, is good I do, gracias," she replied. A nurse led her to a side room where the two made up three beds.

"Excellent recovery of their eyeballs, undamaged, I should be able to get their eyesight recovered by morning, if, and this is a big if, we can somehow remove these glass eyes without poisoning the girls," the doctor explained.

"Good, if they can see and have their faculties back by morning, that will go a long way," Alister replied. "I presume you have been Detecting Traps?"

Jim and Deiter echoed, "You bet!"

"Didn't find anything! That's the trouble with Dominus," Doctor Caterwall explained. "He is always changing his methods on us. No traps, but have a look for yourself. However, please note on the x-rays the presence of foreign objects, there in each glass eye, in their backs, on each ankle above those metal shoes, and at the ends of each arm."

Fortunately, the girls heard nothing of this, they were now sound asleep, a byproduct of his potion to recover their minds. Alister very carefully checked for traps, covering every inch of their bodies. Like the others, he found none. Next, he reviewed the x-rays. "Darn, darn, darn!" he exclaimed. "You are right. Let me examine them more closely." He cast an Identify spell, Amanda and Pam followed suit. Deiter and Jim were seconds behind them, though they were not sure at first what they were identifying.

"See, there are traces around the small sphere within the glass eye," Alister pointed out.

"Yes, I see it now. Isn't it one of those In Case Of This Then Do That spell?" Jim asked. Deiter now saw that Jim was right; he'd been too slow in identifying the presence of that spell, one that he had yet to learn.

"Let's get Mary Ann down here and have her take a look. She is the best person I know of in matters of this spell," Alister said. A few minutes later, dressed in mismatched socks, hair flying in all directions, Professor Mary Ann began carefully studying her star pupil, Ashley.

"Yes, I believe the spell went as follows, 'In Case Someone Tries to Remove the Glass Eye, Explode.' It is so tiny for a bomb," she explained.

"Poison. The girls were told it would poison them if anyone tried to remove them," Alister replied, satisfied that they had indeed worked out the spell.

"Wonderful, just wonderful," Doctor Caterwall complained bitterly. "We can fix them up pronto, only they die if we make the attempt."

"If they could only see," Jim said, "they could manage to get by while we worked out how to nullify these poison pills."

"I agree with Jim," Deiter added, "if the Idiot Mind is gone and they can see, they will be better able to cope with the rest until we can find a way. They are only glass eyeballs. I have an idea, if you want to listen to it."

"Sure, fire away," Alister answered him. Pam wondered if he was not actually letting Deiter work this out for himself, while Alister had already worked it out, much as he often did with her and Sleuting.

"It is simply speed of execution, in this case. You know—the old magic trick. Put a glass of water on a tablecloth and ask someone to pull the cloth out without spilling the water. The key is to pull the cloth fast enough so that it overcomes the force of friction between the bottom of the glass and the cloth. Here, nothing is holding these fake glass eyeballs in place. So if we can yank them out sufficiently fast, the exploding things will burst way outside of their eye sockets, causing them no harm."

"I believe you have hit upon it. However, we don't know how caustic this poison is, and we don't want to get poison spread all over this emergency room. The question is how do we remove them fast enough?" Alister replied.

"Hey, I know," Kathy decided to speak up at last. She had been sitting quietly, potions at the ready. Now she had an idea. "Why not cast a Force Wall around the glass eye, bending it to totally surround the thing. Then, when you remove it, why, if it explodes, the explosion will be contained with the Force Wall."

"Hey, that's better than my idea!" Deiter exclaimed. "Way to go Kathy!" She beamed. Seldom had she gotten praise, being only an average student until she had gotten to Potion Making I last year. Now she shone like a star, and she knew this was her field of expertise.

Beads of perspiration dripped from the doctor's forehead as he slowly and with the greatest of care began to slide his Force Wall behind one of Lindsey's glass eyes. He did not want to jar the object in to thinking it was being removed nor did he want to cause any further damage to her eye sockets. After five long minutes, he had the glass eye completely surrounded. "Okay, here we go," he said. He gave a quick yank and pulled the glass eyeball out of her head. As expected, something inside it caused a small explosion, which was contained within the protective barrier. The ball itself was destroyed. Glass shards lay in pieces, and a funny colored liquid covered it all. They all realized that Lindsey would have had all these shards buried in her eye socket with the poison spreading everywhere had they just removed it.

"Delius, I believe this is your area," Doctor Caterwall suggested, handing him the remains held tightly within the Wall of Force, now shaped as a sphere.

"Yes, I will get right on it. One poison identification coming up. Care to join me in a bit of research, Miss Townsend?" Kathy looked shocked that a Professor would actually ask for her help. Eagerly, she headed off with Delius to the student potion making labs to analyze the poison.

Twenty minutes later, all the glass eyes had been safely removed. Now Doctor Caterwall set to the real work of healing their original eyes and the optic nerves, which had been severed by the magical spells. Because the eyes were in such good shape, having been refrigerated, he knew this would be the easiest of cures for these girls. An hour later, both girls had their eyes bandaged and were properly clothed for the night. Carefully, Deiter and Jim carried both girls and put them into the beds beside Juanita's bed.

Around eleven that Sunday night, Kathy joined Pam and Amanda in their bedroom. "We did it—isolated the magical concocted poison. A tiny amount will kill you. Tomorrow in Potion Making, Professor Delius will help me brew up a big batch of antidote potion, just in case." Kathy was on cloud nine. She had done something quite useful and was very pleased with herself.

"Terrific, Kathy!" Pam was quick to lavish well-earned praise on her. She remembered the long, tedious hours she had spent working with Kathy on science and math. Now, Kathy found something in which she excelled over everyone else, which pleased Pam as well.

Chapter 15—Back to Classes, Mostly

Early the next morning, before everyone normally headed down for breakfast, Pam, Kathy, Audrey, and Amanda raced to the Infirmary to check on Ashley and Lindsey. They found both girls awake. The nurses had just finished helping them use the restroom and had dressed the girls. Lindsey and Ashley were sitting on the edge of their beds, awaiting someone to feed them.

"Hi Lindsey, Ashley! It's Pam, Amanda, Kathy, and Audrey here," Pam announced. "How are you feeling today? We had quite a time finding you this time and rescuing you."

"Thanks, my head hurts, but I guess that will pass. Idiot Mind got us good," Lindsey replied. "Did we say anything really stupid, you know, that we should know about?"

"Yes, we must have been very stupid, but did we say something, like well you know, really embarrassing? I don't think I can stand being teased just now," Ashley added, looking more or less in their general direction.

"Well, Lindsey," Audrey said hesitatingly, "you did tell Deiter that you loved him. Twice. You couldn't stop kissing him when he found you."

"I didn't? Did I?" Lindsey's face turned red.

"Yes, I'm afraid that you did," Pam said stoically.

"What about me?" Ashley asked again, afraid that she had said something equally embarrassing.

"You're cool, Ashley," Pam admitted. "Doctor Caterwall says you will probably have your eyesight back today. That's good because it's Monday, and we've got classes again."

"Oh no! I am going to miss classes again!" Lindsey wailed.

"Rats, I was working my butt off just to stay up," Ashley added. "Now I will be so far behind that I'll never catch up. You don't suppose that they will hold us back a year, make us take fifth year over again next year do you?"

"Oh, I don't believe that will be necessary, Miss Stokes-Compton," the friendly voice of Alister broke in on the teens.

"Not unless you plan to lie in bed for the next seven months." The girls giggled.

"Seriously, I have brought you all breakfast, if your friends would be so kind to help you two eat. I believe that they will take copious notes for you today. Hopefully, by tomorrow you will be able to get back to your studies some way."

While Pam began feeding Lindsey and Amanda, Ashley, Lindsey asked, "Are we really going to be able to see again soon? I mean I recall Dominus telling us something about there being poison things all over us, like in our eyes and shoes."

"Quite right about that. Instead of traps, this time Dominus concocted a special poison, lethal in small doses. However, Miss Townsend here and Delius have managed to isolate the poison and will be brewing an antidote today in Potion Making Class."

"Wow, you did that, Kathy?" Lindsey replied, very impressed with Kathy's skills.

"Yes, last night, while they were healing your eyes. Strange thing. After he removed your eyes, he just left them lying on the floor, and Juanita put them in the refrigerator in case he wanted them later on. I think she figured he just forgot them or something," Kathy explained. "So Doctor Caterwall was able to reuse them, but I'm not sure how."

"Say where is Juanita?" Pam asked.

"One of the nurses took her down to see the kitchen," Ashley replied. "She wanted to get started early, helping to fix breakfasts for everyone. She is really a terrific person and took care of us when we needed it."

"Well, she will be one of our cooks from now on. I've hired her," Alister grinned, though the two could not yet see him.

Suddenly Lindsey became very serious. "Alister, Pam, can you stick around a while? I think I have finally discovered a way to stop Dominus and his Restricted Wish spell." Pam nearly fainted! She's spent hours researching this! Alister nearly choked on his egg.

"Certainly," he coughed to clear his throat. "We need

miracles like these, if we are to stop Dominus. When you are ready, you have my undivided attention!"

"Mine too," Pam managed to squeak. She looked at Lindsey, who was in terrible shape. Yet, in spite of everything that had happened to her, she still kept alert and had a way to stop Dominus's most powerful spell.

Before long, Amanda, Audrey, and Kathy headed off to classes, promising to take many notes. Pam would need the notes too, at least for their first class.

"Okay, Pam and I are here, Lindsey. Are you ready to tell us?" Alister asked, scarcely able to conceal his excitement and wonder.

"When we were walking down the street, I heard the words appearing in my mind. 'I wish that Miss Lindsey Barron be brought here before me naked and with her arms removed at her elbows, nicely healed, but when she arrives, she will be under my Idiot Mind spell and under my Paralyze spell.' I think that there was a second part or a second wish to get Ashley," Lindsey explained, rubbing her throbbing head. Idiot Mind spells frequently produced headaches during the recovery period.

Ashley added, "Yes, I heard something like that too. If I recall right, it went, 'My second wish is that at the same time Miss Ashley Stokes-Compton be brought here before me naked and with her arms removed at her elbows, nicely healed, but when she arrives, she will be under my Idiot Mind spell and under my Paralyze spell.' Something like that anyway."

"Cool, Ashley, then you heard the casting too. I believe that the victim of his Restricted Wish spell also hears the wish as it is spoken while casting. As it was being cast, magical energies were flowing to me from his wand. I realized that I could deflect that energy beam, dispel it outright, throw up a wall of huge resistance forcing it back or even better, twist it all up or even disperse the energies. I believe that if one did anything at all to that energy flow, the Restricted Wish spell would fizzle and not detonate. I was going to try, but then I sensed Ashley was going to be part of it too, and I couldn't leave her to face Dominus alone. As it turned out, that was wise."

"No kidding, sis. Neither one of us could have managed alone," Ashley answered. "Thanks Lindsey. I owe you one."

"Now that is interesting, Lindsey. As you know, I've also been the victim of Dominus and his Restricted Wish spell. I too heard the words as he cast them, but didn't realize that I had the power to do something about it. It happens so darn fast, you know," Alister explained.

"No kidding, lightning fast," Lindsey replied.

"Hey, we saw him really age this time! Right after we arrived there stark naked and paralyzed, we saw him get greyer, and these lines appear on his face," Ashley added.

"Bags under his eyes too," Lindsey added.

"Okay, thanks. Pam and I will research your suggestions further. We'd best let Pam go to classes." Pam gave each girl a hug and left, thinking all the way back about what Lindsey had said. It seemed to make good sense. Only the how bothered her. How does one deflect the magical energies?

"How's my patients today?" the kind voice of Doctor Caterwall broke into their hearing.

"Much better, but we have big headaches, though," Lindsey replied, looking sort of in the direction his voice had come from, not realizing that he was now closer to her.

"You are not as short of breath today, I see," he replied, startling her by being now so much closer to her than she had expected.

"Well, we are rested and have not done anything physically exerting. Besides, I think that we are becoming more used to wearing the corsets, doctor," Lindsey speculated.

"True, true, I also gave you both a larger dose of red blood cells to carry more oxygen than normal. That ought to ease things a bit. Eat lots of liver, dears," he added. "Now then, let's remove the bandages and see how the eyes are recovering."

Jim, having finished breakfast, wandered into see how Ashley was doing. Thus, when Doctor Caterwall first removed Ashley's bandages, Jim was the first person that she saw, bringing a huge smile to her face. He grinned back; his prayers were answered; Ashley could see again.

"Things are a little fuzzy," Lindsey replied to his

questions.

After a thorough exam, he gave his prognosis. "Looks like they are nearly healed. By tonight, your eyes should be back to normal again. However, please keep eye strain to a minimum for a week, okay?" Both girls readily agreed very, very glad that they could see once more.

"Now then, all is not so good otherwise," the doctor continued. "As you know, Dominus has booby trapped the re-growth of your arms, the removal of your melted corsets, and the removal of your shoes, though I must admit that I have never seen steel shoes, much less heels like these. Here, let me show you two the x-rays. You will have a better understanding of what we are facing." He showed them their x-rays, pointing out the small objects, which contained the explosive charge and poisons.

"Any attempt to undo the corsets, remove—if we can ever figure out how—your shoes, or make any attempt to re-grow your arms will trigger these small balls to explode, sending poison throughout your body. Here is one of the glass eyeballs after we removed it." He showed them the shattered bits of glass covered with an oily substance, all still behind the protective Force Wall.

"It was Miss Townsend and Mister Cross who worked out how we could safely remove them; it worked. However, those methods will not work for these other five poison implants. They are imbedded within your flesh. No way to get a Force Wall around them. We all will be researching various ways and means, mind you. However, I don't see any solution coming very soon. None of us has ever seen anything remotely like this. It is going to take us time to work this one out. I do hope you two can somehow get by until we can work out a safe method of extraction."

"Are we talking days or longer?" Ashley asked, slightly shaken up by his seriousness.

Doctor Caterwall sighed. "Ashley, Lindsey, I would truly love to tell you it would be mere hours before we all here have worked it out, but if I said that, I would lying to you. Days, very likely. Weeks, probably. Months, gosh, I hope not! Yet, it may well take that long. We might get lucky and have it worked out later today. Realistically, girls, it may well be weeks before I am confident that I can safely remove them. I give you my word that I will spend every waking hour of every day on your situation, excepting when others need the doctor. Is this acceptable to you?"

Lindsey sighed, "It will have to be. Thank you all for working so hard on our problem. Honestly, Ashley and I can use our magical spells now to help us get by. I can still cast my phantom hands and so learn to cast new spells. So can Ashley. Wearing this horribly tight corset is most uncomfortable, and we need to use the bathroom frequently, but we can manage. Just keep us with the red blood cells. It is awful only to be able to say a word or two before gasping for breath. However, I just don't know about these shoes. Maybe since we can now see and in our right minds, we'll be able to walk a little. After all, Dominus constantly insisted that we were to practice walking quite a lot, implying that we would eventually be able to walk in them. If we can't, I guess we can just Teleport everywhere instead of walking."

"You guys work on a cure, and we will work on getting by until then," Ashley agreed. "Only someone please fetch us our school clothes and our wands. I'm going to need some practice again."

A half hour later, the two girls finally looked like themselves, as much as was possible. They opted for jeans hoping that would help hide their steel shoes somewhat from the stares of others. However, with their reduced waists, neither their blouses nor jeans fit at all well, no matter how they fiddled with their belts or sashes. Next, they began using their spells to hold and cast simple spells.

"Make phantom hands, well lower arms and hands, Ashley, that's how I used to do it when I was a first year here," Lindsey explained.

"It looks a little weird, Lindsey, your wand seems to be floating in space in front of you," Ashley stated the obvious. She tried to mimic her sister and soon had it down. "Yes, we can cast this way. Clean!" she commanded, making the proper wand motions with her phantasmal hands, which really was just a clever use of their Move Object spell. "Say, it's easier to do if you just pretend your hands are attached to your elbows, sis. See?" She demonstrated for Lindsey.

"You are right; it is a lot easier to do. Guess they will just have to get used to us having short arms," she giggled.

By ten they were both hungry again. Their stomachs were so constricted that only small amounts could be eaten at one time. "I think we're going to have to start eating about every two hours," Ashley concluded.

"No problem. We can get sandwiches to bring with us to class. Just stick them into our book bags," Lindsey concluded. "Each time we get a meal, we also get something for the in-between meal. That should work out okay, don't you think?"

After eating a small sandwich, both were full once more, at least until lunchtime. Doctor Caterwall checked on them once more. "I didn't tell you this in front of the others, but there is one thing we could do which would partially solve your problems."

"What?" asked Ashley. Doctor Caterwall looked awfully embarrassed and ill at ease. Ashley had a flash of insight and added, "Oh, I get it! You could amputate our feet and arms and then regrow the missing limbs."

"Well, yes, that's what I was thinking. Only problem is the regrowing potions and how they would interact with the embedded corset. If there were no problem with the melted corset, then yes, in a week or so you would have your feet back and hands. Unfortunately, there is no way to amputate your back. That sphere capsule is lodged solidly into your backbone, right up against a vertebra. There's just no way to operate on that one; the risks are too great."

"Dominus must stay up late at night to dream these tortures up," Ashley commented dryly. "Wish he had something better to do than figure out better ways to harm people."

"You'll get no argument from me on that one," the doctor chuckled. "The real reason I came by was to ask both of you if you can remember the command words that he used during the spells to implant the poison capsules and to turn your shoes into steel? I've been utterly unable to locate either spell in my library."

After thinking hard, both shook their head no. Lindsey justified, "We were pretty out of it by then, paralyzed, blinded by the replacement glass eyes, and turned into idiots. I didn't get any of what he said when casting. Sorry."

"Me either," Ashley added, looking a bit morose about having failed to memorize the key words.

"That's understandable girls. You were pretty traumatized at the time. I was just hoping to get a clue. Say, have you tried walking yet this morning? I am very worried that you will not be able to get around on your own. I can't imagine anyone walking in shoes like those, though I don't know how you girls managed those high heels at the Inaugural Ball, for that matter."

"No, we've been working on getting dressed and getting used to casting without our arms and hands, doctor," Lindsey replied. "I suppose that we ought to get on to that part. I suspect that will be the most difficult thing to manage."

Suddenly, Lindsey cried out, "How utterly stupid of us, Ashley! Morons we are. Duh! Magic, we are not making use of our own skills!"

"Huh?" Ashley replied, startled from her own inward thoughts.

"Morph Self—we ought to just morph ourselves into someone else! I bet all of our problems will be gone!"

"Duh! Me thinks we are still under the Idiot Mind spell! Righto! I should have thought of that too. Who should we become? Let's try it, Lindsey, but who will be change into? I mean, we can't become another Amanda and Pam. That would be too confusing for everyone."

"Hey hold on a minute you two! Do not morph yourselves! That may well trigger the poison capsules to explode!" Doctor Caterwall's shocked expression and urgent tone scared the two girls.

Lindsey's face became hot. "Oh! I didn't think about that."

"Right, the In Case of spell may well trigger if your body forms become normal," he replied using a gentler tone. "Ask me before you try anything else, please."

"We promise," Ashley agreed, still a bit shaken by his

startling pronouncement.

"Okay, I will leave you two to it. It's back to the library for me. If you need anything, let one of the nurses know or Message me in the library. I suppose I'll find Alister there too. He sure is taking this rather hard, you know. He is getting older, and I keep telling him he's taking on too much stress. Well, you know him; he'll never rest until this Dominus business is handled. In a way, I think he feels responsible for the whole thing. He was the Governor when Dominus was here. Herbert told me. Evidently, they had long talks about whether to expel Dominus or not. I probably should have kept my mouth shut about that. You'll excuse me." Doctor Caterwall made a hasty exit to avoid saying more.

"Now that is interesting," Lindsey noted. "Did you see the way he looked when he revealed that to us? Say, we ought to see if we can get Herbert to chat with us about Dominus."

"Cool idea. The more we can find out about him, the better my divinations will be. Lindsey, I'm ready to work flat out on divining his every move. After what he's just done to us, I'm fighting mad, Lindsey. He treats us as if we were, well, useless playthings made for his amusement or something. What did he mean about us becoming eighteen years old?" Ashley asked.

"Right now, he thinks of us as kids. I'm sure of it. When we are eighteen, we are legally adults. I think if we were eighteen now, he would have turned us into his play toys, like those we've been rescuing. I'm glad he didn't mess with our breasts as he did with Nadia. That would be horribly embarrassing to go class with breasts that humongous. It's going to be bad enough with these weird shoes. At least, no one can see the corsets. Can't miss our lack of arms, though, but we've both been through that before. I guess we better start trying to walk in them."

Slowly the two stood up, working hard to keep their balance. However, as Lindsey suspected, being able to see made all the difference, though had she had arms, she could have kept her balance better. "Boy, we don't dare make a mistake in these," Lindsey commented as she walked to the other side of the room. "With these little arms, I can't grab on to anything to support myself when I need it."

"Yes, it is wild. I keep trying to grab on to something, but there is no way to do it! I'll bet trying to go up or down stairs in these shoes is really going to be tricky," Ashley replied. "But it is a whole lot easier when you can see what you are doing. Just go very slowly. Maybe we can manage this after all."

The two kept doggedly at it the rest of the morning. At first, their feet cramped and pain shot through their feet, but eventually their feet became numb to it. However, to keep from stumbling, they had to watch where they were placing each step very closely, especially since they could not grab something if they started to fall. More than once, each had to fall gracefully, using a Gentle Fall spell, cast sans wand. That is, having made a mis-step and losing their balance, they made their body fall, slumping to the ground to avoid getting hurt.

At lunchtime, all their friends brought lunch to them. Pam explained, "I think the professors all believe you two will be attending class tomorrow, because they are all just reviewing things today. I think they don't want you two to miss anything important."

"Yes, and Pam and I have the afternoon off," Deiter explained. "Actually, I asked them if we could, seeing how it was all review anyway."

"Why?" asked Lindsey. "I could use the review."

Deiter blushed, "Well, I told them Pam and I would like to help you two learn to walk in your steel shoes. They agreed that one of us should always be right there with you, supporting you so you don't fall down, or anything. From now on, wherever you need to walk, my arm will be around you, Lindsey. Pam's will be around Ashley. Well," he face reddened, "except when you need to go to the bathroom, that is. Pam volunteered to take you there. We'll just switch partners. I hope you don't mind. If you would prefer someone else, let me know, Lindsey. I mean you don't have to have me, because Amanda also wanted to do it for you. I kind of talked her out of it."

"I'd love to have you helping me Deiter. Thanks, I hope you don't mind going incredibly slowly though. Ashley and I have been practicing this morning, but we still go so slowly," Lindsey replied.

"Actually, we are terrified of going up or down steps in these. We are walking on our toes you know. If we just had our arms and hands, we could grab on to things. Thank both of you for coming up with this plan. Having someone holding on to us will make it lots easier," Ashley added.

"That makes sense. Governor Alister wants us to make sure you two can get around safely with our help," Pam admitted. "I'm glad Deiter asked the professors if we could have the rest of the day off to help you two."

"Well, if Deiter needs a break, let me know," Amanda broke in. "I wanted to help you too, but Deiter can be most persuading when he wants to be. I'll be available when you are ready to head into the girl's part of the dorms, Lindsey." She flashed a smile towards Deiter, who grinned back at her. Of course, Lindsey wondered what was going on between those two, but decided to grill Amanda later tonight.

"Oh, save some of our lunch for us to eat later." Lindsey explained, "We now need to eat about every two hours. As you can see, we are both full now, and half is left. I guess we should always go around with doggie bags with us." Everyone giggled at her jest.

"I'm amazed that you can even feed yourselves," Deiter commented.

"Actually, it is doggone difficult this way," Lindsey admitted. "Before when I was only missing my hands, it was fairly easy to manipulate. Now with only my upper arms, it is tricky and awkward."

"No, downright hard!" Ashley added her sentiments.

"Will you allow us to feed you?" Deiter asked. "I mean if you will not be too embarrassed with it, I would love to be your hands at dinner. Or anywhere else for that matter, Lindsey."

Lindsey sighed, but made a decision. "Honestly, Deiter, I would be really pleased if you would do it for me. Before, I had to be independent in all things. Right now, I can barely breathe; the shoes make walking horribly tough, and, combined with everything else, it's almost too much to handle all at once. If you really don't mind, I would be very grateful,

Deiter. Thank you." Amanda flashed a knowing smile at Pam; she thought that Lindsey would accept his offer.

"Well, if Lindsey doesn't mind, I sure don't," Ashley added. "That is, if you don't mind, Pam. I hate to be a bother and a burden on others. When I had no arms at all, I was fiercely independent, had to be, but like this, it's like sis says. We can barely breathe at all, and walking is a nightmare. Trying to cope with the little things like eating is almost too much to bear. Darn Dominus and his sadistic mind anyway!"

"I'd love to, Ashley. Really, none of us mind it at all. I hope we don't seem too awkward doing it though," Pam replied, voicing her big worry about it.

"Just don't get catsup on my nose," Ashley jested. They all laughed.

As they chatted away and finished their lunches, Governor Alister dropped by. He looked old, Lindsey thought. Age lines marked his face. He looked as though he had not slept all night. "Ah, I see you both still have an appetite, albeit I'm told, a smaller and more frequent one." The girls flashed him a big smile.

"I stopped by to tell you that Doctor Caterwall and I are still working on the problem. He told me that he told you about amputating your feet and arms. Please, don't take that seriously just yet. No morphing either. We are now convinced that the infusion of the re-grow potions will be seriously impacted by the melted, embedded corset material. Lord knows what the result would be. However, if you find that you can't get around in those shoes or can't manage to do any new spell casting, and if we have given up hope of ever finding a way to undo this mess, then we would consider taking that drastic an action. I hope it does not come to that. I'm terribly sorry for having to put you through this continual torture, Lindsey, Ashley. For once, Dominus is proving to be smarter than Doctor Caterwall and me. I'm truly sorry." He sighed and looked more miserable than either had ever seen him.

Lindsey didn't quite know how to respond. "It's okay. We're managing pretty well so far. Say, I was wondering something. Are there any limits on how many times one can get their hands re-grown?" This brought a smile to the old man's face.

"Now that is a question I can answer, Lindsey. No, there are no limits on that, but please, let's not do it again after this time, shall we?" The girls giggled, while Deiter smiled.

"I've heard that Pam and Deiter have volunteered to be your constant walking companions. Thank you two. I'm putting you both on notice, Lindsey, Ashley. I don't want either of you walking anywhere on this campus by yourselves. When you need to walk in those steel shoes, I want someone at your sides at all times. It is far too risky for you to walk by yourselves. If you should fall, there is some slight chance that might cause one or more of the poison capsules to break. That is my greatest fear at this time. Promise me that you will not do any solo walking." Both girls did so, only now they had another thing to worry about.

"The capsules—they break easily?" asked a most concerned Deiter.

"Son, we just don't know, and I really don't want to risk their lives finding out. Hence, we take a bit of a precaution here. Of course, you two realize that you will not be attending PE until this matter is fully resolved?"

"Yes! We get out of PE," Ashley teased.

"Rats, just when I was liking softball," Lindsey jested.

"You can attend when they begin first aid studies," Alister added, ending their smiles. "Until then, you have a free period, though you must allow Deiter and Pam to take you where you wish to spend that period." They promised and he left. Soon the others left for their one o'clock review class, leaving Pam and Deiter to assist the girls.

"Well, we'd best get practicing," Lindsey sighed, knowing it was time to face walking in these impossible heels once more. "Deiter, let's see if we can work out the most efficient way for you to support me while I walk. Pam, you work with Ashley. Let's see if we can figure this out. I guess we should take a stroll around the campus, but we'll need our jackets, right?"

"You bet. It is downright cold outside. Supposed to snow a bit tonight," Deiter replied, waving his wand, summoning his jacket and Lindsey's as well. He helped her put

260

it on. "Golly, it looks weird on you, Lindsey. Really long sleeves with nothing in them, weird."

"No kidding, really weird! Oh well, one more inconvenience to bear. Try putting your arm securely around my waist," Lindsey suggested. Slowly and awkwardly, she began walking out of the Infirmary building. Pam with her arm securely around Ashley, followed right behind her.

"You are right. This is very slow going, but you are managing, Lindsey," Deiter complimented her.

"It's lots easier when you are supporting me, Deiter, but I still have to watch very carefully where I put each step."

After a bit, Deiter said, "You know that Alister cancelled the Halloween Dance, don't you?"

"No, why?"

"Because we were all too upset about you and Ashley. We were expecting to go on a rescue mission at any moment. Half of the school was upset about your abductions. He's rescheduled the dance for this Saturday. Will you go to the dance with me, Lindsey?"

"I don't know if I can even dance in these heels. I'd be dancing on my toes, but I'd be very disappointed if I didn't go, even if I just have to sit and watch the others dance. Thanks for asking. I hope I don't spoil it for you."

"Lindsey, just being with you is all I ever want." After a pause, he asked quietly so Pam couldn't hear, "Say, did you mean what you said to me when I was rescuing you?" Lindsey didn't answer right away, so he added, "I know you were under an Idiot Mind spell, but you said that you loved me."

Lindsey was expecting this, she sighed. "Just because I was being an idiot, Deiter, doesn't mean that I wasn't being sincere. I've been thinking about that. I have never admitted this to anyone, but I think I am in love with you, strange as that may seem. I hope you aren't offended by it."

He leaned over and gave her a kiss on her cheek. Whispering in her ear, he said, "I love you too, passionately! I dream about you every night, Lindsey, but I never thought that you would love me too! Not after the awful way I treated you in our first years here. I promise to always be the very best I can be for you, Lindsey, always. You are the greatest girl in the whole world!"

Lindsey smiled, "Not so great at the moment. I can barely walk and breathe, let alone work with my hands like this." She wiggled her arms inside the long sleeves of her jacket. Both giggled at the strange effect.

"Lindsey, I promise you one day I will rid this world of Dominus. I'm slowly becoming an Eliminator. You'd be surprised at what Wilma has already taught me. However, I still have nightmares about killing that Death Stalker when we rescued those women in Georgia. It was an accident. I meant to injure him with the cold spell, not kill him. So I won't be killing Dominus, but I'm not going to put him back in prison so he can escape again either. Somehow, I'll find a way to rid our world of that sadistic, evil man. I just don't know how just yet, but I'm working on it."

"Say, you are walking pretty well in the heels, Lindsey," he noticed that she was doing a bit better, now hazarding an occasional glance at the campus around them.

She smiled. "Because I got a good leader holding on to me."

"Hey Lindsey," Ashley called from behind her, "I've just timed our speed. No way are we going to have enough time to walk between some of our classes. We are going to have to use Magical Doors."

"I was afraid of that. We have to go so pitifully slowly just to keep from falling down. Guess our companions will have to cast the spells for us helpless ladies." All four laughed heartily. Deiter well knew that Lindsey could cast that spell without her wand or even saying the words. She could cast it right as she was walking along.

"Dominus is not going to ever stop us!" Lindsey added when they all stopped giggling. "I guess we ought to try the stairs. After all, from now on we are going to be using the tunnels. I don't think it will be possible for us to walk in the snow in these shoes. My feet are freezing cold already. We don't even have socks on, and this steel is getting as cold out as the air."

As they headed for the nearest tunnel entrance, Deiter said, "Girls, leave this to me. I think I know how I can get your feet warm. Question: do you like the way the steel looks? I mean, it doesn't even look much like a shoe."

"Er, no, Deiter, they look ugly. That's one reason we are wearing our jeans so low—to try to hide them as much as we can," Lindsey answered him honestly. Deiter opened the door to their dorm, and they went inside. "Let us sit a spell. My feet are throbbing."

They sat down on a bench. Lindsey and Ashley wanted to rub their feet, but felt only cold steel. Meanwhile, Deiter enlarged his shrunken laptop and brought it out of hibernation. "Look at these shoes. Last night I did some web surfing to see where he got the idea from—got to be from shoes that look like this. I think this pair most closely matches yours. What do you think?"

"Boy those are indeed fetish shoes. Yes, I think this is what they looked like before he shrunk them and turned them into steel." Lindsey stared at the screen, wishing Dominus had not turned them into steel.

"Okay, you two stay here. I have to go get a package," Deiter said with a wry smile. Don't move from here." He dashed off forgetting to create a Magical Door. Ten minutes later, a door appeared and he stepped through, carrying two boxes.

"Okay, now for some creativity. First, we put these warm socks on your feet. Here Pam, put these on Ashley. Just cut them in the back so they can go up over the heel, like so. Shortly, both girls were wearing heavy winter woolen socks over their steel heels. He opened one box, while handing the other to Pam. "Ta da!" He held those same exact shoes, only slightly larger.

"Boy those look fetish indeed!" exclaimed Pam. "But what do we do with them?"

"We get creative, that's what. First, we break off the heel, like so." He got out his pocketknife and began surgery on the back of the shoe. Twenty minutes later, he finished up. Lindsey now wore the black patent ballet shoes over her socks over the steel heels. Deiter cast his shrink spell on the leather so that they fit tightly against the steel and socks.

"My feet are warming up already!" Lindsey exclaimed.

"I wonder if we can still walk in them?" Deiter helped her up, and they walked around the area a bit. The modifications worked perfectly. They also made far less noise as she walked, plus her feet were getting warm rapidly. Deiter then fixed the other pair for Ashley. Pam and Ashley then took an experimental walk and pronounced Deiter a genius.

"Now we look presentable, really we do. I felt so embarrassed walking in steel shoes. Now they look like mere fetish heels, like real shoes. Plus my feet are finally warm! Thank you Deiter! I could kiss you!" Ashley exclaimed, very pleased with the results.

"Don't you dare, sis. He's mine. Go get your own fellow!" Lindsey teased. All four rolled with laughter, until Ashley and Lindsey began gasping for breath in their tight corsets.

Next, they attempted the stairs. Had they had hands, this would have been relatively easy to accomplish. Now they found themselves utterly dependent upon their two helpers. "I can only do stairs with you holding me, Deiter. No way could I do this by myself. I can't bend enough to look down to see the steps, and I can't hold on. But either way, my knees are taking a beating! Perhaps it will be best if we use Magical Doors to go down or up, otherwise it's going to take us eternity to go one flight up. I have to stop to catch my breath every few steps."

"No kidding, Lindsey! I knew steps were going to be hard without hands or arms to hold on to the railing, but going up with this tight corset, I can only do three steps before I have to stop or faint!" Ashley explained to Pam and her sister.

"You know, if we are going to ever get justice out of Dominus, we should make him live like this so he knows what it's like—what he has been doing to us," Ashley continued, vocalizing something she had been thinking about for the last two hours.

"Plenty of women would agree with that statement, I'll bet," Pam added.

"I can see Dominus now: breasts as big as his head, no arms at all, glass eyeballs, a fourteen inch waist corset melted into his skin, wearing steel ballet heels like yours. Wouldn't that be a sight?" Deiter chuckled at the whimsical image he'd painted. "He'd sure get a dose of his own medicine. But would you two feel like you had gotten Justice if Dominus ended up this way? I've been thinking about the new States Justice Department and all that they are attempting. That's why I was asking. At first, I thought: yes. He gets to see and feel what it's like to have done to him what he's done to so many other women. Now, I am not so sure. That will quickly wear off. Is that real justice? Like what they were talking about at the meeting?"

"Yes, I can't help but like to see him treated as he's treated us, just so he knows what it's like—how awful it actually is," Lindsey replied. "But you are right, Deiter, that bit of satisfaction is short lived. It might be part of the overall Justice, but there has to be more. Look at all the pain and suffering he's caused us and the murders of others. No, real Justice has to be more significant than that, though I wouldn't mind him experiencing firsthand what he's making us go through."

"Cool, Lindsey. We agree. I didn't have much confidence in my own opinion, probably because he's not done this stuff to me. You can count on me to help you two and all the other women get *real* Justice, only we have to figure out what that might be," Deiter said passionately.

"We'd best get them walking some more, Deiter," Pam broke in. "They need as much practice today as we can give them. Tomorrow they have to face going to classes for real."

As suppertime approached, the four made their slow way to the dining room. Naturally, hundreds of their classmates wanted to look at them. Some said how sorry they were; some offered any help. Both girls took this in stride. Both allowed Deiter and Pam to help them manage their dinner, making the two pack two doggie bags for later. Lindsey then silently cast Move Object on the bags, putting them in their dorm room.

Because they moved so slowly compared to the other students, Lindsey suggested they stay seated until most had left. "I don't want to be a traffic jam." They giggled once more. Just then, Jim arrived, bringing two guests along with him, Nadia and Jolina.

"We heard what happened to you, and we just had to come and give you a little advice," Nadia explained. "When you wear corsets this tight, you need to eat more roughage, lots of lettuce, stuff like that. We've worn fetish heels like this too, but only for short times." Nadia gave her friends numerous tips to make their lives a little bit more pleasant, for which both were very thankful.

"We heard that you are having the dance this Saturday instead of last Saturday," Nadia said with a sly glimmer in her eyes. "Since you have to wear the corset and heels anyway, why not dress the rest of you so that you look fetish and not weird?" She then told them which of Lindsey's outfits that Nadia had given her would work best with their current waists and heels. "Trust us; you will look absolutely fabulous in spite of this horrible situation. You deserve that much, Lindsey, Ashley. If you want some help with the outfits, Alister has given us special permission to come back Saturday afternoon and help you two dress right."

"What have we got to lose?" Lindsey replied. "Thanks. We're yours to dress," she teased.

"Say, the way that Deiter has fixed up your steel heels is a stroke of pure genius!" The boy sat up straight, proud of his minor achievement.

"You are coming to the dance with me, Princess," Jim said. "I won't take any excuses. You are my Princess and I, your Prince." Ashley giggled.

"Of course, Prince Charming," she teased him and batted at him with her short arm. He merely gave her a loving kiss on her forehead, all the while her little arms were batting at him.

"Okay, we got to go—Alister business," Jim announced. Nadia and Jolina promised to be back around three o'clock on Saturday.

Later that night, the two girls allowed Amanda and Kathy to help them get ready for bed and even tuck them in. "Without the use of our feet or lower arms, everything is so difficult, plus we can't bend much at all," Ashley lamented. "Thank you for being our nursemaids. You are going to get a work out with us, it seems."

266

"I'm only glad that we can help, Ashley. Honestly, I know both of you would do the same to help us out if we were the ones in the pickle," Kathy replied.

"Darn it! I can't even pull my own covers up," Lindsey commented, after struggling a bit with her short arms. "These are next to useless," she wiggled them.

Ashley agreed, "It was easier having no arms at all than like this, only they do help us keep our balance a little bit. I do hope they get us out of this mess soon."

As Lindsey fell asleep, she wondered just how she was really going to manage all her classes tomorrow.

"Wake up sleepy heads," Kathy called out. Lindsey and Ashley struggled to get out of bed.

Struggling with such short arms, an inability to bend much at all, and the impossible shoes, a frustrated Ashley called out, "Little help here!"

"Me too," squeaked Lindsey. "I can't even manage to get myself out of bed like this."

Bags packed for their morning classes, dressed, and hair brushed, they headed down for breakfast. Pam had her arm around Ashley, while Amanda did the same with Lindsey. Out of habit, Pam headed for the stairs. As she steadied Ashley, she realized her goof. "Oops! I forgot. No stairs. Sorry."

"Well, I'm started down. We might as well keep on going. Down is a whole lot harder than up," Ashley replied. "It's more like trying to feel your way down the steps, because I can't bend quite enough to see where I'm putting my feet. Plus I have to make real sure my toe is completely on the step by feel alone. Not much feeling is coming through the steel shoes."

"I'm sorry Ashley. I'm still mostly asleep myself. I can make us a Magical Door," Pam suggested, feeling miserable about putting Ashley through this bit of torturous step descending.

"No, I'm just complaining. Sorry, I'm grouchy before I eat. Slow and easy does it; we're half way down now."

While feeding the girls their breakfast, Deiter announced, "Say, I just heard that Juanita is now in the Infirmary getting her legs regrown! She's going to be a cook here once she is healed."

"Great!" Lindsey replied. "We should stop by and give her some encouragement this evening."

"Just say when," Deiter grinned. As soon as they were done eating and doggie bags filled, Deiter opened a Magical Door to their English classroom. With his arm snugly around Lindsey, he stepped her through to the room. Pam with Ashley in tow was right behind them. They were early, which was just as well, because they moved so slowly to their seats.

"Thanks, Deiter. I'm afraid you are going to have to get my book out. Darn, I can't even take notes like this." Suddenly, Lindsey began to be afraid that this was not going to work out at all.

However, once everyone else arrived and Professor Cho Lin began, she forgot about her plight. She became fascinated with the brief synopsis of the next famous novel they were to begin reading tonight. It was called *The Lord of the Rings*. Before she knew it, the class was over. While the others were heading off to PE class, Lindsey and Ashley decided they ought to go to the Library, where they could get a start on this new huge novel that spanned three books.

Pam created the Magical Door and a minute later, they escorted the two to seats. Deiter got out the first volume from Lindsey's backpack and placed it in front of her. "Bye for now. Back in time to get you for the next class." Pam did likewise for Ashley.

Sitting by themselves in the otherwise nearly deserted Library, the two looked down at their novels. With a struggle, they managed to get the books opened to read chapter 1. Turning pages became exceedingly difficult, even with their spells. "Maybe this isn't going to work," Ashley suggested. "Besides, I need to go to the bathroom pretty soon, and I'm getting hungry again. What do we do?"

"We could walk ourselves to the restroom. There are no stairs," Lindsey suggested. "I wonder if I could manage to get your jeans undone with Move Object? I've never tried anything that complex and intricate, though."

"Can I help?" Lillian Angel, the Librarian asked. She had been told to keep an eye on them.

"Hi Lillian. We, er, sort of need to use the restroom. I hate to have to ask you, but I don't think I can manage such complex motions with my Move Object," Lindsey admitted, her face flushing with embarrassment.

"I know I can't," Ashley volunteered, certain that she would be utterly unable to get Lindsey's jeans off. Now if she had the use of her feet and toes that would be quite another matter entirely.

"Well, come on, I'll put my arms around both of you and off we go. There are only a couple of sixth years in here now anyway. Come on; let's go."

Around ten minutes to ten, a Magical Door opened, and Deiter and Pam stepped through, the door vanishing after their passing. "All set for Calc class?" Deiter asked.

"Get us there fast so we can grab a bite of our sandwich first. We're starving," Ashley replied. Lindsey cast the Magical Door this time, and with the assistance of the two, they arrived very early. Hastily, Deiter retrieved Lindsey's sandwich and held it for her to gobble. Pam did likewise for Ashley.

Fortunately, they couldn't eat much at a time and soon were full once more. With their books placed before them, Lindsey panicked again. "How am I going to write out the solutions? I can rather hold the pencil. No, I will try to use my phantasmal hands, only it is going to be very slow going."

When they packed up to head to Earth Science class, Lindsey lamented, "I've only got done half of the problems that you two have finished."

"Hey, that's double what I got done," Ashley said gloomily. "At this rate, I will have to stay up all night to get one day's worth of school work done!"

Much later, with lunch finished as well as a restroom break, they took their usual seats in Huan Su's spell research class. Huan Su began in a surprising way. "Today and for the rest of this week, we are going to all tackle the various spells that Dominus must have used on Lindsey and Ashley. Specifically, class, we are looking for antidote spells that will remove the poison capsules from within their bodies without triggering the In Case Of enchantments. Also, to a lesser extent, we need a spell that is the opposite of Altering Leather to Steel. We suspected a Melt spell was used to implant these poison capsules, but the trick is to find a way to undo the In Case Of spell. I know everyone wants to help these two, so as an added incentive, I will grant an A for this term to whoever comes up with a workable way to remove the capsules without endangering their lives any further."

To Lindsey's surprise, the whole class yelled and cheered. Peaches called out to the two, "We are all going to do our very best for you two. Hang in there!" Everyone dashed off to the library, but it took the four several minutes to follow them all there. Lindsey and Ashley soon discovered that they were useless doing spell research. They really needed hands to manipulate the many books and pages for rapid searching.

While their classmates dashed about the stacks grabbing book after book, skimming through pages, the two barely managed to flip a couple of pages. This was the low point of the day for these two girls, who eventually stopped even trying.

Potion Making II went a little better. Here they could use their Move Object spells to add the ingredients, stir the brew, and so on. Nevertheless, they were far too slow and barely had the ingredients mixed before the period was up. However, Delius came by and said, "Good going, you two. I'm going to cast a Fix spell on both your pots. Tomorrow, I will cancel the spell, and you can continue right where you left off." Both girls expressed their gratitude for this bit of kindness and leniency. "By the way, you are giving the whole school a lesson in courage, forging ahead no matter what the obstacles may be. Very well done, both of you. I'm proud of you both. Most students would just have given up and lay on their beds waiting for a cure to be found."

On their way to Spell Casting class, Deiter whispered to the two, "Wow! I've *never* heard Delius ever say that about *anyone* before!"

Lindsey smiled briefly before admitting, "Er, we need to use the restroom and eat a snack before class starts. We just aren't going to have enough time. We're going to make you two late as well!"

Pam cast her spell and got the two into the restroom,

feeding them while they went. Deiter created another Door spell, so that the instant they were done, Pam could step them back to him. Meanwhile, he created a second door to their seats in Spell Casting class. They made it just in time. Professor Jerry Thornby was just walking to the front desk, as Deiter got his and Lindsey's spell books out. "That was close," he whispered, "but you two did it!"

"The next few weeks, we will be working on alteration spells that have their uses in particular circumstances, though one is only for historical purposes these days. Wizards and witches since the dawn of time have been interested in changing one thing into another. In the ancient days, the objective was to turn just about anything in to gold. You've already learned how to turn stone to mud and mud to stone. Now we want to change water into dust, so that one could dry out something or to change dust into water for use when you are dying of thirst in a desert. I know Emilio will enjoy this spell. He's into desert survival." Several classmates chuckled, and he smiled.

"Several centuries ago, creatures called basilisks roamed the earth. Their gaze often turned one into stone. Likewise, the ancient Greeks had their Medusa, which, as the tales go, would also turn anyone who gazed upon her head into stone. Thus, historically, changing stone into flesh and flesh into stone was important in those days. Of course, no such creatures exist today; they are all long extinct, if they ever existed at all. Probably the spell's best use is to help get rid of mice, turning them into stone when they scamper about your bedroom or kitchen." Several girls giggled. He expected such.

"Of course, far more relevant today would be to find the spell that Dominus used to alter leather into steel, so that we could help free Lindsey and Ashley, by casting the reverse spell. Unfortunately, such spells are not in our Grade 6 spell book, though I understand that Professor Huan Su is having you all research that spell. Obviously, Dominus found it somewhere. Good luck in finding it. Now then, first we will begin with water to dust and dust to water. Next week, we will attempt the flesh to stone and stone to flesh. However, you will be given a mouse to change back and forth. If you are successful, the mouse will feel nothing and suffer no harm, unless you fail to turn him back to flesh once more. Let's have one member from each team come up and get your cup of water. You have until Friday to complete this pair of spells."

Deiter and Pam brought back a cup for their partners, who had managed to retrieve their wands with their Move Object spells. "Deiter, please open my book to the right page," Lindsey asked.

"Already on it, love," he placed it in a good position so she could read it and practice its casting. "Actually, we both can practice this at the same time, since we are not likely to get it quickly if he is giving us until Friday to do it right," he said. "Let me know when you want me to flip the page."

"Flip the page! Deiter, that's it! I remember that there was just such a spell in my book of Teacher's Spells—you know Pam, the one you got me for Christmas. Tonight, Ashley, you and I need to learn that one, then we can use our wands to flip pages!"

"Cool! I was never more miserable than in the Library this morning," Ashley admitted.

Deiter read the spell's description and began practicing its casting. Lindsey took her time and read it thoroughly, before trying. She knew that she needed to get the wand motions down pat with her phantasmal hands before even trying to cast it. By the end of the class, Deiter was elated. Five times he changed the cup of water into a cup of dust and back again. At last, Lindsey was ready to try it herself, confident that she could manage to make the required motions.

"Wow! You did it on your first try, Lindsey! Way cool! Now see if you can get it back again," Deiter encouraged her. Unfortunately, she had not yet read that part and it would have to wait for tomorrow.

"Hey, I got the dust back to water once," Ashley exclaimed, "but Pam, she is super; she got it done both ways several times." Pam smiled, but again wondered if their success was not due in part at least to their visits to the Beyond.

After a quick trip to the restroom, the four arrived in the dining room, where Jim was waiting on Ashley. "Hi

Princess. I'm here to feed you and get you to and from your elective class. Pam needs to go to hers, so I'm her relief person. I hope I will do," he teased her.

Later, when Jim and Ashley were alone and heading for Professor Mary Ann's classroom, Ashley stopped him and said, "Jim, I had a miserable day. Can you please just hold me tightly for a bit? I need it."

He did as he asked, "Honey, anytime, just let me know. I love you. I'll do anything for you. You are the bravest person I know."

"Jim, I'm scared I'll be stuck like this forever. When I had no arms, I used my feet and got by just fine, but like this, it's horrible!"

"I know, I know. I've been to five libraries around the country today looking for the counter-spells. Alister has us all hopping about like mad on this one. You have many people working to find a cure. Just hang in there. If you need me to hold you, I will hold you as long as you want."

"Thanks, Jim. I hate to be such a bother to everyone. Will you be here when I get done in an hour?"

"You bet I will be here, Princess."

She smiled, "Okay. I want you to sit and hold me for a long time after that. I can't face trying to do all that homework just yet. I feel so helpless like this."

After seeing her safely into Mary Ann's office, he nodded to the Professor and left. "Professor," Ashley said calmly, "I want to spend all our time now Divining what Dominus is going to do. I don't care what the risks to me are. I want to help stop him big time, starting now."

Her eyes darting around the room, her hair flying in all directions, Professor Mary Ann was nervous. "I—I believe we're safe here." Having said that, Ashley noticed that she seemed to calm down a bit. "I rather expected that you would be very angry and desirous of taking on a larger role. I have something for you to read. It's by Mabel Pruit." At the mention of the former Rat Pack member, Ashley perked up and leaned forward to read the passage, thankful that she didn't have to try to hold it and turn the pages herself. She read the following:

Controlled Divining: You must train yourself to put
yourself into the mind of the Divinee, as if you were
sitting right there in the back of his or her mind,
hearing, seeing, sensing, thinking all that the Divinee
is perceiving and thinking at the moment of
divination. With evildoers, malcontents, and
perverts, one's own disgust of their viewpoints and
actions tends to get in the way of the diviner. Let go
of your values and experience what the Divinee is
experiencing as they see and sense it. M. P.

The stern voice of Mary Ann asked, "Can you do this
and are you *willing* to do this, Ashley?"

"Yes, but I don't know if I can do this with him, you
know. I *aim* to work at it as long as it takes. I have to stop him
from doing this to other women and girls." She waved her
short arms around. "Honestly, professor, I was far better off
before—when I had no arms at all—than like this. These are
almost useless, and I can't use my feet and can just barely walk
or breathe. He has to be stopped, and I don't think anyone else
in the world can do it, so I have to work at it until I can. What
do I do first?"

A half hour later, Ashley had finally let go of her
disgust, revulsion, and hatred for this man. Suddenly, she
seemed to slip inside his head! Later she would describe it as
somehow just sliding into his mind from behind. He was mad,
really mad. Now Ashley found herself keenly interested and
became absorbed in her silent observation of Dominus.

"Darn those governors anyway. I bet anything that
Alister was behind it, since our spies reported that many of
these leaders met in secret at Bradbury's School of Magic
several weeks before they announced it. I smell the
interference of Alister Broadwell behind this. Darn him
anyway, the old fool. Well, he blocked my perfect plan. He was
probably forcing that stupid teen Ashley to divine for him. He
can't divine his way out of a box given a blowtorch! Well, I've
taken her and that accomplice of hers, that Barron girl, out of
the picture now. They won't be interfering anymore on his
behalf."

Ashley sensed another man entering the room. She had flashes of a fancy business office; she smelled fresh leather or rather she sensed Dominus smelling it. Vision turned on! She was now seeing what Dominus saw! Ashley recognized the man walking up to Dominus, Ames Selig, a Death Stalker. His face looked ashen, and Ashley sensed what Dominus was sensing: the man was very frightened and did not want to be standing before Dominus.

"Boss, they're gone. Complex has caved in. They are not there," Ames said, his voice shaking and cracking, as if he feared Dominus would slay him on the spot. Ashley felt the most powerful surge of anger flowing through her body, far stronger than any anger she had ever felt in her life!

"What?" Dominus shrieked in a falsetto voice. His anger seethed. Ashley felt herself fighting to contain it, valiantly restraining herself from lashing out and slaying Ames on the spot. No, she realized this was what Dominus was feeling. "You are sure no bodies lay in the rubble?"

"No, boss. I spent an hour casting spells. There is no flesh anywhere in the ruins. It's only partially caved in so we might be able to rebuild it, sir," Ames replied, his voice still shaking, but Ashley sensed through Dominus that Ames began to calm down slightly. Dominus had not killed him on the spot, and Ames found that encouraging.

"Darn that Alister! Has to be his infernal meddling. I thought I had that place totally secured. I wonder how he managed to locate them there? I will have to go there myself and study the spells cast." Dominus calmed down somewhat, "Well, Ames, they may have regained physical custody of my future toys, but they will never be able to get them whole again. My new enchantments will totally prevent the removal of my devices or the re-growing of their arms. If they are stupid enough to try, the poison developed in South America will kill them in seconds, though I hope that doesn't happen. I'm *so* looking forward to their eighteenth birthdays, when I can finally add them to my play toy collection! They will look stunning with boobs as big as their heads, better than Nadia ever did. Of course, I will add a few more modifications to their looks then too. Such sweet pleasure they will give me then, ah."

"No, they will never figure out these new spells of mine. So, no matter that they've been temporarily rescued, they are going to have a perfectly miserable time of it. Small payback for their constant meddling in my affairs. Now I won't have to worry about supporting them and can concentrate on getting around this roadblock on my Golden Path. Oh, those two will suffer good. Those shoes was the most brilliant idea that I have ever had! By the time they turn eighteen and I am ready to turn them into my toys, they will be very adept in walking in them." Dominus let loose an evil laugh.

"Boss, what's our next move?" a different voice spoke up.

"Alister wants the whole country of norms turned into my zombie puppets, so let's give him his wish. Only this time, we'll use a shell game. Get them to figure out the production quantities needed to cover New Jersey, Massachusetts, and Rhode Island. We'll convert those next. Always use an ever-expanding perimeter. Make plans and preparations to build five new production plants here in Georgia, only when the equipment arrives, we'll actually send it overseas. Let's setup five new real plants in other countries in secret, say Singapore, Paris, Amsterdam, London, and Cape Town. Those will be the real production units, not the fake ones here in Georgia."

"But boss, how will we keep that darn Idaho militia from intercepting the pill shipments?" asked the new voice.

"Simple, Ben. Since I can't use the US Army as planned, I'll get our President to order them to provide secure deliveries in the future. Let's see those Idaho boys take on the whole US Army!" Again, Dominus laughed evilly.

Mary Ann carefully jogged Ashley from her semi-trance state. "Dear, it's past seven. We should stop for today. Jim's here to take you back."

Ashley jerked her head and opened her eyes. She was very dizzy and disoriented for a bit. Then, she exclaimed, "Mary Ann! It worked! It really worked! I got all sorts of great information on his plans! I have to talk with Alister immediately! Wow! Oh wow! That was way, way super cool! I really was there, in his head. I could see, smell, and hear what he did. Gosh, he was angry when he found out that we escaped his prison."

"Magnificent job, Ashley!" Professor Mary Ann exclaimed. She sent a Message for Alister, who came running into her office. Of course, he went over to Ashley's chair and the two exchanged hugs. Fifteen minutes later, she finished telling Alister what she had overheard.

Tears streamed down Alister's face, tears of joy and hope. "I have never been so proud of you students before. Ashley, words cannot express how deeply indebted our whole country, indeed the world, is for your efforts. I will get everyone working on your information right way. With your help, we may yet be able to stop Dominus. Thank you, Ashley."

Ashley had torn emotions. Yes, she felt proud of what she had been able to Divine, but she also felt horribly vulnerable and nearly helpless, so dependent upon others, more so than ever before in her life. The reality of her predicament came smashing back into her consciousness the moment she tried to stand up to go back to the dorm with Jim. Teetering and wobbling, her little arms flailed wildly, until Jim put his arm around her waist, holding her tightly and stabilizing her. Jim cast a Magical Door and helped her step through it.

"Where are we?" she asked, fighting to keep from crying. "Oh, the Formal Gardens."

Jim helped her sit down on the bench and put her coat on, zipping it up for her. Long sleeves flopped beside her, where her lower arms and hands used to be. Jim then put his arms around her and held her tightly. She rested her head on his shoulders. Neither said anything. Words were not needed or desired. She just needed to be held by someone she loved and that loved her.

After a bit, she heard muffled voices. Nearby, Deiter and Lindsey were also snuggling, taking some private time for themselves. "Oh, hi you two," Deiter said, as he saw Jim and Ashley. "I brought Lindsey here after our elective courses were done. Lindsey's kind of in the dumps, but I'm cheering her up." He carried Lindsey over to the same bench, and the four sat together for a time.

Ashley saw that Lindsey had been crying. "What's happened, sis?" she asked, worried about Lindsey, forgetting her own mess.

"I had an awful time in Dispelling class. I can't move around to dodge anything at all. I get so out of breath doing the least bit of work. This corset is so tight that I have a hard time concentrating on what I'm supposed to be doing. I really made a mess of things tonight. But Deiter has been so understanding, he just held me for the longest time, until we heard you two arriving. How did your class go?" Lindsey tried to pull out of her emotional slump by putting her attention onto Ashley.

"You won't believe what I managed to do tonight!" Ashley said with a newfound enthusiasm. She related all that she had seen and heard while Divining Dominus.

"You mean he doesn't expect that we will ever be able to get out of these things and get our arms and hands back? Not until he comes for us when we are eighteen?" Lindsey asked nearly petrified. Her nightmare was growing worse by the minute.

"Yes, that's what he sincerely believes. Only he did say that by then we would be experts at walking in these stupid shoes. So I guess the more we do walk in them, the better we will get," Ashley tried to sound a hopeful note, though she didn't quite see how this was possible.

"Ballet dancers spend hours working at it so they can stand and walk en pointe or do pointe work in their ballet performances," Deiter suggested. "I surfed the Net a bit and found some information on it. I know these are not quite the same thing. Pointe shoes don't have heels, but maybe it will get easier for you." He was also trying his best to encourage both girls, even if it was only a little.

"Well maybe," Lindsey admitted. "Ashley, just don't try walking in the snow. I did a while ago and found out I can't even take a step without slipping."

"No surface area to speak of," Deiter added. "Slippery shoes, that's for sure. I suppose we should get back to studying now. Fifth year has more homework than I can manage."

Lindsey teased him, "And you have two good hands to

do it with, not like us now!" He gave her a hug instead of replying. A minute later, the four stepped through Lindsey's Magical Door into the Yellow Hall study hall. Jim said good night to Ashley and left, heading for Alister's office. Ashley first had to tell everyone what she had learned about Dominus and his plans, before she could finally settle down to do any serious homework.

Both she and Lindsey only grew more and more frustrated as the evening wore on. Being minus both their hands and lower arms was proving a difficult obstacle to overcome with their magical spells. By the time the group broke up for the night, both girls had finally finished their math, but still had all their other subject's work to do.

After Pam and Amanda got them both ready for bed, they decided to sit at their desks and try to get their reading assignment for the morning English class done. It was after midnight when the two finally went to bed. Trying to be as quiet as they could and holding onto each other, they made it to Ashley's bed. Lindsey insisted on getting Ashley properly tucked in, "Tomorrow you can tuck me in." On her knees and using her arms and Move Object spell, she manage to get Ashley covered up.

Now she had to awkwardly walk to her bed all by herself, arms waving about, well not as much as she had been waving them, she noted. Amanda had the covers already pulled down, so getting in was easy enough. She gave up on getting herself properly covered however. She couldn't bend enough to see what she was doing and her short arms were useless anyway. She fell asleep feeling more miserable than she ever had felt in a very long time. Dominus sure knew how to torture someone, of that she was certain.

Working until midnight each night, the two were able to keep up with their math and English homework. Earth Science they allowed to slide; they were just too slow. Their own spell research projects for Spell Research I class moved at a snail's pace compared to the progress they had made during September and October. Still, they did add some spells to their growing list. Reading became a little easier for them, once they mastered the new Turn Page spell; they could hold the book open and read more easily.

Potion Making progressed, though they each took over twice as long as anyone else did to complete a potion recipe. Spell Casting was the only class that they did well in now. By the end of the week, both were readily changing water into dust and back again. Both were confident that next week they could handle flesh to stone and the reverse spells.

After the fiasco in her Dispelling elective, Professor Delius took a different approach with her. Now they began working on her identification of spells that she did not know. A gut feeling on whether a particular spell should be absorbed or countered or allowed to detonate was now required. This Lindsey could manage, though she really wanted to get back to the live action course that she had been doing.

Friday afternoon in Spell Research class—actually they were in the Library—Deiter and Pam combined for the first breakthrough. Quite excited, Deiter came to Lindsey with some news, "Look what I found in the shoe industry! Plastic to Leather and Leather to Plastic! See they make plastic models of new shoe styles and then change them into real leather shoes to see how they fit and all that. Some companies, especially in China, use the reverse, taking US shoes and turning them back into plastic models, which they then slightly alter. I got us halfway there to getting your shoes off your feet!"

"Great going, Deiter!" Lindsey said, hopeful that at last someone was making some progress.

Pam broke in on them, also quite excited. "Hold on a second, Deiter. Look what I've come across in the auto industry. Plastic to Steel! They make plastic models of parts, and then change them into the real thing, steel. It works in reverse too. I bet if we put these two together, we have a way to get the shoes off. Steel to Plastic followed by Plastic to Leather! Eureka! We've found it. I bet anything this combo is how Dominus got them on your feet in the first place!"

"Thank you both a million times!" Lindsey exclaimed.

"Woo hoo, you two! Thank you, thank you!" Ashley added, suddenly feeling pounds lighter.

"Well, don't get too excited just yet," Pam said

solemnly. "We don't dare try this on your feet. That would trigger the explosion of the poison capsules. We still have that one to solve, but at least we are making progress." Indeed, word quickly spread to all their classmates here in the library. On their own, everyone let out a loud cheer. Lillian Angel smiled and didn't bother to quiet them down. She, too, was pleased for this first step.

Friday night in Study Hall, Lindsey and Ashley agreed that they would spend most of the weekend trying to catch up on the whole weeks' worth of Earth Science. Ashley explained, "We are able to do math and English during the week. So if we can do the science stuff on the weekends, maybe we will be able to keep up, unless we get more papers and lengthier assignments to do."

"Agreed, sis. Nothing but Earth Science on the weekends, well, excepting the dance tomorrow night," Lindsey pointed out.

"Say," Deiter wanted to cheer them both up a bit more, "I've noticed that you both are getting better at walking. Good going. I won't have you missing the big dance by saying you can't walk, love. I'll carry you there, if I have too."

Lindsey and Ashley both giggled. "You wouldn't dare?" Lindsey teased him back. Deiter got up and picked her up. Now they all began laughing. He kissed her and sat her back down.

"I'm not kidding, love. You have been doing miles better than on Tuesday, really you have," he insisted. Lindsey hoped this was true, though she didn't really believe it.

Saturday afternoon, Amanda was in the dumps again. Ahana had shooed her away so that he could practice with his pals for the dance tonight. Pam was off doing more research in the Library along with Tom. Kathy and Emilio were working with Professor Delius to finalize their batches of poison antidote. Amanda stayed with Lindsey and Ashley to help them with whatever they needed, but when Jolina and Nadia arrived, she became intensely curious about just how her friends were going to look after the two fetish women were done with them. Nadia wore her favorite satin form-fitting green dress with matching high heels and striped green and white corset over the top of the dress, while Jolina wore a similar dress and corset, sky blue in color. Both dresses had the smallest of walking slits, but with their extreme heel heights, this was plenty of room.

"First, we strip you both, Amanda, you work on their hair. We'll take measurements and do the rest. You two will be knock outs at the dance tonight!" Nadia promised. Lindsey noted that both women were extremely pleased to be doing this for them. This was something the two women loved to do, not just because Lindsey and Ashley had been instrumental in saving their lives.

As the supper hour approached, Nadia and Jolina finished their transformation of the girls. Amanda just gasped at their final look. Lindsey now wore a long, form-fitting light blue satin dress with a striped blue and white outer corset. Her arms were bare and the dress stopped well short of her ankles, showing off the ballet shoes she was forced to wear. The sharp contrast in width around her tiny waist was very pronounced and the dress had only a small walking slit. A silk blue scarf was tied around her neck, accentuating her dress.

Ashley was similarly dressed. Her satin dress was a pale pink with matching pink and white outer corset and a pink silk scarf around her neck. "There, you two look positively smashing!" Nadia exclaimed. Both girls walked over to the full-length mirrors to see just how they did look.

"Wow!" Lindsey exclaimed. "I do look really good, don't I? Gosh, my waist looks phenomenally small, doesn't it? Wow."

"Oh, I do like this look!" Ashley said, doing a turn to the left and right. "You're right, our waists are absolutely striking. Well, no one is going to miss the fact that we're forced to wear that tight corset of Dominus, will they? It leaves nothing to the imagination."

"Oh yes it leaves plenty for their imagination, dear," Nadia teased her. "Wait til your boyfriends see you looking like this! If they don't go nuts over your outfits, there is something horribly wrong with them." The girls giggled.

"It is not as bad as I thought it was going to be," Ashley commented, "wearing this second corset over the top of the dress. It's only a little bit more confining is all."

"Right, it is just snug. The one that he melted into your body—that one is just awful. It's inches smaller than the one he melted into me," Nadia explained.

"Well, you had an adult waist, Nadia. These are still growing teens. Still, that man should be shot for what he is putting you two through," Jolina emphasized. "Well, we should get you down to the dining room where your dates await you. Then, we have to be off. Another big night at the dance hall. Couple more years and you two can be regulars there too. If you want a job, we'll be more than glad to give you one."

"Thank you both!" Lindsey moved over slowly to Nadia and gave her a hug, then Jolina, while Ashley followed suit. Lindsey created the Magical Door to the dining room. Amanda held the door open for them. Nadia put her arm around Lindsey, and the two stepped through to the dining room. Jolina with Ashley followed right behind them. Amanda brought up the rear.

Ahana, Deiter, and Jim were already there waiting for their dates to arrive. "Oh my god, Lindsey, you look incredible! Wow!" exclaimed Deiter, eyes nearly popping out of his head. "You look like a goddess or something."

"You've outdone yourself this time, my Princess!" Jim, equally awed said to Ashley as he moved to her side. "Wow, you look fantastic, sexy, beautiful, just fabulously gorgeous!"

Nadia whispered to the girls, "Told you so. Bye-bye for now." She and Jolina left, making their own Magical Door to the parking lot, where they teleported back to Denver. The boys escorted their dates to the table, but half the school strained to get a good look at them. Finally, Ashley had Jim walk her out into the middle of the room, and she did several of the poses she had learned how to do at the two photo shoots.

"You are supposed to be looking at me," Amanda chided Ahana, who was openly staring at the two girls. He blushed noticeably.

"But Amanda dear, they look just incredibly fabulous, don't you think? How can any guy keep their eyes off of them?

Okay, okay, I'm sorry that I booted you off this afternoon. We have so little practice time together that we have to take it when we can. I'll make it up to you, my love." Amanda felt appeased after he also told her that they had rehearsed a new Antique Rock song especially for the two girls, *Behind Blue Eyes*. "Look, if you want to sing or play an instrument, we can use you in the band." Amanda now had something to think seriously about!

Jim hastily took photos of both girls, actually taking so many that he filled up his camera's internal memory. He promised to send those of Lindsey to Deiter. As the dinner began, Lindsey put her arm on Deiter's shoulders. "I hope you don't mind feeding me. These stubs aren't useful for much at all. If only he had just taken our hands," Lindsey lamented.

"Helping you is just about the highest honor I could have," Deiter bubbled. "You are a total knock out tonight. I just cannot get over how super you look, though I know it must be very uncomfortable for you."

"Not that bad, really, Deiter. I thought it would be too, but that corset of Dominus is the worst thing, along with the shoes. I can't take big steps anyway now, so the tight dress doesn't matter the slightest. I hope you don't mind me rubbing my arm on your shoulders and back; it's about all I can do, except hug you with them."

He kissed her forehead, "I love you, Lindsey."

She blushed and took a last bite of supper. She was already full, so was Ashley, but everyone else was just getting started. "Benefit of feeding us, Deiter, is that we can't eat much." Both chuckled. "Save me a doggie bag please."

Shortly after six, the tables were cleared, moved out of the way, and Ahana and his three fellow band members took their positions. "Are you ready to rock?" Ahana yelled. The response was deafening. "All right, first song is dedicated to Lindsey and Ashley, our fashion queens for this dance. It's an Antique Rock song called Behind Blue Eyes." Pam let out a squeal. She knew that song, and she clapped and yelled.

Ahana began strumming and singing, "No one knows what it's like. . ." Both girls were more than a little worried about how well they could dance, but at once, they found that they could wiggle and shake with the best of them. Their footwork, however, was drastically reduced. Also, they kept running out of breath after one song, to say nothing of their feet. Quickly, they discovered a good pattern: dance one and sit the next one out. By the time that ten o'clock came and Alister interrupted to announce that this would be the last slow dance, once more Lindsey swore that someone had sabotaged time! It should only be seven at the latest.

For the last slow, romantic dance, Deiter held Lindsey tightly to his body; she put her arms around him, resting her head on his shoulder. As they moved as one, she found herself whispering in his ear, "I love you. Thank you for tonight." Although in these heels she was now several inches taller than him, she leaned down and the two embraced. Nearby, Jim and Ashley were tight together, passionately kissing as well.

When the lights came back on full, the hundreds of students began filing out. Kathy and Emilio came into the dining room. "Wow, Lindsey, Ashley! You look fantastic!" Kathy exclaimed, sincerely impressed with their newfound sense of high fashion. Both had missed the dance, however.

"Thanks, feet are killing us, but we did it," Lindsey replied. "Are you just getting here?" She suddenly realized that she had not seen Kathy all evening.

"Yes, Emilio and I were working with Professor Delius. We've been conducting an experiment, my idea really," Kathy answered her, scarcely able to contain her exciting news. "It works!"

"What works?" Ashley asked, slightly confused, having just gotten in on the conversation.

"Remember when I said that I helped create the poison antidote? Well, this week, we managed to synthesize that poison, perfect match. Tonight, we tried my idea. We injected a rat with the antidote first, then we injected the poison. I know it sounds silly, backwards, but I thought if we got the antidote in it first and then the poison came—well, it worked, the rat was just fine! Don't you see what this means? We can give you the antidote, and then we don't have to worry about the poison capsule bursting. I know it is very risky, but so far it's the only thing anyone has found."

"Kathy, you are amazing!" Lindsey replied. "You are the best potion maker ever!"

"Only problem," Emilio added solemnly, "is if it doesn't work, you're dead. I keep telling them this is very risky."

They chatted until everyone else had left the dining room. At last, Lindsey cast her Magical Door, and with the help of Amanda and Pam, the two girls made it safely to their room. All chatted away, while Amanda and Pam undressed the girls and got them ready for bed. For the first time in days, Lindsey got a good night's sleep. Just knowing that a way had been found to free them, no matter how risky, did wonders to her morale.

During the next week, Pam and Deiter were the first students to successfully change the mouse into a stone mouse and back again. Lindsey was a little ways behind them, owing to her slowness. By the end of the week, the whole class succeeded with this mostly historical spell. Deiter asked about whether or not he could cast it upon Dominus and turn him into a stone statue. Everyone thought this would be an excellent use of the spell, until Professor Thornby explained that if cast upon an unwilling victim, there was a good chance they could dodge the spell's effect, especially top wizards such as Dominus.

Chapter 16—Thanksgiving

The second Friday in November, at dinner, Governor Alister asked Lindsey and Pam to come to his office after eating. "Of course, Deiter and Jim can escort you. I still don't want you walking around by yourselves."

A bit later, the boys helped their girlfriends into the soft leather chairs in Alister's office. He asked them to wait outside. This was to be a private discussion. "Lindsey, Ashley, I regret to inform you that we still haven't found the proper method to remove the poison capsules. I've made you spend two agonizing weeks like this, while everyone has been in search of a remedy. I'm sorry to have put you through it. Still, we've not uncovered any good answer."

"However, thanks to Miss Townsend and Professor Delius, an antidote is ready, and as you know, they've performed experiments on rats to prove it works. Well, let's just say that it works on rats. We do *not* know if it works on humans. At this time, we are left with three choices, and none do I really like."

"First, you could allow us all more time to try to find a really safe remedy. That would mean more daily torture for you to endure, and there is no guarantee at all that one would ever be found. Dominus has really outdone us all this time."

"Second, we could administer the antidote and attempt to surgically remove the five capsules, knowing that in doing so, they will likely explode and spread their poison throughout your bodies. This option I really do not favor. Your lives, even as constrained as they are now, are worth everything to me."

"Third, we could attempt to re-grow your arms and legs, after we amputate them above where the capsules are located. However, there is no way we can do this with the capsules in your backs. What will happen when the potions hit the melted corsets, none can say for sure. However, Doctor Caterwall has been doing some experiments on rats, and while there have been unexplained side-effects, they were not life threatening ones, as the exploding capsules certainly represent."

"I wish I could give you a better set of options, but alas, I can't. You don't have to make up your minds right away. Take as much time as you like to decide, then let me know. What do you think?"

"Say," Ashley had an idea pop into her head. "Why don't I try to Divine what would happen with each of the three choices? Duh, I'm supposed to be a Diviner after all." Alister grinned.

"Go for it, Ashley. I don't really like anyone of them really," Lindsey suggested. Ashley closed her eyes and relaxed. She focused on the third option, re-growing their appendages. After sometime, she saw a vision of herself before a mirror and gasped.

"Oh, if you re-grow while we still have the corsets melted into us, we will end up with hands and feet just fine, but something unexpected happens with the corset. It's like our shape changes. I mean right now, it slopes down to our very tiny waist, which is fourteen inches around. After the potions are done, that thin line, which is now so small, has grown to nearly three inches wide. We would have a whole band around our waists that is only fourteen inches around. Plus, the thing becomes a hardened shell, and we won't be able to bend throughout the whole area the corset occupies."

"Gosh, that sounds even worse," Lindsey exclaimed, rather frightened at this vision. "I mean we can barely breathe now. I can't imagine how much worse that would be!"

"Well, let me see what I can sense with the others," Ashley suggested. Minutes later, she shrieked and came too. "Well, option two is no good. You will be successful with the ones in our arms and feet, but when you go after the one in our backs, it explodes and we die. I think it's the amount of poison and the close proximity to our hearts. There isn't enough time for the antidote to work."

"Jeesh, that's even worse, Ashley! How about choice one?" Lindsey pleaded.

Ashley concentrated. Lindsey watched the big clock's minute hand slowly moving. Her sister didn't move a muscle as time slowly passed. Lindsey was about to give up hope, when Ashley finally opened her eyes. Seeing the big grin on her sister's face, Lindsey suddenly felt a little hope flooding into her mind.

"Yes, that's the proper course to follow, sis. Deiter and Pam will fix us up; they will be the ones who work it out, and then the doctor can regrow our arms and hands. However, it won't be for weeks, I think. It happens during Thanksgiving break, you know, when we have four days off from studies."

"Yes!" Lindsey punched her hand into the air in a victory sign, but only her upper arm went up, however.

"We've somehow managed so far these past two weeks, so I guess we can manage another two, especially knowing that a real cure is coming," Ashley said encouragingly.

"Very well done, Ashley, well done indeed. I'm continually amazed with your Divination powers. You realize that you are rapidly becoming the foremost Diviner on this planet?" She beamed, glad for his praise and for finding out that there would be a remedy coming, one without ramifications.

"I suggest you best not tell Deiter and Pam about this divination. It might cause them undo stress," he cautioned. "Pam has taken this all very hard." They agreed. "I'll let you two get back to whatever now. Just between you and me, I think this is the wisest course of action to follow. Patience has its rewards."

A short while later, they told everyone in the study hall their decision to wait a little longer to see if someone came up with a safer remedy. "I'm all for that, Lindsey!" Deiter said, "I love you too much to see you get permanently harmed or even killed! But can you two get by more weeks like you are? I mean it must be just awful."

"With your help and Pam's and Amanda's and everyone's help," Lindsey said with a twinkle in her eyes that he had not seen since they had been abducted, "we are succeeding. Thanks."

For the next two weeks, Lindsey and Ashley continued with their successful study actions. That is, they would work all evening on their math assignments, and then stay up until midnight or later to get the reading done for English class. On the weekends, they worked hard to catch back up in Earth

Science. However, they continually lost ground in Spell Research. Potion Making slowly became a disaster for them. By the end of November, they were ten potions behind the rest of the class—ten hard potions, not the easy ones from last year.

On the bright side, Spell Casting continued to be bright for the girls. This next week was spent learning how to cast the Major Invulnerability spell that their staves could cast. When they successfully cast this spell, they were immune to all Grade 4 and lower spells! This was a most valuable spell to learn. Lindsey managed to pick this one up easily, and by the end of the week, she had it down sans wand, sans words. Deiter began calling her "Miss Hotshot," which pleased her.

The next week, they learned another protection spell, Total Magical Barrier. When this spell was cast upon a person, no magical spell of any kind could pass through the barrier, either in or out. Thus, while surrounded by the barrier, the wizard could not themselves cast spells. Yet, it made them immune to all magics. Ashley pointed out to Pam that this spell would be one way to defeat the Restricted Wish of Dominus. Of course, Pam also pointed out that then you wouldn't be able to work any magic against Dominus either, a strong downside.

During this time, nothing new was discovered by anyone concerning a remedy for the girls. Beginning two days before Thanksgiving, Lindsey noted that Pam and Deiter were spending a lot of time in hushed, animated conversations between themselves. As soon as anyone got too close to them, both hastily shut up. Lindsey thought this a bit strange, though.

The day before Thanksgiving, Governor Alister made a school wide announcement. "It is with regrets that I'm forced to cancel our Thanksgiving Day trip to Telluride. After what happened to Miss Barron and Miss Stokes-Compton, it is far too risky to allow any of you to wander the streets of Telluride, outside the magical protections of our school. As you know, we still haven't found a remedy for them. I sure don't want any more of you to suffer the way that these two have for nearly a month now. Instead, I have arranged for a formal dance on Thanksgiving evening. Girls, wear your finest dresses; boys, your finest suits. Slow waltzes will predominate. Hopefully, this will be sufficiently romantic to substitute for the movie theater and its grade D movies that you are so fond of sitting through during Telluride Day."

Pam chuckled, as did many others. No one watched the movies; it was time to kiss and make out. Fond memories of Monique returned to her. Throughout the dorms, many cheered, including Lindsey and Ashley, who loved the dances. A number of boys, however, groaned and complained.

Thanksgiving morning, Pam was more mysterious than ever. "Please, will you all do something for me and not ask why?"

"What is it?" Amanda asked.

"I suppose, unless I don't like it," Kathy said, a bit reserved.

"I'm game," Lindsey said, while Ashley nodded that she would.

"Will you all go down to the study hall for, say, the next half hour? You can help Lindsey and Ashley do their Earth Science homework. They need all the help they can get with it. Just don't come back for a half hour. I know we need to get ready for the big dance, but please just give me a half hour here in our room totally alone."

"Sure thing. Amanda, will you do the honors?" Lindsey held out her short arm. Amanda grinned, grabbed their science books, and put her arm around Lindsey, who opened her Magical Door to the study hall. Kathy did the same with Ashley. A minute later, Pam had the room all to herself. She hastily sent a Message and then vanished up through the ceiling.

"What is Pam up to anyway?" Amanda asked Lindsey, as she opened Lindsey's textbook for her.

"Dunno, but I'm not into studying right now. I wonder what I ought to wear to the dance. I don't suppose that the really expensive Inaugural Ball gown will remotely fit, not with this waist line," Lindsey replied.

Ashley giggled, "Not a chance, Lindsey. About the only thing we can wear is one of your fetish outfits with the corsets. However, going as a maid is not going to work." All four girls giggled. In the end, they decided to wear the same outfit that they wore to the belated Halloween dance. The half hour passed rapidly. Lindsey waited for Pam to send them an okay to return Message.

When they returned, Pam was smiling, but said nothing about whatever she had been doing. "We best head for the showers early, since all the other girls will want to use them too." A bit later, they were all showering together, though many of the girls were staring at the semi-visible lines of the melted corset and the girls' tiny waistlines, to say nothing of the steel shoes.

As before, Lindsey and Ashley had to allow their friends to dress them. Pam was wise to allow them lots of time to get ready. None of the girls had actually done this by themselves before. Nadia and Jolina had dressed them. By suppertime, all the girls were ready. Amanda and Pam wore their Inaugural Ball gowns, while Kathy wore the elegant gown that Ashley had given her, the one she had worn in the photo shoot. This dress was one of Kathy's prized possessions! All five looked radiant and stunning as they stepped through the Magical Door into the dining room.

True to his word, Governor Alister had decorated the room romantically. Drapes hung over the walls, the fresh scent of flowers spaced evenly down the many rows of tables added to the ambience, as well as the burning candles on the tables. The overhead lights were dimmed. Deiter presented Lindsey with a lovely corsage; likewise, Jim pinned one to Ashley's dress.

Roast duck with almonds was the main course, though Lindsey and Ashley had their boyfriends tuck half of their meal into doggie bags, which Lindsey then shrunk into a very tiny size and had Deiter stow in his pocket. She knew she'd be starving in about two hours. While she waited for the others to finish their meal, she began to wonder whether she could actually waltz in these heels.

Rock and roll dancing was easy; formal dancing was not. She would have to move her feet, and she realized that she had an awful time trying to take even one step backwards, walking on her toes with that steel heel behind her foot.

As soon as the dance music began, Lindsey realized just how bad this was going to be. Deiter whispered, "Just move; forget about trying to do the actual dance steps, just move anyway you can, and I will follow. We'll make this work somehow, dear." Lindsey finally relaxed and did as he asked. She spied Ashley and Jim looking at her feet. Her sister was having the same difficulties as she. By the second waltz, Lindsey forgot about everything but being in Deiter's arms, moving with him as one. She even forgot to eat again after two hours! Ten o'clock came in an instant for her, as it always seemed to do when she was dancing.

She and Deiter embraced through most of the last dance. As he bid her good night, he whispered, "Listen to what Pam has to tell you tonight. It may work." He would not elaborate, leaving her in mystery.

Once in their room, Lindsey, still in her tight dress, sat down, taking the load off her aching toes. "Okay Pam. What's this thing that Deiter says you need to tell me?" Ashley collapsed on her bed as well, only with the double corsets, she couldn't easily get back up, began laughing about it, and then couldn't catch her breath for a bit.

Pulling her expansive folds of satin out from under her, Pam also sat down. Kathy and Amanda did likewise, becoming very curious about Pam. Perhaps now they would find out what she had been doing in secret this morning.

"Well, Deiter and I worked out a way that we think will work to allow you to safely get rid of the poison capsules, the corset, and the shoes all in one move. I tested the procedure on myself this morning and can vouch that in theory, it works—well it works with clothes, that is. However, because of the risk of poisoning, we want Kathy to be ready with the antidote potions, just in case, but I don't think it will be needed. Right now, it is too complicated to explain, and I'm tired. Tom kept me dancing every dance, and my feet are killing me. I guess I should wear these high heels more often. You two did splendidly tonight, Lindsey, Ashley. Incredible."

Lindsey gave a bit of a laugh, "Ha, all I could do was sort of move my feet, not much like a waltz, but Deiter was really good with me. I wish we could have these dances every weekend."

"If we did, we'd never get any homework done," Ashley teased her sister. "Really, we are getting quite used to these shoes, walking on our toes. According to Nadia, it is supposed to be quite fetish, these shoes, that is, bedtime shoes. Maybe one day I can find out." All the girls giggled over this innuendo. "Someone help me up and out of this dress, please? I'm exhausted, and I can't seem to sit up by myself." They all giggled again. A bit later, Amanda tucked Lindsey in, while Pam tucked Ashley in for the night.

Next morning, after breakfast, instead of a long study day, Pam and Deiter were again conversing in private. Lindsey and Ashley sat at the now empty table waiting patiently and anxiously. Could this be their freedom day? Kathy had run off to fetch her antidote potions.

Deiter finally explained what they were about to attempt. "We are going to take you to the Beyond. Then, when Pam brings you back, you are to concentrate on the single idea of coming back with just your normal body, flesh and bone, no clothes, no shoes, no capsules, no foreign materials, just yourselves. You will come back to your bedroom. If all goes as it did with Pam yesterday, you will arrive naked. That's why she wanted you out of the room. I'll send your clothes along afterwards. It worked yesterday. Pam arrived stark naked in your room. I had all her clothes left in the Beyond with me."

Deiter and Pam then launched into a lengthy explanation of the Beyond for Ashley's sake. "We don't want to tell others about this taboo subject, so it is best that Kathy doesn't know just what we are really doing. However, Pam, Kathy, and I think the safest thing is for each of you to take one antidote potion just before we do it, just in case it isn't fast enough. But I think it will be. Teleportation is nearly instantaneous, and the In Case Of spell needs a bit of time for it to realize its detonation criteria have been met. By then, you should be safely back in your room, and the capsules can explode harmlessly in the Beyond. That's the plan. Are you still willing to try?" he asked hoping they would agree. Naturally, both did, more than ready to get free from this diabolical trap of Dominus.

Pam and Deiter did their Half-teleport to the Beyond. Both then knelt down, pretending to look under their beds. Lindsey and Ashley saw their heads and arms protruding down toward them from the ceiling! "Way cool!" Ashley exclaimed.

Both lengthened their arms until they reached the two girls, who raised their short arms up to meet them. "Now what?" asked Ashley.

"Up into the Beyond," Deiter called out, lifting Lindsey out of their room and into the Beyond, where she stood beside him. Pam did likewise with Ashley.

"Unreal!" Ashley commented, realizing that her mouth didn't open, but her words came out anyway.

"Thought rules here," Pam hastily thought to the two. "Think and it happens. I always feel more secure with a solid road under my feet. Here, like this." A road appeared beneath the four, much to the relief of the swaying two girls.

The two experimented a bit and discovered that thought really did work up here in the Beyond. Ashley began doing cartwheels through the space, though there was nothing that defined the space. "Okay, we best get on with it," Pam cautioned.

Once more, she and Deiter explained what they wanted the two girls to concentrate upon, as they were brought back into their dorm bedroom. Lindsey focused all her attention onto returning with nothing but her body, no clothes, no shoes, nothing that was not part of her body. Once Pam was sure she was fully concentrating, Pam stepped both Ashley and Lindsey back into their room. She was ready to call out to Kathy for antidote potions at the first sign of poisoning, however.

"Oh god! My feet won't bend!" exclaimed Ashley as she arrived onto their carpeted floor, stark naked. "Oh my waist! I can breathe again! Oh! It's gone! The corset thing—it's gone!" Ashley sat down fast before she fell. Her feet were rather rigid from having been so confined for a month.

"Wow! It worked!" Lindsey exclaimed. "I can breathe at last!"

Hearing their voices, Kathy came rushing back into the

room, ready to administer more of her antidote potion. "Oh my!" She stared at the naked teens in surprise. "Oh! The shoes, the corset! They're gone!" she exclaimed, totally startled.

"How do you feel? Any signs of poison in you?" asked a worried Pam.

"I feel so much better it's not funny!" Ashley replied.

"Me too. I feel fine. No, better than fine! Such a relief to be able to breathe again," Lindsey added.

"Okay, Kathy, get Amanda and get them dressed a little. I'm going to get Deiter, and then we must get them to Doctor Caterwall right away!" Pam insisted. She stepped out of their room into the empty hallway and Half-teleported to the Beyond, where Deiter was getting frantic with worry.

"It worked! They are fine. Come on. Let's get them to the Infirmary pronto," Pam explained. Deiter had already gathered up their clothes, which had remained with him in the Beyond, putting them into a canvas sack. The two decided to arrive back on campus behind the Infirmary building, where no one would likely be able to see them suddenly materializing. From there, Deiter opened a Magical Door to their dorm and a moment later, the two entered Yellow Hall commons.

"You wait here, and I'll help get them down," Pam said. While Deiter dearly wanted to see Lindsey, he knew that he couldn't go into the girl's side of the dorm. He would just have to wait it out.

Shortly, a Magical Door opened, and the girls appeared. Lindsey and Ashley were being Levitated by Amanda and Pam, while Kathy hovered over them. "We're okay, Deiter!" Lindsey explained immediately. She saw Deiter's face turn pale when he saw her lying down. "It's our feet. They won't go flat anymore so we can't stand up. It worked perfectly! Thank you! Thank you!" Deiter insisted on holding her hand, while they all cast another Door into the Infirmary.

"What? How? Oh my goodness! It's a miracle!" exclaimed a shocked Doctor Caterwall, as they entered the Emergency room. "How did you?" he didn't finish his sentence though. Deiter interrupted him, hoping to avoid answering the obvious question of how.

"Pam and I have them this far. No poison capsules are in them. Can you please fix them up," Deiter begged anxiously.

At once, the doctor went to work. Explanations would have to wait. "Okay, first, to the x-ray machine. I must verify those poison capsules are out of their bodies. Yes, I see the problem with your feet. I expected as much, encased in those steel shoes for a month. However, the healing potions will handle that, girls. Not to worry."

Twenty minutes later, he had satisfied himself that the poison capsules were indeed gone. Governor Alister and Professor Cho Lin had arrived in the meantime. "I hear you two pulled off a miracle, according to our fine doctor," Governor Alister teased Deiter and Pam, while the girls were off being x-rayed.

The two had a problem to face: should they tell them about the Beyond or not. Both knew well how other wizards had handled Greeley's discovery of the Beyond. Deiter and Pam had already discussed this at length during their several private chats. Deiter was terrified that if they told the complete truth that both of them would be grounded, be ordered to desist from using Teleport spells, ostracized, or just plain not believed. Pam, even more worried than Deiter, had at last come up with a way out. It was she that answered Governor Alister's questions.

"We used a special variation of the Teleport spell on them, sir," she began. "Right in the middle of the movement, we had them concentrate on arriving with only their physical bodies. That is, no clothes, no shoes, nothing that was not an intrinsic part of their bodies. Deiter assisted on the sending end, and I was on the receiving end, since they arrived naked." She hastened to add this detail, knowing that they would also be in big trouble if Deiter had seen the girls naked. "It worked; their clothes, the poison capsules, the shoes, the corset thing, all got left behind. Then, Amanda, Kathy, and I helped get them dressed, and with Deiter's help, we levitated them and brought them here." This was nearly the truth of the matter, if one discounted the role that the Beyond had played.

Professor Cho Lin rubbed her hands through her hair. "I don't see how this was possible. Teleport spell?" She looked confused, if not baffled.

"Well, congratulations are certainly in order, Miss Betts, Mr. Cross," Alister said. "Sometime, we will have to have a lengthy discussion on this whole process that you two have devised. However, now is not the time. We need to get the girls healed and caught up with their studies. There are only a few weeks left before the end of the term."

"Don't worry, we plan to spend all of our free time helping them catch back up," Pam volunteered, thankful that Alister was not going to press her for more details just now.

"Okay, the girls are ready for their many potions," Doctor Caterwall announced. "This is becoming routine. You all know the drill—what they will need for the next few days."

The girls giggled, and Deiter grinned. Pam suggested, "Okay, we will go get their things and their computers. I'll have them rigged up for voice activation in short order. We'll all spend the next few days in here with them; besides, we all need to review anyway."

The doctor advised, "By Monday, they should be able to attend classes again, though I don't want them lifting anything heavier than a pencil until midweek, mind you."

Their whole group setup a full time study hall in the Infirmary. "We must get you two fully caught up before Monday morning," Pam stated flatly, as she began assisting them with their math assignments. Deiter constructed a book holder so that they could read their novels. Pam and Deiter only left the two alone when they went to fetch meals for everyone or at night. The days passed quickly, and they achieved their goal. On Monday, the girl's arms and hands were solid enough for them to hold a pencil or pen, but nothing heavier than their wands.

When Lindsey and Ashley entered their Literature class at eight a.m. on Monday morning, their classmates broke into spontaneous clapping. "We are all glad you are healed and back," Peggy West called out.

"You bet!" Peaches added above the noise. Professor Cho Lin smiled and allowed the class outpouring of sentiments, before she finally called them to order.

"Now then, can anyone answer why, after Boromir

attempted to steal the ring, Aragorn was not angry with Boromir when he found the fighter dying from the many orc wounds?" she asked. At once, the class was back on track, diving into the motivations behind the men. Lindsey found herself reflecting on her own recent situation. She still did not harbor hatred in her heart towards Dominus or Simon. True, he had really caused her grief, pain, to say nothing of the discomfort, but she still didn't hate him. Rather, she found herself feeling pity for the man, who obviously had serious mental problems. How can you hate an ill person, she wondered? He had to be stopped, true, stopped cold in his tracks, but not with anger.

Yet, Ashley did. Ashley now harbored a good deal of hatred and anger towards him. It went beyond the murdering of her parents. Of late, Ashley had been working hard at divining his next moves. At night, she often heard Ashley curse him, when she thought no one was listening. Even Deiter now seemed to hold much more hatred of Dominus in his heart, she thought. While her mind accepted these facts, her heart told her this was going to fester and eat away at them. She had to find a way for Ashley and Deiter to come to grips with this anger and hatred, and let it go. Could there be anything in these novels that might help her reason with them? Her mind wandered off in search of an answer.

She didn't find one. On their way to their next class, Kathy chatted away, "Well, with this trip to Telluride cancelled, we're going to have to scramble to find times to do our Christmas shopping. I was going to suggest that we all go together, once we get home for the vacation, but I guess Governor Alister won't allow that, considering what has just happened to you and Ashley, Lindsey."

"We can shop online," Pam stated flatly, as if everyone had forgotten they had computers. "Lindsey, you are awfully quiet. Are you all right?"

"Yes, just fine," Lindsey lied. She couldn't really say outright what was bothering her, that she was worried about Ashley and Deiter and their growing hatred of Dominus. "You are right. I don't think we dare chance going out shopping. We've just had an awful month, and I don't want another one like that any time soon."

"How about never again?" Ashley added, "Darn Dominus anyway. One day he will get what he deserves!"

"In spades!" Deiter added angrily.

"Yes, but we ourselves are not strong enough to go up against him," Pam pointed out. "Besides, now he has the government and the US Army on his side." That sobered them all, ending their conversation.

During Spell Research class, Lindsey had a bright idea. She went in search of the spells that Doctor Verner used to help erase patient's emotional traumas and scars from their mistreatment and abuse. After a half hour of hunting, she finally found *Common Spells for Mental Healing*, by Abzog Mortimer. It looked promising, and she sat down to read it carefully. Lindsey found the little book fascinating.

Handling Loss Spell: used when the patient has lost a loved one and is grieving more than should be expected, when the patient has lost something and is reacting abnormally to that loss. Can also be used to lessen the usual grief the patient experiences when he or she loses something or someone. Vital Note: the spell forces the patient to re-experience the moments of that loss. It has been found that sometimes the current loss is dependent upon an earlier, unseen loss of a similar nature. The spell automatically handles this situation by locating and handling any earlier loss incidents.

This spell looked promising; she carefully documented it in her new spells database before continuing.

"Ah, this is even closer!" she whispered her excitement over finding just the spell she needed for Ashley and Deiter: Erase Unwanted Emotions Spell. The name sounded right at least, she read the description.

Erase Unwanted Emotions Spell: permanently erases the root cause of unwanted emotions, such as grief, fear, anger, and hatred. Note: the spell is useless if the person is currently experiencing the emotion because of what is going on around the person at this time. For example, it is natural to have fear when a grizzly bear is charging towards you and you have no defense. However, if the person is experiencing severe fear and there is nothing in the present time environment to warrant such fear, the spell will erase the root cause of that fear.

Lindsey smiled and dutifully copied everything about this spell into her database of new spells. She promised herself that she would learn it and cast it on Ashley and Deiter sometime during their Christmas break. However, there were four more related spells, including the spell that Doctor Verner had used to erase the women's emotional trauma. By the time to leave the library, she had all the spells copied and had taken down the book's MAG-ISBN number so that she could order herself a copy of this invaluable little book.

Chapter 17—Revelations

The first Monday in December arrived, only two more weeks until the long Christmas vacation. Always before, Lindsey had nearly everyone's presents picked out or purchased. Not this year. Both she and Ashley were swamped with homework. The past month had cost them dearly, especially in Potion Making II, to say nothing of Spell Research. Neither had minded much getting out of PE, but now they were required to attend, because Betsy was beginning their first aid studies. Both girls had lost their catch up hour.

Making matters worse, they had finished the Grade 6 alteration spells and found that Professor Delius Dogs was now about to teach them their necromancy based spells. As they all filed into the spectral room, which never ceased to give Lindsey goose bumps, Deiter commented to his friends, "Well, now we get to learn some really powerful spells. I've looked at the book, and these are going to be power spells, Lindsey."

"Oh get real, Deiter!" Pam broke in before Lindsey could think of a reply. "Cause Death—how wonderful! Now you can play God and go around killing people. No thank you, Mr. Cross! I don't want anyone dead, not even Simon Mac Fluide. Captured, yes; dead, no."

Undaunted by Pam's outburst, Deiter added, "Yes, but you could use it to kill rats and rabid dogs and such. It isn't limited to people, you know." Unconvinced, Pam just gave a huff and took her place, wondering how she could fake learning these spells and if they would prevent her from obtaining her A in Spell Casting.

Lindsey noted that Professor Delius' hair was more greased than normal, when he strode ominously into the classroom. His face seemed grimmer than ever before. "He doesn't look quite right," Ashley whispered to Lindsey.

"Page 95! No talking!" he barked antagonistically. "Today, it is my great privilege to attempt to teach some of you what are perhaps some of the most powerful necromancy spells. With a wave of your wand—and the proper, precise incantation, of course—you can instantly kill living creatures and people. Yes, you can kill a whole crowd of normals with this spell. However, least some of you think this would be useful in our current crisis," he stared straight at Deiter. "Put all such notions out of your head. The spell has severe limitations when it comes to killing other wizards and witches. None of you in this class needs worry about accidentally killing your fellow classmates. You see, once you have been able to cast Grade 6 spells, you are immune the Cause Death spell— that is, unless you are taken by complete surprise with it or are under the effects of the Idiot Mind spell at the time. Dominus cannot be slain by this spell, though I have been able to pick off a few of his henchmen with the spell."

"Once cast, you point your finger at the person or creature you want slain, and your wand will activate. You continue to point rapidly at each of the other persons or creatures until you sense the spell has finally discharged. The number slain is the variable. With normals, depending upon the luck of your casting, anywhere from six to a hundred can be slain with one casting. You might be able to get from two to four grizzly bears with the spell. You might be able to slay up to thirty first year students, but no more than a half dozen third years and only a couple fourth years. The more powerful the person or creature, the less of a chance you have of killing them."

"Now I can sense many of you are revolted by the whole notion of this spell." Lindsey thought that was the understatement of the year, but kept quiet. "Girls, you are walking down the street, and some thugs come up intending to rape you. With this spell, you can stop them dead in their tracks. Perhaps you come across an armed robbery; three men are threatening to kill a store owner. With one casting, the gunmen are eliminated."

"Or perhaps you are out walking on the plains, Miss Whitewater." Amanda flushed as he picked on her. "A rabid wolf comes charging at you. One cast and the wolf is terminally handled. Or perhaps you have a mouse infestation; one casting and the infestation is eliminated. Very useful spell, Cause Death, but one not to be taken lightly! I caution you the

Department of Magical Misuse closely monitors all usages of this spell; abusers will be apprehended and jailed. You cannot go around wantonly killing people."

"Then why hasn't the Departments arrested the various Death Stalkers?" unable to restrain herself any longer, Pam burst out without raising her hand. "Surely they have killed many people with this spell." Her disgust with the whole idea of this spell was obvious to all. Lindsey saw many other students nodding in agreement with her. Peaches, however, wasn't among those.

"Because in this class of forty of you, perhaps only five of you will be *bright* enough to learn to cast this spell!" he retorted. "Besides, the Death Stalkers have to be found first, Miss Betts. As you well know, that has proved exceedingly difficult to accomplish." She flushed.

He paced the room for a moment, and then continued, "This spell is reversible. That is, by casting it in reverse, you can bring another person or creature back to life. Some call this reincarnation, however. Unfortunately, the person's current body is dead, so their new body will be quite different. While they still retain all their memories and such, their body will be new, even perhaps of the opposite sex. Not even their age can be predicted, but you will have given them new life, which is the whole point of this spell."

"Professor?" Andy raised his hand. All eyes turned to the budding archaeologist. Deilus nodded, and Andy continued. "Cause Death is understandable, I mean, you can kill both people and creatures with guns, knives, and many other ways. Yet, isn't this reincarnation historically in the realm of God? Many religions believe that each of us is a spiritual being and that we inhabit these bodies. I know you didn't use the word resurrection, but reincarnation. Still, don't the organized religions have a problem with our using this spell? Kind of like cheating death or something."

"There are many ways to, as you say, cheat death, Mr. Rains. This is but one of the possibilities open to wizards and witches. I encourage you to use your research hour to investigate other such spells. Hint, check on one of the Grade 9 spells. As far as religion goes, yes, they do not take kindly to our use of this spell. Things get rather messy for the resurrected individual, whose new body is nothing like their previous body, and many complexities and confusions enter. Use this spell wisely, as you have no control over the sex, age, or even appearance and form of their new body." Little did he know just how correct this would be several years from now.

"Now then, enough of this banter. Let's get down to work. You have two weeks to attempt to learn Cause Death and its reverse, Bring Life. One of the partners come up here and retrieve a mouse cage. We will practice on mice. Once you have slain it, Bring It Back to Life." Dutifully, Deiter rose to get the critter for Lindsey. His face had lost its enthusiasm for this spell.

A bit later, while he and Lindsey stared at their mouse scampering around the small cage, he admitted, "Lindsey, I think I've changed my mind about this spell. I mean, promise me that if I am killed, then you won't try to Bring Me Back to Life. I don't think I could handle suddenly becoming a woman or an old man or even a baby. Besides, if we cannot kill Dominus with this spell or even most Death Stalkers, what's the point of it? We've got lots of spells to handle rabid wolves and such."

"I promise, but the same with me. Promise you won't try to bring me back to life either; it sounds just awful," she replied.

By Friday, Peaches had the spell down pat. "Gang, I have a great use for Bring Life. I have a really great dog, Sammy, but he is getting really old. When his body dies, I can Bring him back to Life in another dog body, and he can still be my trusty pet. You know—he will remember me and everything." Lindsey had not thought about this aspect and began to see alternative uses for the spell, at least the reverse spell. However, it was not enough for her to attempt to learn how to cast it. At the end of the two weeks, six in the class had been successful with these spells.

That Monday evening, the group headed off to their electives right after supper as usual. Lindsey wondered if Professor Delius would harangue her about her poor performance with the Cause Death spell. She entered the Hall of Necromancy a bit hesitantly this evening. She went straight to the large hall in which the mock battles took place. Here, she had been practicing her Dispelling under Professor Delius' watchful coaching.

He looked grimmer than usual, far worse than earlier today. Something was definitely bothering him. Lindsey was just about to ask him, when he looked up and spoke. "Lindsey, I have some bad news for you about our Dispelling Theory class. I knew it would come to this eventually, and it has. There is no easy way to say this, Lindsey," he used her first name, she noted, dropping all pretense of formality.

"Over two years ago, Governor Alister came to me to beg me to teach you Dispeller Theory. I told him then that I knew almost nothing about it and most certainly could not actually do any real dispelling, save the Dispel Magic spell. He was most insistent, saying that of all the professors, I was the most skilled in dealing with students, because so many refuse or have such a hard time learning necromancy based spells. I finally agreed and checked out every Dispeller book I could find in the Library of Congress."

"I know that I have given you a hard time, these past years, but I was just trying to get you to be able to do what it said a Dispeller ought to be able to do. To my surprise, you have been able to master those skills. Now, however, I am at my wit's end. We've covered everything that I have ever found out about Dispellers and how they work. I can teach you no more. I will be honest with you, Lindsey. All these incredible things that you can do, such as identifying a spell from wand motions, from a few spoken words—none of these I can do myself. If I have seemed overly demanding and harsh these past years, I am truly sorry. I just have no feel for how best to teach something that not even I can do. Now we are at an impasse. I've no idea what else we can do or should do."

"You mean you can't do what I've been working so hard to do?" Lindsey said shocked. "Wow. I thought that you could. Well, that's silly of me. After all, if you could, then you would be a Dispeller too. I feel rather stupid now. Well, it worked. I've learned to do things that I thought at first were impossible, so you did okay with me." After a pause, she added, "So there is nothing more for me to learn about Dispelling? Does this mean I am as good as my dad was?"

"Sorry, I never knew Samuel Barron, Lindsey. Yes, everything the theory books say or hint that a Dispeller can do, you are doing regularly and well. I guess we will just have to end our evening elective class," he added. "That is, unless you have some ideas to try or want more practice in some areas we've already covered."

Lindsey suddenly realized just how Professor Delius was treating her! He was talking with her as if she were his peer or better—as if she were a grownup, full witch, so totally different than the way he had treated her when they had had their first evening class years ago.

"There is one more thing that I would like to try, professor. Like I told Governor Alister, when Simon was casting his Restricted Wish on me and on Ashley, I thought I knew how to foil his casting by dispersing the magical energies. I would like to try that and see if it does work. I've been thinking that it might also disrupt other spells as well. I know that no one here can cast the Restricted Wish spell, but perhaps we can experiment with other spells, professor."

A few minutes later, Lindsey found their roles reversed in many ways. Now Delius was taking orders from her, and she was in the driver's seat, so to speak. "Okay, I'm ready. I have my major protection spell up, so you can't hurt me. Try firing a Ball of Fire at me, and I'm going to see if I can disrupt it the same way that I think I could cause the Restricted Wish spell to fail." Dutifully, from across the room, Delius waved his wand, intent upon sending a large Ball of Fire at Lindsey.

She concentrated and saw the magical energies forming, though she knew at once from his wand motions and from his chanting precisely what spell he was going to cast. As the energies formed in response to his command, she carefully began disrupting them, pushing them to either side, forming little curlicues of energy flows. To both their utter amazement, his spell sputtered. A few flames emitted in all directions from his wand, doing nothing of significance.

"That was incredible, Lindsey!" Professor Delius called out, clearly impressed with her action.

"It really works!" Lindsey called back, very pleased. A completely new vista of Dispelling beckoned to her.

"We should work on this aspect a whole lot, Lindsey," Delius took charge once more. "Do you realize just how powerful this actually is? I mean you did not have to issue a counter spell, chant, or even use your wand! None of this is in any Dispeller Theory book that I have ever seen!"

For the remainder of the hour, he shot all manner of spells at her, most all of which she managed to disperse. The few with which she failed to act sufficiently fast detonated harmlessly on her; the protection spell kept her from harm. Lindsey was ecstatic as she headed back to the dorm to tell her friends about this new action. Delius raced over to talk to Governor Alister about it as well.

Deiter entered the large conference room in the Admin Hall, ready for more Eliminator theory from Pam's Aunt Wilma. "Why so somber, this evening?" she asked, noticing the young lad looked a bit morose, not his usual eager self.

"Oh, it's those necromancy spells that Professor Delius was teaching us today, Cause Death. I mean, at first, I thought learning those would be just perfect for an Eliminator."

"But now?" Wilma astutely probed.

He sighed, "I'm not so sure."

"That face in death still bothering you?" she asked pointedly. Wilma was referring to the Death Stalker who Deiter had accidently slain with his Blast of Cold spell when they were rescuing the women held prisoner in Georgia.

"Yeh, still have nightmares about it. Maybe I'm not cut out to be an Eliminator after all," Deiter admitted. "I mean, I don't really want to kill anyone, just capture them, which is not what an Eliminator does, now is it? They are supposed to eliminate the threatening persons."

"I see. And what does the word eliminate mean?" Wilma asked quite pointedly.

"To kill," Deiter replied without thinking.

Chuckling to herself, Wilma conjured a dictionary. "Silly definition. Come; let's look up eliminator. Ah, one who eliminates," she read aloud.

"See I was right; it is one who kills others," Deiter

continued.

"Let's look at eliminate, shall we?" Wilma nudged him, pointing out the word.

Deiter read, "To get rid of or remove." He yawned.

"Where does it say to kill?" Wilma asked.

"Well, if you kill, you are certainly ridding or removing the opponent," Deiter replied.

"Yes, but is that the only thing one can do to rid or remove a threatening opponent?"

"Oh, well no. I mean, if I disarmed him or stunned him or trapped him in some sticky webs or paralyzed him, that would also rid or remove him," Deiter admitted.

"Or her," Wilma added. "You seem to think all Death Stalkers are men. There are some women, though not many, given Simon's low opinions of women. Besides, Bill West seldom killed. He preferred to capture the Death Stalkers alive so that they could stand trial for their crimes."

"I see. Well, I feel better about it then," his melancholy evaporated, as he realized that elimination didn't mean just killing. Then, the question that had been haunting him ever since he started this elective class returned to his mind, probably jarred by the mention of Bill West, the famous Rat Pack Eliminator who had captured Dominus so many years ago.

"Say, Wilma, there is one thing that I have been meaning to ask you ever since we started. Why do you know so much about the art of Eliminators anyway? I mean, you are just Pam's aunt and a mother and all that."

It was Wilma's turn to sigh. "Well, I told Alister this day would come. I guess it has. Deiter, you have earned my trust because of what you have done for Lindsey and Ashley. It's time that I shared my secret with you, but you must promise me never to divulge this information to another." Deiter was keenly alert and rapidly promised her. What was she going to say?

"Deiter, I *am* Bill West or rather that is my disguise that I used in the Rat Pack," Wilma explained.

"No, you can't be?" Deiter protested. For years, he had idolized the famous Bill West, Rat Pack Eliminator.

Wilma cast her Morph spell, and Bill West now sat across from Deiter. "When Sam Barron formed up the Rat Pack, he was terribly concerned about the safety of Monane and me. Already, the world knew about Mabel Pruit and her incredible divination skills. No hiding her, which eventually cost her and her family their lives. Sam ordered Monane and me to take on a disguise as men, even procuring a supply of DNA from some derelict men who lived in San Diego. At this point in time, we both are running low on our supply of Morph potions, so we usually use the Morph spell whenever possible."

"Monane is one of the world's best trackers, though Amanda is rapidly becoming her equal. Sam and I thought that this would be the downfall of Dominus and his gang, because we know that Dominus holds witches in low repute, believing that they are weak and inconsequential in the grand scheme of things. However, I did capture him once and aim to do so again, if only the opportunity arises. I do admit that I had a hard time not changing back into myself just to taunt Dominus, once I had him captured. I'm very glad that I resisted that temptation, seeing as he is now free once more. Had Monane and I not had our little disguise, we would likely have been slain a long time ago, just as Sam and Mabel were."

"So Monane is Able Monument, or rather the other way around," Deiter replied, stunned by the revelation. "Incredible! Now so many things that have happened over these last five years suddenly make sense! Wow! So you have been looking after Lindsey all these years too. No wonder you always seemed to be there when she was in trouble with Dominus."

"Yes, she knows of our identities, as does Alister." Quickly, Wilma told Deiter just who also knew her secret identity, Lindsey's group and Alister.

"Golly, not even Professor Cho Lin knows or Delius," Deiter added.

"Nope, only Alister and the kids know, and of course their families, the Compton's and the Whitewater's. Already, I worry that far too many know our secret, but it cannot be helped. Pam figured it out a while back, clever Sleuth that one."

"Anyway, Deiter, if Bill West doesn't have to kill to

eliminate, neither do you. Let's get back to Eliminator Theory, shall we?" Wilma suggested. Deiter threw himself wholeheartedly into learning all that she could teach him, but he couldn't wait to tell Lindsey about Wilma! So much now made sense to him.

In Divination Theory class, Ashley became annoyed. "I'm unable to see through his eyes anymore, Mary Ann. I can't get into his mind, something is blocking me."

"Are you relaxed, concentrating?" Mary Ann asked, beginning to go down the list of necessary actions that a Diviner must take to perform adequately.

"Yes, yes, I can get into his head—one of the Death Stalkers," Ashley replied.

Suddenly, she brightened up, "Oh! He's on to me and now has some anti-scrying devices on his person, just as Lindsey and I wear. I think he thinks that I have been getting useful information on his plans from himself and is trying to stop me. Well, I'll just look in using the others in the room. I don't have to look from his point of view, now do I?" Ashley was back in business, trying to glean useful information to pass on to Mary Ann, who would pass it on the Idaho Red Brigade and Erin Saks, who would use it to interrupt the flow of the Saude Dourada and its manufacture.

While Ashley had no real idea of the effectiveness of the countermeasures Erin had been taking, nevertheless, she took time each weekday evening to attempt to divine as much as she could about Simon's current plans. She slid in behind the head of one Death Stalker. Dominus was holding a conference.

Now she could see Simon, his face was curled with anger; blood vessels in his head were enlarged and pulsating. "Darn! How the heck did they find out about Singapore?" One man, evidently the one who reported something to Simon, was visibly trembling.

"Dunno sir. We did everything just like you ordered. They hit us by surprise as we were loading the container ship with the equipment. Just too many of them. We lost ten men to the Idaho Brigade, to say nothing of all that equipment. It's insured isn't it? I mean, we can order some replacements?" the man tried to smooth things over, hoping Dominus would not take his anger out on him personally.

Simon fairly screamed, "Five times we've attempted to ship the equipment abroad, and five times it's been waylaid by this darn Red Brigade! How the heck do they know my plans?"

"Boss, it must be that Compton kid. She must be divining us somehow," the man who Ashley was using as her medium spoke up, startling her. It was a weird sensation to be looking and listening through another person, and then having them suddenly speak.

"Yes, that has to be it, Boss," another man in the room added quickly, seeing this as a viable way out of the violent fit anger in which his leader currently displayed. "Perhaps she is becoming as good as old Mabel Pruit used to be. If so, we must take enormous precautions."

Simon sighed; his anger left him, his temples relaxed. "Yes, that must be it. While I've taken precautions to keep that meddling kid out of my head, she could be inside anyone of your heads right now! Dispel Magic!" His wand activated. Ashley was shot out of the head of the man who she had been using; her spells cancelled.

"Ouch! That hurts!" Ashley called out. Instantly, Mary Ann was at her side, looking her over for injuries. "Simon dispelled my spells. Gosh, that feels awful when you suddenly get your spells canceled. Well, he can't keep me out for long!"

"That's the spirit," Mary Ann said encouragingly. Ashley relaxed and rejoined the man whom she was using to spy on Simon.

"It's time that I used the US Army. Let's get another shipment ready for Singapore, only this time I will have President Snow send along a division of troops. Let's see this silly brigade take on a whole division. Perhaps that will be the end of the Idaho Red Brigade," Simon laughed covertly. His men joined him.

The hour was up. Mary Ann gently roused Ashley from her intense divination concentration. Hastily, Ashley relayed this startling bit of news, and Mary Ann, looking far more worried than normal, hastily sent a lengthy message to Erin Saks.

Ashley headed off to the dorms and her friends, but the

four ran into each other at the big underground chamber below the dorms. Pam, Ashley, Lindsey, and Deiter all came together from different side tunnels. Simultaneously, Lindsey and Deiter exclaimed, "You'll never guess what happened. . ." Both stopped mid-sentence. Pam grinned, but was intensely curious.

"You first," Lindsey said diplomatically.

Deiter blurted out what he had just found out about Wilma being Bill West. "Well, it's about time that you knew," Pam replied. "Honestly, I've felt badly about leaving you in the dark about them. Now we don't have to keep it a secret from you any longer. That's a relief."

"Yes, I'm sorry that I couldn't tell you before," Lindsey looked apologetically at Deiter.

"I know; that's all right. At least she now trusts me and that's terrific. Say, what were you going to say," he asked. Lindsey blurted out her news about how to dispel any spell being cast just by fiddling with the energy flows coming from the opponent's wand.

"Do you suppose that we can learn to do it too?" asked Ashley. "If I could, then I wouldn't have to worry about Simon kidnaping me again."

"Me too," Pam added. Deiter, likewise.

"Dunno, but we can sure try when we have time," Lindsey sounded a hopeful note. "I think you have to be able to see the energy flows, though. Let's experiment over Christmas break." All agreed and headed up the stairs to the study hall.

On Tuesday, Pam followed up on the hint given by Professor Delius. She checked out a Grade 9 Standard Spell Book and began looking through the table of contents. Slow Time caught her eye as did Wish, but she forced herself to continue looking for something that might tie in with what Delius had said yesterday about reincarnation and the like. Then, her eyes lighted upon Create Clone. "Bingo!" she whispered and began reading the preliminary description of the spell.

With this spell, the wizard or witch can create a clone of anyone including themselves. The clone will have all the memories of the host donor up to the instant of the spell casting. Hence, said clone will be able to cast all the spells that its host could cast at the time of the clone creation. A gram of DNA material is required for the clone's construction. The clone will be an exact duplicate of its host, complete with all memories, knowledge, and skills of its host.

"Well, that is interesting, but not too useful," Pam muttered. "What's Simon going to do, make a bunch of clones of himself? Will the real Simon please stand up?" She laughed at her own joke so hard that Angel had to give her a shh warning.

On Friday, Professor Delius asked Ashley and Lindsey to stay a minute after Potion Making class. "As you both are aware, I have made many concessions to both of you concerning the making of your potions. However, you both are still so very far behind the class that you have no chance of passing." Lindsey's face fell. Ashley shrugged; this she already knew and figured that she would be stuck with retaking the class next year.

"I have talked this over with Governor Alister, and he has given his consent to my proposal. If you two will delay your Christmas vacation by three days, during that time, we can work on making potions all day long. After three eight hour days, I would expect that you should be totally caught up to the rest of the class."

"Sure! That would be great! Then, we won't have to take it over next year," Lindsey replied eagerly, thankful for this unexpected kindness from Professor Delius. Ashley agreed as well, having just had an image of walking into next year's class as a sixth year joining all those fifth years, a disgraced witch.

As the two walked fast to catch up to their friends, Ashley whispered, "I'm glad we have this chance to catch up. Honestly, I couldn't face the utter disgrace of having to take Potion Making II over again. I'd take something else instead." Lindsey grinned.

Chapter 18—The Holidays

"Lindsey and Ashley are arriving." The monotone voice of the magical announcer bellowed its warning. It was the fourth day of Christmas Vacation, and the two were finally coming home. Amanda, Audrey, and Pam anxiously awaited their arrival and were in the Compton's front room waiting impatiently for the two to arrive.

Of course, Monane, Wilma, and Lloyd accompanied the two, just in case. "Hi everyone," Lindsey called out, walking in her front door, followed by Ashley. Already, they had moved their duffle bags from their porch into their rooms. After hugs, Lena, carrying Jonathon, walked into the room to welcome her two daughters home. More hugs ensued.

"We're rather busy around her," Lena explained, as they all sat at the kitchen table, Ashley rummaging for some snacks. It was around ten in the morning. "All of our apartments are now full, can you believe that?"

"Ours too," Amanda hastened to add.

"Wow! All from New York?" Indeed they were, mostly families who ran into troubles there and needed a fast exit.

"You are just in time for the dance tonight at B & B's," Pam changed the topic. "It's rock night again. Tom's taking me."

The girls spent an hour catching up on all the news around the ranch. Unfortunately, Nadia and Jolina were off in Denver with Barnaby and Bailey, but were expected for dinner. Finally, Amanda, who had been trying to find a way to get Lindsey's attention since her arrival, said, "Lindsey, let's go to your room a minute. I have something important to tell you. It can't wait." Pam gave Amanda a glare, and Lindsey guessed that Amanda had already told Pam about whatever this was about.

Ashley and Pam began playing with Jonathon, so Lindsey led Amanda to her room. "What's up? I've only *not been* here for three days," Lindsey teased. Indeed, she and Ashley had been working eight-hour days making potion after potion. Both girls knew that potion making was not something that they wished to pursue!

"I've a confession to make, well sort of. I've been practicing my Tracker skills, as Monane asked me to. I chose to watch Deiter. I don't know why, I just did. Maybe because he just found out about Wilma and Monane. Anyway, I have. Lindsey," Amanda gushed in a terribly serious tone, "Deiter is doing something really weird, really, really strange!"

"Huh?" Lindsey was taken aback. "What do you mean?" she thought was a good reply.

"I'm supposed to be following magical energy lines, you know, like the ones left when we send a message to another. Anyway, I was watching Deiter, and he's been using the Teleport spell, well sort of. I'm sure that is the spell, only it is not working right. Monane wanted me to follow the energy trail from its source to its destination, as if I were tracking a Death Stalker or Simon or someone. Well, I did. They have always begun at his house in Colorado Springs, but when I follow the trail, it just ends. I mean there is no destination point. He just vanishes!"

She went on, "Honestly, this is *not* the way Teleport works. He should be arriving *somewhere*. At first, I thought he might have gotten into trouble, been hurt, or been captured, so I told all this to Pam. She, well, she's been miffing me, telling me to mind my own business and that he's all right. Now I don't want to look like a fool over this, so I cleverly talked to Monane about Teleport spells. She's confirmed that when you Teleport, there is a clear source location and a very clear destination point, always, without fail, period."

"But Lindsey, Deiter has done this weird thing five times now! Do you suppose that he is making some horrible error in his spell casting? I don't know what to make of this. I haven't gotten brave enough to ask Monane about it, though. She was very clear about how the Teleport spell worked."

"Has anyone checked on Deiter? Asked him if he is okay?" Lindsey asked, not quite grasping what had been happening with Deiter.

"Well, yes. Pam Messaged him last night when I could stand it no longer. He sent me back a message saying he was just fine and would be joining us tonight. He wants to take you to the dance, naturally," Amanda replied.

"Strange. You say he starts a Teleport at his house and then doesn't arrive anywhere?" Lindsey asked, beginning to understand what Amanda must be seeing.

"Yes, but there is more. Twice now, I have seen his energy trail in reverse. That is, he comes back to his home, but there is no source point. I swear there is no source point, only the destination point. How can this be? Deiter must be really messing up his Teleport spell. I'm worried that he may end up killing himself or something, you know, like we heard about wizards arriving underground and dying at once."

"I'll check with him and make sure he's doing it right, Amanda. Thanks for the head's up. Say, you can see magical energies. Maybe you can learn how I can disrupt spells too," Lindsey sounded a hopeful note. Amanda seemed relieved, and the two rejoined the others.

Pam then headed to her room, but asked Lindsey to join her for a minute. "What did Amanda tell you? Was it about Deiter?" Pam asked.

"Yes, something about his Teleport spell going awry," Lindsey replied.

"She's on to him and us! She is seeing our Half-teleport spell to the Beyond. She confided her observations in me two days ago. I've had a hard time trying to dissuade her that there is nothing wrong. She's as tenacious as a bulldog on this one, Lindsey. I'm sure she will be asking Deiter about it, probably tonight when we go to the dance."

Lindsey chuckled, "You know it's darn hard to keep anything secret around us! I think we should tell her about the Beyond, maybe take her there, if she wants to see for herself. After all, we four now know just how beneficial that is in the casting of our alteration-based spells. What do you think?"

"Yes, but what if she gets deathly ill, like Deiter did when he first saw the Beyond?" Pam argued.

"Well, Ashley didn't get sick nor did I. So maybe it will be okay. I'll ask Deiter about it tonight," Lindsey replied. "Say, what are you working on?" Lindsey just noticed an enormous pile of papers in several large piles spread out over the floor of

Pam's room.

"Oh, Earth Science! I just realized that we are way, way, way behind in that giant research project. Now we only have four more months to get it all done and prepare our speech to the class! Some of this is my initial attempt, but I admit, it is going all wrong. Do you think the he'll allow us to change our topics at this late a date?" Pam asked, knowing what Lindsey's reply would be. She would echo what Professor Jasper had told them that first day.

"No, he was pretty insistent about our changing topics once he's Okayed them. I'm afraid you are stuck with it, Pam. Anything I can do to help out?" Lindsey volunteered, knowing that she probably would not be of much use at all, besides which, Pam had just reminded her of her own project, equally late.

"Not really," Pam said dejectedly, resigned to flunking Advanced Earth Science. "Now the rest of this is interesting stuff. I got to chatting with my dad and Mary Hampton, you know the lawyer who is living with us. Dad and Mary suggested a new line of research. You see, eventually, Simon is going to be apprehended by the authorities. Once he and his Death Stalkers are eliminated, millions of people are going to want Justice. That's the new thing—turns out this obtaining of Justice is taking off like a rocket. Apparently, the concept is going over beyond all expectations. Anyway, with millions wanting Justice, that's assuming we can find a way to get them off the heroin pills, dad and Mary suggested that all of Simon's many holdings be confiscated."

"Now that is proving to be a complex request. Just as soon as one company hears about the Department of Justice taking over another company, liquidating it, and using the funds to pay retribution to those Simon has injured or killed, they will very likely transfer all their monetary assets overseas into secret bank accounts and then vanish themselves. Dad and Mary have suggested that we have a plan all set up. The instant that Simon is captured, thousands of Justice personnel will take over the many companies and corporations that Simon owns, preventing them from liquidating their assets and capturing them as well, though some may not be guilty of any real crimes."

"So I'm working up the master listing of every holding of every one of Simon's vast companies and corporations. He has his hands in nearly everything imaginable! Some of these are very hard to trace so I've got my work cut out for me on this one. Thankfully, Tom's volunteered to help me with it. At least, we have had one break. Look at this; I've been making a time line of his life. He was born in 2138 to Ross and Jacqueline Mac Fluide. He has a sister six years younger, Michelle. He entered Bradbury's in 2150 and graduated in 2156. He was captured in 2163 by the Rat Pack. Now what is very curious and has given us a terrific break is that in 2156, Ross actually divided his extensive corporate holdings, giving Simon at least half of his enterprises. Our guess is this was his graduation present from his father."

"It seems that right around that time, both Jacqueline and Michelle died. I've found her death certificate, Jacqueline's that is. However, we can find nothing about Michelle after that date, presumed dead as well. Shortly after that, Ross must have retired. He apparently transferred ownership of all his many holdings, which were at least the size of what he gave to Simon, to one R. B. Folquet. Thus far, there has been no dealings between the two giant corporations—none whatsoever."

"So now we know just which companies Simon began with when he graduated in 2156. What Tom and I are doing is coming forward in time, isolating all the various deals, buyouts, and transactions that were done. I'm confident that in time, I will know precisely every financial detail of Simon's extensive enterprises. One day, the many people that he's harmed will get Justice, at least financial reimbursement anyway. That's better than nothing," Pam concluded.

"Wow. That's incredible. I leave you alone for three days, and you have found out tons! Way to go, Pam," Lindsey was very impressed with Pam's results and did not restrain her praise.

A bit later, while changing her clothes and putting her stuff away, she Messaged Deiter telling him about Amanda's observations. His reply was what she expected. Deiter suggested that it was time to tell her about the Beyond and take her there too. Deiter was quite predictable, Lindsey noted to herself.

After lunch, Audrey began asking them what they were going to wear to the rock dance this evening. Soon, the girls began chatting about just what to wear. While all agreed on jeans and tennis shoes, which top became the topic of intense discussion. Their decisions were cast aside after the arrival of Nadia and Jolina, along with the twins. Both women looked as fetish as ever; both attempted to get the girls to dress fetish for the dance.

"Golly, you two are certainly growing. My, you are definitely filling out," Jolina explained over supper.

"I know," Nadia added. To Lindsey she said, "We just can't get over it—how all of you young ladies have been filling out these past months. I guess if we were seeing you every day, we'd not notice it so much." Lindsey had no idea what she was talking about. She was still herself, but stared into the mirror for some time after supper and while getting ready for the dance. In the end, they decided to do fetish on another night.

B & B Dance Hall was packed, so much so, that Deiter and Lindsey gave up trying to dance and took a seat at the table with Nadia and Jolina. "I can't believe this! There are so many of us that we haven't got room to dance properly," Lindsey complained.

"We know. We have hired R. B. to enlarge the space magically; that's much cheaper than trying to make a larger building. Hopefully, next weekend, it will be double the space," Nadia explained. "Sometime during the vacation, we need to take you to get fitted for the maids of honor dresses. We've picked out our white wedding dresses. Wait til you see what we are going to wear!" The excitement and joy in Nadia's eyes was a wonder to behold, Lindsey thought to herself. They agreed to do it on Monday, as long as Monane and Wilma could accompany them. A bit later, the two older women went to check on how the refreshments were holding out, leaving Deiter and Lindsey alone for the first time.

Quickly, they discussed the Amanda Situation, as Deiter now began calling it. "Honestly, we should do it soon, just in case we run into any troubles. You know, if she has some ill effects, there will be time enough to recover before we have to go back to school." After a bit of a discussion, both agreed to do it tomorrow around ten in the morning.

At 10:15, Amanda arrived in the Beyond for the first time. After a lengthy explanation, Deiter Half-teleported her there, with Ashley, Lindsey, and Pam tagging along. Lindsey quickly thought a solid road beneath their feet, which helped to stabilize Amanda, who looked terribly confused at first.

"Oh, this is really, really weird, but cool, mind you. I feel like I'm doing something terribly wrong, you know, something highly illegal or taboo," she thought, and the others heard.

"True, we can't say a word about this to others. Look what the wizarding world did to poor Greeley. We certainly have a very different point of view of the world now. We've discovered this is why we can cast alteration spells so well and so quickly," Deiter thought to Amanda. He went on to explain their test done with Ashley and how they had been able to use the Beyond to remove the poison capsules from Lindsey and Ashley over Thanksgiving. Now things began to make sense to Amanda, who had never understood just how Deiter and Pam had helped Lindsey and Ashley.

"You think and it is so?" Amanda asked. Deiter nodded. Suddenly, Amanda was doing enormous cartwheels through the Beyond!

"This is way cool!" she thought to the others. "You can do almost anything here. Wow. Look at me!" Now Amanda appeared to be upside down to the others, grinning like a cat. A while later, they reappeared back into Lindsey's bedroom, deciding that only a minute had elapsed.

"Thanks, that was incredible!" Amanda gushed. "Oh, I ought to look at our magical energy trails!" Her Tracker responsibility reasserted itself. "Bingo! Our trails are just like what I saw with Deiter the last three days. Sorry, Deiter, not really spying on you, but Monane gave me orders to practice following energy trails, and I chose yours. No one around here is allowed to do much traveling, as you well know."

Deiter grinned, "No offense taken. Now we should see if

this improves her skills with alteration spells. Amanda, try disarming me." Deiter's wand flew across the floor, as did the other's wands, which were originally in their pockets!

"Whoa, way super cool! I did a Deiter!" Amanda exclaimed, referring to Deiter's first attempt at the spell, in which he accidentally disarmed the entire class. "Maybe now I can learn dad's Make Permanent spell that you all have picked up. I'll ask him about it tonight. Say, who all knows about the Beyond anyway?"

"Greeley and us," Pam explained. "No one else has ever dared to see the Beyond, calling it taboo. Even Governor Alister considers it a taboo subject. We don't dare tell others about it, Amanda. We could get grounded or worse, ostracized like Greeley, driven out of the wizarding world."

"Okay, mum's the word," Amanda agreed, though she felt a bit sheepish about it.

"I've been doing some experimentation," Deiter explained. "I took a tip from you ladies and made myself invisible. Then, I tried looking in on various places around the world. It is really cool. You can peer into anywhere you can conceive. Pretty darn cool, though I'm not sure if that has any real uses, unless you were a spy or something like that."

"They don't see you then?" Pam asked, curiously.

"Nope. Not like Cho Lin seeing Lindsey's head hanging down from the sky or that child who saw you, Pam. They don't see me because my Invisibility spell is in effect. Works perfectly," Deiter proudly replied. Then, he changed the subject, "Say, have you got any plans for a big Christmas party or anything? It's rather boring at my folks."

Just then, Audrey came by the room, overhearing Deiter's question. "Hey that sounds like a cool thing to do! Let's have a big party here. Oh, Lindsey, mom's looking for you. Wants you to watch over Jonathon for a while." The gang headed to the front room where the playpen was now located.

"We should have it on Christmas Day," Ashley continued making the party plans. Invite all the folks staying here and on the Whitewater complex."

Suddenly, Audrey turned grey. "Oh no! That would be a really bad day to have it. Something is going to happen on

322

Christmas Day! Something bad." She just had one of her premonitions. She added hastily, "Christmas Eve is better and safe."

"What is going to happen on Christmas?" Pam wanted to know. So did everyone else. Audrey just shrugged her shoulders, and the others knew her well enough not to ask further questions. She had no other data.

"Okay, time for Diviner action," Ashley joked. "You all work on the plans, and let me go see what bad thing is supposed to happen. We make a good team, Audrey."

"Not really. I can only tell when something bad might affect me, not anyone else, sorry," she admitted, though she need not have. All knew her limitations.

"Someone should be with you, Ashley, you know, just in case," Lindsey said, her voice full of concern.

"I'll go with her," Pam volunteered, and the two headed for Ashley's bedroom.

An hour later, those in the Compton household had been convinced to hold a party on Christmas Eve. Now all that remained was to invite all the others who were staying here and over at the Whitewater ranch. That took all of ten minutes. The girls set to work making plans for the party, and Deiter became very bored. Fortunately, Emilio and Kathy arrived, having received Lindsey's message about the party. Emilio and Deiter excused themselves and headed for the TV room and the game console.

Meanwhile in Ashley's room, Pam watched the apparently sleeping Ashley. She was startled by Ashley's voice, "Audrey's right! I see two diverging paths ahead. Something may happen of great significance on Christmas Day. I bet anything it has to do with Dominus or Simon. I'm going to concentrate on him first. If it isn't him, I'll try again."

A half hour later, Ashley finally awoke from her semi-trance state. "Well, it's Simon again. He's going to steal something called the Hat of Argo, whatever that is. Why would he want to steal a hat is beyond me. Must be important, this hat, I mean. Maybe we can Mag-Google it and find out more."

Pam dashed to her room next door and rapidly typed in the query. "Bingo, Ashley. There is just such a thing. Here it is." She read the text, though Ashley, looking over Pam's shoulder, also read it.

The Hat of Argo is a most powerful relic from the past. Created in 1610 by Argo of Venice, the hat bestows Class 4 Diviner potentialities on its wearer. This priceless relic is housed in a hermetically sealed glass container at the National Museum of Venice."

Pam also noted the super-security devices protecting the hat, which looked like an ordinary Renaissance hat. It was purple in color.

"Well, that explains a lot," Pam declared flatly. "Once Simon gets a hold of this hat, he will be able to divine all our opposition moves and so counter them. Then, there will be no stopping him ever! Governor Alister must know about this at once!" Ashley rejoined the others to tell them what she had discovered, while Pam sent a number of detailed messages to several wizards, including her father.

Later that afternoon, Pam received a Message back.

Pam, thank you for this timely tip. Be sure to thank Audrey and Ashley for me. I have talked with Antonio Peza, in charge of the museum security there. He assures me that all safety precautions have been taken to prevent any theft of this relic. He assures me that it cannot be stolen. However, I have my doubts and am suggesting that the Red Brigade take up a watchful position around the museum, just in case. It must not fall into Simon's hands! A.

As the group prepared to head off to the B & B Dance Hall—it was live band night, and Eli's Rockers were playing—Pam told the others what Alister had told her about the museum security. At the dance, still wearing their jeans, the group tried to dance and cheer Ahana and his band, though the crowd seemed even larger than last night. Deiter made a strange request, though. "Lindsey, would you mind dancing with Tom for a few minutes? I want to dance with Pam, er, well talk to her. It's important."

A minute later, a perplexed Tom began dancing with Lindsey, who tried to explain what was going on, though she didn't have a clue. Deiter seemed urgent in his desire, so she had agreed.

"Pam, sorry to butt in like this. This relic hat—it is important isn't it? What would happen if Dominus gets his hands on it?"

"Well, he would become as good as Ashley at predicting future events. He'd know our plans as soon as we made them and could counter them. Honestly, Deiter, I think that Ashley sees him taking over control of the whole world, once he gets the hat. Why?"

"Okay, I kind of figured that might be the case. We have to stop him from getting his filthy hands on that relic hat. Thanks." He moved back to Lindsey's side, Tom grinned and hastened back to Pam.

Once more, the evening passed entirely too quickly for everyone, except Amanda, who longed to hug and kiss Ahana. She did so the minute he ended the last set. "Missed me, I see," he teased.

"It's murder being out there in the audience, turning down dozens of offers to dance, when all I want is you, handsome," she teased back.

"Well, then you are just going to have to get your music skills up to speed and join the band, like I've said before," he playfully chided her once more.

"All right. You win. I'll do it, starting tomorrow," Amanda agreed.

The next day, Deiter didn't come around to help with party planning. Amanda also excused herself, spending the day with Ahana, trying to work out how she could fit into their band, and then practicing. Fern came over to spend time with Audrey, "Now they both kicked me out," Fern said disgustedly. "Honestly, musicians!"

"Well, you can help us plan the Christmas Eve party," Audrey suggested, and the two joined the others making plans and ordering the decorations.

"I thought Deiter was going to lend a hand today," Pam asked during a soda break.

"He was, but last night he said something came up, and he won't be by until this evening," Lindsey replied. "He wouldn't say what it was, though."

Around seven that night, the monotone voice

announced, "Deiter Cross is arriving." Lindsey headed to the door to greet him. "About time," she scolded him as he entered carrying a small black box. "You missed all the planning. So tomorrow you need to help us all bake pies and Christmas cookies."

"What? Bake? Pies, cookies?" a perplexed Deiter looked forlornly at her. "I don't know how to do either."

"Well, it's much like potion making, so you will do fine. Come on in. What'cha have there?"

"Something for Ashley. It's important." He followed Lindsey inside; quickly the girls joined them in Ashley's room. Pam was quite curious about the box.

"I have something for you, Ashley. This is your department. Ta da," he opened the box, revealing a purple Renaissance hat!

"This isn't what I think this is, is it?" Pam found words first.

"Yes, I made a switch. No way was I going to allow this to fall into the hands of Simon! The Hat of Argo. Try it on, Ashley. See if it works. I left a dummy identical looking hat in its place," a very proud Deiter explained.

"You stole it? Like a common criminal?" Pam blurted out. Though a bit harsh in her pronouncement, Lindsey felt that Pam said it all.

"If Christmas Day comes and goes without Simon taking any action to steal it, I will put it back, and no one will be the wiser. Yet, if Ashley's prediction is true, Simon is going to steal it, but he will only get the imitation one I created early this morning. Go ahead, Ashley, put it on and see if this is the real one. Perhaps they had a dummy one on display as well. If so, then I still have to find the real one before Simon does," Deiter explained.

Cautiously, as if this was a crumbling million-dollar paper hat about to disintegrate, Ashley put it onto her head. Though many centuries old, the fabric was magically enchanted and not at all fragile. It seemed to fit her head properly. All eyes looked at her. She shrugged. "Nothing is happening, though I suppose there must be a command word or something to get this hat to work properly," Ashley suggested.

I am too working properly! You just haven't asked me anything, but then you don't need me for that matter. A voice appeared in her mind, startling her.

"It's talking to me!" she whispered. Deiter's eyes opened wide; a broad grin appeared on his face, along with a smug look of superior success.

"What's Dominus Malefic or Simon Mac Fluide up to anyway? He is trying to steal you from the museum," Ashley thought to the hat.

Hum, well I'll be! Yes, he's trying to steal me, but you've beat him to it, I see. Yes, I can see that it is better that you have taken me than him. But what I don't see is why you need me? You are as good as or better at this than I am.

"Er, Deiter, my friend here took you to keep you from falling into Simon's hands. I'm doing pretty well as a Diviner, though I'm still learning how to do it all properly," Ashley thought back.

This Simon fellow is a nasty man. I can see that now. Don't worry, if he had taken me and tried to get me to work for evil purposes, I would have stopped talking to him. Please don't take me off your head for a while. I have not been worn for so long now. I feel I am behind the times.

"When were you last worn?"

In 1939 by a man who went by the name of Adolph. Nasty, insane fellow. I refused to speak to him. What's the use of creating me if no one uses me? Answer me that if you can.

"I can't, but I promise to tell the museum people about it. Perhaps one of the staff there will wear you occasionally. It's worth a try. They think you are a priceless relic, and are guarding you and protecting you for the ages. After all, you are many centuries old now."

Hum, is that significant? The number of days since my creation? Perhaps so, perhaps not. Ah, I see, Christmas Day is to be the time of my theft. I am getting a clear picture of it now. Are you?

"Yes, I am too. Oh, look, they are expecting trouble. I have to warn Governor Alister to get Erin out of there. He'll be killed!" Ashley began to take the hat off.

*Wait. I will tell you one thing that you have missed. Simon Mac Fluide is not **the** Simon. Bye, been wonderful chatting with you. Let's do it again sometime soon.* Ashley took the hat off and looked up at the faces of her friends staring at her.

"Anything?" Deiter pleaded.

"Yes, yes, this is the Hat of Argo. It chatted with me. We both saw that Erin and his men will be killed if they try to intervene. Dominus is expecting them to try to prevent him from taking the hat. I must warn Alister and get Erin out of Venice right away," Ashley spoke rapid fire. Then, she sent a lengthy Message to Governor Alister.

While she was occupied with this, Pam asked, "Okay buster. Just how did you manage to steal this hat from the museum? I know that it was under very heavy security. Out with it this minute."

"Can't. Best if you don't know, then only I'm in trouble, not you," Deiter replied stalwartly. Lindsey gave him her best pleading look, and his stoic face melted slightly. "Okay, I had a little help from the Beyond. That's all I'll say at this time. After I put it back, I'll explain in full. Okay Pam?" Pam nodded. She now knew just what Deiter had done and how he had done it. Her mind was racing with the possibilities this offered them.

Governor Alister had barely received Ashley's message when the door warning announced, "Alister Broadwell is arriving." Ashley dashed to the front door, calling out, "I'll get it. He's coming to see us. Rodent Pack business." She hoped no one would pay him any mind for a little while anyway. As she opened the door for him, she put her finger to her lips and led him on back to her room, where everyone was gathered.

"What's this all about? You didn't? You did," he began, and then sat heavily down onto Ashley's bed.

Deiter spoke up. "I had to sir. Dominus will be stealing it. He is expecting Erin to try to stop him and is laying a trap. Both the hat and Ashley saw Erin being killed if he goes to Venice and tries to stop Dominus. Don't worry. I put an identical hat in place of this one. No one will be the wiser, especially Dominus when he tries to wear it. I will put the hat back once Dominus has stolen my fake."

"How did you get by their beefed up security measures?" Alister asked.

"You don't want to know, sir. That way, if anything happens, it's only me that takes the fall," Deiter tried to explain his position in simple terms.

"Do we know that this is the actual relic, the Hat of Argo?" he asked. Lindsey noticed that his face was heavily lined with age. He must be under a tremendous amount of stress, she guessed.

"I put it on," Ashley spoke up. "Yes, it is the Hat of Argo. It rather speaks into your mind and picks up your thoughts. It is lonely, I think. It hasn't been used since 1939. Honestly, it was made to be used and has been just sitting around for hundreds of years now."

"What all did it tell you, Ashley. This could be very important," Alister replied, all the while staring at the hat.

"Well, I believe that it has the skill of a Class 4 Diviner. It says I am its equal and don't really need to wear it. Okay, I'll tell you what it told me." She saw the exasperated look on Pam's face and knew that she was not actually answering Alister's question.

A couple of minutes later, Pam looked startled. "What does it mean that Simon is not Simon?"

"No, it said Simon is not *the* Simon. I don't know what it meant by that," Ashley replied. "I'm just as baffled by that as you are. I've been inside his head, even seen some of his memories, before he began wearing the anti-scrying devices like we wear. He is Simon Mac Fluide, so I don't know what the hat means."

"Honestly, sir, I will put it back after Simon steals my fake hat," Deiter spoke up, wondering if Alister would assign him to detention or expel him from Bradbury's.

"What's done is done," the old man sighed. "Okay, I will call off Erin, since now there is nothing there to protect. If Simon does break in and steal the relic, then we will all hear about it. If so, then your actions, Mr. Cross, could be said to have been totally warranted and justified. However, if Dominus doesn't actually steal it, then, well then we are in big trouble. Until then, I believe I should take charge of the relic and keep it safe in the vaults at Bradbury's where Simon can't get at it, should he discover that we now have the hat."

Carefully, Deiter put the hat back into the specially made box he had made to keep the hat safe and sound. Alister turned to leave, "Until this is handled, let's keep this just between us. The fewer that know about what you have done, the better, if you take my meaning." They nodded and he left.

"Well, I think that he let you off the hook for now, Deiter," Pam glared at him, "but if we are wrong, you will probably get expelled or worse. How did you manage to steal it anyway?"

Deiter, still worried, brightened up. Throwing out his chest, he proudly explained, "The less you know the better, but I will tell you this. I made good use of our new spell. I conjured a duplicate hat and made it permanent, swapping my duplicate for the real hat. Pretty clever, eh?"

Pam had to admit that he had made good use of spells, but she added, "Still, it is stealing, and there are likely to be repercussions, you know."

Beginning to worry once more, Deiter said sheepishly, "I'd better be getting home now."

"Be back here at nine in the morning; you've got to help us bake lots of pies and cookies," Lindsey teased him.

By nine thirty the next day, Lindsey could see why Deiter was not doing at all well in Potion Making II. He had a terrible time following a recipe; he kept omitting steps, losing his place, or just plain making measurement errors. At last, the girls ordered him out of the kitchen, putting him in charge of fixing the decorations. This he could handle well and was thankful for the reprieve from kitchen duties. Emilio and Kathy arrived around ten, and the two boys worked together on the decorations. At noon, Jim came by, bringing the Christmas tree, the same live one they had used before, and they spent the afternoon decorating it, though it had grown significantly through the years.

By suppertime, the whole house smelled of pumpkin pies, chocolate pies, custard pies, and a myriad of different types of cookies.

At seven, their many neighbors began congregating in

the spacious front room, which was decorated in the spirit of the season. Outside, snow was falling; inside was warm and festive. Lindsey did not know most all the new families that had moved in temporarily to their adjoining apartment complexes and those of the Whitewaters. Several men, women, and children were obviously still recovering from the heroin addiction of the pills. Those looked somber, and many had the shakes. Still, gratitude seeped from many, many eyes. Between all these new families, a dozen young children brought new life to the party. Several younger ones asked her about Santa Claus: had anyone seen him? Would he find their stockings now that they had moved? Holding Jonathon, Lindsey couldn't help but assure them that Santa would find them somehow.

Deiter, constantly at Lindsey's side in the throng, which filled their front room, got into the spirit as well. He, too, saw the hardships that had been forced upon the innocent children, some of which were still recovering from heroin pills. He whispered to Lindsey, "What if their folks are unable to get them any presents? You know, being driven from their homes in New York, they might have lost everything. Here we are promising them that Santa will find them. What if? Well, you know."

Lindsey looked at Deiter; this was a side of him that she had never seen before. These younger children were victims too, and Deiter was touched by their plight. They were not yet sorted out into potential magic users or normals. Yet, Deiter was genuinely concerned. "Well, they are certainly having a ball at the party. This was sure a good idea for the kids and everyone else, but I see what you mean. Some of the parents look downright haggard. I bet many have lost their homes, jobs, money, everything except their lives—probably had to leave everything behind just to escape with their lives."

"That's what I mean," he replied.

"What's that?" the teasing voice of Nadia broke in on their conversation. Dressed in a bright red, form-fitting, satin gown with a green corset and green spiked pumps, Nadia was sipping a cup of eggnog. She had moved over to chat with Lindsey and overhead Deiter's reply. Hastily, Deiter explained what he meant.

Nadia smiled and whispered in his ear, "What say you and I do a little shopping after the party is done? Our little secret."

He grinned and replied, "You are on!"

"What are you to whispering about?" Lindsey interrupted them, slightly annoyed at being left out. Obviously the two were planning something.

"Nary you mind, my pretty," Deiter said coyly. "It's between Nadia and me." This annoyed Lindsey even more, but she couldn't get him to say more, as three smaller girls came up to see Jonathon.

"We sometimes babysit him, you know," said one six year old girl with brown hair tied with Christmas-colored ribbons.

By the time the party ended around nine, Lena was ready for its conclusion. She and Polly sat exhausted at the kitchen table, as Lindsey and Ashley joined them. "Well, that about does it on the pile of cookies and pies! Honestly, I was petrified that we would run short. I've never tried to feed so many people," Lena exclaimed.

"Me either, Lena, but the joy on so many faces made it all worthwhile, but my feet are in need of some serious attention," Polly replied. "Next time, Lindsey, we are going to make you girls the official hostesses. You can do all the serving!" Both women chuckled.

"Mom, Polly, thanks for everything. The party was just perfect. We got so many thank you's that I lost track. I think it made their Christmas," Lindsey stated factually.

"Well, that is an understatement," Polly replied. "These people have been through utter hell in New York. Some lost everything, barely able to escape with their lives. It's the least we can do for them. Honestly, the situation in New York and DC must be absolutely horrid indeed."

Fred joined them, "Yes, dear. It is. Wizards and witches run everything now. Normals have become slave automatons, doing mindless work. Ah, but they are all healthy and earning money, no crime," he added quite sarcastically.

"Dear, will you and the others mind cleaning up the

mess?" Lena asked. "I'm going to put Jonathon to bed and take a long, long, hot bath."

The teens began casting numerous Clean spells, but Deiter and Nadia were standing in one corner of the living room whispering once more. "Excuse me, Lindsey. I have to run an errand with Nadia. I'll be back as soon as I can."

"What? And abandon me to this really big mess to clean up all by myself?" Lindsey teased in mock protest.

Teasing her right back, Deiter said, "But dear, you have Ashley, Pam, Amanda, Ahana, Audrey, Fern, Emilio, and Kathy to help you. Surely, you won't miss me." Both chuckled. Deiter, his arm around Nadia, left, heading for her apartment home. Lindsey did not see both leave and Teleport away.

"Just like Deiter to split when there is real work to be done," Pam stated flatly. "Come on; we need to get the place cleaned up and all the presents brought out for the morning."

Around eleven, Nadia and Deiter returned, their faces bright, but slightly red from the cold. Nadia allowed Deiter to finish their secret plan, while she joined Barnaby, who patiently was waiting for her return.

"Well, I'm back. Say you all did a good job fixing everything up. Now then, I could use a little help here," Deiter said. He dumped the contents of the small duffle bag that he was carrying onto the floor and canceled his Shrink spell. A mound of presents, gaily wrapped, lay on the floor.

"What's all this?" asked Lindsey. Pam, Ashley, and Audrey looked just as surprised as she did.

"For the kids. Nadia and I wanted to make very sure that Santa came for the children. Only I need some help getting these to their trees in their rooms," Deiter explained. "She and I went shopping. I'm afraid I really had no idea what to get the girls, so Nadia picked out presents for them, while I got the boys some toys."

Lindsey just grabbed Deiter, hugged him, and gave him the warmest kiss imaginable. "Thank you!" Rather red-faced, Deiter smiled, while the other three teens giggled at his embarrassment.

"Okay, Move Object time," Ashley interrupted Lindsey. "How do we know who gets what?"

Deiter had to push Lindsey off himself to reply, "Each has a letter on it. Blue is boys. Pink is girls. 'O' is older kid. 'Y' is younger kid." With Ashley putting her unique talent to good use, an hour later, the presents had all been moved beneath the various trees in the adjoining apartment homes and those on the Whitewater complex.

At last, Deiter gave Lindsey a good night kiss and left for home, before his parents' curfew time, just barely. "Well, Deiter sure surprised me tonight," Pam commented, as the four girls got ready for bed. "When we first met him back in first year, I swore he was the most heartless boy I had ever seen."

"People can change," Audrey said quietly, "sometimes for the better."

Christmas morning the many families exchanged their gifts and enjoyed their private time together. Around ten, Fred got a phone call and interrupted everyone's happy mood. He turned on the big screen TV, "It's Dominus again. He's attacked a museum in Venice, Italy this time."

As everyone gathered around the screen, the face of Hugo was explaining, ". . . around eight this morning. He bypassed all the security by drilling a hole straight through the marble outer walls and steel protection panels, making a straight tunnel to the vault that held the relic. Yes, Dominus now possesses the Hat of Argo, a relic that turns its wearer into a Class 4 Diviner! The Italian authorities have launched a countrywide search for him and have asked the President of the United States for help in regaining their precious relic. They only want their hat back or so their consulate claims, when one of our reporters interviewed him an hour ago. The White House has not replied to our many inquiries, but the Press Secretary has told us to expect a live speech from President Snow within the hour."

KMAG switched to a commercial and Fred turned it off. "Wonderful Christmas present," Fred sneered sarcastically. "Now he will be able to divine our every move!"

Ashley was about to say something when the monotone voice announced, "Alister Broadwell is arriving." The teens dashed to the front door, just as the voice added, "Deiter Cross is arriving."

"Did you hear the news?" the voice of Amanda startled them, just arriving on the teleport pad, followed by Ahana. Lindsey opened the door to let them in, observing that Deiter and Alister were greeting each other.

"Heard the news," Deiter exclaimed as they entered.

"We need to meet," Governor Alister said solemnly, and Ashley led him into the kitchen. The front room was a mess of wrapping papers and presents lying about. Shortly, R. B. joined them, along with Fred and Lloyd. After accepting a cup of tea, Alister said, "Well, you've all heard the news, but sometimes the news is not precisely accurate. It seems that Dominus has in fact stolen the fake hat that Mr. Cross here put in place of the real Hat of Argo."

"What?" exclaimed a very surprised Fred Betts. Lloyd stared at Deiter, as did Amanda and Ahana.

"It seems that Mr. Cross decided to act on his own. After hearing the divination of Ashley's, he somehow managed to fabricate a duplicate hat. It seems, R. B., that this past summer's lessons of yours have been put to an unusual task. Yes, he conjured a duplicate hat and made it permanent. We'll not ask him how he could have possibly gotten into the secure vault at the museum and performed the switch. Yet, he did so two days ago. The real relic, proven to be so by Miss Stokes-Compton, is now safe in the school's vault."

Deiter sat up so straight and tall that Pam thought he might crack a rib or fall over. "That's incredible, Deiter!" Fred commented. "Son, I don't know how you did that one, but it has saved the world from Dominus! Do you realize what possession of that hat would have meant?"

"Yes, sir. That's why I did it. If Dominus gets that hat, he will be unstoppable," Deiter replied.

Alister resumed, "I have just finished a long chat with the museum's director. Indeed, he was shocked to learn that Deiter was able to steal it right from under their noses, amid their top-notch security arrangements. He reviewed their surveillance videos and did see two hats appearing in the sealed vault for the briefest instant. Nothing more. The approach used by Dominus caused tens of thousands of dollars of damage, but bypassed all security measures. He was overjoyed that we have the hat safe and secure. He has agreed to keep up the pretense of the hat having been stolen by Dominus. We agreed that later on when it is safe to do so, the relic will be quietly returned to him. As far as the world knows, Dominus has stolen the real relic. Thus, Mr. Cross, your theft will be ignored, though begrudgingly the director did ask me to thank you. He was very upset that both Dominus and you were able to get around all their security measures, as well you might expect."

Just then, a very worried looking Mary Hampton came into their kitchen. "Alister, have you heard? Are we all compromised?" Pam knew immediately where her fears originated. If Dominus did indeed have this Hat of Argo, then he would soon be able to divine all those working to stop him and take decisive action against said parties. Undoubtedly, all the other conspirators also had the very same fear.

"Ah, Merry Christmas, Mrs. Hampton," Alister disarmed her fears at once. "It is indeed a merry time, for Dominus has the wrong hat. He stole a fake hat that was on display, not the real one which, I am proud to say, lies securely in our school's vault. The museum director has instructed me to keep it safe until such time that it is safe to return it to the museum in Venice."

The relief on her face was apparent to all. "Oh, thank heavens for a Christmas Miracle! How ever did you manage to get it? I know that you talked to them, but I thought you said they swore it was secure?" Mary replied, sitting down before her legs gave out as the tenseness left them.

"The fewer that know the details of that the better. Let's just say that a Rodent Pack member acquired it for us in a timely manner. When it is safe, I will tell you or rather let him tell you all about it."

"Fair enough. Say, probably everyone's going to need to hear this," she hinted. "After all, I was starting to plan where we might evacuate to this time."

"True, true. I was just about to Message everyone. Please, keep it a secret that he stole a fake hat, though. As long as he thinks he got the real hat, the Hat of Argo is safe. If you

336

all will excuse me, I best return to Bradbury's and let the other Pack members know about it. The real question is how many of the governors should know. I'll keep you informed. Thanks for the tea." Lindsey walked him to the door to see him off.

"Deiter is not going to get into trouble over this is he?" she asked as they stepped outside.

"No, no he isn't, Miss Barron. In time, he may receive a reward for his timely intervention. Enjoy your fleeting holidays. My, how does time fly by so quickly?" He spoke a command word and disappeared. Lindsey, relieved, rejoined the others, who were still chatting about the news.

Mary was saying, "Pam, I found those records you were seeking, the ones that were not computerized. They add another ten companies to your list. Let me know what else I can do for you. It is such a mammoth project: finding out the entire assets owned by Simon Mac Fluide. He's done a good job hiding them."

Fred could not help but brag a bit about his daughter, "Not nearly a good enough job to keep them from my Pam!" Pam grinned, and her face flushed. She didn't like being the center of attention. Lindsey realized that even her father now treated her as a peer!

"Thanks. I'm determined that when we all take down Dominus, we will be able to immediately confiscate every last one of his holdings and assets so that we can use them to help all of those he has harmed all these years," Pam replied. She and Mary disappeared into Pam's room to go over the documents. Slowly things returned to the Christmas Day relaxation.

The girls all took turns thanking Deiter for his presents. He had given Lindsey, Ashley, Pam, Amanda, and Audrey each a magical ring that could store three emergency spells. He'd spent nearly all of his savings on them. "I really wanted to get you a ring with a Full Wish spell in it, but they cost so much that I couldn't even buy a tenth of one of those. The last time Dominus kidnaped you, all your possessions were left behind, but just in case the next time they aren't, put some key spells in your rings that will help you out." One by one, each of the girls gave him a thank you hug and kiss. All five were very impressed with his generosity and his willingness to do all in his power to keep them safe from harm. Even Pam was very surprised with his gift to her and was feeling a bit guilty about her gift to him, a book called *Creating Better Potions for the Beginner*. Still, if he read it, maybe it would help him in Potion Making class, she justified.

Deiter then began telling them what his father had given him, a Winchester rifle, a course in gun safety, and a course in marksmanship. Just as he was finishing his explanation, the monotone voice announced, "Santa Claus is arriving."

"What?" Lindsey called out, surprised by the unusual announcement.

"Probably the man in the red suit who came to Alister's big meeting with the governors," Pam concluded as they raced to the front door. Sure enough, there stood Santa Clause in his complete outfit, with bulging belly.

"Come on in, Santa. Just don't let the neighbor kids see you," Lindsey teased.

"Not to worry, I will be invisible to other prying eyes," he said as he entered, and they all sat down amid the mess in the front room. "I can only stay a short time. I have come to give Miss Ashley Stokes-Compton here a present." It was indeed Erin Saks, the leader of the Idaho Red Brigade Militia, the group that had been actively raiding Aetna Pharmaceuticals and the company's attempts to create more manufacturing plants around the world.

"This latest business with the Hat of Argo has given us all a real scare, Ashley. Had he gotten that hat, we would have been doomed. Yes, I sent two spies to watch over the museum in Venice. He brought fifty Death Stalkers with him, all prepared to battle us. He really did anticipate that we would be there to prevent his stealing the hat. We would have walked right into the trap, if it had not been for you. It is now very, very real to us just how valuable you are in our efforts to thwart Dominus. We also realize just how vulnerable you are, so I came today to give you a little present."

He handed her a magical scroll and explained, "Ashley, this scroll contains only one spell that can be cast only one time. To cast it, you simply read the words clearly and decisively. It is a Full Wish spell. If you get captured again, use it to free yourself or if you do not have it with you, have someone you trust read it for you to get you rescued immediately. And no, the reader of the spell will not physically age by casting it. The creator of the scroll incurred that aging penalty when he wrote it some fifty years ago. May it help keep you alive and safe."

Ashley took the scroll as if it was the most delicate, valuable item in the entire world. She was stunned, as were the others. Pam found her voice first, "A real Full Wish spell? This scroll must have cost a fortune!"

"P-P-Pam, here, you hold it. I don't trust myself to use it. I would just goof it up. You are the smartest of all of us," Ashley said, her hand shaking slightly. She was in awe about the whole thing.

"Probably the wisest course, since your friend, Pam, is not likely to be captured with you. Dominus really wants you out of the picture, so to speak, Ashley," Erin replied.

"I, I, I don't know what to say," Ashley managed to say.

"Just keep the hints coming. That's all the thanks we need. I need to run now. Perhaps one day we can put aside all disguises and chat like normal people again. I look forward to that day. Until then, happy holidays to you all." Still speechless, Lindsey followed him to the door and watched him Teleport away. Jim arrived a moment later and followed her inside.

"Hi all, back from the emergency Security meeting. What's up, Princess?" Jim said, seeing a still shocked Ashley staring at the scroll now in Pam's hands. Everyone else was staring at it as well. Pam explained what had just happened.

"Good gods! A real Full Wish scroll! I never thought that I would ever see one of those!" Jim exclaimed. "They cost a fortune! Now Dominus can't get his hands on you again! Thank you Erin wherever you are!" Jim was relieved and elated at the same time. "Whatever he does to you now, why, we can undo in a moment, right Pam?"

"Yes, I wonder what these cost and how readily available they are," she replied. Pam was so excited that she forgot to use her wand as she cast Move Object, summoning her laptop from her room to her lap. The girls chuckled as the laptop appeared, its power cord dangling in the air, along with the mouse.

Suddenly, Lindsey realized just what Pam had done. "Pam, you didn't use your wand! You just cast Move Object sans wand!" she exclaimed. At once, the others suddenly realized it as well. Pam looked completely dumbfounded.

As the realization formed in her mind, her voice squeaked, "Oh my!"

"Super cool, Pam!" Deiter praised her. The others joined in all at once, so much so that again she was embarrassed. Hastily she typed in her query, hoping to defuse so much attention now on her once more.

"Here is a start. Says Full Wish scrolls are exceedingly rare. The last one was sold on MagEBay for 1.3 million dollars back in 2150, twenty-seven years ago now. Gosh. There are a zillion requests from would be buyers asking for such a scroll, but no sellers." The group crowded around her, reading the screen over her shoulders. Pam then MagGoogled the Full Wish spell. They all read along with her.

The Full Wish spell is classed as a Grade 9 spell, primarily because no higher grades have ever been defined in which this spell could more accurately be placed. The difficulty level of casting is almost beyond words in terms of conviction, for this spell requires the utmost conviction of the caster, far, far beyond that required of any other spell. After all, the casting of this spell will permanently alter and readjust the reality of the entire universe and thus requires a level of conviction of the caster that no other spell remotely approaches.

"Wow!" Pam muttered.

"Intense!" Ashley added.

"Impossible," Audrey whispered.

"Incredible," Lindsey exclaimed.

"You will get a chance to try to learn it next year, as sixth years," Jim explained to the group of fifth years. "Though don't get your hopes up. Professor Thornby says that one student in ten thousand actually succeeds in learning this spell, if that many. He said that no Bradbury student has ever learned it."

"Wow," Pam said once again.

"Say, let's give it a go next year," Deiter said encouragingly. "That would certainly help us capture Dominus. I mean we could wish for his capture and all that."

"Well, Erin certainly gave you an incredibly valuable present, Princess," Jim said lovingly to Ashley. She was still too much in shock to say much at all.

Pam then put the precious scroll into a velvet bag and showed everyone where she would keep it, in her laptop bag. "After all, I'm never without my laptop, so if anything happens to me as well, the rest of you know where the scroll will be located. I certainly hope that we do not need to use it though."

"Me too," squeaked Ashley, whose voice was still not back to normal.

"I wonder where he got it?" Jim mused. No one had any ideas about that.

"I think that we should tell Governor Alister about it," Pam suggested. "After all, he was under incredible stress that whole month when you two were rescued and we were all searching for a way to undo what he had done to you." Lindsey recalled just how awful Alister had looked for over a month until Pam and Deiter had finally discovered how to get the poison capsules out of their bodies safely. Pam sent him a Message, but none saw the incredible relief that appeared on his face when he read her message, none but Professor Cho Lin who was standing before him in his office.

Later that evening as Lindsey and Ashley, who still shared the same bedroom, prepared for bed, Lindsey remembered her new spell, the one she wanted to try out on Ashley and Deiter. Carefully, she reviewed her notes on the Erase Unwanted Emotions spell, which permanently erases the root cause of unwanted emotions. "Ashley, I learned a new spell at school that I want to try out on you. I know that you now really hate Simon with a passion, and that you get so angry just talking about him. I think I can cast the same spell that the doctor cast that erases the trauma behind things like this. After all, when we next run into Dominus or Simon, I don't want you irrationally angry. After all, who can reason with an angry man or woman?" She teased her sister a little.

"I know I get so angry just thinking about him that sometimes it takes me half of my elective class to get calmed down enough to do any divination. Will it hurt?" she asked timidly.

A bit later, with a Silence spell cast upon their room so that any screaming or such from Ashley would not be heard, Lindsey began her casting. As soon as her wand activated, she knew it would work, and Lindsey watched and listened to her sister.

Ashley began reliving some of their encounters with Dominus and or Simon. However, as painful as they were, they flew by, and Ashley kept reliving earlier and earlier experiences. To both girls' utter amazement, suddenly Ashley was reliving one of her hospital stays when she was three years old. There, the doctors were removing the last remnants of her arms. As she lay there recovering, she stared at a prominent wall plaque that read: This children's wing was donated by Simon Mac Fluide in memory of his loving mother and sister, 2157 AD.

Suddenly, Ashley brightened up, "Wow! I stared at that plaque for days. I couldn't even roll over, no arms. I kept thinking what a wonderful, loving person this fellow must be for donating such a nice place to take care of me and all the other kids there with me. Well, I guess it is time for me to change my opinion of that. But I wonder why Simon did that—so out of character for the Simon that we know."

Lindsey observed that her spell had discharged and knew that the spell had done its thing. Neither was the slightest bit sleepy now, and Ashley just had to tell Pam what she had just discovered in her past.

A sleepy eyed Pam listened to Ashley, then commented, "Lindsey how did you do that? Have you learned a new spell?" Lindsey then explained that she had learned this one and told Pam about it. Satisfied, Pam then took her laptop out of hibernation and added a new entry into the Mac Fluide time line that she was creating.

"Well, that does seem strange. It sure doesn't fit in here

at all. Tomorrow I will look into that some more. There ought to be records of that, I expect." Ashley felt acknowledged, and she and Lindsey headed for the kitchen to make some cocoa in hopes that would help them get sleepy once more.

Sipping from their warm mugs, Lindsey commented, "You had it so much worse than I did. You know, I could see your little body lying there, no arms and all, so helpless. You had to grow up with none at all. I mean, I at least had arms, just no hands. I could sort of pick up things and carry them, but you, gosh Ashley that must have been just awful for you."

"You had mom to help you all the way. I had no one, just foster folks who only cared for the paycheck they received. I had to be tough to survive at all. That's why I've never taken anything from anybody. Running into you and mom was the best thing ever in my whole life. I just hope that I can be half as good a mom as mom is to us. Say, you didn't have it so easy either. Mom was showing me some old photos of you when you were just going to school. You had it hard too."

"Yes, yes I did, but I'm so lucky to have found you!" The two sisters hugged each other and headed to bed.

The next day, when Deiter dropped in to spend time with Lindsey, he got more than he expected. Lindsey explained what she had done with Ashley last night and said, "Now I want to cast it on you. After all, when we go about trying to capture Simon, I need you in prime condition, not full of rage and anger."

Deiter sighed, "Yeh, I know, I know. I just don't know what comes over me. Will it hurt?" Lindsey wondered why everyone thought this would somehow hurt them. A few minutes later, safe and secure in the Silenced bedroom, Lindsey cast her spell.

Rapidly, Deiter began reliving his various experiences that directly or indirectly involved Simon or Dominus. As far as Lindsey could see these were all relatively minor, compared to what Ashley had endured. Then, Deiter was back in his early childhood, his father continually lecturing him.

"Deiter, one day you are going to be a mighty wizard, strong and powerful, a true Black Hall graduate, just like me and perhaps the greatest wizard ever, Dominus Malefic. He also went to Bradbury's School of Magic, just as you will be doing in a few years from now. Always remember, a Cross is strong, mighty, powerful; we act with decisiveness, just like Dominus. Yes, I admit that he perhaps crosses the line sometimes and is now in jail for that. Still he is well worth emulating as the most powerful wizard of our times. You would do well to follow his example. Never show weakness, be strong, be powerful, be a Black Hall powerhouse."

Deiter started laughing, "Dad told me that crap at least once a week ever since I was six years old. The day the bus came to take me to Bradbury's for the first time, he reminded me of it again. No wonder I was picking on you heartlessly that whole first year! God, Lindsey, can you ever forgive me?"

Her spell had discharged, and she knew it was finished. Lindsey smiled, "Silly, we wouldn't be here if I hadn't already forgiven you."

"Oh!" he looked genuinely startled, though he realized the truth of her statement.

However, Lindsey was now pondering an observation that she just made. "You know, it seems that always the anger and hatred goes back not to some time when the person did something bad to you, like I thought it would, but rather back to a time when you liked or loved or admired the person you now hate or are violently angry with. Strange. Deiter, it's as if you can't hate someone unless you first had affection for that person. Perhaps it is also proportional to how much you loved or admired the person first. You know, the more you love someone, the greater the hatred that comes afterwards."

"Heavy philosophy, Lindsey. I'm afraid that's way beyond me."

"Remind me to ask the doctor the next time we run into that old German, will you?" she asked. He agreed and thanked her as well. For some reason, he felt lighter and more cheerful than he had in a long time.

His mood changed a few minutes later, when they joined the others. Pam had suggested that they all work together on their enormous Earth Science projects. After all, none had done anything on it yet, and once school started, they would only have a few months before they would have to make their class presentations.

As suppertime approached, Lena commented to Lloyd, "I guess they really do have more homework to do. I've never seen them all studying like mad during the holiday break." Lloyd grinned, remembering his fifth and sixth years at magic school.

Chapter 19—First One Thing and then Another

Dominus waved his wand and shot a Disintegrate beam at the Hat of Argo, lying on the floor. He'd spent the entire day trying to get it to give him divinations. He'd checked to see if it was magical, and it was most definitely radiating magic. It had to be the hat. Yet, it failed utterly to communicate with him.

In disgust, he had several of his most trusted Death Stalkers put it on to see if it would communicate to them about the future. Relieved, but also angry, the hat remained silent to all wearers. At last he cursed, realizing his great, improvised plan had failed. His beam found its mark, and the hat disintegrated.

"So much for that relic!" He spat on the remains that had not entirely disintegrated. "Okay, nothing ventured, nothing gained. Now then, where are we on our plans?"

Melvin Hoggs, dressed in his finest business suit, stepped forward, his laptop at the ready. He had been waiting for just such an opportunity to present his case, to get on the good side of his most admired leader. "Sir, if you will allow me to make a short presentation, you may find this most interesting." He knew that he was sticking his neck out because Dominus respected his other Death Stalkers far more than he had thus far shown Melvin. It was now, if ever there was a time.

Almost taken by surprise, Melvin found Dominus giving him the go ahead over several other Death Stalkers, who were about to answer their master's question. Melvin cleared his throat and began. "Sir, I have been compiling a very precise table of our shipments, both of pills and of new and used equipment, beginning at the launching date of the National Health Care program. If you will note, I have carefully logged the date, the contents of the shipment, whether it got through or was intercepted, and the day of the week of the interception, if it was hijacked."

Dominus growled; the list was extensive, and the column indicating interception contained an alarming percentage of checkmarks. "Bear with me, sir. This is important. If you will notice, initially, the pill shipments got through, up until the time the manufacturing plant was bombed and heavily damaged. After that, shipments began to be intercepted at an alarming growth rate. Most of the attacks came on weekends and in the late evening hours."

"Now here is when you decided to open up new pill manufacturing plants in other locations. Notice that there is a distinct change in the patterns of interception. I've listed the projected duration of each equipment shipment, its origin point and intended destination point as well. As you can see, everyone was intercepted somewhere along its route. Yet, there is a distinct, undeniable pattern here." He watched the eyes of Dominus carefully. Everything hinged on his reaction. Dominus, who was only paying half attention to his accountant, suddenly fixed his gaze on Melvin and his laptop screen.

"Notice that all attacks occur during week nights, usually late at night, not on the weekends any longer. In fact, none was hit on weekends. Further, said attacks always have occurred at remote locations along the route of travel. From this, several facts are glaringly obvious," Melvin said clearly and distinctly. Dominus smiled. He began to see some as well, now that all the data was so carefully organized.

"First, news or divination of said shipments must be coming to the culprits sometime during the week, probably also in the evenings. Several of the travel routes were quite short, only a day in a couple of cases. They had to receive the information and had time to act, to get into position, and to attack the shipment. Ergo, they must be getting the tipoffs in the early evenings of weekdays, not on the weekends."

"Second, the attacks are at remote locations, which means collateral damage is tremendously lessened, and the news of said attacks take longer to reach the authorities, who likewise cannot reach the sites quickly, giving said perpetrators maximal time to wreak their havoc and slip away undetected and unscathed."

"Yes, I can see that, but how does this help? I see our latest secret shipment just before Christmas was also lost," Dominus growled.

"I am not quite finished, sir. This leads me to two possible speculations. If your statement that there is a budding Class 4 Diviner now attending Bradbury's School of Magic is correct, one could conclude that this student is divining our shipment dates and routes, feeding the data in secret to the Red Brigade each evening. We know students party on the weekends, but work on their schoolwork during the weeknights. It tends to fit the pattern rather well. That being the case, changing our planning and shipping strategies to move the merchandise only on the weekends might be one way to foil this divination." Dominus smiled; he liked the analysis thus far.

"On the other hand, if there is no Class 4 Diviner at work here, that can only mean that somewhere in our organization there is a traitor, a spy at work, feeding the data to the Red Brigade. In my humble opinion, before you attempt another shipment, you should find out which it really is. If you will read the bottom line on the screen, you will see my suggestion on how this may be accomplished. However, only you and I will have seen that suggestion. It is imperative that only you and I see it, if it is to work. Once you have read it, I will delete that line." Dominus read, smiled, and nodded to Melvin. At once, the line vanished.

"Now then, I have two other plans which we can implement. One will rid us of this infernal Red Brigade permanently, and the other will allow us to get more plants operational. However, there is no immediate crisis. The Georgia plant is still producing enough pills to meet the demand in New York and DC."

Melvin switched to another window. "Again, no one but me has seen these plans. I have been carefully working with other staff on them, though I have been careful to only divulge a small part of any plan to any one individual. None on our staff knows the full details of either plan."

"Melvin, you are a genius. I love them, simple, direct, and diabolical. A man after my heart. Your latter plan I have already been contemplating myself and know that it will work, although I have been a bit reluctant to go to it. Perhaps I have been a bit too egotistical to use it. How soon could we implement the first plan? I'd like to rid ourselves of this infernal, meddling brigade that no one seems to know where they are located."

"Sir, we must handle the secret plan first. We must know the source of the tips. Besides, my best estimates are that it will be late February before the manufacturers will be ready to ship another complete production factory to our locations. We've rather exhausted all available suppliers of much of the equipment. This gives us time to determine the leak."

Dominus frowned; there was no getting around the destruction of so much plant equipment. "Gentlemen, let it hereby be known that I'm formally adopting the three plans of Melvin Hoggs. Let's get down to business here. We can commence operations on the first plan today." Several of the Death Stalkers gave Melvin a hateful glance. This accountant in a business suit had just compromised their coveted positions. True, he was a wizard, but that hardly counted.

"Gentlemen, I have an urgent errand to attend to, so while I'm gone, I want you to assist Mr. Hoggs in any way that you can. Follow his orders to the letter. I will be back in a few hours. And no, I don't want any bodyguards accompanying me. This is a private matter." Several looked shocked. Dominus never went anywhere these days without his private bodyguard army of wizards protecting him.

Once he had gone, Len commented, "Melvin, I sure hope you are right about all this. If you aren't, well, I've seen Dominus kill the goofer-upper." Melvin took that as a threat, not a warning. Undaunted, he proceeded to outline what he needed first, companies and contact names abroad.

Dominus headed down to his planning central desk. There, he wrote out two complete sets of shipping orders. One set, he sent via a Message to a shipping clerk in New Haven, Connecticut, with an electronic follow up copy. The other set he fired off in triplicate. Then, he returned to the main office, carrying the second set with him. He put on an air of cheery success, intended only for show.

"Ah, gentlemen, I have found us a Christmas present! I've located a startup company in Amarillo, Texas, that has a complete set of the very equipment we need to get a new, small factory up and running. They were glad to part with it, since they were overly optimistic in their initial plans. I've prepared the shipping orders. Send these through our lines. By golly, we'll get at least one new factory up in Amsterdam by February. The components are still in their original shipping crates. As soon as a rail car can be sided there, it can be loaded and sent by rail to the Port of New York, where a container ship will meet it. Find us a suitable container ship quickly. It should be there by New Year's Day."

The President of Aetna Pharmaceuticals breathed a huge sigh of relief, while his fellow Death Stalkers cheered, pounding their fists into the air, signaling victory at last. "Now let's get some tight security on this shipment, boys. We don't what this one to get ambushed along the way," Dominus chided them. Six left at once to see to the many details.

Dominus gave a slight head nod to Melvin, who replied similarly. During the next ten days, he worked closely with Melvin in secret, sharing not a word of their plans with anyone else. On December 31, a messenger arrived with a pair of confused dispatches. He read them over and flashed them to Melvin.

"Well, we can relax a bit," Dominus announced to his throng. "Both shipments have arrived right on time."

"You mean the whole factory is now being loaded for Amsterdam?" one aide asked.

"Well, not exactly. They shipped us a load of rocks, per my orders. It was a fake order, designed to see if we had a traitor in our midst. I'm very relieved to say that there are no traitors on our payroll. You see, I handled that shipment the exact same way we've been handling all the other equipment purchases and shipments, which have all been hijacked. If we had a traitor in our midst, this one too would have been stopped somewhere along the line. No spies among us." The assembled managers and Death Stalkers breathed a huge sigh of relief with this highly encouraging news. Many had been secretly speculating that there was a spy among them.

"Further, we know that the kids are on break from school. Hence, we don't expect to have Broadwell forcing divinations from that Stokes kid. Indeed, my secret shipment also got through unscathed. She is not divining on her own, but probably being forced to do it at school, under Broadwell's direct orders, I'll wager. Gentlemen, we now know what it is that we are up against, a Diviner. Now we must take all manner of preventative measures to block said divinations and to use it to somehow entrap the darn Red Brigade, but that will have to wait until they are back in session once more."

"From now on, it will be one continuous shell game that we play. We will setup many different transactions, purchases of equipment, shipments, and such. None of you will know which of these are the real shipments and which are the empty shells. I'm afraid that it has to be this way until I can get sufficient anti-scrying devices for every critical position in the pipeline. Sorry fellows, but we cannot let a stupid kid interrupt our plans any further. Already she has cost me well over a hundred million dollars, though insurance is covering the monetary losses. Nothing can easily replace the lost factory equipment or time. We've wasted over two months when we should have been converting another two states over to the Health Care Control program."

"Boss, you want us to take care of this Stokes kid for you?"

Dominus glared at the man. How had she managed to escape from his underground prison? His poison capsules had been defeated, but how? He'd taken every precaution that he could devise, not only to keep their location from being discovered, but also from getting their arms regrown, their eyes replaced. He'd dreamed up the most diabolical means to keep their mobility to near zero, and yet, despite all this, both kids were back to normal in short order! Oh, if only they were not still just kids! One more lousy year, and they would turn eighteen! Then, then, he promised himself, then he would show them who was their master! Oh, how they would beg and plead for sweet death to put them out of their misery. Oh, how he would relish not giving in to those divine pleadings.

In a low voice, full of more malice than any Death Stalker could imagine, he replied, "If so much as one hair on her pretty little head is harmed, you will wish that you never were born!" Then, Dominus screamed loudly, "No one is to attack them; no one but me. She is mine! Do you hear me? Mine to destroy utterly!" The man who made the suggestion sunk down in his chair in an effort to become invisible.

Dominus calmed down. "We need that bitch a while longer. We will be using her to confuse our enemies and using her to ambush the Idaho Red Brigade and wipe them off the face of the earth. Time enough to get her later on, just seventeen more months and she is mine forever. Now we have work to do."

Dominus now saw the spring unfolding before his eyes, right on target. While he would continue obtaining more plant production equipment, getting it shipped, and plants operational here in the US, all this was but a shell game, and a game that would culminate in the capture and elimination of the Idaho group. The real acquisition of production plants was being handled overseas by Melvin, quietly and discretely. No one else in his organization knew exactly what Melvin was doing or planning. Dominus gave him a target of having ten production plants going by midsummer, a goal Melvin thought was easily obtainable, given sufficient funds.

By fall, Dominus estimated, the US ought to be awash in Saude Dourada, enough to convert the entire eastern half of the country. Once that was done, there would be little anyone could do to stop him. Already he had hundreds of overseas wizards and witches applying for positions with his organization here in the US. A year, maybe two, and the wizarding world would finally be taking its rightful place in the world—the norms too, for that matter.

"Why did I pick such a hard Earth Science topic?" wailed Ashley. Her sentiments were echoed uniformly around the kitchen table, where the fifth years were frantically trying to get a handle on their various research topics.

"We are all doomed," Pam lamented, "I guess we all will be together next year retaking Advanced Earth Science together."

"How awful," Deiter commented. "A Black Hall student forced to retake it again. I will be the disgrace of my Hall!"

"What about all of us in Yellow Hall? We're about to set a new record on the number of fifth years who flunked!" put in Ashley.

"Well, how about taking a break, Lindsey, Ashley," the cheerful voice of Nadia broke in on their study laments. Tomorrow, they would be heading back for the spring term. Neither teen hesitated a second, only too glad for any opportunity to leave their dismal study mess behind them. Both followed her clicking heels into the living room, where Jonathon sat in his playpen, being mostly ignored by the teens for the last week. His face brightened up as he saw the three enter, followed by Jolina.

"Hi there Jonathon, Nadia and Jolina have a present for you, little fellow," Nadia cheerily said, while Lindsey, who looked at Ashley, retrieved their brother. She sat him on the sofa beside Nadia, who held a well-made, small book.

"Nadia and Jolina have written a little book for you. See, you cannot tear the pages. It is called *Where Has Peter Bear's Blue Ball Gone?*" Ashley noted that the cover proclaimed Nadia as the author and Jolina, the illustrator. Jonathon cooed. Nadia began to read.

"Peter Bear lived in the woods with his mother bear, father bear, and his older sister bear."

"Can you see which is Peter Bear, Jonathon?" she asked. He cooed and pointed to the little bear playing with a blue ball.

She flipped the page and read on, "One day, Peter Bear lost his pretty blue ball. It was nowhere to be found. Peter Bear was sad."

Jonathon, who was starting to talk, said, "Where ball?" Nadia shrugged, as if to say she didn't know.

She turned the page again. "Peter Bear wanted to play with his ball, but he did not know where it was. It was lost. 'Oh dear,' said Peter Bear, 'whatever can I do?' Yes, Peter Bear had a problem. He thought and thought and thought."

"Then, Peter Bear decided he could pretend that he

never had a ball. After a minute, this made him feel very sad." She pointed out, "See he is crying." Jonathon made an understanding noise.

On the next page, she read on, "Next, Peter Bear decided that he could ignore his lost blue ball, and he went outside to play. But now he missed his blue ball more than ever!"

"Later, Peter Bear decided that he could go play with his sister and make mud pies. He could avoid even thinking about his blue ball, but that didn't work either." She pointed out that Peter Bear was playing with his sister, but was still thinking about his ball.

Jonathon said, "Where ball? Find ball."

She continued, "Even sadder, Peter Bear went back into his house and decided that he would run away, flee. He wouldn't have to think about the ball ever again. He went outside, but now he felt very sad; he didn't want to leave mommy, daddy, and big sister. He cried even more."

"Finally, Peter Bear decided that he should do something and went to look for his ball. 'I will find it. I wonder where I left it?' he said to himself. He looked under his bed. No ball. He looked in his toy chest. No ball. Can you see where his blue ball is at?"

Jonathon cooed, "There!" pointing to a blue ball hidden just inside his closet door.

"Right! Peter Bear finally opened his closet. There was his pretty blue ball waiting for him, right where he had left it yesterday. Peter Bear was very happy. He went outside to play with his blue ball. Peter Bear learned his lesson, attack and face your problems. The End."

"Read again," Jonathon exclaimed, trying to flip the pages himself. Nadia, trying to hold back her tears of joy, did so. And again, and again. After the sixth time through, she gave him the book to play with himself; he was one happy little boy.

"It's our first published young children's book," Nadia explained.

"Just came out today. I hope it is a success," Jolina added.

"Congratulations! Incredible, did you see how Jonathon took to it!" Lindsey exclaimed.

"That's way, way super cool!" Ashley added. "Wow. You two really did it! Amazing. Are you going to write more? I liked it too. It's just the way I felt growing up—you know, attack, never give in and succumb. Wow."

Both women beamed. "You bet we are. We owe it all to Lena. She was the one who encouraged us. We've always secretly wanted to write children's books, uplifting ones. She told us to try it. I can't believe that we succeeded!" Nadia explained, wiping the water from her cheek.

"Sure is a big hit with Jonathon. Look; he's still looking at the pages," Ashley commented. She gave both women a big hug. Lindsey followed suit, but also silently Messaged Lena to come and see the new book as well. A couple minutes later, they reread story, much to Jonathon's appreciation, and she too had tears in her eyes.

Hugging both women, she said, "Very well done, you too. Incredible. Thank you both."

"No, thank you, Lena. It's all because of you. We would never have gotten up the courage even to try if it had not been for you. Lindsey gave us back our lives, and we are going to give back uplifting stories to children and help make people happy through dancing," Nadia explained.

That evening, after packing her many bags, Lindsey spied her dad sitting with Jonathon on his lap. He was saying, "Where's that blue ball? I don't see it. Oh there is it, good boy." The two were having a good time with the cloth bound, nearly indestructible little book. Lindsey felt at peace.

That same evening, Dominus waved his wand and cast several spells to prevent anyone from overhearing his conversation, trying his very best to prevent scrying by the infernal Stokes kid. Melvin cast similar spells of his own. Satisfied, the two men sat down near Melvin's laptop. It was midnight, another aspect sure to make scrying more difficult.

Melvin cleared his throat, as he often did just before launching into an extended presentation, a nervous habit he'd had since grade school. "Sir, I wanted to bring two things to your attention, if you have not already noticed them. First, we now have Amsterdam online; their first major shipment should be ready for transport by February 1. I believe that this has been completely unnoticed by the enemy."

"Yes, Melvin, very good work and planning on your part. Well done. At last, we are making some progress." Dominus begrudgingly acknowledged the accomplishment of his new business associate, who had come to him after the fiasco of the western governors that unexpectedly supported this National Health Care Program.

"Work is progressing on five others. Second," Melvin continued. Dominus found this incessant necessity of his to numerate his points incredibly annoying, but didn't interrupt. This was why he, not these others, would eventually rule the world. "Work is progressing on five other production plants around the world. The screen shows the various stages of completion of them."

"Third," Melvin continued, as Dominus fiddled with his jacket's sleeve, "have you considered purchasing some of the plants of the major pharmaceutical manufacturers in and around the New York area? There are quite a few there that are still pumping out massive quantities of drugs used by normals, insulin, various pain killers, and medical drugs of all kinds. I've met with a few of their senior staff. Until the western governors threw their total support behind this Health Care Program, they were unconcerned. Most figured the country would rebel or protest or refuse to go along with the program, keeping them in business. However, now they are getting rather nervous, if that's the correct word. When the program is fully implemented nationwide, they will be out of business completely. Overseas demand for their products, while large, can be handled mostly by their overseas plants. Many of their senior staff are becoming very worried indeed. Perhaps now it the time for take-over moves. It might be an easy way to gain more plant production facilities."

"Too costly. Right now, they think that their companies are still of great value. Soon, we can acquire them for a penny on a dollar. If we really do need their capacity, I will have the President nationalize them. Let them fight the government instead." Dominus snickered loudly.

"Right. Fourth, I am a businessman, not a politician. Are you aware of the incredible turmoil that is happening in the remaining states? I know that it is being kept out of the mainstream news by Presidential Order, but I had to make a trip to Los Angeles last week. I was shocked to see the reality of the political scene there."

"Hum, what did you see?" Dominus became quite curious. Just how observant was this upstart businessman anyway?

"The governor and the state organizations, along with this new States Justice Department are seen to be wholly behind the National Health Care Program. Yet, the larger businesses, well those that I talked to anyway, are dead set against it. They claim the results of having automatons, their words mind you, as workers and management is devastating. No norm can ever be allowed to hold any position above menial worker because their brains can't handle it! The only way to stay afloat, they claim, will be to hire those of the wizarding world to fill those positions. By their estimates, only one in a hundred can be filled, leading to a total collapse of their businesses. Worse, most of the companies' top executives and owners are normals. Hence, nearly uniformly, the major companies are fighting the states continually, and doing everything they can to change the mind of the governor. Lobbying and even massive bribes have never been this blatant or widespread."

"The average man in the street, if you believe all the talk shows, is also up in arms over the governor's support of the program. In LA alone, there are now fifty different local militias forming up. I heard that the same is occurring in nearly every populated area. How can the elected officials withstand such a groundswell of total opposition and remain in office and effective? Aren't they headed for a crisis of unprecedented proportions?"

"Yes, I do believe that Governor Alister Broadwell's Grand Plan is about to backfire in his and his follower's faces. Explode may be more like it. We will do nothing but sit back and watch the fireworks. After all, President Snow has promised us the full support of the Army, should we need to resort to more forceful means," Dominus fed his follower some tidbits of information that he suspected Melvin might not have known.

"Ah, I see. Well, yes, that will be a big help in countering all these local militias. But what about the very real concern of all the businesses and corporations and their need to replace millions of highly skilled salaried, research, and management positions?" Melvin expressed his greatest concern about this whole endeavor, hoping to get some idea of what Dominus had in mind.

"In time, they will be replaced with other wizards from abroad. However, we will not need researchers into more and better drugs, for example. Those can be discarded as compost. What do we need bigger and faster jets for anyway? We just Teleport. It's drastically cheaper and ecologically friendly. That's a joke, by the way. Norms don't need to travel, just perform their daily tasks as they are told. So the airline industry can be allowed to disappear as well. Honestly, Melvin, if you think about it, the only industries that we really need to keep operational are those that handle food, clothing, shelter, and commodities. After all, we must have our TV sets, music players, phones, and computers. But do we really need computers that run faster and better than those that we have now? Aren't the computer programs and applications doing just fine today? Why do we need more research and development in those areas? We don't. Just keep on making the same things that we now have for replacements. No, probably half of the companies across the US are just plain excess baggage. Those we will allow to disappear. Make sense?"

Melvin nodded; now that it was put into perspective, it did make sense. After all, why go to all that trouble to take a commercial flight? Only if you were a total masochist would you fly instead of Teleport. Besides, it is vastly cheaper to truck food across country rather than fly it. Certainly, there would be a major period of restructuring of companies, but then the economy would right itself. He was satisfied for the moment.

Chapter 20—A Long Haul Until Spring

At the start of Spell Casting class, finally, the moans from the students stopped. All morning long, the professors greeted them back, piling on a mountain of homework, uniformly at least it seemed that way to the students. They had a bit of a respite in Spell Research class, finding it refreshing to get back to searching the library for new and sometimes cool spells. Then came Potion Making II. Professor Delius seemed to delight in making their first day back from break horrid. Assigning a very difficult potion and one that created a putrid stink; moans gave way to gags and a few vomits.

Now, things would finally become interesting once more with new and powerful spells in Spell Casting class. Professor Huan Su greeted them, introducing himself to the several newer transfer students. "This month, you have but four spells to learn to cast, powerful, elegant, and highly useful spells, major evocation spells indeed. First is the Punching Fist." Deiter recalled that this was the one used when they raided the Georgia mansion to rescue the imprisoned women. A giant fist appeared before the face of one of the Death Stalkers and began punching him as if he were a punching bag. Deiter sat up very straight in his chair, listening to every word from Huan Su.

"Next, we will cover the Advanced Lightning Strike. This spell goes beyond a normal bolt of lightning in that you, the caster, can cause it to split or fork into several branches and thus strike more than one opponent or enemy. Yes, these are intended to be offensive. While the Punching Fist is seldom deadly, the Advanced Lightning Strike often is quite deadly."

"Yet, advanced evocation magic is not confined to just these offensive spells. Rather, the next spell is perhaps one of the most widely used spells in our entire arsenal, the In Case Of spell. Many of you have seen this one in use over the last few years. For example, In Case I get Disarmed, Teleport me home. In Case I am badly wounded, Teleport me home. For you ladies, In Case someone molests me, Teleport me home. In Case I am Disarmed, Summon my Wizard Staff. Ah, the uses I have seen for this spell. In Case I forget my umbrella, Summon my umbrella. Yes, I've seen that one too. However, the spell will not work In Case I get Wished somewhere, Teleport me home. It fails in the presence of a Restricted Wish spell, I am afraid to say. There are some limitations."

"Finally, we will examine how to evoke a powerful Guard to watch over some key chest, possession, or similar valuable. If anyone attempts to get close to the object, the Guard then attacks them. It can most definitely kill thieves. Governor Alister used many Guards during your first year here, when he was guarding the Rod of the Apocalypse. They very nearly killed Dominus when he stole the rod. So we have lots of work to do this month. However, we will begin by reviewing the Major Protection and Magical Barrier spells. I will need you to have them cast upon you so that you are not harmed by the giant fists or the lightning strikes. Let's get to work. Show me that you can cast these two spells."

"Now we are into some serious magic!" Emilio commented to Kathy.

"Most useful spells!" Pam said to Tom.

The two hours literally flew by the eager students. Just as the end of the period came, Deiter finally managed the incantation to bring the Punching Fist into existence, pounding a well-protected Lindsey with it. She was thankful for the Magical Barrier spell, which totally protected her from being a punching bag. Deiter walked tall from the classroom this first day.

After supper, Lindsey joined Professor Delius in the Hall of Necromancy for her Dispeller Theory class. She felt a little awkward and was hoping that perhaps Delius would simply end her training, since he'd run out of things to teach her. However, such was not the case. For an hour, Delius cast spell after spell at her, while she exercised her new skill to disperse the magical energies as they were forming. It required an intense concentration on her part, however, and she was sweating profusely when they ended.

"Unbelievable, Lindsey, just incredible. I would never, ever have thought such Dispelling was possible. Yet, seeing is believing. You realize, don't you, that I have been casting all the spells that I know at you tonight."

"Er, I didn't know that. It takes my total concentration to do it. I'll feel much more comfortable when I have done this to a Restricted Wish spell." Delius knew precisely what she meant. If Lindsey could do that, she'd no longer have to fear the diabolical tortures of Dominus.

"I think that tomorrow I will have another join us, giving you two of us at once to handle. Are you up for it?" he asked. Lindsey knew better than to say no, for he'd just go ahead and do it anyway, since she deflected every one of his spells this evening.

"Professor, I was thinking, I would like to see if Ashley can learn to do this too. You see, I was going to try to disperse Simon's last Restricted Wish spell, but I sensed he was going to get Ashley too, so I didn't so I could be with her. If I knew that she could also disperse it, then maybe we won't get captured by him again."

"I understand. No, I couldn't leave a loved one either. She is doing some vitally important divination work now, but I will talk with Mary Ann and see. No promises on when, but we'll give it a go." She thanked him and headed back to the dorm and the mountain of homework still facing her.

As she walked down the long tunnel, a Magical Door opened and Deiter stepped out. "Hi, good timing. How did it go with Delius?" His arm slid around her waist and she smiled. "You are soaking!"

"Tell me something I don't know! I had a work out. He shot every spell he knew at me. I was pressed, but I dispersed every one of them Deiter. Now if I could just know for sure I can also do it to his Restricted Wish, I would feel immensely better about it all."

"You're kidding me?" he looked at her, slightly confused. "He shot real spells? You could have been seriously hurt!"

Lindsey giggled, "Not very likely anymore. Deiter, I can

see the energy of the spell as it is forming, and I can alter it as I chose."

"Gosh, you may be the world's greatest Dispeller ever!" he exclaimed.

"Don't know about that, but I aim to help put Simon and his Death Stalkers where they belong," she declared.

"Hi all. May be difficult to do that," Ashley appeared from an adjoining tunnel, also heading back from her Divination Theory class. "What an awful night. I spent an hour getting nearly nowhere at all! Simon is on to me big time. He has anti-scrying spells and devices all over himself, the room, and now even his Death Stalkers too! I guess it has just been too easy until now. Mary Ann says that I must overcome these new obstacles, but I don't see how yet."

Just then, they entered the dorms and Yellow Hall's study hall where their friends were waiting for them, homework piled around the tables. Pam looked exceedingly glum, however.

"Pam's elective is done," Amanda announced to the new arrivals. "Professor Cho Lin hasn't got anything more that she can teach her about Sleuthing. She said that if Pam wants to know more, she is going to have to go to CSI school when she graduates Bradbury's. Bummer."

"Sorry Pam. I guess you now have more time to catch up on your other homework," Lindsey tried to put a better light on the situation.

Pam faked a smile. Amanda added, "I am about done too. Monane says that there is very little left that she can teach me about Tracking. I can use more study time, that's for sure."

"Well, I may be joining you both soon as well," Lindsey added, then related what happened this evening. Deiter knew that he had mountains to learn from Wilma and enjoyed every minute of it and thus kept quiet.

Around nine, a Message flashed before Pam's eyes. "Oh. Governor Alister wants to see me. Back in a bit," she said, very surprised, and concerned that none of her dear friends had received a similar note. What can he want of me, she wondered all the way to his office.

"Ah, good evening Miss Betts. Have a seat." Gosh, he is

looking very rundown, she noted. They'd been so busy getting the students off the bus and settled in, to say nothing of their own problems, that she hadn't actually looked at Alister. She began to worry about his health.

"Professor Cho Lin has informed me that you have achieved all the skills that we can teach you about Sleuthing. Congratulations are in order." A tea set appeared, and he offered her a cup.

"Now that you have a bit more free time, Pam, the Rodents Pack needs your assistance. As you probably have heard from Miss Stokes-Compton, Simon has gotten wise to her divination attempts. He has very likely acquired or cast anti-scrying and similar spells. Professor Mary Ann believes that he also has his rooms and his close associates likewise protected. This will make divination vastly more difficult, but not impossible. In the meantime, it is imperative that the Rodents Pack take effective actions against this National Health Care Program. To date, we have been able to keep their overall production so low that they can't expand into other states."

"With divination now more problematical, I would like you to use other means to ascertain Simon's plans and suggest ways that pill production can be arrested. Are you game for this new challenge? Please, only work on it during the hour that you have been using for Sleuting Theory."

"Sure thing. I'll get on it tomorrow night then. Do I report things directly to you?" she asked, wondering how she could do this, when Ashley, the Diviner, could not.

The instant that Pam reappeared in the study hall, all her friend's eyes were on her. "Well?" Lindsey hinted. Pam suspected that they had done nothing at all while she was gone, except speculate on what Alister had wanted. She told them her new assignment. Ashley was very relieved to hear that Pam was also working on trying to figure out what Simon was doing. Until now, it had all been on her shoulders.

The second week in January, Ashley was allowed to accompany Lindsey to Dispeller Theory class. Since her divination work was severely hampered, this was a good time for her to learn to disperse Simon's Restricted Wish spell, if that were possible for her. After working with her all week, Ashley was adequately dispersing spells, though slowly. This gave both girls confidence that they would no longer be subject to Simon's spell. Lindsey was relieved on Friday night when Ashley was easily able to disperse each spell Delius sent her way.

Mid-January, Pam finally had a breakthrough in her evening researches. She discovered a financial transaction in which Aetna Pharmaceuticals had recently purchased Hage, a small Dutch manufacturer of anti-depressants. After a bit more research, she found shipping receipts showing small shipments of medicinal heroin were now being delivered monthly to this company. Obviously, this company was now going into the production of Saude Dourada. This she reported to Governor Alister. Now she began to focus her research efforts to overseas pharmaceutical companies.

Twice a week, Professor Delius increased the number of opponents that Lindsey had to face down in her Dispeller Theory exercises. By the end of January, he had twenty other students all casting spells at Lindsey at the same time! While it required the utmost concentration on her part, Lindsey dispersed all spells being sent at her, almost like a machine gun. News of her incredible action spread around the school, and she found many other students staring at her, when they thought she might not be looking. While she found it annoying at best, she endured it. She knew that her mission was to keep her companions alive so that Simon could be captured; this she would do no matter what it cost her.

The third week of January, Spell Casting class turned hilarious for everyone. Class started out serious enough with Huan Su explaining the In Case Of spell. "You can join any other Grade 6 or lower grade spell to this one. For example, In Case I am disarmed, Teleport me home. You cast first the In Case Of spell, followed at once by the action spell desired if the situation triggers. Once you set the pair of spells up, they last until the situation is activated or you chose to cancel them. It does not automatically cancel after a period of time, as in the duration of many other spells."

"However, you do need to be very careful about the 'of' clause. For example, you cast In Case I get hurt, Teleport home. Okay, on the surface it sounds fine. You are walking down the street and stub your toe, which hurts or you accidentally hit your elbow on the corner of a desk. The spell activates and you are Teleported. Why? You are hurt, you see."

"Now sometimes you can pin it down to a very specific thing happening, an unequivocal thing, such as getting disarmed, falling off of a cliff, drowning, being blinded. Other times, it is a relative thing, such as badly wounded, totally confused, very sick, or being attacked."

"Now then, it is time to begin practicing this one. I want you to cast In Case I Get Tickled, then Color Tickler's Hair Green or any color of your choice." The whole class giggled, particularly the girls. Once you believe you have the pair installed, your partner's task is to trigger the spell by tickling you."

"Whoa, this is going to be fun, Lindsey," Deiter commented and madly flipped his book's pages to the spell details. Lindsey was still laughing, along with most of the girls.

With a passion not seen in a long time, Huan Su watched his students dive eagerly into the spell. In fact, this was a challenging spell to learn, but he had years ago worked out this fun way for the students to approach it. By turning it into a fun session and one that had their interest, he'd discovered his students picked up the spell many times faster than usual. Yes, this was a tough spell to master fully, but a highly valuable one indeed. Hence, he had worked out his playful method.

As the end of the two-hour period approached, many began having success. "Okay, it worked. Lindsey, try to tickle me," Deiter said finally. Smirking, Lindsey began tickling his sides. To her amazement, she found he was terribly ticklish indeed. Just as he flinched and began to laugh, his spell activated and Lindsey's long brown hair became flaming orange. Both roared with laughter.

Nearby, Pam's spell activated and Tom's short hair turned pink, much to his dismay. Ashley's hair turned bright red as Amanda's spell activated. Peaches' spell activated, turning Andy's hair a royal purple. The class was rolling in laughter as the period ended.

For the rest of the week, as students scrambled from class to class, to lunch, and to supper, suddenly a fifth year's hair would change color, a loud farting noise would break the hall noise. or an awful stink suddenly enveloped a pair of students. Eagerly, the fifth year students continued to set up all manner of silly In Case Of spells on themselves, egging their friends to trigger the spells. Yes, they did indeed have frivolity for several days.

More importantly, by the end of the week, all were now casting deadly serious In Case Of spells. Deiter now never went anywhere without having In Case I am Disarmed, Summon my Staff in effect. Lindsey, Ashley, Amanda, and Pam now kept In Case I am attacked, Summon my staff on them. Slowly but surely, these teens were becoming prepared for the real world outside of magic school.

At the end of January, Pam cast Protect My Laptop. If anyone tried to hack into her laptop without her permission, the spell would activate, creating an opponent, which would attack the perpetrator. If the person was a normal, they would very likely be killed by the attack! However, she gave all of her friends the deactivation word, just in case they needed to retrieve the Wish scroll in her keeping. Lindsey now recognized that around her large ranch complex, Lloyd and Fred had installed numerous Protect spells. She could now identify that peculiar residual magical energy that she had seen on numerous occasions.

The first half of February, they once more found themselves being taught by Professor Mary Ann. She had two powerful divination spells to teach them. These, she particularly enjoyed teaching. Lindsey noted a distinctly happier countenance on Mary Ann's face during these ten sessions, though she still looked as scattered as always. "First, we are going to learn how to See True, that is, to see what is really there, piercing through any and all disguises, magical or otherwise. This is a most powerful and useful divination spell, as you can easily see. Not even Invisibility will shield one from your view."

The whole class threw themselves into learning this spell. Mary Ann had each partner cast Invisible on themselves and then move to a different place in the classroom. The other partner then cast their See True spell to locate their invisible partner. Midweek, when all had this one down fairly well, she then had the partners Morph Self into Another and had the casters find their partners once more. Again, by making this one fun and enjoyable, the students learned it more quickly than normal. The festive mood changed the next week, however.

"This week, we are taking up a very difficult spell, Know History. You come upon a person, place, or object and wish to know more about it. Take this ring here for example. Please cast Detect Magic on it." The class did so, discovering it was radiating magical energies. "Now, please cast your Identification spell on it to determine what it does. Again, over thirty spells fired off rapidly, followed by the usual intense studying of the ring.

"Professor, I'm not getting anything," Pam stated flatly, unused to having one of her key Sleuthing spells inoperable.

"Precisely. None of you will get any useful information from that spell used upon this ring. Sometimes, this happens. Now if you can cast Know History, you may get some highly useful information. Let me demonstrate the spell on this ring." She cast the spell and then recited what the spell told her about the ring.

"The spell relates as follows: First President, husband second, given to you, in my absence, safe. Yes, it always comes out as silly rhymes, limericks, and such. Can any of you decipher what the spell is telling us?"

Dead silence. Many squirmed in their chairs. At last, Deiter commented, "Well I don't see any use for a spell that speaks in riddles. Totally useless information, that's all."

"There, there, magic is not always black and white, Mr. Cross. Anyone hazard a guess?" Professor Mary Ann continued to ask.

Finally, Pam raised her hand. "Professor, First President may be referring to George Washington. His wife, Martha, may be the original owner of the ring. Maybe he gave it to her to keep her safe when he was not there, a Protection Ring perhaps."

"Precisely correct, Miss Betts. Well done indeed. Yes, this is the very ring the George Washington gave Martha to protect her during his many absences. It is one of my most cherished possessions. Now please form up into teams of four students each. I only have ten items that we can use for this spell. All are rather rare and valuable, you see. Have one member of each team come up here and fetch one for your group. Under no circumstances are you to tell other teams what you have identified, should you get it properly identified."

"One final note, passing this spell is not required for a passing grade in Spell Casting Grade 6. We have over thirty students in this class. I will be very surprised if five of you can make effective use of this spell. It is a very tough one, not only to cast, but also, as Mr. Cross has so clearly pointed out, tough to decipher. Nevertheless, I expect each one of you to give it your best attempt; that is what matters the most."

Deiter brought a pocket watch back to Lindsey, Ashley, and Amanda, his new team members. "Duh, it's a watch. Are we done now?" he said rather annoyed by this spell. The girls giggled—just the effect he wanted to make anyway. By the end of the week, Deiter had managed to get the spell cast properly twice, but was wholly unable to derive any meaning from what he heard in his mind. Lindsey and Amanda got the spell to work rather rapidly, but also were unable to work out what it said. Ashley, on the other hand, shone with this spell. Her initial casting happened almost the very first time she tried to cast it.

She heard, "Haste makes waste, or so it is said. Kites and lightning formed its making. Will it be seconds or minutes?" Eventually, Deiter, Lindsey, and Amanda also heard this short message. Apparently, the spell always gave the same message, Ashley concluded rightly.

Pondering its meaning for two days, Ashley finally

guessed, "Professor Mary Ann, I believe this watch does something to time for the bearer. Perhaps it was made by Ben Franklin; he did experiments with flying kites in a thunderstorm."

"Precisely so," a proud Mary Ann acknowledged Ashley, who was the first student in the class to get this far on their object. "Now how does one activate its magic?"

"Well, perhaps you turn the watch back a little or a lot and it does its thing," she suggested, that being the only sense she could make of the last part.

"Give it a little try, just a little please," Mary Ann grinned. Ashley took the watch, moved the minute hand back one minute, and looked up.

Weird! Everyone was just where they were a minute ago, doing what they had already done! Even stranger, they seemed to be moving in slow motion, and she could not understand the words they were speaking. Lindsey's voice was a low, drawn out bass! Yet, she was moving normally! It was so strange, that Ashley got up from her seat and moved to Mary Ann's desk so that she could look back on the whole class, all of whom seemed affected. Suddenly, everyone was moving and talking normally once again.

"Hey, Ashley! How the devil did you get up there?" Deiter called out, shocked to see Ashley, who a second before was sitting beside him, now up by the professor's desk.

"Wow! Way, way super weird!" Ashley exclaimed. "You all were moving really slowly. I couldn't even understand what you were saying because you were talking so slowly!"

Professor Mary Ann said, "Well done, Ashley. The watch reverses and slows time down for a brief period. I think you can imagine how useful this could be in certain situations."

"Can I try it?" asked an eager Deiter.

"I'm sorry. Only if you correctly guess an object are you allowed to use it once. All these magical items belong to Bradbury's School of Magic and are for use in this spell. Keep trying, Mr. Cross. Maybe you will get the next one."

He didn't, of course. Both Pam and Ashley worked out what five of the objects did. Surprisingly, Peaches got one herself, and Andy, another, due to his extensive archaeology training. One other transfer student, whom Lindsey did not know, identified another one.

The remainder of the month was spent outside with Professor Blake Smith, learning to Conjure Animals and Snare Creatures. He had them begin small, conjuring mice and then snaring them. "The animals you conjure will be expecting to attack your enemies at once. Ladies, don't worry, the animals are not actual animals, if your opponent's kill them. In any case, these magically created ones will disappear within minutes or sooner. Yet, when you find yourself being attacked and have no one to protect you, this spell gives you something to help fight for you."

"But Professor, what good are mice? Unless I'm being attacked by cock roaches or something," Pam asked, rather annoyed with the spell.

"Ah, Miss Betts, eager to get on with it I see. Well, we are beginning with animals that you are most likely to be able to conjure. During the week, we will attempt to conjure larger and larger protectors. Keep practicing and you will soon see." He teased her as he always did with his students. She sighed and dutifully conjured another pair of mice.

By the end of February, most of the class was able to conjure giant bears to fight and protect them from harm. Lindsey even managed to conjure two giant horses, whose hooves were quite deadly. All found that snaring these much larger, vastly more powerful and dangerous animals quite a chore indeed.

During the long, dreary month of March, Professor Cho Lin worked them on their advanced illusion based spells. These culminated in their ability to create an illusion that was permanent in nature until dispelled by the caster of a Dispel Magic. These illusions were quite real, in that they not only impacted sight, but also sounds, smells, even tactile senses were present. While fun and entertaining, Lindsey didn't see what use they would be to her. Many shared her position, though Cho Lin did her best to try to show them clever uses of the spell, uses which convinced another person to relay some key information that they might not have otherwise.

On the other hand, Amanda and Pam were more interested in the details of the False Clue spell, as such directly affected their ability to Sleuth or Track. Lindsey took a little interest in the spell, since someone might use it against her. Most students became very bored with these spells, however.

These were the highlights of the ten long weeks. Mostly, the students crammed on their traditional courses, reading upwards of fifty pages each night, doing dozens of math problems, and trying to grasp the advanced topics connect with their study of Earth. As April 1 approached, finally Professor Jasper began to give them long study blocks in which to work on their science projects, much to the relief of Pam in particular, who was convinced they were all going to flunk Advanced Earth Science for sure.

Chapter 21—Spring Strike

"Lindsey! Your mother is down at the parking lot gate!" a worried looking Deiter walked into the study hall, piles of books shrunk to fit his hand.

Lindsey jumped up, ready to dash there. Ashley, too, looked shaken; she'd not had any dire premonitions about her mother. She began to follow Lindsey.

"April fool!" Deiter called out jovially.

"Deiter!" exclaimed Lindsey, as her fright and worry gave way to total annoyance.

"You—you—you," Ashley began, completely unsure how to finish her exclamation. It didn't help that Emilio and Kathy were giggling away.

"Got you both good, didn't I," Deiter continued his playful ribbing, piling his books onto the table beside Lindsey's mound, then canceling his Shrink spell.

"Just for that, I won't help you the slightest tonight," Lindsey finally found a way to get even with him. Deiter feigned a horrible, hurt look, which only cracked up the others even more. Even Pam managed a grin, though she was trying to ignore all their antics. Studies were plainly quite serious these days, she thought.

"Hey, look, things have got to get better, easier," Deiter tried to shift the topic. "Have you all noticed that we only have four more spells to learn in Spell Casting class?"

Only Pam had. "Oh no! They are enchantment and charm based spells!" Lindsey lamented as she peeked at the remaining pages in her book of Grade 6 spells. That could only mean that they would be having Professor Janice Smith as their teacher, the only teacher Lindsey had little respect for, the only professor who had given Lindsey a horrid time her first year here, when she had no hands.

Ashley, imitating Professor Janice, remarked, "Lindsey, make sure your wand activates!" That broke everyone up, including Pam, who roared with laughter.

They were not laughing come Monday when Professor

Janice, wearing her trademark cherry red lipstick, walked into their Spell Casting class. Of all the professors, she was the most attractive. She sat on the desk and made sure that her nylon-covered legs and heels were visible for the boys, many of whom couldn't take their eyes off her.

"It is my pleasure to teach you your remaining Grade 6 spells. These are quite powerful spells, you see, easy for you to mess up. So I will be watching you closely. As always, proper wand activation is pivotal in getting these complex spells to work." Her eyes and many others in the class drifted onto Lindsey, whose face flushed involuntarily, as it had during her first weeks at Bradbury's as a first year.

"Some of you brighter students may wish to take up the occupation of Magical Item Creation, when and if you graduate. The very first spell that is needed is, of course, Enchant an Item. For example, you have decided to create a magical ring to hold spells. You have just spent three thousand dollars for a suitable, fine quality, gold ring. Now you must enchant the ring so that further spells can be cast into it. If you botch this spell, you must start over, having wasted the three thousand dollars. I'm sure that some of you will do this repeatedly, waste fine quality items. So study this spell well."

"Governor Alister has kindly loaned us thirty-three such quality rings for you to enchant. Come up here and get yours, then let's get to work. Honestly, this is the easiest spell we are going to learn in this term. The others, I'm afraid, you are going to find much, much more difficult." Deiter retrieved one for Lindsey so she could avoid closing the distance between her and Professor Janice.

By the end of the week, only six in the class could not actually get their rings enchanted. Poor Emilio was one of these. Try as he may, he never quite got the spell one hundred percent correct. Always it fizzled. That Professor Janice continued to smirk at his efforts didn't help one bit, but actually lowered his confidence further. As they left class on Friday, Emilio commented, "Well, I guess that I'm just not cut out for enchanting things."

Kathy came to his rescue though, "It's just Professor Janice. She has it in for you this term. I'm sure that if you practice it on your own, you can do it, Emilio." Pam agreed with her, and he felt a bit better about his failures.

On Saturday night, Governor Alister called another meeting of the Rodents Pack. Eagerly, the teens filed into his large conference room, wondering what the latest news might be. KMAG continued to report only the Presidential party line, though many students had taken up listening to the many talk shows, in which the true situations were discussed, many in revolutionary terms.

"I wanted to take this opportunity to bring you all up to date. As many of you know, Simon has taken numerous anti-scrying precautions, but that has not stopped Miss Stokes-Compton, Miss Betts, or us. First, I must compliment Miss Stokes-Compton on her timely divinations. It seems that Simon had laid a trap, hoping to eliminate Erin Saks and the whole Red Brigade. Yet, she thought that premonition was too easy for her to have had and divined deeper, seeing the underlying trap. Disguised as a big shipment of equipment and pills, an entire US army division was onboard that train, ready to wipe them all out. Thanks to her warning, Erin took no action, foiling that attempt."

"Now then, as far as new pill production facilities go, we have not been as successful these last few months as I had hoped. Simon, wise to our countermoves, has apparently been secretly acquiring smaller facilities abroad. However, thanks to the diligent Sleuthing from Miss Betts, we have discovered some of these. One is in the Netherlands, and I am sad to report that it is now online, pumping out the pills."

"However, due to the quantity of pills, they are being forced to ship them here either by cargo ship or by air transport. Erin has risen to the challenge, and we have intercepted a fair number of those pill shipments. Alas, I'm afraid that they now are likely to have sufficient stock that more states can be brought into the program. We've learned that President Snow is likely going after Connecticut, Massachusetts, and Rhode Island next. Expect major problems in those states to develop in April or May at the latest."

"We have been asking our supporters abroad to attack

or damage the known facilities, but as yet, they have not been successful. I have been reluctant to allow Erin to take his forces overseas and attack the plants there. The political fallout is too steep a price to pay, just yet anyway. I am hopeful that others in the Netherlands can see the larger picture and will take action. If Simon controls all the US, he is sure to extend his dominion over other countries, if only they can see that. I have been working vigilantly to make this clear to those I know overseas. Time will tell if I have been successful."

He chatted a bit more, took a few questions, and then the meeting was over. As they walked back to the dorms, enjoying the crisp, spring night, Pam commented, "Boy, Governor Alister really looks worn out."

"He's under a whole lot of stress," Ashley pointed out. "He's trying to lead everyone against Dominus. It's no wonder he looks haggard." The teens discussed this a while longer, before hitting their research project for science class.

As the last two weeks of April loomed, the weather in the afternoons was warm and sunny. Consequently, Professor Janice held the two-hour long Spell Casting class out of doors, near the formal gardens. "These last two weeks, some of you will be learning the Fear Strike spell and the Group Suggestion spell. A successful Fear Strike will cause a group of your opponents to flee in terror, get very ill and vomit, or simply lie down and fall asleep, effectively handling them. With Group Suggestion, you can convince an entire group of people of some fact. Just how successful you will be depends upon how unreal the suggestion is. If you try to suggest that they are all dead, none will believe it. With the sun shining brightly, if you try to suggest that it is raining, they will not believe that either. However, if you suggest the warm sun is making them sleepy, as many of you students are right now, they will all believe you and start falling asleep."

Indeed, Kathy had to nudge Emilio awake. He was drifting off; the warm sun was shining on his head and chest. Instead of working with one spell until they all had it down, Professor Janice had them working on both spells. For some students, this resulted in total confusion, which she seemed to enjoy watching. Pam spied this, particularly with Kathy and

Emilio and ordered them to work only on their Group Suggestion spell.

By the end of the third week of April, members of the class were starting to fall asleep on the grass, laugh hysterically, run around in small circles, and other humorous things as commanded by those who were successful at casting of Group Suggestion spells. None laughed louder than Professor Janice, who always seemed to enjoy seeing the students in unusual predicaments.

By the following Wednesday, Lindsey and her friends had both spells mastered. However, since others in the class were still practicing them, Lindsey decided to see if she could throw off the spell's effects on herself, without actually disrupting the caster's spell. As they began their two-hour class, Audrey commented, "Lindsey, we should not be here today. Something bad is going to happen to me."

Lindsey glanced around, but saw nothing but the budding flowers and green grass. Even the trees in the Dark Forest were coming out. She could see nothing that would cause trouble. However, Ashley stopped her practicing and began using her divination skills instead. She had come to trust in the vague premonitions of Audrey. At last, she began to see. "Lindsey!" she said, "I see a wall of men attacking us! How can that be?" The two girls looked around, but saw no men, nothing but a beautiful spring afternoon.

Professor Janice called out to Ashley and Lindsey, "Concentrate you two. Let's see wand activation." Lindsey grumbled, but activated her wand, casting Clean on her shoes.

Ashley, on the other hand, was very worried. Defiantly, she decided to cast her Group Suggestion spell. Her wand activated, but her command was, "Everyone, stay totally alert for trouble. We are being attacked." Professor Janice, who had been looking for another round of silly actions from the group of students, was totally surprised to suddenly see everyone looking around, this way and that, wands at the ready, as if they were being attacked or about to be.

Just then, Amanda spied movement across from the Dark Forest. "Over there!" she called out. All eyes moved to the west and the trees and more distant wall. Boom! A loud explosion shook the ground.

As the shocked students looked, part of the outer, grey granite, stone block wall crumbled. Swarms of men wearing black pants, shirts, with black masks over their faces, rushed through the breach, wands waving. Professor Janice had her back to the wall and was slow to turn around, but she too saw the swarm of men coming at them. Before she could issue any orders, a ball of fire detonated, catching Emilio and Kathy off guard. Both were badly burned and fell to the ground.

That convinced Lindsey this was no practice session. Immediately, she concentrated and began dispersing other magical energies coming their way. "Blast them; I'll hold them off," she shrieked. Deiter and the others began firing off spells as fast as they could shoot them. Balls of fire appeared among their attackers; bolts of lightning struck some, knocking them off their feet. Clouds of poison gas deluged some. Disintegrate beams took out chunks of ground, as the men in black dodged out of the way. Lindsey made sure that none of their attacker's disintegrate beams were successfully cast, of that she made certain, concentrating heavily on that spell, making sure she disrupted those.

Fifty men swarmed through the breach, casting spells wildly in all directions. Magical doors opened up all around Lindsey's class. Professors and other students swarmed out to their defense. Lindsey spied Fern rushing out, shooting off a Ball of Fire as she arrived. Lindsey concentrated for all she was worth, eliminating twenty or more spells each volley, but that meant thirty got past her, however. Screams of pain came from all sides, though she dare not break her concentration, least more spells get past her.

Something hit her arm—pain! She ignored it and wiped out another five spells. Explosions or spell detonations thundered across their campus. However, because the older students had been practicing spell combat under Professor Delius, all the older students had some idea of how to conduct themselves on a battlefield. They were not a bunch of scared schoolchildren nor were they total novices to real spell combat situations. The fifty invaders soon discovered this aspect. The students worked together! Some shot Dispel Magic spells to remove protection spells the invaders had on themselves. Those were followed immediately by power offensive spells, many of which got through because of the success of the Dispel Magic spells. Several Disintegrate spells removed some men's limbs, as they failed to dodge out of the way sufficiently quickly.

Still, the attackers could not figure out why nearly half of their spells failed utterly to detonate! While there were a few Staves of Power on the battlefield occasionally absorbing spells, that would account for only a few. They were losing nearly half of their offensive spells! While they had expected resistance—this was a school of magic after all—they had not anticipated what they were experiencing. Already half of their men were out of the battle, lying wounded or dead.

As suddenly as it started, the battle ended. Those still standing heard an order and Teleported away, leaving behind their fallen. While Governor Alister and the others stood staring at the suddenly silent field, the bodies of the fallen men vanished. Many called out, "Where'd they go? What just happened?" Similar comments echoed from all sides. At last, Lindsey broke her concentration and turned to look around her. Many of her fellow students were lying injured on the grass around her. Six hundred students had swarmed out to help defend the school, along with all the professors.

Over the eerie silence, Governor Alister's voice boomed. "Check your fellow students. Rush any critically injured students to the Infirmary immediately. If you are slightly injured, walk there and form a line. Those uninjured, help those who need it. First years, front and center. Lend a hand going from fallen to fallen. Move!"

Lindsey turned to Deiter, who was at her side. "Deiter, you're wounded; you are bleeding!" She saw blood oozing down the side of his face.

"Your arm, Lindsey, it must be broken! I'm okay, really I am," he replied. She looked down at her left arm, which was bent at a weird angle. Now the pain surged through her body, and only Deiter's strong arm kept her from hitting the ground hard.

She heard Pam call out, "I'm all rite—just my node."

She turned to see Pam's nose bleeding profusely. Tom's right ear was bleeding, as he held onto Pam. Audrey was unconscious on the ground, but a heavily bleeding Peaches still stood over her, protecting her from additional harm. Andy and Amanda were standing over Ashley, who was also unconscious on the ground. Both their clothes looked badly burned.

Governor Alister was now leaning over Ashley. Lindsey fought to retain consciousness, leaning heavily on Deiter. "Stunned. Get her to the Infirmary," his disembodied voice sounded. Stunned—then she was alive—perhaps not seriously hurt. Her mind tried to focus. Now he was over Audrey. How did he get there so fast, she wondered. "Also stunned. Infirmary," he spoke commandingly.

Now Alister was moving to another fallen figure. Lindsey twisted around to see. Someone had been in front of them, but who? Her mind struggled to work—too much data too quickly, but mostly pain, searing pain. Who? Then she recognized the robes of Professor Janice, who had steadfastly refused to retreat and had stood her ground, protecting her class from the onslaught. Now she could see—burned—burned badly—no hair. The pretty face seared. The notion that Professor Janice might be dead flooded into her mind.

No, Huan Su was Levitating her. Cho Lin was opening a Door. Gone. Must be at the Infirmary. Must be alive still. Lindsey's mind tried to assimilate facts. Then more pain. She sat down. Deiter allowed her. "Darn it! I can't see well," he commented to no one in particular.

"Let us help," a soft, timid voice of a first year broke in on her mind. Three first years had come up to them. She allowed two of them to help her up, while another helped Deiter rise. Following the lead of the young ones, Lindsey's feet began to move—move toward the Infirmary.

"Guess we held them off," Lindsey finally managed to put together a sentence.

"You bet we did! I thought that we killed at least half of them, but then their bodies vanished. I don't get that part, but then I can't see too well now, too much blood is in my eyes," he replied.

"We saw it! They really came at you heavy! We thought you all were going to be killed!" one first year girl tried to explain, while keeping Lindsey upright and moving slowly southward. "Gosh, your arm looks really bad!"

Several normal staff members went rushing past them, on their way to inspect and begin repairs on the hole in the outer wall. To Lindsey, it seemed the green grass was full of small insects all making their way southward toward the Infirmary. How many were hurt, she wondered.

Just outside the Infirmary, lines of wounded students began assembling. One nurse came by and instructed a first year to hold a bandage tightly against Deiter's head to stem the bleeding. She heard Pam's funny voice saying, "I'm all rite, my node. Wad happened?" She turned to see the nurse giving her a bandage to hold against her bleeding nose.

"Here, Lindsey, drink this," the voice of the nurse said. She drank and the world turned dark. She was sound asleep. She didn't hear the voice command Levitate, nor did she hear Move Lindsey to Table 1.

Food. Lindsey smelled food! She was starving; she opened her eyes. "Hello sleepyhead," Pam called out. "Everyone, she's awake now." The dull throbbing in her left arm brought back the wild battle to her mind. Lindsey sat up and stared around the room.

Some thirty students, most from her class, lay on makeshift cots low to the floor. Her arm was heavily bandaged. Pam's voice was back to normal, "Your arm got smashed, but it's healing now. Supposed to be vastly better by tomorrow. It's around suppertime."

"Ashley? Audrey? The others?" Lindsey tried to formulate her worst fears, but only names came out. She was still groggy and disoriented.

"I'm fine, well nearly so," Ashley called out nearby. "I got stunned early on, missed all the fun. Audrey got smashed, broke her jaw, but she is still resting, can't talk right now."

Ahana added, "Amanda and I took a bit of a beating, Fist Gloves, no less, but we're fine."

Lindsey relaxed a little, and then was brave enough to ask, "Did we lose anyone? Any of us get killed?" She dreaded the answer, so many vicious spells were flying; she just couldn't stop all them.

"No. Governor Alister claims that is the biggest miracle that he has ever seen!" Pam replied. Lindsey sighed, deeply relieved.

"I told him that you were stopping all their deadly Disintegrate beams so we could focus on delivering damage to them," Deiter called out from across the room. "We're all in here. The whole class got pretty banged up, one way, or another. No one is seriously hurt, excepting Professor Janice."

"Speak for yourself!" moaned Emilio. "I got fried and so did Kathy. We are in great pain!"

"Yes, but you will be fine by morning," Pam tried to encourage the two. "Honestly, that's what Doctor Caterwall says. Seriously, Lindsey, how many of their Disintegrate spells did you stop anyway?"

"I hope all them. I lost count. I tried to stop those and others that I knew would be really bad for us, but I couldn't stop all fifty at once," Lindsey lamented.

"Pretty darn incredible, Lindsey. Let's hear it for our Rodent Dispeller!" called out Peaches. To Lindsey's wonder, some thirty plus voices chanted Dispeller Barron! Dispeller Barron! Then, they clapped as best they could, given their own injuries.

Peaches continued, "Now we've all seen just what a *real* Dispeller can do, Lindsey! Even Governor Alister says that we all ought to have been killed. Yet only Professor Janice is badly wounded, but she'll be fine in a week or so."

Lindsey called out to everyone, "Yes, but we are a team. You all killed nearly half of them. I saw them fall! Say, what happened to all those we killed or wounded?"

Amanda answered, "Governor Alister and Professor Mary Ann ascertained that Dominus must have used a Restricted Wish spell to remove their bodies so that they can't be identified. No one has any proof of who it was that attacked the school. Monane came by and verified their findings. I ought to have seen it myself, but I was not in so good a shape when it happened."

"No kidding! They used a lot of Slice spells, once they

found out their Disintegrate spells were not working. Many of us got some nasty cuts. We need to practice dodging more," Deiter added.

"But why? I don't understand why they attacked the school," Lindsey asked aloud, before she realized that she was just vocalizing her many thoughts.

"Six million dollar question," called out Andy. Many echoed his sentiments.

Pam, of course, had a different opinion. "Well, once Governor Alister arrived, over half of the men began attacking him. It is a wonder that he was not injured. I think that they were after him and the school was just in their way."

"Yes, but he's the head of the school and the best wizard here," protested Peaches. "That would make him the most dangerous wizard on the battlefield. Naturally, I would concentrate on him first." Pam couldn't disagree with her argument; it was rock solid as well. Still, Pam firmly believed that the school was attacked solely to get at Governor Alister.

Just then, dozens of first year students came into the large room, rolling steel carts piled with dinners. "Yes! Here comes food!" Emilio called out, forgetting how much he was hurting.

Carefully, each first year brought a plate and glass to each person and insisted on helping them with their meal. Lindsey noted that the same girl who had helped her off the battlefield came to help her eat. She asked, "Does it still hurt bad? Your arm? I mean it looks lots better now. I was very worried. I'm Sheela, Sheela Blackstone, Brown Hall."

"I can't move it, but it's lots better. Thanks for helping out. It's rather hard doing this with one arm. Glad you weren't injured, Sheela," Lindsey replied, between bites of the cheeseburger.

"The professors ordered us first years to stay out of the fight. We wanted to help, but honestly, what is one magical missile going to do against all those super powerful spells? We all did get to help everyone afterwards, though." She chatted away, giving some appearance of normalcy to the dinnertime.

As they were finishing up, Doctor Caterwall entered, wiping off his bloody hands. "I need to make my rounds, but first, I want to report that Professor Janice is finally doing well. As you know, she was badly burned several times before she went down. I now expect her to make a full recovery, though it was touch and go there for a while. I see you have all found your appetites, a very good sign." Emilio grumbled a little, several others managed a slight chuckle.

As he began to make his rounds, Governor Alister and the other faculty members entered, having finished supper with the rest of the school. "Well, I see you all are looking much better this evening. I'm told that you should all spend the night here, however. I want to extend my heartfelt thanks to every one of you students. You fought bravely and did not give up even an inch of ground to a vastly superior force. Very well done. However, there are a few questions that I and the staff would like to ask you, if you are ready to talk about the attack." Seeing no objections, he continued. "First, were any Disintegrate spells cast by the enemy? This is a very crucial question."

"Sir," Lindsey volunteered, "I dispersed every one of those that I could. They shot plenty of those at the start. I figured those would be the most deadly of their attack spells, so I focused on not letting any of those get through. Plenty of other spells got by me, sir. I couldn't stop so many spells at once."

Governor Alister sighed; his body definitely slumped. However, Professor Cho Lin and Delius exchanged knowing glances. "Alas, I had hoped that none were cast. This presents a different light on the attack. Since they were using Disintegrates, they were indeed, as Professor Delius insisted, out to kill us, students and professors alike. That makes the whole attack even grimmer. However, in that case, Miss Barron, we have all witnessed a Dispeller show that exceeds all Dispeller shows in recorded history. It is nearly unbelievable that a single Dispeller could block or render ineffective some twenty Disintegrate spells cast nearly simultaneously, as Professor Delius suggests. The many rugged hours that you and he have spent working on doing just this have paid off handsomely, Miss Barron. Today, you have saved many student lives, perhaps many professors' lives as well!"

"Yes, but we are a team," Lindsey protested. "All I did was hold them off so the others could get in some attacks to stop them. They killed half of them, didn't they?" Pam smiled. She knew that Lindsey was throwing equal credit onto everyone else who fought back.

"Indeed, the teamwork I saw today makes me cry. When one of you fell, your friends formed up around you and protected you. As a result, not a single student was killed. That is the biggest miracle I can imagine. You all should be incredibly proud of your actions today and those of the many others who swarmed out to aid you. I want you to know that as of now, twenty-five security men will be on patrol around our perimeter, twenty-four-seven! Never in history has a school of magic been so attacked. I promise you that it will never be allowed to happen here again."

"Professor Delius and his mock battles gave us an edge," Pam broke in. "Without those practice sessions, I wouldn't have known what to do out there. Thanks to him, I was rather prepared. We ought to do more mock battles, sir."

Delius smiled at the unexpected but highly accurate compliment. Governor Alister managed a grin. "Yes, Miss Betts, you are quite right in your assessment. The teamwork among yourselves and the many others that rushed out to assist was a marvel to behold. Together and united, we are strong. You all proved that again today. Not a single student fled the battlefield or faculty member, for that matter." Lindsey realized he was making a direct reference to Professor Janice. "Now I ought to allow you to get your rest and let the many healing potions work their magic. We'll talk more later."

As things settled down for the evening, Pam whispered, "He's right you know. Janice didn't Teleport away. She held her ground the whole time. I would never have predicted that she would do that."

"I know. I am surprised by that too," Lindsey whispered back. She may be covertly hostile to students, a tease for boys, but she didn't desert them when it mattered. Lindsey began to see Professor Janice in a different light.

Across the country in near the outskirts of Macon,

Georgia, Dominus paced the stately, oak floor of the large living room, waiting for news. Two days ago, he'd finally reached a decision. It was nearly May and still he was far, far from his vitally needed goal, enough pills to begin converting more states. He was unsure how much longer he could delay the President and her Health Care Program. He was supposed to be able to bring more states online six months ago. Yet, every attempt of his to build more plants in the US, buy more plants overseas, all had been thwarted, blocked or attacked by this Erin Saks and the Red Brigade, all under the control of Governor Alister Broadwell!

He'd taken every precaution possible against this new Class 4 Diviner. Yet, only the fresh, new ideas of his business associate, Melvin Hoggs, had made any difference. Their plan to ambush Erin had failed utterly; they did not show up to hijack the train. Every attempt to acquire new production equipment from within the US had failed, trains blown up, plants somehow burned to the ground—the list went on and on.

Only Melvin's overseas plans were working, at least mostly. Their new Dutch plant was online and had produced a large quantity of pills. While the first shipment made it to their secret warehouse and was sufficient to bring the next three smaller states into the National Health Care Program, the second shipment was at the bottom of the ocean, sunk under mysterious circumstances. Now that plant had been attacked by Dutch rebels, but was still partially operational. Three more plants were just now beginning production. It seemed at every turn, Dominus detected the silent hand of Broadwell interfering, blocking him and his goal.

It had to be Governor Broadwell. There was no one else. "Stupid coward, using kids to do his dirty work," he'd spat on the floor. Yet the realization finally came. He would have to take Broadwell out of the game. His grand scheme was being sacrificed solely because he insisted on personally torturing his age-old enemy personally. At last, he realized that he, too, would have to make sacrifices, if he truly wanted his Golden Path to come to fruition. Thus, he'd finally consented to listen to the suggestions of his Death Stalkers.

Len Striker had come up with the plan, a simple plan. Smash a hole in the outer wall, rush in probably dealing with a few school kids first, but then leveling everything against Governor Broadwell, when he appeared on the scene, which would be an absolute fact. He would be there rapidly, vainly trying to protect all the school kids. It would be a simple matter to Disintegrate his head, end of problem, end of covert resistance, end of all their troubles. On paper, it seemed simple.

Melvin cautioned him that no magic school had ever been attacked openly and that the population at large would be outraged when they found out who attacked helpless schoolchildren. To prevent this, Dominus agreed to use his Restricted Wish spell once more to retrieve all those who were unable to Teleport away once the battle was finished. They would leave no trace of themselves behind. All would wear masks. It was imperative that none of them ever be identified—leave no trail that led back to the Death Stalkers or himself.

Wanting no slip-ups, Dominus appointed Len Striker to Field Commander and left the details to him, but insisted that Len take a very strong party with him. Len had protested, "Boss, they are only kids!" Dominus overruled him and insisted that Len's Strike Force had fifty men, total overkill as far as Len was concerned. Dominus resisted issuing an order of "Bring me back his head." Besides being melodramatic, such orders would potentially interfere with Len's field tactics. Dominus would have to settle for the simple news that Broadwell was dead. He rationalized that he could "live with that."

Ten minutes after the initial C4 explosion that ripped apart the protective outer barrier around the school, Dominus issued the retreat order. He found that he simply could not stay away from the battlefield. He'd taken up an observation point in the old line shack in which he'd held Sam Barron's kid prisoner five years ago, during his failed attempt to retrieve the ancient rod relic. From here on the tall mountainside, with binoculars, he could at least see the death of his archenemy Broadwell. Quietly, he cast his spell and then returned to his mansion in Georgia, where the fifty were already there waiting him.

Dead bodies lined the floor. Dominus listened to the report from Len Striker, his badly burned Field Commander. "Boss, we caught a class out on the grass learning spells. I don't know what happened. We were never able to get by them! I just don't understand what happened! None of our Disintegrate spells worked, not one, boss! Not a blasted one! I've never seen anything like it. I mean those kids—they just swarmed out of the other buildings and joined the attack! Kids! They should've run for cover and hid! Hundreds of them counterattacked us, Boss. What the heck happened there? They are only kids!" Len was terribly shook up, badly burned, and very confused by what had happened. None of it made any sense to him at all, none. They should have been able to eliminate that handful of kids there on the grass rapidly.

A voice called out, "Fifteen dead. Ten more ain't gonna make it." Someone handed Len a healing potion, which he drank without thinking about it. His mind raced to make some sense from this catastrophe. "Boss, could those kids not have been kids at all? Maybe they were Erin Saks men in disguise," Len vainly suggested the wild idea bouncing around his confused mind.

Now several other men began agreeing with Len. If those were not school kids, but the Idaho Red Brigade, then everything would suddenly make total sense. They had gone up against an entire section of highly trained soldiers, not mere schoolchildren. Rapidly, the survivors around the room accepted this idea. So much so, that Dominus' hesitation in replying only fueled their conviction that they had been taken by surprise by Erin Saks.

Dominus looked over his mental memories of the battle. He'd seen Sam Barron's girl standing tall, as if she were completely oblivious to the battle raging all around her! Dominus did not see her cast a single spell the entire time! No, she appeared totally frozen, rooted to the ground. Typical of a girl, he concluded. Just as he was about to snicker at his image of her, Dominus saw her eyes!

For the very first time in his life, a cold fear began to

seep over him. He recognized that look, that look! He realized she was silently casting spells! That she never even raised her wand scared him even more—that she did not need the use of her wand in the middle of a huge battle registered in his mind. Fear now flooded through his entire body, a fear that he had never known. Something Len said came to mind, "None of our Disintegrate spells worked." Dominus finally realized what had happened there on that battlefield. A Dispeller! "No," he forced himself to see the truth of it, "the most powerful Dispeller the world had ever seen!" Fear swept over him in waves!

Dominus fought to keep his body from visibly shaking. A master leader, he knew that he could not outright tell Len and the men what they had faced. He'd lose them all at once; they would flee into hiding. He also knew he could not keep his shaking hidden much longer. "You did well. I have to think!" He waved his wand and stepped through his Magical Door. Then, he Teleported to his subterranean hideout in Singapore. Alone in the dark, damp basement, Dominus collapsed onto a sofa, his body shaking uncontrollably. His armpits stank. Fear overwhelmed him, but the darkness hid his body. For a time, he could not think.

Chapter 22—End of Term Jitters

Monday, things returned to normal, well mostly. Professor Janice was still bedridden. Other professors filled in for her, covering her many first year classes. She had requested that no students visit her, but on Friday morning, she had asked to see Lindsey only. Lindsey arrived to see her professor's face so heavily bandaged that she was unrecognizable. Only her eyes and mouth were visible from her neck up. The woman's eyes told Lindsey that she was in a great deal of pain and probably under strong painkillers. "Only talk a brief minute," Doctor Caterwall insisted. Lindsey nodded, approached her, and bent low.

Professor Janice whispered, "Alister told me what you did out there. I wanted to personally thank you. Now go, but please don't tell anyone how badly I look."

"Thanks for helping us all stand our ground, Professor. I promise I won't. Get well soon. If you need anything, let us know," Lindsey replied.

Doctor Caterwall motioned for her to leave. "She's barely able to talk at the moment. I must keep her stress level low." Lindsey nodded and left, living up to her promise not to tell the others about her condition. She did tell her friends that Professor Janice wanted to thank her, though.

Spell Casting class was officially over, as was Spell Research and PE. With three hours thus freed up, everyone used the time to work feverishly on their huge research project for Earth Science. Even more time came their way because by the weekend, both Math and Literature classes were also finished, leaving only Potion Making and Advanced Earth Science to go.

"I know I'm going to flunk Potion Making," Emilio moaned. It was early Saturday morning. Everyone was gathered in the study hall, frantically reviewing all their notes for Monday's Potion Making final exam. "I only got half of them done right all year! I just know he is going to make me make one of those I already can't make!"

"Don't feel bad, Emilio," Pam lamented dolefully. "I will be there with you. I don't see how I can pass it either." She had failed to achieve an 'A' on one third of the potions this term and was certain that she wouldn't make it as well.

"Honestly, I don't see how you all get into so much trouble with these potions," Kathy replied, trying to help. "Look, just do what I do. As I do a step, I put a little checkmark beside it. That way, I don't lose my place."

"I tried that last time, but I accidentally checked the wrong step, and it all came out botched," Emilio explained.

Changing the topic, Ashley commented, "I saw Professors Cho Lin, Huan Su, and Delius heading for Governor Alister's office when I came down this morning. I wonder what they are up to? Probably more interesting than these stupid potions." Lindsey's mind, looking for any excuse not to dwell on these awful potion recipes, began speculating on some imagined meeting. She wondered why they had not been invited, which, for some reason this morning, seemed to annoy her.

Professor Delius wiped his hands through his greasy hair. "Then, it's confirmed, Alister. Dominus sent his Death Stalker army to kill you, right here on the school grounds."

Alister sighed. "Yes, yes, Delius, there can be no doubt about that now. I've gone over everything with Mary Ann. She is totally convinced as well."

"Well, it does make sense, Alister," Cho Lin spoke up. "You are coordinating all the resistance movement against Dominus. Only an idiot could not come to that conclusion."

"Yes, but I had hoped that Dominus would not harm the children. What have I done? I don't care how you look at it. I've placed all our students in the gravest peril!" Alister pointed out his grave mistake. "I apologize to all of you. In hindsight, I shouldn't have done that."

"You really had no other choice, Alister," Cho Lin defended him. "No one else in the country is nearly his match except you. If you had not stood up to him, then where would the whole country be? Lost, all of us lost."

"That's not the point, Cho Lin, and you know it," Delius

chided her. "By his mere presence here at the school, he is placing the safety and well-being of eight hundred plus students at risk! That's the point. We were phenomenally lucky that Lindsey and her group were outside in the precise location when the attack came. Think of what would have happened if Janice had her first years out there practicing Sleep spells! We would have been sending thirty students home in pine boxes!"

Cho Lin didn't reply. She knew he had a very valid point. Instead, Huan Su spoke up, "The question now is what do we do about it? It is my opinion that with ample States Security men on guard at all times, any recurrence can be prevented."

"You honestly think that will deter Dominus?" Delius sneered. "Get real, Huan Su! Next time, he'll come with hundreds of men, bomb us into oblivion, poison us, or use any number of diabolical methods. He wants Alister dead. As long as Alister is at this school, the kids are in jeopardy period!"

"Delius is right, you know," Alister commented sadly. "My presence here at Bradbury's is placing them all at risk, each and every day. Yet, there are the students to consider, Miss Barron and Miss Stokes-Compton, perhaps even Miss Betts. The real question that I have been pondering is does Dominus realize what those girls have become? We all saw the greatest act of Dispelling ever recorded, to say nothing of the Class 4 Divining, or even the incredible Sleuthing. Does Dominus realize the full potential of Miss Barron? I'm certain he is fully aware of Miss Stokes-Compton; no hiding that one. Miss Betts is more of a thorn in his side. No, I am very much frightened for Miss Barron. She has become the key to everything now."

"What do you mean, Alister?" asked Cho Lin.

"Until now, I had hoped to keep the incredible skills of Miss Barron a total secret. Then, in some distant surprise attack, with her aid, we capture Dominus and his gang, ending his reign of terror. However, after that battle in which she demonstrated very clearly her incredible skills as a master Dispeller, perhaps the world's best, Dominus must now know her true potential. If I were him, I would concentrate all my efforts in eliminating her. She represents the only serious threat to him personally. Miss Stokes-Compton may be able to thwart his plans, but Miss Barron now has the potential to stop him in his tracks utterly. If I were Dominus, I would be petrified of what Miss Barron might do."

"So you think that he will now go after her?" Cho Lin's voice grew rather shrill; worry lines suddenly appeared upon her forehead. "Like drop a bomb on their ranch or something?"

Alister shrugged his shoulders, but didn't answer her speculation. "Should I go or should I stay? I owe it to Lindsey to do everything in my power to keep her safe until she graduates. We all do. But in staying, do I bring trouble to her and to other innocent students? Can I live with myself if an innocent student dies?" He sighed.

"Whatever I do, we do, we cannot and must not abandon Lindsey. I was instrumental in bringing her here to Bradbury's in the first place. I encouraged her to develop her Dispeller skills and made it possible for her to learn the art. I simply cannot abandon her now."

He continued, "We are possibly at that last point in time in which Dominus can be stopped from becoming master of the world. I firmly believe that Lindsey alone may be our last chance."

Cho Lin piped in, "Well, then that's that. You certainly can't protect her if you are not here at Bradbury's, Alister. You can't go away now."

"The matter is settled," Delius added solemnly. "We should put our heads together to see what additional protections we can devise for the safety of all the children."

Complicating matters was the May Day track meet against Brown Hall and the following day's soccer game against Black Hall. Lindsey chided herself for not having paid much attention at all to their team. She ought to have held practices, ought to have attended the other spring contests, ought to have done this and that. In the end, it didn't matter. With the addition of the speedy twins from New York, Yellow Hall easily beat Brown Hall, winning all three events.

392

Similarly, the soccer game with Black Hall was a letdown.

She had promised to let everyone on the team have a chance to play. In fact, she herself did not start, coaching from the sidelines. The team did so well, that Lindsey never did put herself into the game, which set a new record for Bradbury's. Yellow Hall won the game without their captain even playing in the game, and they took the trophy once more. Of course, Black Hall was upset, because it seemed to them that Lindsey was teasing them by not even deigning to play in the game. Deiter found this hilarious.

Sunday brought them all back to the reality of their science projects. "Well, I'm going first," Emilio told everyone. "Just got it Okayed from Professor Jasper." Pam looked at Emilio, awestruck by his pronouncement. She was miles from being ready to make her presentation.

Emilio unshrunk his model and began, "My project was to see if I could work out the design of a self-sufficient desert ecosystem. This past summer, I got to see how one could build a home that is nearly entirely self-sufficient." He began to explain his ideas, many of which were extensions of R. B.'s designs. He had added a water reclamation system and several more features. "My biggest problem still unsolved is how to grow sufficient protein, though I don't like soy pizzas. They are not really pizzas." The class roared with laughter.

Andy went next, making what Lindsey thought to be a rather dull presentation of rock strata and its age. That one could date something in the ancient past from mere rocks seemed a rather pointless exercise to her, but then she had no interest in archaeology.

Tom's thirty-minute presentation of his computer simulation of climate changes was more interesting. Kathy woke all the girls up. "Does the weather affect personality? You bet it does! Can you imagine living in a place where it is cloudy every day? How about a place that is sunny all the time?" Kathy held their interest all the way through, though in the end, Lindsey realized that she really had not proved much of anything. It was mostly subjective, not objective. She wondered if this would affect her grade.

Audrey convinced all the girls that plants grow better

when you talk nicely to them and give them lots of encouragement. The boys uniformly thought this was all bunk, but she had many charts to prove her point.

Lindsey's turn came. "You are what you eat." A strong opening line, she thought. "Is there any real difference between organically grown food versus commercially grown food using pesticides and growth formulas? I set out to see if there is any difference. There is. Chemicals are absorbed and stored in the plants. We then eat these. You all know what happened to me when I was born. Mom drank tainted water. However, commercially, the concentrations are low." She displayed her chart. "What I found out is that very long term studies are needed to show if these lower concentrations will have adverse effects on our bodies. Short term, they are safe, but no one knows about long-term exposure. Some chemicals are stored in the body and build up, until they are at unsafe levels." Again, she had a chart to show several. When she finished, she didn't think that she had convinced anyone either way. However, it was done and that alone was a huge relief.

Everyone found Amanda's report on the aftermath of the hurricane that Dominus parked over the southeastern part of the country quite interesting. At first, vast quantities of plants suddenly sprang up in a lush of growth, making a one in a century spectacular spring. However, the next year, the dry area was back to its usual dry state. She presented a series of findings of the unusual plants whose seeds only sprout in wet times such as this one had been. Later, Ashley's dire predictions of global doom and gloom from long-term effects of the de-forestation of the Amazon didn't cheer anyone up.

Pam went last, giving her several more fanatic days to get her project done. It still was not finished when her turn came at last. "My topic is the migratory paths of birds: genetics, inheritance, or learned. Everyone knows that many species of bird fly south for the winter and then back north for the summer. Often, the birds follow the same route year after year. I wanted to know just how they know the route to follow."

Unfortunately, Pam had reached no real conclusion, though she presented many arguments and even a sample video when a man flying an ultra-light in the shape of a giant bird led some endangered birds south for the winter. Professor Jasper had to cut her off after thirty minutes. Pam felt sure that she had botched the whole thing.

"Well, you did choose a really hard one," Lindsey consoled her. Pam felt miserable and hung out around the posting board, waiting for their grades to appear. They did, the next day. "How'd you do?" asked Lindsey, writing down her own grades.

"It's a miracle. I'm really slipping, Lindsey. I squeaked by barely. I got a 90 in four subjects: Advanced Earth Science, Potion Making II, Literature, and PE. That's four by the skin of my teeth!"

"Pam, that means you got all A's again, doesn't it?" Lindsey said in an exasperated tone of voice.

"Well, yes, but," Pam replied.

"Well, so did I," Lindsey answered her. "So much for your doom and gloom, Pam."

"Hey, look at that! I got an A in science. Kind of makes up for my C in Potion Making, doesn't it?" a cheery Emilio broke in on the two. "Guess I don't have to take that over next year. Kathy already told me she got nearly a perfect score in Potion Making II. I bet she will take Potion Making III next year. Not me! I don't want to go anywhere near that stinking lab."

"You will have lots of company," Lindsey teased. "Other than Kathy, I don't think any of the rest of us will go near it either. I wonder what our classes will be? Sixth year is supposed to be even worse than fifth year, though I cannot imagine how it could be so."

"Well, we have to have PE and literature; those are state requirements," Pam pointed out.

"Ugh, more stupid novels, I'll bet," Emilio groaned.

"No, it's worse than that, Emilio," Pam explained. "It's poems." He let out a yowl. No one laughed, however.

Pam noticed another smaller note. It read: See your councilor for your sixth year schedule. Around ten that morning, Lindsey and her gang headed for Professor Cho Lin's office to get their new schedules, after which all were planning to visit the bookstore to get needed books and supplies.

"Ah, the whole crowd at once, I see," she teased them as the large group filed into her office. "I have your basic schedules done. Kathy and Emilio will be continuing in Basic Calculus, Professor Herbert wants to make sure you both are up to speed at this level of math before you graduate. The rest of you are in Calculus class. Here are your schedules."

Eager hands grabbed theirs and eyes skimmed down the courses.

```
 8:00 PE
 9:00 English Literature and Composition
10:00 Calculus
11:00 Elective
 1:00 Spell Research II
 2:00 Spell Casting Grade 7
 3:00 Spell Casting Grade 7
 4:00 Spell Casting Grade 7
```

"Wow! Three periods for spell casting!" Pam noted.

"Yes, half of every day is devoted to magic," Professor Cho Lin replied, as she always did. Some sixth years always made that comment. Now then, the electives must be worked out on an individual basis. Some of you I can handle. Lindsey, Ashley, Pam, you are to report to Governor Alister's office. He wishes to make some elective suggestions for you." The trio looked at each other, said goodbye to their friends, and dashed off to the Admin Hall.

"Now then, Kathy, I have a personal request from Professor Delius that you should take Potion Making III. How does that sound?" she asked.

"Wild horses couldn't keep me from that one!" Kathy had found her niche.

Emilio wondered if she had made a mistake. She suggested that his elective be Business Math. He was so confused by the idea that he agreed, wondering why he alone would have two math courses. Audrey took Plant Biology. Deiter was given Eliminator Theory II. Tom got Advanced Programming. Amanda took Music Performance.

"Come on in," the quiet voice of Governor Alister welcomed his expected students. He had already prepared tea, which the three accepted. "Now then, electives. Ashley, yours is the easiest. I would really appreciate it if you took Practical Divination next year. It will round out your special skills. How does that sound to you?"

"Hey, really good. I was hoping you weren't going to suggest more math or science."

"Good. Good. No, I think you need to know everything we can possibly teach you about your art. Now for you two." He looked at Pam and then Lindsey. "I am not a Diviner, but I am a good judge of people. I am about to suggest some rather strange electives for you two. I wish that you would give them serious and careful scrutiny. I am not making these suggestions lightly."

"Pam, let's do yours next. I would like you to take Elementary Education."

Pam's mouth waggled. Advanced Physics, Advanced Programming, Super Sleuthing, College Calculus, these crossed her mind. Elementary Education? She stared back at him, trying to absorb what he had said. Well, she always had been tutoring nearly everyone these past five years. She liked it. "Okay," she squeaked, surprised by her own voice.

"Lindsey, I would like you to take Administration Management as your elective." Lindsey nearly choked. She had not the faintest idea what this was. Yet, if Governor Alister thought that this was vitally important for her to take, she would do it. He had never been wrong about her. She agreed.

"Fine, fine, all three of you. I will send these choices along to Professor Cho Lin, who will give you your final schedules then. Thank you for being so considerate." He cleared his throat and said, "Another matter. During the summer, I want you three to promise me that under no circumstances will you go beyond the ranches without a squad of adult wizards accompanying you. I believe that Dominus now knows just how powerful Lindsey has become. He certainly knows about Ashley. I would fully expect Dominus would make every effort to have you three killed. Let's not give him the opportunity, shall we? I want to see you three back here in the fall and in one piece too," he grinned. The girls giggled, knowing what he meant.

"Ashley, if you do any divination over the summer, Message me with the results, and I will see that they are forwarded. It might be best if you relaxed and enjoyed your summer. Yet if you feel you need to contribute, I will understand that too," Alister said. Lindsey could tell that he was diplomatically trying to avoid telling Ashley what she should do. At that, the trio left and chatted all the way back to Cho Lin's office.

"I don't get it? Administration Management?" Lindsey blurted out. "Why?"

"I can't see Elementary Education either. Has he gone off his rocker?" Pam added, very confused by the meeting.

"Only mine makes any sense," Ashley added. "Maybe he sees a future in teaching for you, Pam. Then, it would make some sense."

"Well, I don't know anything about being a leader," Lindsey added. "Maybe that is what he has in mind with me."

Cho Lin welcomed them back and observed, "Ah, I see that you went along with his suggestions."

"Yes, but I don't understand it at all," Pam retorted. "Elementary Education? Administration Management? Ashley's, I can see hers."

Professor Cho Lin sighed, "I know Pam. I was as mystified as you were when he told me about his ideas. I don't get them either, but then perhaps that's why I'm only Number 2 around here."

"Do we know who is going to teach these courses?" Pam wondered.

"Some we do; some we don't yet. I believe Professor Herbert has agreed to teach Elementary Education, Pam. I will be teaching Administration Management, Lindsey. Mary Ann and several other visiting Diviners will be teaching Practical Divination. Some of the other electives have not yet been picked up, but there is plenty of time before the fall arrives."

They thanked her and rejoined the others waiting for them in the study hall. All were as mystified by Pam and Lindsey's electives as the girls were. All except Kathy, who commented, "I think that Pam would make a good teacher." Pam blushed.

Next came the long lines at the bookstore. They finished at suppertime and had to dash hastily back to the dorms, dropping off their books on the way.

Both Pam and Deiter raced through dinner, wanting to peek at their new books, but on very different subjects. Deiter knew that these were the last spells he would be taught. Anything beyond the Grade 7 spells could be attempted later on his own, but not with much likelihood of success. Pam was curious about the education course.

"Wow! There are only twenty spells in here," Deiter commented a bit later at study hall. He had rapidly gone through the spell book, counting. "Whatever are we doing with three hours devoted to these each day? Must be awfully hard spells."

"Don't forget, Deiter, we also get the chance to see if we can cast sans words and sans wands. Plus we get a chance to learn even more powerful spells," Pam pointed out. "Look at the second half of the book. There are the really advanced spells, another fifteen spells, including the full Wish spell."

"Well, I don't feel so bad having to repeat Beginning Calculus; Emilio is with me," Kathy interrupted the chat on spells. "At least I feel for the first time ever, I'm mostly understanding the math things. Maybe it will be useful later on."

"I can see why I need Business Math," Emilio spoke up. "Kathy and I are getting married when we graduate, and then she is going to open up her own store, Kathy's Potions. So I'm going to have my hands full helping her run the business part."

Tom, wishing to enjoy their last few days before break, suggested, "Pam, would you care to go for a walk in the gardens and enjoy the dusk?" In a flash, Pam's books disappeared up into her room. They were out the door in a moment. Deiter, taken aback, did likewise, Moving his books to his room. He and Lindsey followed them. Ahana and Amanda were right behind them, followed by Emilio and Kathy. Not to be left out, Audrey and Ashley brought up the rear, both lamenting that their boyfriends were not around yet.

Several relaxing days later came the formal end of term ball. The next evening was graduation. Then, it would be home for everyone until the end of August. Lindsey half expected to have a Rodents Pack meeting before they all left, but none was called. The ball passed as usual with the young women wishing it would never end.

Finally graduation night came. Professor Janice made her first formal appearance since the battle. While many students stared at her, no one could notice any perceptible differences in her appearance, not even her hair. Many speculated that she was now using some magical disguises, but no one knew for sure. Lindsey resisted using a See True spell on her, respecting her privacy.

Governor Alister began the celebration as usual. "First, tonight we have the Bradbury Hall Track and Soccer Trophy to award. This year it goes to Yellow Hall once again. Will the team captain, Miss Lindsey Barron, please come up here and bring your powerhouse team with you?" Yellow Hall students clapped, stomped, and yelled their support. Lindsey grinned and allowed her teammates to hold up the trophy high. They had earned it.

"Next, I would like to present thirty-four very special awards. This year, our school was brutally attacked. Professor Janice Blake was holding her fifth year spell casting class right when the attack came. These thirty-three students and professor found themselves at the front line of the battle. Every one of them fought to the end, giving up not an inch of our campus. I would like to present the highest honor that our school can offer, the Bradbury's Distinguished Service Medallion. When I call your name, please rise and come up here. Professor Cho Lin will present you with your medallion. Then stand in a line so that we can all applaud you as a group. Professor Janice Blake." In spite of the caution, Red Hall students stomped and cheered and whistled as their Hall Leader proudly walked up to receive her medallion.

One by one, all members of Lindsey's class were called and presented their medallion. The final applause for the whole group was deafening. Deiter felt terribly proud standing there alongside Lindsey and Peaches. He relished this feeling that others greatly appreciated what he had done. Lindsey, on the other hand, couldn't wait until they could sit back down.

Pam felt incredibly nervous standing there. Most of the others merely enjoyed their moment of fame, knowing that most all the older students would have done the very same thing had they been there. Professor Delius's mock battles had changed the way all the students viewed magical battles.

At last, they returned to their seats and the formal diploma presentation began. Over one hundred twenty students received their high school degree and their magic school diploma during the next hour. Once that was done, everyone mingled with the graduates, congratulating them and wishing them the best of luck. Then, everyone dashed to their rooms for all the last minute packing.

Wisely, Lindsey had already purchased another duffle bag. "Ten bags, stuffed! My how everything grows so!"

"I remember your first year, Lindsey, when you had that tiny backpack," Amanda teased her.

"What's scary is so do I. Everything just seems to multiply each year," she concluded. She was pretty much done, when Deiter sent her a Message, wondering if she wanted a last stroll around the gardens. One by one, everyone slipped out of the dorms for their last stroll among all the blossoming flowers of late-May.

"I'll come by as often as I can this summer," Deiter whispered into Lindsey's ear.

"Please. I'm under orders not to go anywhere without a big escort, so it's going to be lots easier for you to drop by than for me to come for a visit," she replied. "Do you think we will have any real trouble during the summer?"

"Nah, probably nothing at all, Lindsey," he replied. He had no idea just how wrong his analysis would be.
The End.

A Favor to Other Readers

How about helping other readers? Many readers rely on reviews to make the decision whether to buy a book. You can help them make their decision by leaving your opinions and viewpoint in a short review of the positive things of this book. Writing the review and expressing your opinion only takes a few minutes, and other readers will appreciate your efforts.

Click this link: Volume 5 The National Health Care Program scroll down to Customer Reviews; click on Write a Review, and enter your review. Thank you.

Author Information

Visit My Amazon.com Author Page
Vic Broquard Author Page

Follow My Blog
Vic Broquard's Blog

Follow Me on Social Media
Facebook
Google+
LinkedIn
YouTube

Other Books by Vic Broquard

Without Warning (fantasy)

The Trident Series: (fantasy)
>Volume 1 The Trident and the Book
>Volume 2 The Trident and the Scepter
>Volume 3 The Trident and the Resurrection

The Adventures of Elizabeth Stanton Series: (science fiction)
>Volume 1 The Evolution of the Path
>Volume 2 The Great Messiah
>Volume 3 Of Kings and Queens and Troubadours
>Volume 4 Chaos in the Aftermath
>Volume 5 Power Plays
>Volume 6 Age of Exploration
>Volume 7 Abducted
>Volume 8 The Emperor and Empress
>Volume 9 A Job Worth Doing
>Volume 10 Degradation
>Volume 11 The Second Crusade
>Volume 12 When Worlds Collide
>Volume 13 Dark Ages

The Lindsey Barron Series: (fantasy)
>Volume 1 The Rod of the Apocalypse
>Volume 2 The Board of Governors
>Volume 3 The Crown of Moses
>Volume 4 Dominus for President
>Volume 5 The National Health Care Program
>Volume 6 States Justice
>Volume 7 Cross and Double-cross

Zoran Chronicles Series: (fantasy)
>Volume 1 A Dragon in Our Town
>Volume 2 Dragons, Power, Courts, and War

Planet of the Orange-red Sun Series: (science fiction)
>Volume 1 When Kingdoms Fall

Vic Broquard

The Return of the Wizards: Twelve Companions – The Making of Wizards (fantasy)